By the same author:

The Teacher
The Secret
The Angel

Praise for Katerina Diamond:

'Diamond is the master of gripping literature.'
The Evening Standard

'A terrific story, originally told. All hail the new queen of crime!'
Heat

'A web of a plot that twists and turns and keeps the reader on the edge of their seat. This formidable debut is a page-turner, but don't read it before bed if you're easily spooked!'
The Sun

'A page-turner with a keep-you-guessing plot.'
Sunday Times Crime Club

'Diamond neatly handles a string of interlocking strands.'
Daily Mail

'This gem of a crime novel is packed with twists until the last page.'
Closer

'A deliciously dark read, Katerina Diamond keeps her readers guessing throughout as she leads us on a very secretive, VERY twisted journey . . . everything I was expecting from a well-written, pacy thriller.'
Lisa Hall, author of *Between You And Me*

The
Promise

KATERINA DIAMOND

avon.

Published by AVON
A division of HarperCollins*Publishers*
1 London Bridge Street,
London SE1 9GF

www.harpercollins.co.uk

A Paperback Original 2018

2

A catalogue record for this book is
available from the British Library

ISBN-13: 978-0-00-820921-6

Typeset in Sabon LT Std by Palimpsest Book Production Ltd,
Falkirk, Stirlingshire

Printed and bound in Great Britain by
CPI Group (UK) Ltd, Croydon CR0 4YY

MIX
Paper from
responsible sources
FSC
www.fsc.org   FSC™ C007454

To Mum.
We've been through a lot together and
most of it was your fault.

Chapter 1

Tonight was the night. Erica looked in her full-length mirror and checked her dress for the umpteenth time. It was more than she would usually spend but it hugged her in all the right places and she wanted to make a good impression. She scrutinised the bedroom to make sure that it was tidy; she had spent the whole morning cleaning the house, just in case. She hoped this was the one.

Erica had met Warren online; they had been talking for some months now. A couple of weeks ago, he'd started speaking to her on the phone and they had taken their relationship to the next level. She knew he was real because she wasn't stupid; she had been burned by catfish before, people pretending to be someone else, people who were trying to con you out of something. Not Warren though. Erica had pushed to speak on the phone, she had pushed to video call, she had been the one who had gotten intimate first. They had exchanged phone numbers and when she knew he was at work she would send him a cheeky picture of her bra, or maybe the lace band of her underpants that rested on her hip. Warren had told her before that he wanted to go slow, that he wasn't ready for a relationship yet after a particularly painful break-up with an ex-girlfriend who had cheated on him. But she wanted him to know she was serious. It hadn't taken long for Erica to see through Warren's funny and sociable bravado; he was hurting, he was in pain and she would help him heal.

Their conversations were deep, deeper than she had had with anyone else. He always knew the right things to say. It was as though they had known each other forever. Erica had never-thought that she was loveable before, but there was an undeniable connection between her and Warren. The biggest issue was that he lived a couple of hundred miles away, nearer to London than to Exeter but tonight that wasn't going to be a problem.

She left the house clutching her phone in her hand, dreading a notification from Warren to say he was cancelling, that he wouldn't be at the restaurant when she got there. This was the weekend they were going to meet face-to-face, on Halloween. She could hardly believe it was actually going to happen. Warren had booked a local hotel and was going to stay in Exeter for the weekend, somewhere near to her but not with her; he'd said he didn't want to put her under that kind of pressure. He was thoughtful like that; even so, she was hoping he would stay over. This was it – she would finally find out if he was her dream man.

Erica walked through the town towards the cathedral,

looking at all the people in their costumes, feeling under-dressed in her simple outfit. She hadn't dressed up for Halloween in a long time. The streets were relatively quiet, the few children that did engage in traipsing from house to house for sweets had already gone home for the evening. A gaggle of laughing zombies in tiny skirts stumbled past her, on their way to some pub no doubt. Erica smiled to herself every time she thought about the possibilities of the night ahead. She walked into the Mediterranean restaurant on the cathedral square and hung her coat on the rail in the lobby. She fiddled with the red rose pinned to her blouse. Even though they had seen each other before on camera, they thought it would be fun to wear symbolic red roses for their first date. That's when she spotted him.

Erica's heart fluttered as she saw him in the corner, sipping his wine and looking at his phone. She thought how strange it was that they were only just meeting and yet they had already seen each other naked.

As though sensing her arrival, he looked up, and the biggest grin spread across his face. Relieved to see that he wasn't disappointed, Erica walked over. He stood up and held his hand out to shake hers. She placed her hand in his, all the while looking at his knuckles, his fingers, his skin tone. She was trying to commit this moment to memory because she knew it was important. This was the beginning of the rest of her life.

'Warren?' she said, knowing the answer. The smile on her face was beginning to ache. This already felt too good to be true.

He leaned across and kissed her on the cheek. He

smelled of expensive aftershave, something understated and slightly feminine, with a little spice to it.

'It's good to finally meet you, Erica,' he said shyly.

'How is your hotel?' she asked but regretted it instantly, hoping he wouldn't think she was alluding to anything.

'Pretty basic, the bed is quite lumpy and hard. I probably should have forked out for something a little less franchise-y.'

'Lesson learned for next time, eh?' She smiled again. He was even better looking in the flesh. His blond surfer hair hung to his shoulders; he looked like something from *Sons of Anarchy* or a nineties Seattle rock band. His skin was weather-beaten but still somehow perfect. Everything about him was perfect. Why was he looking online for a girlfriend? Why was he interested in her? She could barely understand it but what the hell, this was happening and she was going to enjoy it.

As they both sat down, the waiter came over and took their order. The conversation flowed with such ease that Erica had to warn herself to calm down. Nothing worked out for her, certainly not men, certainly no one as handsome as Warren. She could hear her sister's voice in her head, telling her to be careful, not to fall too fast – something she had told her a million times. Now that Erica was sitting here face-to-face with Warren, her sister's words were the furthest thing from her mind.

After finishing their meal, which consisted of the most expensive white wine on the menu, oysters, a seafood risotto and lemon torte, he insisted on paying the bill and they walked out together. He slipped his hand into hers and their fingers interlocked as they walked along the streets. She didn't want the night to end so they walked through the town together. Instinctively she was taking him to her house. Erica wasn't ready to let him go yet, not after all this time of waiting to meet him. As they left the town and started walking towards the more residential area, he squeezed her hand. Had he figured out where she was taking him?

Warren kissed Erica on the cheek outside her house on the little side street in Exeter.

'Thank you for coming, it was great to meet you,' Erica said.

'Was it everything you hoped for?'

'And then some. What time will I see you tomorrow?' She was testing him, to see if he might ask to come inside – she wanted him to ask.

'I'll text you when I'm awake' he said, backing away slowly, a smile on his face.

She watched him turn and head in the direction of his hotel.

'Wait!' she called out.

He turned around. The smile even bigger than before; he knew what she wanted, and she hoped he wanted it too. He walked back towards her quickly and she took his hand, pulling him towards the house as she frantically fumbled around in her handbag for her keys.

They tugged at each other's clothes as they went up the stairs. By the time they reached the top, they were both in their underwear. She pushed the bedroom door open and they laughed as they fell on the bed, their mouths separated for just long enough before locking back together again. Before she knew it, he was on top of her; she wrapped her legs around his waist as he pushed against her. He pulled away, his chest heaving and the smile still wrapped around his face.

'Do you have a condom?'

'Uh . . . sure,' she said, scrambling for her bedside cabinet. She hoped she had a condom; it had been so long. God, what if they were out of date? Surely the date was just advisory anyway. If she didn't check then it didn't matter.

She found an unopened box and threw it at him. He opened it and pulled out the condom, quickly pulling his pants down and putting it on. She lifted her backside and shimmied her underpants off too. This was really happening. He lay on top of her again and his face hovered above hers. They both held their breath as he pushed his way inside her. His blond hair tickled her face with every thrust. She lifted her hand and tucked his hair behind his ear, it felt strange, synthetic. She would ask him about it after and they would laugh, she would tell him that she didn't care about his hair, she loved him for him. Now that she had properly met him she didn't feel silly for calling what they had love. They'd already been talking online for so long, and knew so much about each other. She did love him.

'Is this OK?' he asked.

She felt his hand on her throat and nodded; they had talked about this online. She knew the safe word

– something else they had discussed. He was gentle anyway, no pressure at all.

'You can be rougher if you want.' She felt his hand close around her throat as he pushed harder into her. She wanted a little danger, something a bit less conventional. They were perfect for each other, this was exactly what she had wanted, exactly what she had told him she wanted.

She started to feel dizzy, combined with the arousal she really was flying now; climax was imminent but she needed to breathe. She didn't have the courage to see it through. Maybe next time. She imagined the weeks they would spend tangled together between the sheets like this. There was no need to hurry.

'Yellow,' she said.

'Just a little more. Trust me,' he whispered in her ear.

'Yellow!' she said again. That was the safe word, wasn't it? Wasn't this the end of it? Wasn't he supposed to stop now? Instead his fingers dug into her neck even harder than before. She was finding it harder to breathe; she started to pound her fists against him but he just carried on. His grip tightened and she felt the tears streaming down the sides of her face. His thrusting was more aggressive now and she wasn't enjoying this anymore. She could hear a faint muttering coming from him; she was too disoriented to make out the words, but when she focused enough to see his eyes there was no warmth there, just malice.

'Stupid fucking bitch.' She heard his last words and the sound of him laughing as she slipped into unconsciousness.

Chapter 2

DS Imogen Grey and DS Adrian Miles pulled up outside the pale green house on Colleton Hill just outside Exeter city centre. Standing in front of them was a row of picturesque terraced cottages facing a thicket of over-grown bushes and brambles, some evergreen and some not so much. From the ground floor Imogen imagined you could pretend you were right in the countryside in the summer. The street was almost hidden from the big red-brick blocks on the other side of the greenery.

'Ready to go?' she asked Adrian, who was wearing his ever-present glazed look. The look of someone who was trying to adjust to life without someone else. Someone trying to pretend they weren't grieving. He obviously hadn't been sleeping; he was probably drinking too much again. She couldn't ask him if he was all right because that wasn't how this partnership worked. He would talk to her if he needed to, she was confident of that.

'Yep, let's go.' He turned the engine off. They got out of the car and looked at the front door, which was being guarded by a uniformed police officer, PC Griffin. He nodded at them both.

'What's the story here then?' Imogen asked the officer.

'Young woman, Erica Lawson, didn't turn up for work yesterday or today. When the boss finally got in touch with her ICE contact, her sister, she came to the house and let herself in. Found Erica upstairs on the bed, called the police immediately.'

'Did she touch anything in the house?' Imogen asked.

'A couple of things, said she let the cat in before she went upstairs and when she saw the body she threw up in the toilet . . . so she flushed it.'

'For fuck's sake.' Imogen rolled her eyes.

'Then she washed her hands and face in the bathroom sink. They've taken her to the hospital to get checked out. She's pretty shaken.' PC Griffin screwed up his face as he spoke.

'Jesus.' Imogen sighed before pulling her gloves out of her pocket and entering the house, Adrian behind her.

Inside, the cottage itself was quaint and traditional in its decoration. There was a smell though, a sweet, unpleasant smell that caught in the back of Imogen's throat. The floral sofa was adorned with a crochet throw and in the centre of the floor was a jute oval rug under an Ercol coffee table. It was all retro shabby chic, duck egg blues and cowslip yellows. The walls were filled with photo frames, with lots of pictures of two women on various holidays together. Presumably the victim and her sister. Imogen was hit with guilt for being angry with the woman who had contaminated the crime scene. Sometimes you had to try to remember that it was more than just a job, that there were people involved, family, loved ones. Maybe she needed a holiday. Case by case, she could feel her empathy eroding.

She gave herself a shake; it must just be tiredness. When this case was over she might see about having a few days off.

They made their way up the narrow staircase in silence, aside from the creaks and groans of the floorboards. Imogen took a deep breath before entering the bedroom. Time to meet the victim.

The body of Erica Lawson lay on top of the covers, fully dressed. At a first glance, you might think she was asleep; her arms were folded across her waist, almost like the classic image of Sleeping Beauty. But when they got closer, it became evident that the woman's eyes were open and her body had started to decay.

Imogen had seen a few petechial haemorrhages in her time, enough to know that this was a case of strangulation: the red dots around Erica's eyes caused by the explosion of the tiny blood vessels that link the smallest parts of your arteries to the smallest parts of your veins. Ignoring the body, the room seemed to be incredibly clean and tidy, immaculate. If there was anything out of place, it wasn't at first obvious. It was cold though, very cold. The window was open. Imogen made a mental note to double check the sister hadn't opened it. Maybe whoever did this wanted to confuse the time of death.

They would have to bring the girl's sister back from the hospital when she was feeling up to it to check if anything had been disturbed. That would happen after the scene had been processed by the crime scene technicians who were all bustling around the room, quietly placing evidence markers and taking photographs.

'What do you think?' Adrian said, breaking her train of thought.

'Well it's staged, that much is for certain.'

'Agreed, obviously.'

'Very controlled.'

'Look at the buttons on her blouse,' Adrian said.

'What about them?' Imogen peered over at the body. Something was off. What had Adrian noticed?

'They're slightly skewed, see? It's like the fabric is twisted wrong. I don't think she dressed herself.'

'Are you thinking she was sexually assaulted?'

'I don't know about that, but I can see that she was dressed by someone else, probably after she died. Everything is just sitting wrong.'

He was right, it did look awkward in places. Looking at Erica's skirt, Imogen could see that it was a back zip that had been done up on the side. She had probably been naked when she died.

'What about the pose?' Imogen asked.

'No idea. Maybe he was trying to respect her?'

'You're going with "he"?'

'She's not the slimmest of women; you'd need a fair bit of strength to dress her once she was dead. I think "he" is a safe bet at the moment. Unless we learn anything else from forensics.'

11

Imogen looked at Erica. She would put her weight at roughly seventy kilograms, around an average size twelve. She was slim-waisted and attractive, obviously very active and naturally quite muscular in the legs. It would be difficult for a woman to be able to handle that kind of weight without assistance. Until forensics showed otherwise, they would work on the assumption that it was a male. Neither of them wanted to say aloud that in most cases, the assumption was usually that it was a male they were after.

'Does it match any other cases we've had?' Imogen asked.

'Not to my knowledge, I'll have a look when we get back to the station.'

'You mean you'll get Gary to check.'

'What about her phone?' Adrian asked one of the crime scene technicians, but she shook her head.

'No phone?' Imogen asked.

'We haven't found one,' the technician said.

'Call us if you do,' Adrian said.

'There are no signs of a break-in either. We think whoever did this was known to this woman,' the technician offered.

Imogen put her hands on her hips and looked around the room some more. It was a small space and they were on the verge of being in the way, so she signalled to Adrian who stepped out of the room first. She followed him, nodding to the technicians, and they headed down the corridor, peering into the bathroom. Another technician was in there taking swabs and samples. They would have to come back when it had been properly processed; there simply wasn't enough room for everyone. This initial assessment would have to do for now.

DCI Mira Kapoor was standing in the lounge when they got downstairs. She had a suitably sombre expression on her face. She always behaved the way she was supposed to behave, said what she was supposed to say when in public. At the same time, she was quite rebellious, at least on the sly, in her office where it mattered. She listened when she needed to listen and she never took any action that wasn't carefully considered. Imogen was quite taken with her, although she still reserved some judgement; she had been burned by her superiors before.

'Poor girl. I want you two to speak to the neighbours and work colleagues, see if you can get a picture of who she was. Later on, you can speak to the sister, she was pretty inconsolable by all accounts and the hospital have admitted her. She's sleeping now apparently.'

'OK, Ma'am,' Imogen said.

As they went to leave, the DCI spoke again.

'Grey, can I have a private word?'

Imogen nodded to Adrian who carried on outside.

The DCI gestured to Imogen to come closer and jerked her head at Adrian's fast retreating back.

'How is he doing?'

'OK, quiet. He's OK though.'

'Do you know if he's been to see the bereavement counsellor?'

'He hasn't mentioned it, but I'm going to guess not.'

'See if you can get him to, please. Last thing I need is him cracking up.'

Imogen nodded. 'I'll do my best.'

'Have you given any more thought to the DI exam, Grey?'

'I don't know if it's the right time.'

She should want it, shouldn't she? Didn't everyone want to advance their career? The thing was that she was happy with how things were at the moment, or maybe she was scared of change; it was hard to know which. Moving up the ladder had always been the plan, but she just didn't feel ready. What was holding her back? Was it Adrian? He would be happy for her and she would be happy for him if the roles were reversed, but at the same time, the dynamic was working for her. Having a stable and dependable friend was important to her right now; she liked being on the same level. Besides, after what Adrian had been through recently, losing his girlfriend, she didn't want to leave him right now. She had to hope this wouldn't be her only opportunity.

'Well, there's an opening and, as I've said before, I think you should go for it.'

'I'll think about it. Thank you.' The DCI nodded, and Imogen left her in the house, stepping outside to see Adrian gazing out into nothing again. She got into the car and he followed, that same haunted look on his face. She wanted to hold his hand and tell him that it would be OK, but that wasn't how they did things. Instead she would continue to be herself, and hoped that would be enough to keep him afloat.

Chapter 3

Connor leant his head against the passenger window as his father drove to their new home. He looked down at the gutter as they moved through the streets, most of the roads covered with russet-coloured leaves. Even the trees here were different to the ones back home. He didn't want to look up at the houses; at least kerbs and leaves couldn't be that different on this side of the world, could they? There was a sense of unease in him; he figured it came from being on the other side of the car, on the other side of the road, on the other side of the planet.

The smooth sounds of Nina Simone's smoky voice filled the space around them. At least his father, Jacob, wasn't trying to hold a conversation with him anymore. Connor felt the car grind to a stop and the air fell silent as his father turned the engine off. He took a deep breath and looked up at their new home grudgingly. They were parked in front of a three-storey red-brick house, with a balcony running across the front and a garage to the side. It occurred to Connor that there wasn't a chance in hell their car would fit in that tiny space even though it was smaller than their car back home.

Without speaking to his father, he got out of the car and walked around to the boot to grab the suitcases. He may as well get on with it. No turning back now. The door to the left of their house opened and a girl came trudging out, head hung low, carrying a black sack; she put it in the wheelie bin and disappeared back inside without looking up or saying a word. Connor's father was still getting to his feet. He pulled himself up and surveyed the area, leaning on his cane with a nostalgic smile on his face.

'Keys?' Connor said.

Jacob rummaged in his pockets and pulled out a hefty lump of keys, tossing them to Connor – not to where Connor actually was, but further, enough to make him stretch, to make him work for it. Grabbing them, Connor walked up the steps and let himself into the house. It smelled old and empty.

Jacob wasn't far behind him, the sound of his left sole followed Connor as it gently scraped across the floor with every other step.

'Get us a beer from the fridge and let's christen this place.'

'Is there even any electricity?' Connor clicked the light switch and the hallway lit up.

'Uncle Joel came and sorted things out for us, said he put some brews in there.'

Connor noticed his father's voice changing already; he had always had an accent that was different to him and the people back in California, but now all traces of any American at all had virtually disappeared. As if Connor didn't feel different enough.

He went into the kitchen, a small and dingy room with a metre square window facing onto a garden that looked overgrown and untouched.

'What's outside?' he asked as his father appeared behind him again.

'Who knows what the olds did to it. Looks like they let it go though. Dad used to spend hours in that garden, in that shed right at the end; he spent more time in there than in the house.'

Jacob put his hand on Connor's shoulder, it was a touch full of force; controlling, making sure his son stayed close. Maybe he was trying to stop him from going outside.

'I wish I could have met them,' Connor said, knowing that would unsettle his father. Any suggestion that growing up with just a single dad wasn't enough for him, that somehow he was missing something from his life, was like poking a raw nerve.

Jacob let go immediately. 'Well, I left for a reason. You didn't miss much.'

Connor waited for his father to be distracted before grabbing a can of beer. He unlocked the back door and stepped outside onto a decked platform. He then made his way down some wooden steps into a wild and unruly mess that came up past his waist. Everything was washed with a cold blue light as the sun faded behind the rooftops. Hacking his way through the stinging nettles, pampas grass and bushes with his arms until he got to the end of the garden, he looked back at his father who stood by the back door. Connor was grateful for the distance between them as he clocked his father's disapproving stare.

He pulled on the door of the shed. The wood was swollen and cracked, but he kicked it a couple of times and jarred it loose. Inside, it was dark and dingy not unlike the house, full of stacked boxes and crates. Connor ventured further, the sparse light cloudy and full of dust.

The boxes nearest the ground had been saturated at one point or another and the bottoms were blown, a mulch of paperwork peeking through the holes. He poked around inside one or two. There were some photo albums and a couple of his father's school reports. He found a small red exercise book, shiny with a black wreath emblem on the front. Inside, some of the pages were stuck together and the words blurred, but he could just about make out that it was a story of some sort. Connor thumbed through it, wondering what his father might have written about in school, what stories he could have possibly told. He couldn't make out the writing very well in this light and so he tossed it back in the box. The air was thick and the more stuff he disturbed, the more dust he could feel in his mouth. Leaving the shed, he pulled the door behind him. He might come back and look around here another time.

Next to the shed, there was a large tree with strips

of wood nailed horizontally to the trunk that went up into the branches.

'What's this?' he called out to his father who had already pulled up a chair outside with a box of beers to the side of him. They had been travelling for a few hours and so it was nice to be outside, even though it was cold. He couldn't begrudge him that.

'Is that still there? It's a tree house. Or it should be. Your grandfather built it. About the only good thing he ever did.' He knocked back the beer. 'It's probably fucked. I wouldn't go up there if I were you.'

Ignoring his father's advice, Connor climbed the makeshift ladder, careful not to spill his beer. He couldn't see his father on the decking anymore. He kept climbing until his hand reached what felt like a platform. He pulled himself up onto it and, sure enough, he was inside a tree house. It smelled musty and there was a hole in one of the corners, but something about it felt good. Connor moved slowly across the floor, unsure how safe it was. There was a window, but it was filthy. Connor pulled off his jacket and tried to rub away some of the thick dirt that obscured his view. He picked up his beer and splashed the window with the liquid, then rubbed hard with his jacket; it was already smelly from the travelling so he didn't mind getting it a bit grubby as well.

He managed to clear a fair bit of the muck off the inside of the window. Opening it, he slid his arm through to the outside and wiped that as well. It was smeared and kind of disgusting, but at least now he could see outside. The tree house looked directly into the neighbour's back garden and onto the rear of their house. Connor smiled as he saw a couple, presumably his new neighbours, kissing against the countertops in the kitchen.

He looked around the tree house and felt a little glimmer of hope. There was no way his father would make it up here – he had a place where he could be by himself, without his father's watchful eye, without the hand on his shoulder, without feeling like he was to blame for everything that was wrong in the world.

Connor shuffled back against the wall and sat down with his beer in his hand, thinking about the different things he was going to have to get used to here in England. His father had always maintained he would never come back, but when his parents had died and left him the house, it seemed like a logical move after the incident back at home. If Connor was honest, he needed a change too. He couldn't carry on being the person he was in California; people had started to notice that he wasn't the same as them, and he couldn't stand that.

He pulled out the Zippo his father had given him as a gift for his sixteenth birthday and struck the wheel with his thumb, watching the flame flickering in the light breeze that ran through the empty tree house. He pulled out a cigarette and lit it before peering through the window again. The woman next door was up on the countertop now, her legs wrapped around her partner's waist, his trousers around his ankles. Upstairs, he could see into what looked like a girl's bedroom; she was sitting at her dressing table, with a lamp on.

It was the girl he had seen earlier when they arrived. As Connor watched, she undid the plait in her hair and started to brush it out.

The loud pops of fireworks in the distance unsettled Connor, and he saw the sky to the east flashing pink. People had already started to set them off in the run-up to Bonfire Night. Looking back at the girl, he could see a blank expression on her face which was reflected in her dressing-table mirror. He wondered if she could hear what was happening downstairs, or outside. The girl stood up and walked over to her window, her face changing colour as the fireworks erupted overhead. Connor shrank back, making sure she didn't know he was in there. For now, he just wanted to watch them – to see what a normal family did. Something he had never known.

The girl had long mousy hair and round glasses, around his age. She stared out of the window into her own garden, which was comprised of a tidy lawn and a decked patio with black plastic furniture and a big orange parasol. Fixating on a point in the distance, she just stared for a while. Her face was empty, not interested, not sad – nothing. After a few seconds, she pulled a book from a shelf in her room and then got into her bed. Connor continued to watch her; she read for less than five minutes and then flipped a switch that turned her reading light into a soft pink glowing orb. It was only then that he realised the dusk had turned to nighttime, he had never known it to get this dark so early back home, it was barely six in the evening.

He turned his attention back to the couple downstairs,

who were still grabbing and pawing at each other desperately until he slumped against her and she pushed him away. The urgency gone, they redressed and disappeared back into the parts of the house that he couldn't see. He watched the sky for a while until the popping slowed to a stop and the sky returned to its lifeless dusky black.

Reluctantly, Connor climbed back out of the tree house and down the tree. It was harder than going up, but still it just reassured him that his father would never be able to make the journey with his leg. He walked back through the garden to his father, who was sitting in the almost-darkness, from the looks of it. on his fourth beer already. It wasn't as cold as he expected it to be, from the stories he had heard it did nothing but rain over here. So far his denim jacket had been enough to keep him warm.

'Anything good up there?'

'Like what?'

'Me and your uncle used to read comics and pornos up there, wondered if there was anything still knocking around.'

'Nope. It's empty.'

Connor pulled at the back door handle to go inside and check the rest of the house out; he hadn't even seen his bedroom yet.

'Listen, Con, this is a chance for both of us to do something right,' his father said.

Connor froze.

'I know, Dad.'

'Try not to fuck things up at school.'

'I'll try.'

'You better try pretty fucking hard; we can't just move to a new country every time you do.'

'I will, Dad, I promise.'

'You'd better get an early night. You need to get proper rest before you start school on Monday.'

Connor took a deep breath. At least here in Exeter he would get to be who he wanted; he would make himself, he would decide what people saw. What they knew and didn't know. He would make sure no one found out about him.

Chapter 4

Adrian was sitting in the interview room opposite Sarah Lawson, Erica's sister and ICE contact. Imogen walked in and sat down opposite Sarah, who looked like a slightly older version of Erica, although her hair was tidier from the photos they had seen. Adrian noted the puffiness around her eyes; she probably hadn't slept since her sister had been found – as she had been the one to find her.

Imogen noted the date and time, plus persons present for the recording, and then nodded at Adrian to start.

'How are you holding up?' Adrian asked, recognising that look on her face. Grief. Since he had lost someone important, the word bereft had taken on a new meaning. Sarah was obviously bereft, missing something, a touch of confusion mixed with sadness. Like walking into a room and trying to figure out what you went in there for, then realising that you would never find it, because it was gone forever.

24

'I . . . I can't believe it.'

'We're sorry for your loss.' Adrian said the hollow words. He could feel Imogen's focus on him as he spoke; he faltered for a moment as Lucy popped into his mind.

'Your sister appeared to be dressed to go out. Could she have been on a date? Did she mention anything like that?' Imogen said, stepping in to speak, to give him a moment.

'No, she didn't say anything about it.'

'Were you not close then?' Adrian said.

'We were. We were really close. I don't know why she didn't tell me.'

'So, you have no idea who your sister was meeting? She didn't mention anyone to you?' Imogen said.

'I swear I have no idea. If I did I would tell you!' Sarah's voice cracked as she spoke. The tears started to gather at the edges of her eyes. She was on the brink of losing it altogether.

'Is there anyone else she was likely to confide in? Did she have a best friend?'

'I was her best friend! I don't know why she didn't tell me if she was meeting a man,' Sarah said again.

Adrian sighed. 'There could be lots of reasons why she wouldn't tell you, Sarah, maybe she didn't want you to know because she wasn't sure it was going to go anywhere. I know this is difficult, but the more you can tell us the better. At this point we are just trying to build a picture of Erica. She's the victim here and there's a reason she was targeted. The more we know about her, the more likely it will be that we can find out why that was.'

'Was she sexually assaulted?' Sarah said, her body tense, as though she almost didn't want to know the answer. 'Did he rape her? I asked but no one would tell me.'

'There were signs of sexual activity, but at this point there is no evidence of sexual assault, we will know more when we get the post mortem.'

'You think they met before? She wasn't the kind of person who would sleep with someone on the first date.'

Imogen handed her the box of tissues that were on the table; the girl took one and clutched it to her, ready for the tears to come out.

'Is there a possibility it was someone from her work at the recruitment agency?' Imogen asked gently.

Sarah shook her head. 'No, she kind of hated everyone there, she was looking for another job anyway. I don't think so.'

'Did she have any hobbies? Go to any clubs? Any cafés she went to regularly?' Imogen said.

'No, she used to get lunch in the theatre; they did these sandwiches she liked and she never had to wait because no one else ever thought to go there for lunch. It was always empty.'

'What about your parents? Is she likely to have told them anything?' Adrian said.

'Our dad lives in Spain with my stepmother; we aren't very close. Mum died five years ago.'

'I'm sorry to hear that,' Adrian said, inclining his head.

'Is there anything else you can tell us that might help find out who she was with?' Imogen asked.

26

'Was she lonely? Was she looking for someone? Did she ever go on any dating sites?' Adrian added.

'She was never without her phone, I used to get so cross with her for checking it all the time, always talking to someone or other; she had a bit of a problem staying in the real world. She wasn't very confident, but she was beautiful; I kept telling her she was beautiful.' The tears started to fall.

'We're going to do everything we can to find out what happened to your sister,' Imogen said.

'It won't bring her back, though will it? I don't really care if you find the person or not. I just want my sister back. I've got no one now.'

Adrian looked at Imogen. It was an unusual comment; it didn't necessarily mean anything, but in these situations people usually demanded revenge. He made a mental note to find out if there were any known issues between the sisters. Her grief was genuine; he was sure of that. He could see it, and he could feel it.

'Can you tell us what phone your sister had, Sarah? We couldn't find it in her home.'

'I don't know, it was a pink thing, she bought a load of jewels off eBay and covered it herself because she couldn't find a case she liked.'

'Any idea where it would be?'

'Well he must have taken it, whoever did this to her.'

'We thought so too, but we wanted to check with you.'

'Did she spend a lot of time at the computer?' Imogen asked.

'She was always on her mobile – like I said, she was

practically glued to it. She had a laptop though. Did you not find that either?'

There was a short silence; they hadn't found it.

'OK, well thank you for coming in and speaking to us, Sarah. We'll get in touch with you if we need to talk about anything else. Is that OK?' Adrian stood up and held his hand out for her to shake it.

'What's the point?' She stood up, looked at his hand without taking it and turned to leave the room.

Adrian put his hand on her shoulder, she turned back to him.

'I lost someone I cared about recently too.' Adrian felt Imogen's eyes burning into him as he spoke to Sarah Lawson, but he needed to say the words, he needed to get this out. 'I know how you feel, I know you want her back more than anything, and if we could do that we would. We can't. All we can do is make sure the person who did this to her doesn't get away with it. She was important and what happened to her shouldn't have happened. Help us to honour her memory by putting the man who did this behind bars.'

She nodded and sobbed. Even though he knew he shouldn't, Adrian pulled her in and put his arms around her in a hug. She had said she didn't have anyone, and he could feel it in the way she clung to him; he felt her chest heaving as the grief engulfed her. The last person who had hugged her was probably her sister, and now she was gone. He had to pull away before he allowed himself to be sucked into his own feeling of loss.

She looked up at him; he could feel that she had understood what he was saying. He hoped that if nothing else, it had made her feel a little better, even though he knew the truth was that nothing would make her feel the same ever again. She would learn to live with the piece of her that was missing; that was all time did. There was no healing, but there was learning to cope with the absence.

Sarah left the room and Adrian followed at a distance. He felt Imogen's hand on his shoulder.

'Miley, are you OK?' She was breaking their rule of asking about each other's feelings, but for once he didn't mind.

'I will be.' Wouldn't he?

Chapter 5

I'm writing this because I have to tell someone and because I don't think I'm going to be alive for much longer. I can feel inside that my time is coming to an end. In a way, I think it will be a relief when it finally happens, but I'm scared about all the things that may happen before. So, I want to tell you a story, my story. For you to fully appreciate the situation, I'll have to start on the day I met him, the day I met them both.

I had just started working at the service station; I would cycle out there at five in the morning and start my shift behind the counter. They would come in every morning and order the same thing and then go and sit at the same table. The taller one with the big smile would order a full English breakfast and a mug of tea, but the quiet one always just had a bacon sandwich, every day for months. It went on like this until one of them finally spoke to me – about something other than just their food order. It was the taller one, as I suspected it always would be.

Did you ever meet someone and just know that this meeting was the first of many? That from the moment your lives came together there was a story to be told, that you had some kind of cosmic business together, something that needed to play out. I knew from almost the first time I saw them both that my life had changed; I felt something shift inside me. I know that sounds like complete nonsense, but I do believe that I was meant to meet them. I even feel happy saying that. Given all that has happened, it seems strange for me to look upon that time as a good thing, but I swear to you, I wouldn't have had it any other way.

He asked me why I put colours in my hair, told me that the purple streak had been his favourite so far. He asked me my name, and then he just kept talking until the quiet one nudged him and he stopped talking long enough for me to walk back into the kitchen, my boss's watchful eyes urging me to get back to work. For the rest of that day I had a smile on my face; I remembered his interest in me and I felt special. I had always been a bit on the awkward side, a bit of an outsider. I was never the girl that people paid attention to. I stayed in the background and let everyone else get on with their business. If I was ever noticed, it was always for the wrong reasons. I didn't really mind my life being that way, at least I didn't until I met them, but for that one moment I felt special, and suddenly I felt angry about all the people who hadn't made me feel special in the past.

From then on, I looked forward to going to work. Every day felt like a new adventure. I didn't know what he was going to ask me next, and that was exciting. I had had crushes before but only on celebrities, never on anyone I knew, and never on anyone who fed my crush, who nurtured and cultivated it until it was a burning fireball of desire. And for all this, I still didn't know his name. He wore a denim jacket, the kind with white wool inside the collar. There was an embroidered patch on his breast pocket with a rocket on it. The first time I called him Rocket, that beautiful grin spread across his face and I guess the name just stuck. His friend silently at his side for each encounter, looking down whenever I glanced his way.

It only took a few months before I was in love with Rocket.

It was a long time before there was even the remotest possibility that anything might happen between us. I guessed that he was just very friendly; his quiet companion seemed to shrug off his behaviour as though it were completely standard, as though everywhere they went he had to listen to his spiel over and over again. His referred to his friend as JD. Rocket would make statements and then turn to his accomplice for confirmation, and JD would just nod and smile shyly. During those first few months, I'm not sure I even heard JD speak twenty words. Rocket did all the talking.

I remember our first kiss as though it were yesterday. It was romantic, even though from the outside it might not seem that way. To me, though, to me it felt as though my heart was going to explode.

The breakfast rush was over and I was taking the rubbish out to the communal bin area. It was hidden away from the public, but as I pushed the sacks into the giant blue wheelie bin, I heard his voice calling out to me from the staff car park. He must have jumped the barrier and come around there. To find me.

My hair flopped in front of one eye and I couldn't sweep it away because my hands were covered in some mystery substance from the lid of the bin. I held my hands out by my sides, aware that they were trembling somewhat, and I just stared at him with my one exposed eye. I felt so stupid, but still special at the same time. He walked towards me and took the pink streak that hung across my face, tucking it behind my ear. Just like that, after all this time, he kissed me and I will never forget the look on his face when he pulled away from me. He looked dizzy; it was the first time I had seen his confidence shaken. I made him feel something, I knew I did.

People started to notice the chemistry between us and it wasn't long before I could see the people I worked with getting excited at watching the romance unfold. There was something so completely inevitable about us. Me and Rocket. Together for ever.

Chapter 6

Imogen was alone, bar a money spider crawling across her forearm. She watched as it climbed down and onto the sofa arm. She was facing the TV but it was off; the only thing to watch was her own reflection in the black mirror.

Two months ago, her boyfriend Dean had said he'd needed some time apart. The schism between them had seemed irreparable but he'd promised he just needed distance and that then they could talk properly. She hadn't seen him for weeks, but this morning she'd received a text from him saying he wanted to see her again, today, if she was available. He must have known she had the day off. He always seemed to know. Nervous, she'd had a shower and then tried to dress in a way that seemed effortless, natural, not as if she had pained over it for two whole hours. She was angry, angry that he had gone and left her there alone in the first place. In the grand scheme of things though, she supposed she owed him.

During his last stint in prison, she hadn't visited him. After that, when they were together, she had forced him to talk about his traumatic past during the course of an investigation. She had said things she could never take back, things that had been recorded. She knew that his leaving was about being alone, rather than *without her*; she knew he loved her still and that made her even angrier. It was a bit presumptuous of him to assume she would still want him after he had been gone so long – she could have moved on, or the chemistry between them might be out of whack now. You couldn't go back, only forwards. All she hoped was that he didn't hang onto the hurtful things she had said. The doorbell rang and she caught her breath.

'Come in!'

She had left the door on the latch; even though he had a key, she knew he wouldn't use it. She stayed on the sofa, waiting.

When she looked up, he was standing in the doorway. He smiled at her, a wide grin, like the time she had first met him, not the broken man she had said goodbye to all those weeks ago. That smile hit her like a hammer. The chemistry was still there.

'Hey stranger.' He smoothed his hair back nervously.

She stood up and walked over to him. Trying to read him was always impossible. He was such a contradiction, so completely open, but full of secrets. She could see up close how nervous he was; he was waiting for her to make the first move and she couldn't bear to think of him in pain. She leaned up and kissed him on the lips; immediately, he pulled her into him, kissing her as though she were a tonic he needed to stay alive.

'I missed you.' She pulled away. 'How are you?'

'Better now. I just needed some space. I'm sorry. I know it wasn't fair of me to disappear like that.'

She waved dismissively, she didn't want to cry and make him feel bad. She wouldn't have been crying because she was upset that he'd had left her, it was more the sheer relief of him being back. But she had a problem and she knew it. Essentially nothing had changed; he was still an ex-con and she was still a police officer. This was still completely unworkable. She couldn't afford to not address that anymore. It really was him or the job.

'We need to talk, Dean,' she said.

'Already? Don't we even get today?'

'We've had too many days. I just can't ignore this anymore.'

He moved past her and sat on the sofa. She couldn't quite believe she was about to do this. He reached into his pocket and pulled out the key to her place and put it on the table.

'You don't have to say it. I know.'

'You can't not be you, you tried. The truth is I love you for who you are. I don't think you can change and if you did, I'm not sure I would feel the same,' Imogen said, hoping he would tell her that she was being silly, that it would all be fine. Even if she knew it wasn't true, maybe they could pretend.

'Conditional love?'

'That's not it. Do you want me to change?'

'Of course not.'

'Well there you go then. One of us has to.'

'It's not because of what you know about me now?'

'What do you mean?' she said. She had found out a lot of questionable things about him during her last big case, just before he'd left. She'd discovered horrific things about his childhood, growing up in care home after care home, being abused by the owners. He had even admitted to killing someone for her. None of that changed how she felt about him.

Dean took a deep breath before speaking. 'The sexual abuse.'

'No! God . . . no, of course not.'

'Not everyone wants to deal with someone who's been broken in that way.' He looked down.

'You're not broken! Don't say that! Please don't think that.' The tears sprang out with as much surprise to her as to him. She hated the thought of him thinking of himself that way.

He patted the sofa next to him and she sat in the hollow. Putting out his arm, he pulled her towards him and they just sat there for a moment. Wondering what happened next. She felt heavy with sadness; knowing that this couldn't continue was a feeling she was used to, but actually ending it was a different matter – she didn't think she would have the guts. Part of her had wished he had never come back, so this moment could never happen.

'What happens now?' he asked, stroking her hair.

'We go on with our lives, I suppose.'

'Just like that?'

'I kept thinking maybe you were right. Maybe if we had some time apart, then it might work out or at the very least all of this would be easier.'

'I'm sorry,' Dean said, his voice strained.

'For being you?'

'For not being able to change.'

'I don't want you to change. I need you to keep being you, just the way you are. There is something very perfect about you. I'm jealous, if I'm honest. Jealous that you can just be . . . so sure of who you are.'

Dean caught his breath for a moment before speaking, trying to stay in control of his voice. 'Don't be jealous of me.'

She looked up and saw a vulnerability she had never seen in Dean before. He looked so lost, maybe this is how he always looked when no one was watching. She kissed him again before sliding her hand across his chest, igniting the fire in both of them instantly. Almost immediately he pushed her back onto the sofa and climbed up so he was looking down on her. They pulled at each other's clothes and forgot about thinking for a little while. Maybe they could have today after all.

Chapter 7

'So, what do we know so far?' Adrian asked for the third time in as many minutes. His focus was a little off these days.

'We found no technology whatsoever in her place, but her colleagues told us she had Facebook and Twitter and all the other gubbins online so the chances are whoever was in her place took it for some reason,' Imogen said.

'Can we get access to her social media accounts?' Adrian said.

'We're trying. Her sister doesn't know any of her passwords. We can only see what's available to see by the public or friends. Her sister let us look from her account.'

'What about the post-mortem?

'It's happening right now, I believe. I could go and check it out.'

'I'll come with you,' Adrian said.

39

Imogen flashed him a look. He knew what she was thinking. She thought he couldn't handle it. She thought the sight of a dead body would send him careering into an abyss of depression. He could still do his job, even despite what had happened to Lucy.

Lucy.

A journalist who had worked on their last case, a journalist who Adrian had very much fallen for. He hadn't even been with her for very long, he reasoned, so the idea that his whole world had fallen apart now she was gone was ludicrous. Things had changed for him, there was no denying that. The biggest change was the fact that his ex, Andrea, and his fifteen-year-old son Tom had moved in with him following the death of her partner, Dominic – who had been exposed as corrupt at the end of Adrian's last case. Adrian had given Andrea the bed and been sleeping on the sofa for the last two months. It was good to have them around. The first few nights after Lucy died were crippling, having other people move in most likely saved him from himself. He worked late most nights and got into work early most mornings. If nothing else, he was scoring some major brownie points with the DCI, if not his own sanity.

Adrian watched as Imogen thumbed through the post-mortem report. She handed the pages to him but he shook his head.

'Just give me the bullet points.'

'Looks like she might have been on a date, she had traces of white wine and oysters in her stomach.'

'Right,' he said.

40

'It's not clear whether she was sexually assaulted – she definitely had intercourse before she died, and there is some minor tearing, but it seems as though it could have just as easily been vigorous consensual sex. Her genitals were washed with bleach, presumably after death which could mean any number of things. Maybe it was an accident and he was trying to remove any traces of himself, or maybe this is part of a larger ceremony that isn't accidental at all. I've not really dealt with anything like this before.'

'Right, anything else?' He didn't want to verbalise his disgust just yet.

'She has also got some half-moon marks on her neck from her nails, consistent with her trying to fight back, pulling at whoever's hands were there. She basically scratched herself.'

'Oh God, poor thing.' Adrian shuddered involuntarily. 'Do you think it was kinky sex gone wrong? Erotic asphyxiation? Breath control or whatever you call it?'

Imogen frowned. 'I suppose that's a possibility, but there's a certain level of calm around the scene. Don't you think? The way the body was redressed – that's confirmed now by the way; she was definitely dressed after death. Something a bit ritualistic about the whole thing.'

'You think it was planned?'

'It just seems too neat not to be.'

'Yeah. Maybe.' Adrian took the sheets of paper from Imogen and glanced through them. 'Says here that they couldn't find any DNA on or in the body. The bleaching

41

wouldn't get rid of fluids, but it would get rid of trace evidence, right?'

'So, what do we think then? Random or targeted? The underwear she had on suggests that she was on a date, coupled with what she ate.'

'Let's find out which restaurants serve oysters then, there can't be that many places around here. Maybe someone saw her on the night.'

DCI Kapoor came over to Imogen's desk; Adrian could feel her eyes on him all the time, waiting for him to snap or something. It was getting tiresome.

'Did you find out anything from Erica's work colleagues?'

'She was single, she had a cat, a few crap relationships but all pretty short-term, most of them guys at work.'

'Where does she work?' DCI Kapoor said.

'Recruitment agency in town,' Imogen said.

'A lot of traffic then, people in and out. What about clients she's dealt with?'

'We have a list.'

'We're briefing on this in two hours. Grey, I'd like to see you in my office,' DCI Kapoor said.

Grey got up and followed the DCI. Adrian wondered if she was being asked to spy on him and then considered that maybe he was being a little egomaniacal about the whole thing and just maybe it was about something else entirely. He would ask Grey later, she wouldn't keep anything important from him.

Looking through the post-mortem for Erica Lawson made Adrian feel like a traitor. He still had a copy of Lucy's post-mortem in the bottom of his desk drawer. For the last few weeks whenever he reached into the bottom drawer, he looked only with his fingers, not wanting to see the name on the report. He felt closer to her with it there in his drawer and he hated the idea of it being filed with all the other victims. It was on his mind every day, but he didn't see how knowing all the details would help him in any way and so he just kept it nearby. He already knew enough.

He shook off the image of Lucy's lifeless body and put Erica's post-mortem down, picking up the crime scene report instead. There were no other fingerprints in the bedroom, not even a partial, and no fingerprints other than Erica or those of her sister in the rest of the house. That implied premeditation, he thought, the wherewithal to know from the start not to leave prints. The door handles were not wiped clean because the other prints were there, which suggested that the killer knew from the moment he stepped into the house what he was going to do.

Imogen returned and sat down next to Adrian, interrupting his thoughts.

'What was all that about?' he asked her.

'The DCI has asked me to act up as DI.'

Adrian raised his eyebrows. 'Oh! Do I have to call you boss now?' He smiled at her; she deserved this. From the moment they had started working together he had been impressed with her dogged determination and work ethic. She would be a great DI.

'You don't mind? You've been here longer than me.'

'If there's one thing I don't need right now, it's more responsibility.'

'She wants me to go in for the exam. There's a permanent DI spot opening up.'

'You should go for it, Grey, you'd be good.'

'I don't know if it's what I want right now.'

'Well, as long as it's not because of me. You do what you have to do. I think you'd be great.' Adrian said. He vaguely remembered a time when he was ambitious, when he'd wanted to climb the ladder and call the shots. None of that seemed to matter anymore though. Maybe it was the grief or maybe it was the fact that he didn't think he was ready yet. He knew that over the last few cases he had made some questionable decisions. He stood by them though, he probably wouldn't do anything differently if he were put in the same position again. He had come to realise he struggled to put the law before his own morality. He needed to fix that before he could move forward in the police.

Chapter 8

Connor had a crude map in his hand that his father had drawn for him for his first day of school. He followed the directions set out on the back of a betting slip that hadn't paid out. The sun was low in the sky, it almost felt as though it were at eye level, burning into his brain as he squinted to check for oncoming traffic before crossing the road.

It didn't help that Connor had been drinking the night before, probably not the best idea he had ever had before the first day of school. A new school, a chance to make a new impression, a chance to wipe the slate clean and become someone else entirely. Could a person reinvent themselves at sixteen? He had no intentions of being the same Connor he was last year, or even last month. Moving to England would be his new beginning; as much as he hadn't wanted to be here, he had to try. He would stop listening to that voice in his head that made him believe that he would fail so why bother, that everything he touched turned to crap. His father's voice. This time he was determined to be different.

School uniform was a new feeling – a cheap polyester blazer and the alien sensation of a tie around his neck. The emblem on the school badge was some kind of bird, like a heron or something, silver and gold. His tie was black with a red stripe through it; he noticed other people with different stripes on theirs, house colours he expected. It was a relief not to have to wear his own clothes – new clothing was way down on the list of Jacob's priorities and Connor wasn't exactly overly consumed by labels himself. Nice not to have to think about how much they didn't have for a change.

He was inside the building now, and he felt claustrophobic already. The size of the school was significantly smaller than the school he had left in America. He tried to make a note of all the exits and remember the layout of the building. He had already been seen by admissions and had some forms to fill out, which he did dutifully. Nowhere to hide. He noticed a few kids looking up from under their fringes, but mostly everyone just got on with it. As they disappeared into their classrooms, he observed that there didn't seem to be the same cliques and divides as there were in his high school back home. Maybe it could be different this time.

He walked through the empty halls until he found the room he was looking for and headed in. The kids were all getting settled into place, pulling their mathematics books out and whispering. There was one seat left at the front left-hand side of the class, so he pulled the plastic chair out and slumped into it. Connor could tell he'd caught some people's attention in the way fresh blood always did.

'I hope you have all finished your half-term assignments because there will be no extensions granted.' Mr Cross walked into the classroom and perched himself on the edge of his desk. He looked over the class, his eyes settling on Connor.

'I'm new here, just started today,' Connor said, aware of how alien his Californian accent sounded, noticing the stir it caused.

'Ah, yes. Welcome, Mr Lee.' Mr Cross stood up and wrote Connor's name on the white board. 'Class, we have a newcomer – this is Connor Lee, who will be with us for the rest of the year. Let's all give him a warm welcome.'

The class started to clap. Connor heard whistling from the back and wished he could leave. He turned to look at his classmates and gave a small wave. There was a girl sat diagonally across from him, and already he could see she had that look in her eyes, a familiar look of lust directed straight towards him. Her hair was a silky white blonde pulled up into a bump at the front with a long sheet of dead straight hair beneath. She smiled and looked down, pretending to be coy, but Connor knew her, or at least he knew girls like her. Escaping his past wasn't going to be that easy if he kept falling in with the same types of people wherever he went.

He turned his attention back to the front and tried to concentrate on the class. Everything about it was different to back home; the tables were arranged in a horseshoe with a block of tables in the centre, unlike the individual desks facing the front that he'd had back in the US. Connor watched as the kids continually ignored the teacher, huddling together in whispers while he spoke. Mr Cross didn't seem to care much either way, he just got on with the lesson. There was a general air of going through the motions, a let's-get-through-this-together type of camaraderie. Mr Cross ran through his well-rehearsed lesson plan and then instructed the class to work from their textbooks until the bell rang. Occasionally, Connor heard the row of girls behind him giggling and got the feeling he was the source of their amusement.

After the class had finished and people began to file out of the classroom for break, Connor looked to see where all the smokers were going. He really wanted to go for a cigarette and he knew that there must be somewhere – there was always somewhere.

'Hey, Connor.' The blonde girl came bounding towards him, her skirt folded up at the waist to make it shorter, the short fat stump of her tie resting on her breasts. She was reminiscent of the cheerleaders in his form back home.

'Hi.' He kept it short.

'I was in your maths class just now, I sat across from you.'

'Oh right, hi. Sorry, my memory isn't so great,' he lied.

'I'm Pippa.' She held out her hand for him to shake; he took it reluctantly, but she seemed even more reluctant to let it go. 'So where do you come from? I haven't seen you around here before . . . plus, you know . . . the accent thing.'

'You know everyone in town?'

'Everyone worth knowing,' she said, blinking slowly with a tiny smile at the corner of her lips.

'Maybe I'm not worth knowing then,' he said.

Connor pulled out the top of the packet of cigarettes from his shirt pocket. Desperate for a smoke, he looked at Pippa with one eyebrow raised in a question. She smiled and grabbed his arm, pulling him outside and down the corridor towards a large grey building at the side of the school field, beside a row of hedges. It looked older than any building in his home town in California.

'Behind here.' She pushed the hedge to the side and slipped in. He followed her to find a couple of other kids hiding behind there smoking too; it was completely obscured from the view of the school windows. Pippa held on to his arm, keeping him to herself.

He took a cigarette out and lit it before handing it to Pippa. She took a drag, then handed it back to him, her eyes just peeping out from under her eyelashes. She was making sure he knew she was interested; it couldn't have been much more obvious.

'What is this place?' he asked.

'It used to be a church or something, like a little chapel, back when this was a religious school. But it stopped being one, like, a hundred years ago and so now it's used for all the sports equipment, the big stuff, for like, sports day.'

'It's cool.' He ran his hand along the brickwork. Some

49

of the pointing crumbled and fell away beneath his fingertips.

'Are you doing anything Friday night?' she asked him, taking the cigarette from his hand again and dragging on it before handing it back.

'Yeah, I'm going skydiving,' he said with a cheeky smile, unsure why he was flirting. He didn't need to.

She cocked her head to the side, knowing full well that he was talking crap.

'A bunch of us are going to hang out, you can come if you want?'

'Um . . . sure. I can skydive anytime.'

Pippa skipped triumphantly backwards and out through the hedge, calling over her shoulder, 'Cool, meet us by the back gate after school on Friday.'

She disappeared and he finished his cigarette, thinking. Maybe things would be better here. Maybe he could make friends after all.

Chapter 9

Connor managed to escape the first day of school unscathed. He was already popular, even before trying out for the rugby team. He liked doing after-school sports – it was a legitimate reason to not be at home, a reason his father wouldn't argue with, a reason Jacob wouldn't see as time-wasting.

Connor had had a meeting with the sports teacher at the end of the school day. He had sought him out, told Connor he was excited to have him in the school, how some fresh blood might shake up the team, along with some inevitable jokes about how American football wasn't really that impressive because they are all padded up. Nothing he hadn't heard a million times before from his father. He laughed along as though he found it as funny as the coach, but he had seen the kind of injuries that could be sustained during what he called football and it wasn't a laughing matter. Padding or not, the sport was serious and the injuries were real. Still, he'd agreed to try out for the school rugby team.

As he walked home from school, he spotted just ahead of him the girl he had seen in her bedroom next door when he had been up in the tree house. She had her head down and eyes to the ground as she moved with small, fast steps. She was on the other side of the road to him, opposite their houses. When she drew parallel with her house, she crossed the road without even turning to check the traffic. Connor frowned. It was almost as if it were him that she was avoiding. He couldn't think why. She disappeared inside her house, and he picked up the pace and ran home.

Once inside, Connor dropped his bag on the floor and rushed out to the garden, quickly climbing the tree until he reached his den at the top. He saw the girl close her bedroom door and slide her backpack onto a chair. She took off her coat and hung it on the door before grabbing a large hooded jumper out of her cupboard and putting it on. She kicked off her shoes and grabbed a book from a shelf next to her bed, then lay down and began to read. Connor pulled his cigarettes out now that there was no way she would notice him.

After some time the light outside started to fade and he saw her reach for her bedside lamp. At the same time, he saw the kitchen light in his own house come on. His father was home. Unwilling to deal with him just yet, Connor decided to light up again and wait until the last possible moment before heading back inside.

'Con!' Jacob called from the back steps. 'Con, are you out here?'

Connor put the cigarette out and shuffled across the floor to the exit. He climbed down, annoyed that he couldn't just be left alone for once. So much for keeping out of his father's way.

'So how did it go?' Jacob asked as he walked back into the kitchen.

'It was OK, how was work?'

'Same shit, different place.'

Jacob took a swig of beer, draining the bottle. He picked up two fresh bottles off the table and handed one to Connor. Connor noticed his father's mood and decided now was as good a time as any to bring up going out the next evening. He had promised he would be different to how he had been back home. He'd vowed to try and mix with good kids and get in with the right people, not people who would try and coerce him into doing stupid things. But maybe those *were* his people, they seemed to find each other. Pippa reminded him so much of the girl he had back home. They didn't look alike, but they were the same type. Not even the cultural differences could hide that desperation to be popular, to be envied and coveted. Connor was familiar with those feelings, although they were gone from him now. All he wanted was to be allowed to be himself.

'Is it OK if I go out Friday? Some of the people in my class invited me bowling,' he said.

'As long as you're back by ten . . . Let me guess, you need the car? Just be careful over here, don't forget you shouldn't be driving for another year.' Jacob rolled his eyes and Connor left the beer on the side, going upstairs before he got embroiled in another conversation with his father. They didn't always end as well as this one.

Chapter 10

Having finished with the list of people who had used the recruitment agency and specifically dealt with Erica Lawson, Imogen was frustrated. Every single person had an alibi for the night of the murder and so it was back to the drawing board. Of course, it wasn't going to be that easy. They had already checked menus of the restaurants closest to her house and moved further afield in a spiral pattern. In order to check for witnesses, they would have to visit the restaurants that flagged as serving the right type of food themselves. They had two restaurants to visit in the city next, they needed to speak to the staff and check any footage that might be available through CCTV. Imogen's stomach growled at the thought of food. It was nearing lunchtime and she hadn't eaten since yesterday. She looked over at Adrian who was staring at some paperwork, although she could tell that his eyes were not connected to the page but instead lost in thought. She wondered when he'd last eaten.

'What say we go down the Guildhall and pick up one of those jacket spuds? I'm starving and I'm not sure I can face the canteen food today,' Imogen said.

'OK. I'm down with that.'

'It's right by the restaurants we need to go to and we can show them the pics of Erica, see if they saw her with anyone,' Imogen said. She felt as though she were overexplaining, but if Adrian suspected she was worried about him, he would shut down. Cautiously, she reached out to pat him on the shoulder.

'OK, you're acting weird. What's going on?' Adrian folded his arms and leaned back in the chair, his eyebrow raised suspiciously.

'I'm hungry, that's what's going on.' She knew he wouldn't take kindly to any show of sympathy at this point, but he didn't look well. He didn't seem to stop for lunch any more, or go home in time for any kind of substantial meal. He looked to be in a permanent state of exhaustion as far as she could tell.

'Bullshit. What's up with you?'

'Nothing!' she protested, in a voice slightly higher than normal.

'You don't need to worry about me, Grey, I'm fine. Just a little tired.'

'Well that's lovely, but I really am starving. Come on.' She walked out, knowing he would be following behind her. She had to remind herself not to be too nice to Adrian. Not to arouse suspicion. He had been there for her before, now it was her turn to be there for him. They were a package deal, her and Adrian. She always felt in safe hands around him somehow – they were more than colleagues; they were friends.

Outside, she opened the car door and got in – less than ten seconds later Adrian was sitting in the passenger seat, resigned to doing as he was told. They drove to the Guildhall and parked in the multistorey before walking to the centre and ordering lunch at the jacket potato vendor. They sat on the low-lying wall and ate in silence for a few minutes. This was all a strange feeling for Imogen, aside from her mother she had never looked after someone before, not like this. She was genuinely concerned that Adrian was hurting and she wanted to make his pain go away. Knowing that she had no control over that, she tried to control the things she could, like making sure he ate. It beat thinking about her own problems.

'OK, you were right, I feel better,' Adrian said eventually.

'Me too. Let's go and see this Carmichaels place and The Bay Tree restaurant then. Let's also hope she didn't travel out of town for her date or we will have a shitload more restaurants to get through.'

'That's the spirit!'

They walked through the arch onto the high street, then down to the cathedral square which was still partially cordoned off due to the horrific fire that had ripped through the Royal Clarence Hotel, the oldest hotel in England, in fact the first building to use the term 'hotel' in England. The hotel had collapsed in on itself after burning for over twenty-four hours in October 2016. Now it was just a façade, the interior completely obliterated. No floors, walls or ceilings, just a charred empty box on the inside. In the corner of the square, tucked out of the way was a small restaurant with a blue exterior called The Bay Tree, and on the opposite side of the square was Carmichaels, a burgundy-fronted restaurant. As much as it would make sense for them to split up, it was better to go to both places together, see if anyone was behaving strangely when they were shown the photo. It meant that one of them could keep an eye on things while the other one did the talking.

They walked into The Bay Tree as the staff were clearing the tables after a lunchtime rush. They offered a reasonable set lunch menu and Imogen made a mental note to remember it if she ever went on a date again. Now that Dean was gone she didn't see much chance of that. There was a Mediterranean smell about the place, lemon juice and olive oil, fresh coriander and salad vegetables. A flustered blonde waitress with pink cheeks and a glistening forehead approached them.

'Table for two?'

'Ah, no thanks.' Imogen flashed her warrant card.

The waitress's eyes widened in surprise, followed by an irritated huff, obviously annoyed at their timing.

'We need to ask you a couple of questions. Were you working here on Thursday night last week?' Adrian said.

'No, I wasn't, sorry, but Tanya was. I'll get her for you.' She seemed relieved that they wouldn't need to speak to her. She forced a smile and disappeared back into the kitchen, scuffing her ballet pumps along the ground as she went.

A few moments later another woman appeared. She looked around thirty years old and had cropped black hair, so pristine that it looked painted on.

'Jenny said you wanted to ask something about last Thursday? Tanya Maslin.' She nodded and folded her arms.

'I don't suppose you remember this woman coming in for dinner last week?' Imogen held up her phone; she had a taken a photo of a photo in Erica Lawson's house. 'She would have eaten . . .'

'Oysters. Yeah, she was here.'

'You remember her?'

'Oh yeah, she was quite tipsy when she left; they drank a lot of wine.'

'I don't suppose you remember who she was with?'

'A man, blond, shoulder-length hair, about six feet two I reckon. He was early forties, I think.'

'That's a good memory you've got there.'

Tanya Maslin shrugged.

'Do you remember anything else about him?' Adrian asked.

'He was cute. Cuter than her.'

'What do you mean?'

'I mean he was a solid nine and she was a six.'

'Wow, OK.' Imogen rolled her eyes.

'OK, a seven. But he was definitely out of her league. Probably why I noticed them. I can't get a date but a girl like that can? Ridiculous.'

Imogen shook off the urge to shout at this woman who seemed to think she was in a position to judge other people, or at least other women. Imogen had known plenty of women like her in her time. Women who saw other women as competition, constantly looking for advantages over them, for flaws to exploit. Imogen couldn't imagine anything more lonely or insecure.

'Do you think you would be able to describe him to a sketch artist?' she asked.

'Maybe. He kept his head down a lot, his hair was pretty unruly as well. I got the feeling he was trying not to be seen; he asked to be seated in that corner over there. Normally when men behave like that it's because they're out with their bit of fluff but, in this situation, I don't think so. I can't imagine anyone cheating with a girl like her. I mean, you usually trade up, don't you? Why do you want to find him?'

Imogen bit her tongue before responding. 'We need to speak to him with regards to an ongoing investigation.'

A look of realisation dawned on Tanya's face. 'Wait, she was that girl in the news, wasn't she? I knew I recognised her from somewhere else too!'

'Do you have their card receipt or anything?' Imogen asked.

'No, he paid in cash. I remember because it's quite unusual and he gave me a huge tip. You don't think it was him, do you?' she said in an incredulous tone.

Imogen didn't get the impression the woman was particularly bothered about having served a murderer. It was more likely that she couldn't quite believe that someone who was attractive would do something like that. She had been quite open about the fact that she thought Erica Lawson was not pretty enough for this good-looking stranger that she had barely met.

'We just need to eliminate him from our inquiries.'

'So, what do I do now?' Tanya asked.

Imogen pulled out her notebook and pen.

'I'll need your contact details, home address and phone number, any mobile numbers you might have. Then we'll contact you and arrange a time for you to meet the sketch artist.'

'I'm Tanya Maslin, as I said. I live at 15, Gladstone Road. I'll write my numbers down for you.'

She grabbed a napkin and took a pen from her pocket, scribbling down three telephone numbers and her email address. She handed the napkin to Adrian, who wasn't paying any attention to her at all.

'Thank you, that's all,' Imogen said before Tanya Maslin disappeared back into the kitchen. Imogen couldn't help but notice how distracted Adrian was; she wished there was something she could say or do that would help him get through this. Maybe he should have taken more time off work, not that that would help. Work was probably the best place for him.

They left the restaurant and took a photo of the exterior.

'Don't suppose there's any point getting forensics down here?' Adrian said.

'We'll tell the DCI and see what she wants to do,' Imogen said.

'You know what this means, don't you?'

'Don't say it.' Imogen felt her body tense.

'CCTV. Now we know where, we're going to have

to see what cameras around here might have on record from last Thursday.'

'Oh God, I can't face it tonight. I'll start in the morning.'

'I'll get started,' Adrian said. 'I've got nothing better to do.'

Imogen kept glancing at him as they walked back to the car; his head was down and he was watching his feet as he walked, lost in his own thoughts again. No one volunteered to watch hours of mind numbing CCTV of an evening, he must be struggling. She knew that he needed to grieve in his own way, but she just didn't think he was dealing with it at all. Just pushing it down and pretending that it was all OK without the girl he had barely had time to fall in love with. She didn't know what to do.

Chapter 11

Connor felt Pippa's hand on his thigh. He edged across the bonnet of his father's car and knocked back the beer he had in his hand. The fact that he was breaking the law made him even more attractive to Pippa; he could see how impressed she was when he turned up in it. He looked over at the group of kids they had come out with – they were different from the kids back home. There was less competition. Granted, though, it was a smaller town and so you didn't get the superstars of high school like he had back at his previous school. The truth was, Connor had been one of the superstars, but he didn't want that again, he didn't want the constant pressure and expectation. He didn't need to feel like he was letting anyone other than himself down if he fucked up and went off the rails.

Connor had had girls like Pippa all over him back then, too. Girls that saw him as a trophy boyfriend, a symbol of their status within the school. Always with a boyfriend, always attached to someone, her self-worth measured by the popularity of the boy she can attract. Right now, Connor knew he was the hot topic. Even if he hadn't looked the way he did, he was unknown and therefore interesting. The kids here were a lot less uptight, a lot less concerned with image and popularity and the cliques didn't seem to be that well defined, unlike the huge school he'd got kicked out of, where not even his football skills could save him.

Connor looked at his watch, aware of the time, aware that his father had told him not to be late.

'Got somewhere better to be?' Pippa asked.

'I need to get home soon.' He swilled the last of his beer, then tossed the bottle into a bush.

'You have a curfew?' she giggled.

'Nah, nothing like that, my dad needs his car back.'

She sidled up to him again, moving her hand up his thigh, edging ever closer to his zip. He looked down and watched closely as though he was watching her touch someone else's leg. Maybe this technique worked on the boys here.

'How can I convince you to stay?'

Connor jumped off the car and pulled his keys out of his pocket.

'I really should be going.'

Pippa looked deflated by this. He knew what she wanted; she wanted him to break the rules for her, to prove that he would get into trouble just to have a little of what she was offering. It was hard to resist, not because of who she was but because of what he wanted. It had been so long since he had felt close to anyone.

'Can you give me a ride home then? I live on Gloucester Road,' she said, undeterred by his efforts to shake her off.

He sucked in a deep breath and exhaled slowly, giving in to the inevitable again. Be normal and do what you're supposed to do, then people won't ask too many questions. He had to fit in; he was already at a disadvantage because he stood out like a sore thumb. There was no reason to draw even more attention to himself by turning down one of the hottest girls in the school. It didn't make sense and people would wonder why. He couldn't have people looking too closely at him – and so he opened the door for Pippa.

Outside Pippa's house, the sound of the car clock rolling over made Connor pull back from her and look at the dashboard. All the zeroes. Midnight – his father would not be happy. Connor's seat was pushed right back and Pippa was straddling him, both of them with shirts unbuttoned. Pippa kissed Connor's neck, making a lot of noise about it. She sat up a little; he looked through the space between them and saw her tanned breasts inside her cornflower blue bra, striking against her white-blonde hair.

'You aren't like the boys around here.'

'Is that a compliment?'

'Oh, hell yes.'

Connor glanced at the clock again as he pushed Pippa off him; she was light but fit under her clothes. He did his flies up. Connor remembered his girlfriend back home, how they would have sex in his car, how she would use sex to make sure he stayed in line. This had been a huge mistake. Connor felt torn between wanting what he used to have and running from it, knowing full well what the outcome had been. He couldn't replace the girl he had lost, the life he had lost, and he didn't really want to. He didn't want history repeating itself.

'You should go inside,' he said, 'I need to get home.'

After dropping Pippa off, Connor pulled into his own drive. The house was completely dark as he walked towards the front door. He pushed the key in as quietly as possible. With any luck, his father had drunk himself into a stupor again and passed out in front of the television.

The door clicked open and he stepped inside. Dead silence. He waited until he could see the bottom step before he attempted to go upstairs. As his eyes adjusted to the light, a weight lodged in his stomach. He noticed the shape of a man, a silhouette to be precise, leaning against the wall at the end of the hallway.

'Jesus Christ!'

The light came on. Connor saw that the figure was Jacob . . . drunk.

'Nope, just me,' his father said quietly.

'You scared the shit out of me!' Connor exclaimed.

'What the fuck time do you call this?' Jacob said through gritted teeth, edging closer to Connor, who instinctively tensed and leaned away.

'I had car trouble.'

'Car trouble? What? Do I look like a fucking idiot to you or something? You think you can just lie to me whenever you feel like it, you little prick?' Jacob's voice got steadily louder as his temper took hold.

'OK, sorry I'm late. I won't do it again.' The sound of his own voice pleading made Connor feel sick. How pathetic. He should just tell him where to go.

'You're damn right you won't! If you screw things up this time you are on your own, I'm not moving to a new house again.'

'I'm not going to screw anything up; I'm just a bit late.'

Jacob moved in towards Connor and looked him dead in the eye.

'No girl is worth ruining your life for, asshole. Keep your dick in your pants and your mind on school.'

Connor sighed. Jacob didn't understand, how could he?

'OK, I get it . . . jeez.'

'Are you trying to be clever?'

'No, Dad, I'm just tired. I'm going to bed.'

Connor took a deep breath and put his foot on the first step. He could tell that his father was looking for an argument. Connor's instinct was always to fuck up and contribute to these inevitable confrontations. He had promised himself when they moved to Exeter that he wouldn't keep doing it, but the tighter Jacob's grip, the more Connor wanted to pull away. He moved up the stairs, unwilling to stay and repeat every argument they had ever had.

'Don't you walk away from me!'

Connor fell onto his hands as Jacob pushed him with full force; the second step jarred against his shin, the bare wood clashing against bone, his leg instantly throbbing. He quickly shielded his head, knowing the places his father liked to punch, and curled into the smallest ball possible, protecting his ribs, throat, face and stomach. Right on cue, Connor felt the full weight of Jacob's trainer as it hit him in the thigh. Connor's eyes closed tight and he hoped that Jacob would keep kicking the same spot as it didn't hurt so much there and it was easy to hide. His father was unhealthy with a bad leg, so the kicking part didn't usually last very long.

Connor heard a metal clinking sound; the sound of Jacob's belt unbuckling and being pulled quickly from his waist. He knew what came next. The hard edges on the side of the belt cut into his skin as it connected with his shoulder. Jacob had wrapped the belt around his fist, either to protect his hands, or to cause maximum damage – the buckle always left the biggest mark.

'Dad, please . . . Please, I'm sorry!' He hated to beg, he wasn't even convinced he meant it.

'I'll make you fucking sorry!'

He hit him a few more times, each time slightly harder than the last, until Jacob ran out of steam. Finally, Connor heard the familiar sound of Jacob's foot dragging as he walked away. He got worse beatings when his dad was sober; at least when he was drunk he ran out of energy faster.

Connor waited until he knew his father was gone before uncurling from his self-imposed cocoon. It didn't really hurt yet, but that was because of the shock. At least he hadn't had a seizure this time. Getting beaten up by his dad was bad enough without the added humiliation of losing control of his faculties altogether.

Pulling himself up, Connor peered into the lounge and saw his father sitting in front of the TV with a beer in hand. As though this interaction had never occurred, as if it were all just a dream. Connor trudged up the stairs and flopped onto his bed, wanting to fall asleep before the pain really started.

As he lay there, he heard mutterings through the wall, coming from the house next door. It was a low sound, an almost drone-like murmur. He realised that any kind of volume would most definitely have been heard through the walls. He exhaled deeply, embarrassed that his neighbours might know what kind of a man his father was, what kind of a coward he was. He couldn't think about it right now.

He closed his eyes and thought instead about the home he had left behind. The home that wasn't really a home anymore, not to him anyway. He thought about his old friends and how he wished he was back there with them. Occasionally, on nights like this, he would try and remember to feel fortunate. He had been told time and time again how lucky he was. He thought about a girl in his old class called Marianne; they had been in school together for seven years. He remembered the last time he saw her vividly – she had been hanging a banner for the end of year summer prom. Standing on a ladder in the cafeteria, obscuring the clock with it. The thing he remembered most about Marianne was that she had always worn yellow shoes in all the time he had known her. He tried to push her out of his mind as he recalled the image of one yellow shoe in the school gym . . . He didn't want to think about Marianne anymore. Sleep. He wanted to sleep and forget, wake up in a new day and deal with that rather than with this.

Chapter 12

It was a long time before he kissed me again, but I wanted it every single day. Whenever I went out to the bins I half expected him to be there but he wasn't. I could tell he was taunting me with it, trying to make me want him even more. It was working; I wanted him more than anything. He was playing a long game and winning.

On my nineteenth birthday I was offered the day off work but I said no – I wanted to go in, I wanted to see him. On that day he came in late, and he was alone. He was holding a bunch of flowers and he told me that Caroline, the girl who worked with me behind the counter, had told him that it was my birthday. That was when he asked me out. A week later we had our first date.

He took me to an Indian restaurant, the nicest one in town, and after we finished our meal he walked me home. The route took us through an alleyway and before I knew it I was pinned against the wall, his body pressed against mine. I couldn't have gotten away even if I had wanted to, which I didn't. We kissed for what seemed like forever and I was flying. I straightened myself out before I got home, before he politely handed me back to my father, who couldn't have been oblivious to what had just passed between us. If he knew though, he didn't show it. It might have been easier for everyone if he had just put his foot down and forbade me from leaving the house again.

I didn't sleep that night; I was so full of excitement, I wasn't sure I would ever sleep again. I could tell in the following days how disappointed my father was in me, but he let me live my own life. He didn't want to be the overbearing parent, he didn't want me to run away again.

Rocket and I became lovers, stealing moments at work and spending every other minute that we could together. He would drive me to work in the mornings – JD would sit in the back seat and say nothing – he never said anything. On Saturday afternoons, we would go to the reservoir and dip our toes in the water until one day I saw a stoat or something in the undergrowth and freaked out. After that we would drive out to the little villages that surrounded the city, each time getting slightly further and further away until eventually we would drive for over an hour before we would stop, looking for that perfect spot for us to hide.

Eventually we found a small town with a river running through it. There was a bend there where the pool of water was bigger, like our own private Garden of Eden. Rocket would lie at the side of the river and watch me swimming in the water, sheltered from the sun by a willow tree that hung over the riverbank. We were hidden from the rest of the world. We never ran into anyone else and this became our special place. I would be frozen when I got out of the water, my skin cold and wet, but he would still throw me down on the grass and make love to me, not caring about his own clothes or the fact that I was numb to his touch.

Those days by the river I felt invincible, as though no one could ever shatter the woman I was becoming. I was stronger for him, or at least I thought I was. I had been so preoccupied with being free that I hadn't noticed my isolation from everyone else. The only world I knew was Rocket. My friends had given up on me. Laughing my absence off at the fact that I was in love and that life never gets better than this honeymoon period. They were right about one thing. Life never did get any better, it only got worse. I was totally complicit in my own demise and I wasn't even aware of it until it was far too late.

It wasn't for a full year that I began to really notice what was happening. Rocket had asked me to move in with him and I'd said yes. He and JD shared a house but JD worked a lot and was never home. My parents helped me move my things, and then we said our good-byes. I assumed I would see them a week or so later, but I didn't see them again for two months, and the time after that it had almost been half a year since we'd met up. In fact, I didn't really see anyone from before I'd met Rocket – this man that I was so blindly in love with that I accepted everything he did or said without question.

JD started dating a bottle blonde and moved in with her; she was pretty but she talked so much. It was hard to imagine him being with a girl like her. Maybe her constant noise took the pressure of talking away from him. Sometimes I caught him looking at me across the room when we were all together. He didn't make me feel nervous or bad though. I couldn't put my finger on it at the time, but I realise now he was checking that I was OK, looking for outward signs of stress or distress. He knew where this was going; he had been here before. But still he didn't warn me.

Rocket would sit next to me wherever we went, his arm always around me, or if he couldn't do that then his hand would be on my knee or my shoulder. I thought this was affection, but I now know that it was possession. I belonged to him, he had plucked me straight from my parents' arms and put his hooks in me. He had never mistreated me, but I had never stepped out of line, I had never done anything unexpected or out of the ordinary. Until then I had never done anything that he saw as questionable. He had moulded me into the girlfriend he wanted – adoring, loyal and fiercely in love.

He got a promotion at work and so he told me I could stop working if I wanted to, but I didn't want to, I enjoyed my job. It wasn't the most glamorous of jobs admittedly, but I liked the hours. I started at 5 a.m., worked for eight hours a day and still had half the day to enjoy myself. I think, looking back, this was part of the problem. Those few hours between when I finished work and Rocket came home from his shifts at the hospital. He didn't know what I had been doing and that bothered him.

His friend owned the camera shop SNAPPO'S and Rocket got me a job there so we could meet for lunch every day as it was near the hospital. I left my waitressing job and started working in the camera shop. I had talked to him before about how much I had always wanted to be a photographer and so he bought me a camera. It wasn't an expensive one, it was an old Russian camera that I had mentioned; it produced imperfect images and that was the kind of art I wanted to create, maybe because I had always felt imperfect myself. I thought Rocket was supporting my love of photography by finding me a job more suited to my interests. Although I missed having my free afternoons, it was good to be doing something different. The manager paid my wages in cash to Rocket, but at least I got my films developed for free as a perk of the job.

In a little over a year my life had been transformed. I had no family around me anymore and it seemed as though my friends were all moving in a different direction to me – it wasn't until much later that I realised they just didn't like him, they didn't trust him. I wish someone had told me, had made me look at what I was getting into, but no one said anything. There was nothing to say, I suppose; for all intents and purposes, he was lovely. I couldn't fault him – there was nothing to fault. He was generous and kind and he was always good to me. Until he wasn't.

Chapter 13

The toilets were empty when Selina walked in; she hurried into the stall and closed the door. They had a ten-minute break before the next lesson and she had a terrible stomach cramp. She held her breath as the exterior door opened and more people piled into the bathroom. The faint aroma of cigarettes, Impulse and hairspray in the air told her it was Pippa, Liza and Naomi. They ran the taps and she listened to them speak, imagining them reapplying the black lines to the corners of their eyes, curling their eyelashes and applying a rosy lip gloss. This was their bathroom ritual, it was how they managed to look preened at all hours of the day.

'So, did he take you ALL the way home then?' Naomi said, her raspy voice instantly recognisable.

'A lady never tells!' Pippa said.

'Right, so what happened then?' Liza's deep and sultry tones were also easy to spot as she jibed Pippa.

'Bitch,' Pippa said and they all burst out laughing.

'So, what did his dick look like?' Naomi said quietly. The laughter continued.

'Naomi!' Pippa called out, indignant.

'No! I mean is he like, circumcised? I heard all Americans do that shit. Is it weird? What's it look like? Are you seeing him again?'

'We're hooking up at the weekend.'

Selina guessed they were talking about her new neighbour, Connor. His arrival at the school had caused quite a stir. Most of the kids in school all knew each other from primary or even nursery school – they were all from similar neighbourhoods, so when someone new came in all eyes were on them. Add to that the fact that Connor had an American accent and he was one of those typically chiselled sporty boys, there was no chance these girls weren't going to get their hooks into him. She looked at her watch; it was almost time for class and she didn't want to be late. She flushed the toilet and took a deep breath before exiting the cubicle to face the girls.

'Have a good listen, Dildo?' Pippa said.

'You're such a fucking freak,' Naomi muttered.

Selina walked up to the sink and washed her hands. She could feel them all staring at her.

'You should let me straighten your hair, you know, it would look so much better than that ratty mess,' Liza said.

Selina pushed past them and out into the hall, finally exhaling properly. Since she had started at the secondary school, those three girls in particular had made her life hell. Having a surname like Dilley didn't help, completely lending itself to the term Dildo, which had been her unofficial name since she had been twelve years old. It didn't bother her as much as they probably hoped it did. She had much bigger things on her mind than those idiots.

Connor stood by the rugby pitch watching the rest of the class. He had been dreading his first sports lesson and for it to come just a couple of days after an argument with his father made him even more nervous. He liked to play sports, but he was worried about the changing rooms afterwards, aware that he had a lot of marks on his body, more than the usual teenager. He knew he could lie about where they came from, but he didn't like the attention. He tried to stay in the moment and just focus on the game for now, trying to discern who the weaker players were. He already knew the rules, as his father had always made them watch matches together and so it wasn't something he couldn't pick up. It was strange not to be kitted out and protected, strange to just run on into danger. Connor liked the idea of it.

Mr Wallis, the P.E. teacher, blew the whistle and subbed Connor into the game. There were only a few minutes left, but he got the ball and ran hard with it, right into the fray. Within seconds, he was under a pile of guys. The whistle blew again.

'Can I have a word, Connor?' Mr Wallis called him over before shouting at the class. 'Everyone back in formation. Start again.'

Connor ran to the teacher, slightly breathless, slightly out of practice. He had been kicked off the team a few months earlier at home and so his physical fitness was not as hot as usual. It wouldn't take him long though, a bit of training and he would be back on top.

'Yes, sir?'

'You sure you're up for this? You'll have to unlearn a few things, and despite what you might think, it's quite different to the football you're used to, not harder – but different. Rugby is tougher in the sense that players play the ball continuously. But with American football, because of all the breaks, you get to play harder when the ball is in play. You'll need to conserve energy at certain times with rugby. You don't need to go full out every time you have the ball. You'll learn soon enough, but if you play like that constantly you're going to end up with some pretty nasty injuries in no time.'

'I can handle it.'

'I'm sure you think you can. But for now, humour me.'

'OK, sir.'

Mr Wallis blew the whistle and the boys stopped playing immediately. They all rushed back towards the school building with much more enthusiasm than they had when playing rugby.

'I read about some of your sporting achievements at your other school and we're lucky to have you here. You just have to keep it together. We play rugby on Mondays and Fridays and then general games on a Thursday, until next term, and then we switch to football – or soccer as you might call it – for spring, then back to rugby in the summer term. We're looking forward to seeing what you can do.'

'Thank you, I'll do my best.'

'I'm sure you will. Now go get showered and changed.'

Connor grabbed his things and headed for the changing rooms. When he got in, all the other boys were out already and drying themselves off which was a relief as it meant he got to shower alone. One of the other boys in the class smiled at Connor as he opened his locker.

'Hey, Connor.'

'Hi . . .' he replied.

'It's Neil. You did great out there, it's good to have some fresh blood on the field. How did it feel without all that padded crap you guys wear?'

'It felt pretty good.' Connor was used to this kind of talk; he had heard it his whole life from his father.

'Hey, I have my driving test soon. If I pass we're all going out. Do you want to come?'

'Sounds cool, sure.'

'Great,' Neil said, 'I'll let you know.'

Connor waited for Neil to turn his back and then slipped into the shower when he was sure no one was looking. He got under the water, the heat of the shower soothing against his bruises. They didn't hurt as much as they should have because he was used to feeling bruised. The first few times it was much worse, but now, he could take it. This was the norm and maybe it was exactly what he deserved. Playing rugby would provide the perfect excuse for the large purple lesions left behind by the buckle on his father's belt; it had pierced the skin as it always did, faded versions of the same marks mottled the rest of his body. There were several marks across his torso. It was the reason he threw himself into football back home. Because people just accept that you get bruised when you play sports. He never got asked any questions, not once.

Connor put his clothes on, his hair still wet, the collar of his shirt cold and damp against his neck. He gathered his things and threw his backpack over his shoulder, both eager to get out of here and anxious to get home. He hoped his father would be out at work today, he couldn't handle the pretence and he hadn't seen him all weekend, not since the beating.

Walking home, he saw the girl from the house next door on the opposite side of the street to him. She kept her head down as she walked. He hadn't noticed her at all at school during the course of the day. She obviously hung in different circles. He could tell she knew he was there, she must have seen him and she didn't want him to speak to her. She walked a little faster and then disappeared into her house. He found himself walking faster to get home, to get to his tree house, to watch her.

Chapter 14

'Nothing,' Adrian said flatly.

'What do you mean, nothing?' Imogen put two cups of coffee on the desk and sat down next to Adrian, looking at the clock – it was a little after ten in the morning. He picked his up immediately and started drinking. She wondered how long he had been sitting here.

'Absolutely nothing on the CCTV, not even her. I've watched everything from around the cathedral and the circle outwards to her house. I even got hold of the surrounding shops. Everything that was working, anyway. It's taken forever and there's not one single image as far as I can see.'

'What about the drawing? The one Tanya Maslin instructed on?'

'Here. Take a look at that and tell me what you see.' He handed her a photocopy of the picture Tanya Maslin had come in to create with the sketch artist that morning before she started work. There was something very familiar about him.

'Isn't that Kurt Cobain?'

'She must have her wires crossed or something. We know it wasn't him at least, he's dead.'

'Well, if you believe the theories, then he's living on a desert island somewhere. Or at least I like to think so.' Imogen had cried when she'd heard that Kurt Cobain had shot himself; she had idolised him as a teen. Now just reduced to being another member of the twenty-seven club, an ever-expanding group of celebrities who'd died at that age – Cobain, Winehouse, Hendrix, Joplin, Morrison. Strangely, all musicians that Imogen had listened to growing up. Twenty-seven, the same age as Imogen.

'According to Tanya Maslin, he was in The Bay Tree with Erica Lawson,' Adrian said.

'She didn't seem like a liar, maybe he really did look like this.'

'Seen anyone like that wandering around town?'

'Maybe he wasn't local.' Imogen shrugged. 'What did the DCI say?'

'She didn't think he was that hot.' Adrian let out a cheeky smile.

'I mean about what she wants us to do with it.'

'Hit the neighbours again, see if they saw him come or go. Maybe the pic will jog their memory,' Adrian said.

'Fair enough. Anything else?'

'Gary has some news on the social media front, but Erica was conspicuously absent from all the usual haunts. He wants us to go see him.'

Adrian stood up and rubbed his eyes. She guessed he had been here all night watching all those tapes, and probably slept at his desk. Worrying about Adrian was definitely a good way to distract her from her own problems. They made their way to Gary's office.

'How are you holding up? You look tired,' Imogen said.

'Home is crazy. It's hard. Andrea is acting like the wife I never had and it's just so overwhelming, I never get any time to . . .' he trailed off.

'Is she looking for her own place?'

'No, she's in major denial about what's going on. We're headed for a big conversation. I don't want to, but I just need some space.'

'You can't have your ex living with you, especially with you guys' history.'

'I can't kick her out, Grey.'

'Well if you ever need a break, you're welcome at mine,' she offered.

As they arrived at the tech lab, Gary shot Imogen a look, a question in his eyes: *is Adrian OK?*

She shrugged almost imperceptibly in response. *As good as can be expected.*

'Welcome! Can I get you some coffee?' Gary asked. 'I bought my own machine, one of the ones with the little capsules. Don't tell everyone though.'

'Just had one thanks. But you'll be getting a lot more visits from me in the future,' Imogen said.

'Why do you think I got the machine?' he said, grinning.

'So, what do you have? Did you find out anything

new about her? Was her relationship with her sister as solid as it seemed?' Adrian asked, skipping past the small talk.

'Sarah Lawson gave me access to their personal emails and texts and as far as I can see the sisters were very close. No big arguments, just the occasional passive-aggressive advice. As far as Sarah Lawson goes, she wasn't aware of any social media accounts Erica had and it's definitely trickier without her laptop to see what websites she was using, but we contacted her ISP and got a full history.'

'And?' Imogen said impatiently.

'She had a Facebook account under a different name. All her own pictures, but the name is Nina Lawless. I searched Nina Lawless and found several profiles on various free social messenger and dating sites. She wasn't stupid though, there was no indication of where she lived from her online photos. You would be surprised how many people post pictures that show their house, street name, all sorts.'

'She was hooking up with people?' Imogen said.

'I don't know how many she actually hooked up with, but she was most active on one of the apps connected to Facebook. It's a social game where you trade on your avatars, your profile photos, buy and raise each other's value, like commodities. It's all done online, like a stock exchange type thing. People from all over the world take part. Everyone owns someone and everyone is owned by some else. You can see her profile here.' He pulled up a profile and some music started to play: 'Where Have All The Cowboys Gone'.

It was a hazy romantic visual of Erica, photos of her sitting on her bed, a little cleavage showing, a little pout, then a picture of her hugging her cat, the camera angled to make her eyes look bigger. The next photo was her holding her hands in a heart shape. Further down the screen was a little bio. Erica was looking for love, or at least some affection.

'So how do we see who she was talking to on this thing?' Imogen said.

'Well it's tricky because it's not a UK-based organisation, but I have requested access to the other accounts that we know of. We should get access to Facebook within a couple of days. This one might take a bit longer, if they even decide to comply. But take a look here.'

Gary scrolled further down the screen and they could see messages posted on the page, her wall; some were obviously first messages from people she had not interacted with before. There were other messages though, fragments of conversations between 'Nina' and various people. Men from all over the country, all over the world. Gary clicked on some of the thumbnails that linked back to their walls; some had pictures of male models that had been adopted as their personas, some had candid pictures of lesser known actors that they were pretending were pictures of themselves. There were greetings from 'Nina' on their walls, too, all friendly, all very generic.

'All these messages seem pretty innocuous though, would he be this obvious? Can you private message in this app?' Imogen asked.

'Yeah, once we gain access we will be able to see the

personal messages, they'll be on this wall here but in red. We can't see them at the moment, they're hidden. I'm working on it.'

'I didn't even know things like this existed. It's weird,' Adrian said.

'It's fun for some people. Not everyone is as good-looking as you,' Gary said.

'Are you on this app?' Imogen asked, worried that Adrian had touched a nerve.

'No, but I have been on games like this before,' Gary said.

'Why are they free? What's the point of them?'

Gary pointed to the screen. 'People buy gifts, the game developers get rich. Here, look, you can give gifts to the person whose profile it is. The majority of the gifts are free, and you can earn tokens to buy bigger gifts, but you can also buy the tokens: a hundred pounds for three hundred tokens.'

'What kind of gifts?'

'So here, for five tokens you can buy someone a daisy, but for a hundred tokens you can buy someone a ruby. Erica has several diamond rings on her profile. They have been given as gifts by admirers. Each one of those cost the person in question twenty pounds.'

'But that's just an image, not a real gift.'

'Yeah, but the more expensive the gifts you get, the more valuable you seem as a commodity.'

'Why the hell would anyone do that?' Adrian said.

'Social media romances can be intense, and these games are very competitive. It's all about displaying how popular you are and how much you're worth in the game.'

'How much was Erica worth? What was her rank in the game?' Imogen asked.

'She was a middle-level player,' Gary said, 'which is actually pretty high. Imagine it in terms of a Hollywood hierarchy in the real world. She would be a supporting soap star, as opposed to an A-list movie star.'

'I don't really understand anything you just said,' Adrian interjected.

'I get it. I may or may not have been on something similar to this in the past. Briefly, mind,' Imogen said.

'Really?' Adrian shot her a look and she scalded him with her eyes, hoping he would understand what she was trying to do. Adrian probably couldn't understand what it was like for Gary, who was lovely but didn't have the same confidence with women that Adrian did. She had witnessed Adrian's effect on the opposite sex on several occasions, mystifying as it was, but Gary certainly had completely different experiences when it came to women.

Imogen noticed that each name had a country flag next to it; she assumed it was the user's country of origin.

'Is there any way to know where the people who visited are from, like exactly?' she asked Gary.

'Maybe, if she had a tracker set into the code. It's pretty standard practice and easy enough to do. It looks like she was well into this game, her wall is quite artistic and stuff, a lot of specialised coding – it wouldn't be unrealistic to assume she had a tracker built in. Once we get the other side of the account it should be easy enough to find out. Although you can fool the tracker by tricking it into thinking you are from somewhere else by using a VPN, but not everyone would even think to do that, so you never know.'

'Can you track on all social media then?' Imogen asked, unfamiliar with Gary's capability or even which code the game developers used.

'It's much easier on these sites where you power your own HTML code and have access to customise themes and designs through the code itself. Not really as straightforward in apps that don't give you that kind of access.'

'And what's this counter for?' Imogen said.

'It's how many visits her page has received since she started on the game.'

'Oh good, it's over a hundred thousand,' Imogen said sarcastically.

'Looks like she's been playing it for a couple of years. There's also a chance that this isn't her first account. There's one thing for sure though.'

'What's that?' Imogen said.

'She definitely had a personal computer or laptop; there is no way she would have been able to maintain this level of involvement with just a phone. So, if you can find that, you will find out a lot more about her and who she interacted with. Nina Lawless has a big online presence. She was pretty obsessed with this game and, the way it works, it makes sense to have more than one profile, so a dummy account to interact with you to make you look more popular.'

'Really? People do that?'

'Yes, any one of these could be Erica's profile as well.

She might have wanted to make someone jealous, make fake money or tokens in the game to send herself gifts. Who knows?'

'You understand all of this? I can't get my head around it,' Adrian said to Imogen, shaking his head.

'Is there any indication of a possible suspect among the evidence we have so far?' Imogen asked.

'I think judging by the way her attacker has managed to avoid all cameras and stuff, we should work on the assumption that he lives quite close to here. At least in the UK. Once we get into the account I can look at her tracker if she has one. I think most people do,' Gary said.

'What if she doesn't?' Adrian asked.

'How about we set up a profile for me?' Imogen said, surprising herself. 'Gary, you would have to be in control and keep an eye on it. But let's assume the guy found her through that. If he knew where she was from, then it's possible that he was specifically targeting someone from this area, someone close to him.'

'Not a bad idea, I guess,' Gary said.

'You can try and connect with the people that she connected with. See if any of them raise any alarms,' Imogen said to Gary, whose face lit up.

'Ooh catfishing, my favourite,' Gary said.

'You worry me, mate,' Adrian said.

'Can you be a convincing girl though?' Imogen asked Gary.

'Can you?' Adrian said to Imogen. Imogen thumped him in the arm, relieved to see the trace of a smile on his face.

'This isn't my first rodeo,' Gary said. Adrian raised his eyebrow; Gary's capacity to know things was genuinely impressive. He didn't know where he found the time.

'OK – make me a profile and I'll send over some suitably cheesy photos,' Imogen said. 'Gary, can I borrow your cat?'

Gary laughed. 'Um, sure? I can take the photos for you if you want? I'll drop by your place with my camera.'

'OK, great.'

Adrian was still staring at the website. 'What I don't get is why use fake photos? Like photos of models and stuff?' he said.

'Because some people collect other people for friendship, and some people collect styles of pictures.' Gary clicked on a profile picture that was electric blue digital art; sure enough the rest of the wall was full of electric blue profile pictures interacting with the user. Almost like little cliques within the game.

'You've got a handle on this though? You know how to play? You can get up to the same rank as her?' Imogen said.

'I can. I kind of love this sort of thing. I'll let you know tomorrow how it's going. Why are we using your photos though? Why not a fake?'

'In case anyone wants to meet, or video chat or whatever.'

'Try to make your pictures a bit naff, don't look too hot or anything. Look normal and like a cat person,' Adrian said.

'What does a cat person look like?' Gary said, that offended tone in his voice again. Was the bromance over? Adrian seemed to be getting on his nerves, or maybe it was something else.

'I don't think there's any danger of me looking too hot,' Imogen said.

'Nonsense, Grey, you're a solid nine.' Adrian got up and walked out.

Chapter 15

'I made dinner.' Andrea stood up as Adrian walked into the kitchen. 'It's nothing special, just a beef stew.'

'You didn't have to do that.'

'I wanted to. You've been so kind . . . after everything. You don't have to stay out of our way you know. It's your house.'

'Where's Tom?' Adrian noticed the table was set for two and felt uneasy at the idea of trying to maintain a conversation with Andrea alone tonight. 'I haven't had much of a chance to speak to him lately.'

'He's sleeping over at Robin's.'

'How's he getting on with the new school?'

'Good. You know he always hated the private school anyway. Here, let me serve you.'

'It's OK, I'll do it. Don't worry.' He pulled up a chair and sat down at the table. The turquoise stew pot stood in the centre; he had forgotten he even had it, it had belonged to his mother, one of the only things he had left from his childhood. It reminded him of the better times they had had together and so he couldn't bring himself to give it away. He was pleased to see it. He had to admit, it was nice to have real food for once. His dinners mainly consisted of takeaways or frozen ready meals. 'Did you work today?'

'Yes of course I worked! The sales are on,' she said defensively. Andrea worked in a local department store, front of shop in cosmetics.

She pulled the lid off the pot and spooned the stew into Adrian's bowl. He closed his eyes and stopped for a moment, remembering where he was in time. Since moving in with him, Andrea had almost reverted to the dutiful girlfriend he'd had as a teenager. This wasn't reality – or at the very least, this reality wasn't possible anymore. He couldn't count the number of times he had wished for this, for them to be together again, but this was different to what he had always imagined. From the moment he had met Andrea he knew she was his destiny, that there would be no way of letting her go and for years after she left him he had pined for her. But that was before he'd met Lucy. Now the love he felt for Andrea was different: less complicated, less urgent. They had been through a lot together and they were good friends, something he had never thought himself capable of with her. He didn't want that to change.

She put the spoon down and sat opposite him, smoothing out her skirt and smiling. She looked as beautiful as ever, except he didn't see her as something he could own anymore.

'We should talk.' He pushed the bowl away from him a little.

Her face instantly tensed and she looked down at her hands; he noticed her nails were short and she had been picking at the skin around them.

'I don't know how to talk about this.'

Ever since the toxic marriage with her husband Dominic had ended so violently and abruptly and she had moved back in with her school sweetheart, the conversation had been nothing but small talk. No mention of all the deception or all the lies, of all the animosity that had been part of their relationship for so many years. He had honestly never believed a day would come where they would be even capable of this much civility, but here it was. They hadn't really spoken about what had happened over the last few months, even years, but Adrian couldn't play this game any longer. He had to confront her.

'Andrea, Dominic told me that you were together before we broke up. How long for?'

'Not long, I swear. Tom is yours, if he told you any different . . .'

'I know Tom is mine, that's not the issue.' It had never occurred to Adrian that Tom would be anything other than his, and the suggestion of it made him feel sick.

'I know it sounds terrible, Adrian, but you have to know you were hard work,' Andrea said. 'You had all these problems with your dad, and I didn't know if you could be who you needed to be . . .'

'What does that mean?'

'I mean, we were bringing a child into the world, and I didn't know what that would be like for you. You realise we were the same age that Tom is now? Not even sixteen. Can you imagine him with a baby? Your family was so dysfunctional. I was worried whether you even knew how to make it work.'

'Were you worried about all of that before or after you met Dominic?'

'Does it matter?'

'It matters. Were those your thoughts or his?'

'I don't know!' Andrea screeched out of the blue. She started to cry. He couldn't remember the last time he had seen her cry.

It suddenly dawned on Adrian that he had been quite selfish about the whole thing. He had been blaming Andrea for bringing Dominic into their lives, but in fact the opposite was true. It was on Adrian, or at least on his father. Adrian's father had been the catalyst for Dominic's behaviour. The men had been friends when they were younger. After an indiscretion that led to the breakdown of Dominic's life, Dominic had been driven to destroy Adrian's father. When Adrian's father was dead and his need for revenge had not been satisfied, Dominic moved onto Adrian and anyone he cared about. He needed to punish someone for the mistake that had destroyed his marriage and his life. Andrea had been collateral damage in the fallout, as had Adrian.

'I'm sorry,' Adrian said. 'I know this isn't easy for you.'

'You can blame me for him if you want, in fact I

would do the same if I were you. If I weren't so easily fooled back then.' She picked up the wine glass on the table and drank the last of it before pouring herself another.

'No. I don't want to blame you.'

'I shouldn't have cheated on you, Adrian. I just want to forget he ever existed.'

'That's going to be very hard. You were together for over ten years.'

'I feel like such an idiot.' She glugged the wine again; he noticed the bottle was empty. She stood up, agitated, and walked over to the window, hugging her arms tightly around her.

'You're not an idiot,' Adrian said gently.

'I just feel like I failed Tom, and you. Will you ever forgive me? For cheating on you?'

Adrian sighed. 'Don't even think about that now. It really doesn't matter, none of it matters. We're all safe and that's what's important.'

'I can't believe I didn't see through him.' Andrea said.

Who was Adrian to judge her? He was a police officer and he hadn't known what Dominic had been up to. All of his dodgy business deals, the people he used and mistreated along the way just to get to Adrian. It must have been so hard for Andrea to accept that she was just a pawn.

'No one did,' Adrian said.

Adrian walked over to Andrea, coming to stand behind her and placing his hands on her shoulders reassuringly. He could feel her vibrating with anguish.

Not because she had been a widow for two months, but because she had found out that more than a decade of her life had been wasted on that liar. He was annoyed at her for giving Dominic an in, but at the end of the day that wasn't going to help anyone. The truth was – and he would never admit this to anyone else – but he felt a little bit vindicated by the fact that he wasn't the only one who'd ever messed up. He had always been the shit parent, the shit boyfriend, the loser. All of that was gone now and he had been given a clean slate. She turned around and sunk into his chest, sobbing. He smoothed her hair with the palm of his hand.

'We don't even have anywhere to live,' she cried into him.

'We'll sort all of that out, and you can stay here for as long as you need.'

'Thank you.'

She looked up at him, her eyes red and glassy, tears streaking her cheeks. She licked her lips and sniffed, trying to regain her composure.

'Come on. I want some of this stew you made.' He smiled at her.

She leaned up and kissed him on the lips; for the briefest of moments, there was the familiar feeling of her mouth on his. The scent of her up close had never changed. He pulled back instinctively, not wanting to revisit that part of his past. He didn't need this complication. Aside from anything else, it was too soon after Lucy.

'Sorry.' She wiped her mouth and ran upstairs.

Adrian shook his head and sat down, picked up his spoon and started to eat. He had to think of something to change this situation. There had to be a way because he couldn't carry on like this much longer.

Chapter 16

It started innocently enough, I suppose, or maybe it had started a long time before I even noticed it. The first time he put his hands on me, I had the bruise for almost two weeks, watched as it changed from black to yellow, his fingermarks on my arm where he had grabbed me. I was tired and wanted to go to bed early, but he had other ideas. The look in his eyes as his fingertips sunk into the fleshy part of my arm shot chills right through me. It was the polar opposite of his smile, so warm and welcoming. For a split second I realised I didn't know him at all.

From that night, I started to notice other things about him, things that I had found endearing before but which suddenly scared me. The way he made sure always to jump up and answer the phone before I could get to it, telling people who called for me that I was tired and resting and would call them back. Little actions that controlled everything I did. If I was home alone,

I noticed how the atmosphere was different to when he was around. I felt like a possession, not the girl I had once been.

It was a little while before he hurt me again, this time with the back of his hand across my face. I waited for the apology, the begging me to stay, but there was nothing – he just looked at me with contempt and the spirit inside me shrivelled even more. As time went on I noticed myself holding my breath, waiting for something to upset him, waiting to be reprimanded.

JD started to come around the house a bit more and I tried to keep the carefree face that I had always employed in his presence, but I could tell that he knew what was going on. Sometimes he would even shrug at me imperceptibly. JD was the only other person who I was allowed to speak to outside of work. I could tell he trusted him implicitly and I wondered why they were even friends. JD seemed like a good man.

Rocket never hit me across the face again, but he did hurt me. Small, malicious movements; a pinch here and there, accidentally burning my arm with his piping hot coffee. I know I should have left him, I knew then, but it just didn't seem like a possibility. I had no one around me to tell me I was being mistreated and so I just continued to let it happen over and over again. I didn't think I had any way out.

It finally came to a head on my twenty-first birthday. We went for a meal together and the waiter smiled at me – he may have even winked at some point. Rocket was so angry, I could feel his eyes on me, blaming me somehow for the interaction. I don't remember exactly what happened that evening as it was all a bit of a blur after we left the restaurant.

I knew, I knew before the dessert even arrived at the table that it was going to be a bad night. He slid a box across the table to me. In it was a necklace, a gold infinity symbol with diamonds in it. He told me it was a promise to me, a promise that I would be his forever, that he would never let me go. The anger behind his eyes promised me pain. He said he would put it on me later with a look that turned my stomach, nothing that anyone else would notice but I did.

When we got home, I made my excuses and went to the bathroom. I locked the door behind me and rushed to the basin to throw up. Infinity. For ever. Was this my life now? Forever scared of what was coming next. Forever hiding in the bathroom.

I sat on the toilet lid with my head in my hands, fingers trembling, wondering when he would finally come for me, knowing that it was as inevitable as the sun rising and feeling as though I needed to get out of there; if I didn't I would eventually end up dead.

He pounded on the door exactly three minutes later – I know because I was staring at the clock. I told him I must have an upset stomach from the meal and he told me to let him in so he could look after me; his voice was soft but the edge was there, the edge that told me he was lying. I had to make a decision on what would be worse for me: opening the door, or not. So, I opened it.

The next thing I remember I woke up in the bedroom and he was on me, in me, my neck was sore and I had *the briefest flash of his hands around my throat. He had choked me unconscious, then dragged me to the bedroom. I couldn't tell at that point whether I was on the bed or not, but I recognised the pale primrose yellow walls. I turned my head, saw the skirting boards and knew I was on the floor. What struck me most was how I wasn't upset or even surprised – he had conditioned me to expect it. I tried to imagine myself accepting something like this two years earlier; if someone had told me that this was what love was then, I would have never hungered for it the way I had done. I was sold a dream that reality could never live up to and my reality was even further from that. I closed my eyes and waited for him to finish, not offering any reaction or resistance at all. When he was done, he left the room, and moments later the front door slammed shut.*

I went to the mirror and looked at my face; my make-up was smudged and I had been crying at some point, I hadn't even noticed. The mascara streaked away from my eyes towards my ears like raven claws. I filled the sink with hot water and considered for a moment submerging my head entirely in the steaming pool, taking my skin off completely – then I might look on the outside like I felt on the inside. Instead I just stood and stared at myself, wondering who I had become. Why hadn't I fought harder, not just tonight but before now? How had I let it get this far? I needed to get away from him but I was convinced that if I ran he would find me. I didn't know what to do.

Chapter 17

Imogen hated photos of herself. She actively avoided posting any pictures online, fully aware of how images had a tendency to float around forever. They had been to a seminar several months ago about the dangers of social media and showing people how to be careful online, how easy it was for your photos and information to be misappropriated. The internet was basically a data-mining nightmare. Everything you typed in was dragged through different algorithms to see what to advertise to you, how to get you to engage, to spend money, to click on links and boost pages with paid advertising. It was all about the reach, how many hits you could get.

Imogen was one of those people who would avoid going on any websites that required you to sign in or download something in order to participate. It was getting harder and harder to do that these days though. Right down to paying household bills, it was so much easier to pay for things online than try and get through to a person on the phone, and good luck with those voice-recognition answerphones.

She picked up her phone and tried to take a selfie, not something she was particularly adept at. The doorbell rang and she breathed a sigh of relief. She opened the door to find Gary standing there holding a cat carrier, with a holdall slung over his shoulder.

'I was joking about the cat, Gary.'

'Oh. Never mind, we're here now.'

'I was trying to take some pictures for the site before you got here, but I'm so rubbish at it.'

'I'll help you. You're going to need at least twenty photos, I reckon.'

'*Twenty?*'

'Well, I'll need some private ones for personal messages, in case it gets that far.'

Imogen sighed. 'Fine.'

'Let's start in the bedroom,' Gary said.

'Not even going to buy me dinner first?' Imogen said and Gary's face flushed red.

They went upstairs and Gary released his cat, Schmiddy, onto the bed – the cat instantly curled up as if he had always lived there, curving his back into the pillows and padding his paws against the duvet cover. Gary carefully took any personal pictures Imogen had in frames around the room out of shot.

'We'll use my camera, it's easier,' Gary said, 'and then I already have the photos. I'll send you a copy of all of them, in case you want them for anything.'

'Why would I want them for anything?'

'Whatever. I would be more comfortable if you had a copy anyway.'

Imogen shrugged. 'OK. So, what do I do?' she sat on the edge of the bed.

'Do you have a book you can pose with?' Gary said

'This one?' She grabbed a book from the top of her chest of drawers and showed it to him. Luckily it was a book Denise Ferguson, the duty sergeant, had given her and not one of her police manuals. She didn't have a lot of time for reading. She kept meaning to make time for it but it never seemed to happen.

'OK – now lie on the bed next to Schmiddy and put the book against your neck as though you've just paused to take a photo.'

Imogen lay back and immediately the cat edged closer to her. Gary climbed on the bed and hovered over her, moving the camera around until he found an angle he was happy with. He posed her arms a little to make her look a bit more natural, and with her free arm he brought it up so it was touching the camera and looked like she was holding it. He took several photos of this pose, some with the lamp on, some with the main light on. Then he got off the bed. She never would have thought of any of this stuff; Imogen was far too pragmatic for this kind of thing. Thank God Gary was pretty much good at everything.

'This really isn't your first rodeo, is it?' she said.

He just grinned. 'OK, can you change your top and maybe let your hair down? I'll just move things around in here a bit if that's OK?'

'Go for it.'

Imogen went to the corner of the room, slipped off her oversized sweater and found a white Aran jumper her mother had bought her, worn maybe once. It definitely looked like something Erica had worn in her profile pictures. When she turned around, Gary had messed her bed up and the cat was sitting at the foot.

'OK, lie here and kind of pose with the cat. Act like you adore him.'

For the next hour, Imogen posed with and without make-up, holding food, hairbrushes, wearing vest tops, dressing gowns, even an evening dress which she struggled to find, eventually discovering it screwed up in a ball at the bottom of her wardrobe in the spare room. They took photos in every room of the house, trying to build up a portfolio of selfies that had to look as though they had been taken over a period of time.

'How many did we get?'

'We did pretty well, I got about forty.'

'Blimey.'

'I'll go and upload them and show you guys tomorrow. I'll try and make some headway with the guys on Erica Lawson's Nina profile tonight.'

'Isn't it too late?'

'No, most of these people do this stuff in the evening. I've got a good few hours' playtime, enough to build your profile and get you noticed. The newbies who know how to play get a lot of attention. A lot of suspicion, too. But they won't be able to link you back to any other accounts or any fake pictures, so that should work in our favour. Some people put a lot of real money into this game, so they take it very seriously.'

'What happens if they think I'm someone who has played before?'

'Well, they'll assume that you'll take yourself to a certain value then bail on the game, leaving them with a dead commodity that won't work for them. The more socially active you are, the more you're worth.'

'Rather you than me. It sounds complicated.'

'I'm looking forward to it.'

'Thanks for your help, Gary,' Imogen said. 'Can I get you some food or anything?'

'No thanks, I'm going to pick up a kebab on the way home.' He opened the cat carrier and Schmiddy just strolled inside and lay down. He must have been the most placid and obedient cat Imogen had ever known, not like the neurotic ones her mother had raised. He almost made her reconsider her distrust of the animals.

'Thanks again Gary, and thanks in advance for the shit Adrian's going to give me over those photos,' Imogen said as Gary put his hand on the doorknob.

'How is he?' Gary asked. She could tell Gary was worried about Adrian and didn't know how to help him. None of them did.

'Trying at least. I think as much as he would hate to admit it, having Andrea and Tom there is keeping him from completely disappearing into grief and depression. He has to behave himself and that's a good thing. Above all else, Adrian worries about screwing Tom up and so I think he's being careful to at least seem to be looking after himself.'

'Well, tell me if you think we need to cheer him up or anything.'

'Will do.'

He opened the door and left Imogen in her own empty home. Wandering through the house, she stepped into the kitchen and looked at the stove. She knew she should eat but she wasn't hungry. Sleep was all she wanted when she was left alone these days. She hated being alone. Unable even to visit her mother in the evenings anymore because Irene was in another country after reconnecting with the love of her life and disappearing on a round the world holiday together. Outside of work, her life had become completely monochrome. She needed a hobby. Maybe she should take up gaming.

She put talk radio on and curled into a ball on the sofa, not wanting to fall asleep to the sound of silence, trying not to think about Dean. She pushed all thoughts of contacting him out of her mind, just like she had every night since the last time he had been here, when they broke up. There were an endless stream of questions running on a loop in the back of Imogen's mind. What was he doing now? Was he alone? Had he found someone else already? Did he miss her? Was he nearby? If she called would he answer? It never ended, like an old broken record player somewhere in the distance.

Eventually the sound of the radio host talking about the politics of the day drowned out her own inner monologue. It would go away eventually; she would get over losing him one day. Just not today.

Chapter 18

Alyssa walked along the river with her dog, Casper, in tow. Casper stopped every few metres, sniffing out any trace of scent that another dog may have left. Alyssa didn't mind though. She was checking her phone almost constantly for updates. She was waiting to hear back from Drew; it had been at least four hours since she had last contacted him and it was unlike him to wait so long to reply – unless something was wrong. She couldn't help but go into a panic when he deviated from the normal behaviour, aware that he could never contact her again and there was nothing she could do about it. One time he didn't contact her for two days and she freaked out, thinking that was it, that she had done something to upset him when she refused to send him a picture of her in her bra.

R U there? she typed.

Sorry, I had a visitor ☺.

Anything important?

No, just a Jehovah's witness. What you doing?

Taking Casper for his constitutional then I'm going to the gym, she lied; she wanted him to think she was toned and full of energy, not the sloth that sat in front of the computer all day at work and then did exactly the same at night when she got home. Her dog walks were the only real exercise she got. That's why she'd got a dog in the first place, to slow down the rapid spreading of her backside.

Do you wear those sexy yoga pants ☺?

I might ☺

I would love it if you sent me a picture of that ☺ Maybe when you get home we could video-chat and you could show me?

Really? You got your laptop cam fixed?

She caught her breath. In the back of her mind something had been niggling at her since they had met: he wouldn't give her his phone number, he wouldn't give her any details about him. She had seen a few photos, but she wasn't sure if he was real or not. Now she might actually be going to see him!

It's the only way you'll let me see you – I guess I had no choice.

It was really happening. Finally.

OK, I have to go, Casper's just done his business. I'll skip the gym. See you on video chat in an hour?

C U later ☺ ☺ ☺ Can't wait.

Alyssa bent down, picked up the dog mess and walked over to the bin, a stupid smile on her face. She wondered what the other dogwalkers must have thought of her, looking so happy to be picking up shit but she didn't care, this was it, what she'd been waiting for.

She had been talking to Drew for a couple of months now. They had run into each other online and hit it off immediately. It was like they were part of the same mind. They shared the same taste in movies, music, books, everything. They spoke on messenger whenever they were online. Sometimes for hours at a time. He made her feel both special and normal at the same time. It was a strange thing to find someone that made her feel normal. Alyssa had never been the girl that guys crossed the room to talk to. She was better online. She was good at making herself seem desirable on a screen. That's why she spent so much time doing it. She knew how to take photos that flattered her. She knew how to make herself look both more voluptuous and slimmer. Her skin always looked like cream in her pictures, whereas in reality it was kind of pasty. She would stand in front of the window, the light in her face acting as a photo editor, washing out all the flaws.

Alyssa had plenty of online admirers, but she knew that they talked to everyone the way they talked to her, hedging their bets. Not Drew though. He spent all his time talking to her. She knew he cared about her; he didn't just talk about himself, he mostly asked how she was doing, and when she complained about anything, he knew the exact things to say to make her feel better. They just fit so well together.

Alyssa walked a little further along the river and then turned around back towards her flat. She was cutting her walk with Casper a little short today. She wanted to shower and do her hair before she saw Drew on camera, before he saw her.

At home, she washed and blow-dried her hair, put her make-up on, contoured her cheekbones and dimmed the lights. She put on a black dress, hoping that it was slimming enough, hoping he wouldn't be put off by her. Hoping their bond was strong enough to get past the superficial. The camera symbol flashed on the screen of her laptop. She was so nervous yet so excited. She took a deep breath before she clicked on the button and then there he was. He was real. He was even better looking on camera than he had been in the pictures. A smile spread across his face when he saw her and all her insecurities melted away.

'Look at you!' he said.

'This is so surreal,' she laughed, unable to contain her excitement.

'You look so beautiful.'

'No, I don't. I can see myself, you know?'

'When are you going to believe me when I tell you how hot you are?'

'Maybe never?' she said but the way he was looking at her told her otherwise. 'Where are you? That doesn't look like your room.'

'I wanted to speak to you about that. I got a huge bonus from work so I bought a new laptop to tell you in person.'

'Tell me what?'

'I'm here, I'm in Exeter. I got the train this afternoon. I'm staying in a totally awful hotel though, I tried to change it, but I couldn't. It's freezing cold in here.'

'What?' She felt suddenly dizzy – what was he saying?

'Can we meet up tonight? I mean, if you don't have anything on. I know I took a risk, and you can say no, there's no pressure.'

'Stop talking! When and where?'

'I don't mind, but can we make it soon? I'm absolutely starving, I've been travelling all day.'

Alyssa looked at him, really looked at him. He was real, that niggling feeling in the back of her mind that told her there was something up with him was gone. At first she had assumed he was a woman or a kid or a much older man, mainly because there was no way a guy like him would be interested in her. But now she could see him on the video, a real life moving person, and he had come here, all this way to see her from Cheltenham. He was so perfect, so completely handsome. She opened her mouth before she even had time to think.

'You could always come here.'

Chapter 19

Connor woke to the familiar sound of the shopping channel blaring through the house. He put his school uniform on. No time for a shower. There was dirt all around the hems of his clothes and he made a mental note to do a wash later. Connor washed all the clothes in the house; if he didn't, then no one did. It was not something on his father's radar of important things to do.

Downstairs was the even more familiar sight of Jacob passed out on the sofa, beer bottles dotted around like a shrine. Connor looked at him, lying there with his mouth slightly parted, the alcoholic wheeze escaping every few seconds, and he thought about how easy it would be to just pick up a cushion and put it over his face. He closed his eyes for a moment and imagined the scene for the hundredth time; in every scenario, his father would overpower him and win. He always won.

As he walked to school he looked for the girl next

door, but she had either left already or wasn't going in. He felt drawn to her and he didn't know why. Maybe because she seemed to actively avoid him. Maybe it was something else.

In chemistry class, Connor assessed his classmates again. He was starting to see the cliques; it was like a three-tiered hierarchy with a few kids floating on the periphery, either through choice or because no one had claimed them. Connor had been claimed by the popular kids and there didn't seem to be much he could do about it. Pippa was sat at the end of the long wooden bench – he could feel her watching him, yet another claim that had been made on him. Maybe having sex with her in the front of his dad's car was a mistake, maybe she thought this meant something more than it did.

He wasn't paying much attention to what the teacher was doing. No one ever got rich doing science, as his father always said. It was all about getting into profes-sional sports. The injury to Jacob's leg was always the basis for these conversations. Connor didn't know how lucky he was, how lucky that he still had the chance that his father had lost. His dad never spoke much about his career in football, but Connor's uncle had shown him news clippings from way back when, from before the incident. Jacob had always implied that his injury was sport-related but Connor's uncle, Joel, had set him straight – his grandfather had done it, Jacob's father. The damage to his knee and foreleg never healed and Jacob was left with a cane for the rest of his life. Connor wondered if he was living the same life his father had led, if one day he would be drowning his sorrows in alcohol and dreaming of a life he never had, forcing his son to follow in his footsteps under an iron rod. He shook the thoughts off and started to listen to the lesson. Even science had to be more interesting than thinking about his legacy.

He was obscured from the teacher, and so while no one was looking, he turned on the Bunsen burner in front of him, watching the flames dance as he played with the settings. He held his hand high over the heat and slowly lowered it until the centre of his palm was in agony. Connor held his breath as the pain intensified; he couldn't pull away now, he had to show his strength, show he wasn't a coward. He clenched his teeth together as the flesh began to sizzle.

'You fucking nutjob!' Someone Connor didn't know was shouting at him across the room. Everyone turned to stare at him. He quickly hid his hand, the pain getting stronger away from the flame. Connor looked up to see the teacher, Mr Pritchard, peering over his glasses, inconvenienced and disapproving.

'Mr Lee! That is not a toy! Please take yourself to the school nurse's office and get that seen to, then come and find me so we can discuss detention.'

Connor stood up and grabbed his bag, his hand throbbing. He left the room, fully aware that all eyes were on him.

At least he knew where to go. The more time he spent at school, the smaller it felt, it was on a different scale entirely to the one he had left behind. It would take less than fifteen minutes to get from one side of

117

the building to the other; back home crossing the school took forty-seven minutes. He'd made a point of finding out how long it took over here. He also knew where every exit was, he had made a point of that, too.

Connor watched Janet, the school counsellor and designated first aid officer, as she carefully wrapped a bandage around his hand. He hoped when he took it off, the blistered skin wouldn't come with it. Janet's hands were soft and caring, careful and tender. He wasn't used to this kind of touch; he wasn't used to being mothered.

'Why are you here, Connor?' Janet said.

'I burnt myself.'

Connor spied his school record file on Janet's desk. They were encouraged to use her first name to foster a feeling of friendship, so they didn't see her as someone that was working against them. Janet's room was nowhere near the staff room or headmaster's office and she was always in there alone. She too was outside the loop, she wasn't one of the establishment – or at least that's what the kids were supposed to think. She was one of them.

'I mean why are you at this school? Why did you move back to England?'

'I'm sure it's all in the file.' He nodded to the paperwork on her desk.

'I want you to tell me. It's more important that I hear it from you.'

Connor found it impossible to maintain eye contact with her. What was the point of running away from his past if people were going to keep reminding him of it? If people were going to keep poking him?

'What do you want to know?'

'Tell me about the incident at your old school,' she said in what he imagined was her nonchalant voice, but he could hear the nervous inflection at the end – he could tell she was more curious than she wanted to let on.

'I was just messing around. I didn't know what was going to happen.'

'You had no idea what the boy was going to do? Just tell me in your own words what happened. I know what the file says, but I think maybe you need to talk about it.'

'I saw a counsellor at my old school.' He shifted nervously.

'It says in your file that you didn't speak to him. Maybe you need to open up to someone? Maybe you would feel better if you got these things off your chest? Did your friend confide in you about what he was going to do?'

'We weren't really friends. He didn't tell me anything and I had no idea he was going to do what he did. I would have told someone. Please, I just want to forget about it.'

'Why did you burn yourself today?' Janet said quietly.

'It was an accident.'

'Do you feel bad about what happened?'

Connor looked Janet in the eye, his eyes glistening; he had to take a breath before speaking again. A lump was forming in his throat, making it hard for him to continue. Connor couldn't admit that his friends were dead because of him.

'Of course I do,' he finally blurted out.

Connor looked away, his eyes watery. He had been asked a hundred times if he had been involved, if he had known what was going to happen. It didn't matter how many times he said it, no one believed him. That's why they had left California.

'Is there anything else on your mind besides the incident in your old school?' Janet asked.

'Isn't that enough?'

Chapter 20

The front door swung open, startling Adrian. Tom walked in and dropped his bag on the ground, a big smile on his face. Adrian wasn't used to having a full house, and he wasn't used to seeing his son every day, but it was great to have him there. Tom had had a lot of adjusting to do in the last few months and he wasn't really one for talking out his problems. His whole life had been turned upside down when his stepfather died, but all in all, he seemed happier for it.

'How was school?' he asked Tom.

'Great,' Tom said sarcastically as he slumped in the armchair and picked up the TV remote.

'Before you turn that on, I wanted to speak to you about something,' Adrian said.

'What?'

Adrian sighed. 'You can use more than one word, you know.'

'What did you want to talk to me about?' Tom sighed.

'Well, it's an idea I had; I wanted to speak to you about it before I spoke to your mother.' Adrian had no idea why he was so nervous. Maybe because he had no real experience in the father-son talks area. His dad was an addict; most of their conversations when Adrian was a teenager involved his father trying to scam money out of him in some way – there was no parenting involved. He supposed he had his dad to thank for his obsession with giving Tom a future though.

'Why?' Tom said, and Adrian shot him a look. 'Why do you need to speak to me before Mum?'

'Because it's your decision really, and I didn't want to put any ideas in your mother's head before I had spoken to you.' Adrian sat down on the sofa and leaned forward, so Tom knew he was serious. That was what dads did, wasn't it?

'What's it about?'

'You're welcome here, always, you know that?' Adrian said.

'I know.'

'But your mother and I, we can't really live together, it's not right. We split up a long time ago now and being in the same house is difficult. We are both very different people now.'

'You want Mum to leave?' Tom said, surprised.

'No, let me finish. You know I've been buying all these collectable toys since you were born? There's even more in the attic.'

'I know.'

'Well, they're worth a few bob. If you wanted, we

122

could sell them to help you guys find a place of your own,' Adrian said.

'But you love them.'

'They were never mine, they were an investment for you. They're just things.' Adrian was touched that Tom had even thought about it like that. Adrian did kind of love them, but only because they made him feel like he was doing something small for his child's future. His ex had married a millionaire and she didn't want anything from him, so him buying these toys and keeping them for Tom had been his way of providing for his future. He had always assumed they would never really be needed because of Tom's new life. He felt good that he had something to offer, that he had done something right and wasn't just forced to feel helpless when everything went to shit.

'So how much are they worth?' Tom smiled.

'I'm not sure exactly; I have several hundred boxed up, all in pristine condition. Some things are worth a lot more than others. The Star Wars stuff alone is worth a few grand. There's a Lego Millennium Falcon that could sell for anywhere between two and five thousand pounds. I have most of the original merchandise from the early Marvel movies, complete sets. There are some numbered art prints that had a limited print run. Collectable stamps, figures, bobble-heads, stationery, watches. Loads of stuff. Aside from that, there are lots of boxed collector's cards up there too, probably worth several thousand quid alone.'

'What? For cards?' Tom said, disbelieving.

Adrian smiled. 'There are serious collectors out there.

Some of those cards are worth a couple of hundred quid on their own.'

'And I get the money?'

'Well, the toys were an investment for your future. Turns out your future is happening a lot sooner than expected. I don't think I want to hand any serious money over to you at this point.'

'So, what then?' Tom asked.

'Depending on how much we get, then it could be enough to put a deposit down on a place.' Adrian knew the prospect of owning a property at fifteen probably wasn't the most exciting thing Tom could think to do with the money, but it was a good investment.

'You mean buy a house with it?'

'Maybe, if we can. I don't know how much money we will get, but your mum could cover what's left of the mortgage, and I'll help too if I can.'

'And it will be mine?'

'Well, it depends, we'll work out the percentage with your mother – if she goes for it that is. You will own a portion and she will, too. If you need a place of your own when you're older then you can sell and split the proceeds in the same way that you paid for it.'

Tom frowned. 'I don't know if I want to spend the money on a house.'

'Let's get one thing straight; I was not planning on giving you the money until you were ready to buy a place, that's always what this was about, it's just happening sooner rather than later because of your situation. Your stepdad's assets are all under investigation and that includes the house, and besides, your mother doesn't want to live there anymore. You guys need stability, and I need to free up some space. There is a lot of stuff here that can go. Anyway, I promise you – it's a good investment.'

'Fine, OK, I understand.' Tom nodded.

'It's no different to owning the stuff, it's just that the money is in a different place. It will still be as much yours as it always was. Just in a different form. A house instead of toys. Things have changed, Tom, and I know you're going to find it tough, but I'm going to try my hardest to make sure you and your mum have a secure future. Eventually things will settle down and your mum will get some compensation once the lawyers have been through everything with a fine-toothed comb. So, don't worry.'

'Thanks, Dad. I'm not worried, I'm glad we're away from Dominic's money. It's weird to say now, but I never trusted him. Living there . . . it never felt right.'

Adrian nodded, relieved that Tom had said that. He didn't want to push Tom to talk about everything that had happened before he was ready and so he had held himself back from asking. Adrian saw a lot of himself in Tom and so he made sure not to push. Adrian had never responded well to that and so he had to assume Tom wouldn't either. Adrian took a breath before continuing. 'I'll get in touch with someone about the stuff then; I know a few big collector shops that might offer something decent for it. The cards we can list online and see how they go. We'll need to take photos of everything and upload them. It might be hard work, but if we get your mum on board I think we can do it.'

'Are you sure?'

Adrian nodded. 'Of course. I told you, they're just things. Your future is more important.'

Tom got up and came over to Adrian, put his arms around him and squeezed. Adrian was surprised; Tom had never been openly affectionate; they were getting closer now that he was getting older. There was a time when Adrian didn't think he would have any relationship with him at all. He choked back the emotion, thinking about his own father and how unlikely it would have been for him to hug him. He must be doing something right.

'You're the best.'

'You're not so bad yourself.' Adrian smiled as Tom pulled away.

'Dad, how would you feel if I didn't go to uni?'

'I think we would have to talk it over with your mother and make sure you thought about it long and hard.' Although Adrian was touched that his son was opening up to him, he knew he couldn't have this conversation without Andrea present, he didn't want to get the blame for influencing Tom. Adrian hadn't been to university and felt like he had done all right for himself anyway, but he also knew that the more options you had in life, the easier it was.

'I have thought about it. I want to join the police. I want to help people, like you do.'

'I suspect your mother will have something to say about that. Anyway, things are changing, there's a proposal that soon police will have to get a degree in policing first, so you may have to go through university after all.' Adrian had joined the police because he needed to get a job with a regular income and some stability. After scratching around working in fast-food restaurants and pubs when Tom was a baby, he joined the police as soon as he was old enough to. Being a teenager is hard enough without adding a baby to the mix. Having Tom so young had shaped Adrian into the person he was now. His life would have almost certainly taken a different path had Tom come later on, or not at all. But Adrian didn't like to think about that. Tom was the best thing that had ever happened to him, regardless of when he was born.

'I don't mind. We can talk her round.' Tom smiled confidently and went into the kitchen.

Adrian wondered how all of this had happened and when the other shoe was going to drop. He couldn't help feeling like this was too good to be true. Maybe because he had allowed himself to think of a future with Lucy, even for a brief moment, and that had been snatched away from him. He didn't want to feel like things were OK, because that was usually when things went wrong. Or maybe he had done his time, maybe he had been punished enough. He had always tried to ignore the Christian guilt that had been drummed into him from childhood. Guilt for things you hadn't done yet but inevitably would do one day. The sins of the father. He had never believed in all of that, but with what had transpired over these last few months he had to wonder whether there was something in it. Maybe he really had deserved it all.

Chapter 21

Connor breathed out heavily as he walked towards the school gates after the last lesson. He had to prepare himself for the rest of his day. It's never easy trying to fit in when you don't care. Connor didn't care about school; it was just something he did to keep his father quiet. Connor didn't care about himself either, it had occurred to him that he only did things in order to get other people to leave him alone. He played football back home to make his father happy; he had bullied Billy Wicowska because his friends thought it was funny. Plus, bullying came naturally to Connor; his father had taught him well. If anything, his father was at least now consistent, it was worse when he was nice to Connor, which he used to be more frequently. The school shooting had put a stop to that. Any pretence of a normal, healthy father-son relationship was out the window.

When news of the attack had broken, while it was

ongoing, Jacob had phoned the authorities and said to the police that he thought his son was one of the perpetrators. Connor had been taken into custody and treated as an accomplice while everyone else had been allowed to grieve. Still, he deserved nothing less. He had pretended to be friends with Billy Wicowska, the boy with no friends, then he had humiliated him. Broken him to the point where Billy took a gun into school and opened fire. Even though Connor didn't pull the trigger, their blood was on his hands.

Connor only went home at night because his father would kick up a fuss if he didn't. He only feigned interest in Pippa because she was slender but curvy in all the right places; he knew it would be considered a cause for concern if he rejected her advances and so he went with it because it was easier than answering questions. So far no one in his class had found out about what had happened back home and he wanted to keep it that way. He couldn't handle being a pariah again.

Pippa, Liza and Naomi were all waiting by the gate. He felt sick at the fake smile that appeared on his face and the giggle of the girls that ensued shortly afterwards. He couldn't wait to be free from all of this, couldn't wait until he was old enough and strong enough to leave home.

On cue, Pippa rushed over and planted a kiss on his cheek before waving goodbye to her friends. She was so needy, so desperate for everyone to see that he was hers. He resisted the urge to wipe her from his cheek.

'Hey Connor.' She squirmed provocatively, trying to

look both cute and sexy at the same time. She reminded him yet again of the girl he had been dating back home in America, Harper – the last image he had of her was that of her unconscious body being loaded into an ambulance. The pale blue cardigan she had been wearing that day soaked in blood. She was pronounced dead four hours later.

'Hey, Pippa.'

'I missed you in class.'

Connor had come in late that day with a throbbing head. He'd been called to see Janet the counsellor for throwing up in P.E after a pretty insubstantial tackle. He had missed all his classes that afternoon; still, his father was off work today, so staying at home wasn't an option.

'Good night?' Pippa nodded at his sunglasses; he'd almost forgotten he was wearing them.

'What I remember of it,' he half joked. The truth was he'd drunk a lot last night, and parts of the evening were missing. He had fresh bruises and a cut on his forearm that he didn't remember getting. The one thing he could rely on his father for was always having booze in the house, making the oblivion-like sleep the only thing he had to look forward to most nights.

'You busy?'

'Just heading home.' He hoped she would take the hint.

'Can I walk with you?'

'Sure,' he said, trying to hide his reluctance to accept.

As they walked, Connor noticed the girl from next door walking on the opposite side of the road. She looked behind her to see who the footsteps belonged to, or maybe because she heard Pippa's laugh.

'What you looking at?' Pippa shouted, showing a side of her that Connor could have easily predicted – bitchy and entitled, allowed to shout at the other girls because, in her mind, she was at the top of the food chain. Reminding him even more of Harper, without absolving himself of any blame. She had been a facilitator of the bullying, offering him rewards for his aggressive behaviour, but constantly making him prove himself to her, making sure he stayed compliant with the rules of their clique. These friendships were always conditional, you had to be part of the pack. The girl looked at them both before disappearing into her house, she had that same lost look that Billy Wicowska had had, not obvious but not that well-hidden. Maybe that was the look that bullies hunted for. Was that how Connor looked when he was alone with his father? He stopped outside his house.

'Well, this is me.' He put his hands in his pockets, hoping this would deter her from embracing him.

'Can I come in?'

The car wasn't there. His father wasn't home.

'It's in a bit of a mess, we haven't finished unpacking yet.'

Pippa skipped up to the front door, leaning against it with just her shoulders, hips jutted out slightly towards him. He was almost embarrassed for her.

'I don't mind mess.'

He couldn't even say no to her, he cursed himself for not being stronger as he put the key in the lock and she pushed the door open with her backside. He would have to think of a way to get rid of her before his father came home.

Inside, Pippa sat down on Connor's bed and made herself at home. Connor was a little put out, although he did admire her in a way. She thought she was so desirable that he couldn't possibly say no to her, the thought didn't even occur to her. She probably thought she was doing him a favour, like she was making all his wishes come true. They were all the same, girls like her. Connor knew that he only had to reject her and her thin skin would shatter like the fragile glass of a light bulb. Instead of staring down at her or sitting next to her on the bed, Connor turned his computer on and sat at the desk, waiting for it to start up.

'I see you're neighbours with freak girl.' She sat forward, a little knocked by his disinterest but not enough to leave.

'Who?'

'Selina Dildo. Take my advice and stay away from her, she is majorly fucked up.'

Connor pulled out a pile of CDs from a packing box and started to look through them.

'Fucked up how?'

'You still buy CDs?' Pippa said.

'Most of these were my mum's.' He pulled out David Bowie's *Hunky Dory* and put it in the disc drive. 'What about Selina?'

'What about her?'

'You said she was fucked up. How is she fucked up?'

'My mate Naomi's boyfriend Ricky was taken out

of school and moved by his parents because she stabbed him in the arm with a pen last year – like full-on, blood gushing, ink poisoning and everything. I totally saw her do it.'

'Why did she do that?'

'She reckoned he tried to finger her or something, but everyone knows that's bullshit.'

'Is it?'

'Have you seen her?' Pippa's face was full of disgust, a disproportionate amount. 'Besides . . . Naomi and Ricky were proper solid.'

Connor sat on the bed next to Pippa and lit up, hoping the seven minutes it would take for him to smoke it would give him enough courage to ask her to leave. The more time he spent with her, the less time he wanted to spend with her.

'Your parents at work or something?' she said.

'I only live with my dad.'

Connor didn't know why his father wasn't home yet, he was just grateful that he had the house to himself. Jacob would make Connor pay if he found him alone with Pippa. He had almost entirely blamed Harper's influence on Connor for what had happened in California.

'Where's your mother?'

'Not here. She left when I was little.'

Pippa moved in closer to Connor.

'So, do you want to get off with me or what?' She pushed Connor back on the bed and kissed him before he had a chance to object, lifting his shirt up and starting to kiss his stomach. She stopped suddenly. Connor knew she had seen the marks.

'Where the hell did you get those bruises?'

Questions, Connor hated questions. Deflection was the only way.

'Rugby, I play a bit rough sometimes.'

Pippa bit her lip and undid Connor's trousers. 'So do I.'

Connor dragged on his smoke and closed his eyes as she kissed her way down. He had to ask her to leave but she was making it difficult for him. If he told her to leave now she would get upset and he couldn't deal with that. His fear of confrontation overrode everything else. Another gift from his father.

Connor watched as Pippa did her bra up, sitting cross-legged at the end of the bed in just her underpants, her uniform on the floor. It was dark already; the winter nights started at around four in the afternoon, making this feel more intimate and romantic than it deserved. It was only a quarter to six. Connor stood up and buttoned his fly, pulling a cigarette out and lighting it again.

'You smoke a lot,' Pippa finally said.

It was now or never, Connor had to say something while there was a break in conversation. 'You should leave. I'll walk you home if you like.'

'Trying to get rid of me?'

'No. Well, maybe, my dad will be home in a minute.'

'You're not allowed girls in the house?'

'Not semi-naked ones, no. Besides, I'm doing you a favour – my father talks a lot, it's embarrassing, you know what parents are like.'

134

'Is he as hot as you?' She shot him a smile as she appraised his body once more.

'That's not even funny.'

She snatched the cigarette from his hand and took a drag.

'Pass me my clothes, will you?'

Connor heard the click of the front door opening and his stomach started to sink. At least Pippa was almost dressed. The door closed with a slam and Connor knew from the depth of the vibration that Jacob hadn't had a good day. He held his finger up to his mouth and Pippa giggled because she didn't understand what was going on. Why would she?

'Con, buddy? You home?' Jacob shouted, filling the house with his presence, shattering the peaceful feeling.

'Meet me downstairs in a second. Make sure you're quiet.' Connor half-whispered, trying not to be strange but feeling afraid at the same time. Pippa brushed her hair into its usual pristine style as he walked out of the room.

He rushed downstairs to find his father at the fridge with a half-empty beer bottle in his hand. One down, at least ten more to go. This was probably the first time in their lives that they hadn't struggled for money. Inheriting the house had made things too easy for Jacob; he had more money to spend on alcohol, his one true love.

Connor backed away into the hallway, leaving Jacob to stare out of the window as Pippa appeared. Connor pushed her towards the front door, still trying not to seem defensive. She opened her mouth to speak, but he planted his lips on hers in a long, slow kiss, and when he pulled away he saw she was fizzing with electricity. Too much to speak. Before she knew it, she was outside and he had closed the door. Crisis averted.

'Where are you?' Jacob called out.

'One minute!' Connor looked in the hall mirror and smoothed his hair down. He should probably get a haircut soon. His father didn't like it when he grew it too long and it was creeping past his ears.

Connor walked into the kitchen.

'Who was that?' Jacob said.

'Who was who?'

'Whoever just left.'

'Just someone from class, that's all.'

'Why didn't you introduce me? Embarrassed of your dad, are you?'

'No, no of course not. She had to go.' Connor explained, trying not to sound nervous in any way, something that always exacerbated the situation.

'Worried I'm going to show you up in front of your girlfriend?'

'She's not my girlfriend.' Connor's heart started to beat faster, he needed to get out of there. His father's tone was denoting that this conversation would only end one way, with blood.

'Pull the other one,' Jacob sneered, pushing past Connor and heading to the front room. 'I can smell her all over you.'

Connor picked up the car keys. Considering how determined Jacob was for Connor not to get into trouble over here, he was still fine with him driving the car; as far as Jacob was concerned, Connor had passed his test back home and that was that.

'I'm taking the car,' he said, leaving before his father had a chance to get a hold of him. He had learned that his father was rarely angry enough to chase him. Sometimes Connor thought he was just doing it because he was bored. It didn't take much for things to escalate though and Connor didn't want to deal with his father's temper right now. It was more of an anxiety than a fear, a general feeling of unease that pricked and spiked when Jacob spoke to him like he was dirt. That was always the precursor to a beating; at least Jacob was considerate enough to give him that opportunity to get away.

The TV came on full blast and Connor knew he had a while before his father was blind drunk. He stepped outside to see Pippa still there, leaning against the car, trying to look sexy, always trying to look hot. It must be exhausting. He wished she would just get the hint and leave him alone, although he had to admit he wasn't even doing that right. He looked over to the house next door and saw Selina watching from her living room window. Connor opened the car door and, without speaking, Pippa got in. As he walked around the car he could feel Selina's eyes on him, so he looked up and smiled, a half-smile, but he saw the panic on her face before she disappeared back behind the curtain. There was something about Selina that was fascinating. She seemed out of place. Just like him.

Chapter 22

One day, Rocket let me go to the library to get some cookery books. While I was there I snuck a look in the reference section – I'd finally put a name to my predicament and accepted that I was in an abusive relationship. I looked at the phone numbers I should call if I was in trouble but didn't write anything down, I was scared he might find the paper and punish me when he realised I was trying to leave. Even being in that part of the library made me nervous, as though he had spies watching me at all times. I committed the number of a local women's charity to memory and left before anyone saw me and reported my whereabouts to him, something that was highly unlikely, but my paranoia about his omnipotence was growing. I remembered as a teen thinking about women in my situation and wondering why they didn't just leave – that made the most sense, right? Except I was terrified. There was nowhere he couldn't find me, I truly believed that at the time.

The next evening, Rocket invited JD and his girlfriend to have dinner with us; dinner I prepared through puffy red eyes. Pretending to be a normal happy couple had been exhausting. I felt suffocated by him, just being in the same room as him had me scared to breathe, unsure what would set him off. Dinner was strained, at least it felt that way from where I was sitting. Rocket made jokes and I laughed as genuinely as I could, my blocked nose betraying my sadness. I spied JD watching me from the corner of his eye. I couldn't tell if I wanted him to figure out what was going on or not.

I cleared the table and as I put the plates in the sink I felt a gentle hand on my back. JD asked me if I was OK and I said yes, I saw his eyes flit to my neck that was marked with Rocket's fingertips; the concealer hadn't quite worked. I told him not to say anything and that I would be fine. We went back out and, to my surprise, JD confronted Rocket without a second thought; he told his girlfriend to take me home. Was it really going to be this easy? Was I finally free? As we were getting ready to leave, I heard Rocket and JD arguing. It started to get physical. From the next room we could hear a ruckus. Things were being broken and in my head was the image of JD lying dead on the floor at the end of it. When they had finished, we could hear them talking and what amazed me most was that Rocket listened to JD. When they emerged from the room covered in cuts and bruises, both in as bad a shape as each other, I was surprised. I had never thought JD was capable of violence, but he had held his own against his friend. Rocket stared at me intently for a few moments before he agreed that I could leave. I could hardly believe it. I took my things and we parted ways. I never went back to that house, I never went back to him.

I stayed with JD and his girlfriend; I had lost touch with my family and was too embarrassed to go back to them and tell them what had happened. I had lost my self-esteem. I felt as though they would think less of me. For days I thought I was dreaming and that I would wake up back there, with him. Every time the phone rang or there was a knock at the door I expected it to be Rocket trying to reclaim me. It never was though. Over the next few weeks I noticed more and more the way JD would look at me. I began to suspect that he was in love with me. What's more, I think his girlfriend noticed it. One night after dinner they got into an argument, I hid in my room and listened as she accused him of sleeping with me when she wasn't around. He denied it but she didn't believe him. He promised her that he had never touched me but when she asked him if he wanted to, he didn't answer her quickly enough. And so, she left.

When JD and I were living alone together in that house it was like a light had turned on inside me – I realised that the path that I had been on was leading me to him, that this was where I was supposed to be. He was loving and caring to a fault. I think JD thought he had put a stop to our relationship before Rocket really hurt me and so they still stayed in touch a little. I could see that he was lost without his friend and I didn't want him to be unhappy because of me. It would be a long time before I could be around him again, if ever. I never did tell JD that he raped me, or any of the other things he did really. Not in detail.

As the months went on, our feelings grew and grew until we finally pronounced our love for each other. He asked me to marry him and I said yes; I couldn't imagine being with anyone else. I felt so safe with him. Everyone had accepted the situation as it was and we had our wedding in June. None of our families were there, I didn't feel like I had anyone but JD. Our wedding was just us two and a couple of witnesses who worked at the registry office. My world was tiny.

A few months later, JD lost his job on the construction site he had been working on because the contract had ended and there were no new projects lined up. Last in, first out. I knew he wanted to save up for a deposit, so we stopped renting and instead moved in with his parents. His relationship with his father was intense and unpleasant; I often felt as though I was unwelcome and his father made remarks to that effect. He would walk into our room whenever he wanted, he would take money from my purse, he was horrible to his wife. His mother was meek and quiet, completely in her husband's thrall, he controlled everything about their lives. I saw JD in a whole new light, I understood his protectiveness over me.

When JD finally found another job, I had had enough; I said I wanted to move, and from then on, every spare penny we had went into an old leather handbag of mine. We didn't put the money in the bank because JD's father often opened his mail and he didn't want him to know how much money he was making and how much we were saving. As our nest egg grew I could finally see a little light at the end of the tunnel for me and JD.

One night we talked about Rocket. I asked why they were so close when his friend was clearly so damaged. He explained to me that they were more than friends, they were brothers, not by blood, but in every way that counted. As children, they had found solace in each other. Rocket had taken care of JD against his violent father and against the bullies at school. He talked about him with genuine affection and I knew that if I wanted to keep JD, then I would have to learn to accept his friend back into my life. I was terrified of being around him again but I was more concerned for JD not having the one person he considered to be family.

It was as though I was so happy that some part of me had forgotten what had really happened, as though I had pushed it aside in my mind and replaced it with an altogether more palatable version. It had been well over a year since we had split up and so I told JD that I was ready to move forward, that we should all be friends again.

Chapter 23

Aside from the incident with the Bunsen burner, Connor had been getting on fairly well at school so far. Better than he had expected to. Apart from the fact that he had been pulled into his social circle rather than choosing for himself. Claimed by the cool kids already, he could see other people in his class keeping their distance from him and he knew why. His friends obviously had a reputation around the school for getting their own way. He was considered one of them now and so he didn't get the random smiles or hello's anymore. He had picked a side.

So far, Connor had managed to keep his past a secret; no one knew about the dysfunction that had surrounded him for as long as he could remember. If they knew who he really was, maybe they wouldn't want him in their gang, but as it was they had no idea. They thought he was like them. That was something he had noticed that was the same. Both here and in America, all the kids were working so hard to fit in with each other that there was no honesty about them; they were all pretending to be fine, or not fine depending on the peer groups they were trying to impress. He was just as bad as the others. He didn't want anyone to know that his father knocked him around. He didn't want them to know about the emptiness inside him.

Sometimes after school he got home to bottles strewn across the table as though Jacob had been drinking all day. It was as if being here, in this house, was too much for him. As if everything he had been running away from was in this building. Connor's father had never spoken fondly of his youth, if he ever spoke about it at all. There was something about this place in particular that was eating away at him and the only way to stop it from swallowing him whole was to drink himself into a stupor every day. What was worse was that Jacob was angry at Connor for forcing him to come back here, for messing up their life in America.

Today when Connor got in Jacob wasn't around. The house was so peaceful when he wasn't there, as if it had exhaled and all the toxins had left. Connor tidied the beer bottles and cans into a bin liner and then sat on the sofa. He pulled a familiar object out of his pocket. It was an old photograph, battered and tattered around the edges, faded and blown, a reminder of a life he could barely remember, aside from whispers in his ear as he fell asleep or a fleeting silhouette in the corner of his eyes every now and again. Mother. In the photo, her face was obscured by her long hair as she looked down at the baby she was cradling in her arms, the smallest trace of a smile visible on her lips. He remembered what she used to sing to him when he was young. The words still drifted through his mind from time to time. *Hush little baby, don't say a word, daddy's gonna buy you a mocking bird*. It wasn't until he was older that he thought about the words and how unlikely they were.

Connor looked up. A tiny beam of light cut through the darkness just outside the front of his house. He stood up and went to the window to see his neighbour, the woman – presumably Selina's mother – wandering around with her slippers on. She was wearing a short animal-print nightdress and a furry neon pink fleece coat, and her bleached hair was tied into a messy bun on top of her head. Every time he saw her she had a vaping cigarette in her hand. She seemed to be looking for something, an animal maybe. But he could see she was shivering and so Connor thought he should probably go and find out what was going on.

As Connor opened the door, he heard the woman calling out.

'Tequila! Come on baby! Come inside!'

'You lost someone?'

Instinctively she snapped up straight, chest out and knees dropped so that her silhouette was more flattering. She stared at him.

'So, you're Jacob's kid, are you?'

'You know my dad?' Connor asked, surprised.

'I've known him a long time, I grew up around here, too.' She winked and puffed her fake cigarette, eyes always on him. She made him uncomfortable.

145

'Who are you looking for?'

'My cat, she's white and fluffy with a diamanté collar. Worth a lot of money, so I need to find her.' She sucked on her bottom lip as soon as she'd finished her sentence.

'I'll help you look,' Connor offered.

She flashed him a smile and batted her eyelashes. She was attractive, but she was another one of those women who would fall apart if she wasn't the centre of attention. Nothing like the image of his mother that he had just been looking at. Nothing like how he imagined a mother should be.

Connor pulled his boots on and stepped outside. Even fully clothed he was freezing; he looked at her bare legs and shivered. She mistook his look and a self-assured smirk appeared on her face. At that moment Connor saw his father walking back to the house. He was carrying two bags from the corner shop. Connor groaned quietly to himself and braced for whatever would happen next.

As Jacob approached, a white cat darted out from some bushes and ran inside the neighbour's house.

'Bloody thing!' Selina's mother remarked under her breath, before shooting one of her smiles at Jacob as he stepped into the light.

'Diana,' Jacob said, nodding at her. Connor noticed his father's eyes run over the woman's body involuntarily.

'I met your boy,' Diana said. 'Reminds me of you, Jacob – same wicked smile.'

'Where's your old man tonight?' Jacob said.

'Passed out on the sofa last time I saw him.'

There was a moment of silence. 'Well, goodnight,' Jacob said finally.

'Aren't you going to introduce us?'

'This is Connor,' Jacob said reluctantly, sounding almost ashamed, probably itching to get inside, to get to his beer.

Connor knew how his father wanted him to behave; he wanted him to nod politely then go inside. He was almost tempted to start up a conversation, but the fact was he was tired and wouldn't mind having a smoke in the tree house before bedtime. Neil from school had got him some grass and God knows he could use the hit right now; his whole body knotted every time he saw his father, the tension running through his shoulders like the edge of a serrated blade.

'Hi. Nice to meet you, Diana,' Connor said before leaving.

Diana's mouth was wide open, ready to start talking. She was more interested in Connor than Jacob, maybe to make Jacob jealous, maybe because she was clinging to some notion of youth. Who knew. Connor didn't want to stick around and see his father make awkward conversation around a woman; he had seen it before and it made him wonder how the man had ever had a child in the first place.

Connor walked straight through the house into the garden. The light from the kitchen only lit half of the overgrown path, but his eyes adjusted to the darkness by the time he reached the tree. He had to feel for the makeshift ladder with his feet as he climbed up and into the tree house. It was a little lighter inside as the tree house was raised and the light from surrounding houses acted as lamps.

He rolled himself a joint and opened one of the beers he had stashed up there, it was colder than the fridge anyway. The moon was high and bright tonight and the face on the surface looked more real the more Connor smoked. He heard his father call out to him, but instead of answering back, he pulled his earbuds out of his pockets and put them in his ears, turning on the music player on his phone. There wasn't a chance in hell his father would make it up this ladder so Connor would just wait until his father was asleep before going back inside.

Selina was sitting at the dressing table in her bedroom, applying a thick layer of white face paint to her skin. Connor watched as she erased her face completely; from this distance all he could see was a white oval, her long mousy hair pulled back into a ponytail. She stared at herself for a few moments as though she were seeing her reflection for the first time.

Picking up what looked like a black eyeliner, she started to draw; at first, he didn't know what she was doing, but then he saw the single black tear she had put on her cheek. He looked at his phone, scrolling through until he found the song he wanted. She was drawing a Pierrot clown on her face; he put 'Ashes to Ashes' on his player and for that moment he felt as though she was somehow a figment of his imagination, only there to feed his need. He recalled the Pierrot in the music video, in the sea, and he imagined himself to be back in California, where it was never this cold. He felt more connected to this girl than he had to anyone else since he had arrived in the country, maybe partly because of the music. In that moment it was as though they were the last people left on earth. He wanted to get stoned and watch her forever. He couldn't feel his fingers now and it was getting harder to control them enough to roll another joint. He felt strange but not strange enough.

Grabbing another beer, he drank it in one. When he looked back into Selina's room, she was wiping the face away and he wondered which one was her real face, the sad clown or the sad girl. The grass was strong and so he lay down; the moonlight lit the sky enough for him not to be afraid. Darkness scared Connor and he didn't know why. Since the shooting it had got worse. Sometimes when he was waking up, he could feel, taste and smell the cupboard he had been hiding in as if he were still there. He remembered the feeling of waiting for the door to open and the muzzle of a gun thrust in his face. The dark smelly cupboard in the science block being the place where they would find his body. He had been so sure that he was going to die. The dizziness washed over him and he closed his eyes, the faint sound of gunshots in his mind.

When Connor woke up, he couldn't feel his legs. His head was muggy and there was a cloudy feeling, not helped by the fact that he was frozen. He looked at his phone and realised he'd been asleep for several hours, it was after eleven. He looked out towards his house and saw all the lights were off bar the flickering of the television set, which meant his father was probably unconscious in the lounge. The neighbours' house looked strange and Connor couldn't understand why. His eyes weren't fully adjusted and his mind felt altered, so he stared at Selina's bedroom. As if he had been woken by a cry in the dark, he saw the thing that was bothering him; a shadow moving across Selina's room.

It was too big to be her and that muggy feeling in Connor's head began to expand and thicken until it was bouncing off his temples from the inside. His stomach swirled as his eyes acclimatised even more, the clouds rolling away from the moon until it lit up her room. He saw the bedcovers lift and the man of the house climb in, the bed too low to see anything else – but Connor knew, he knew the things he could not see.

He rushed to the opening of the tree house as the realisation hit him fully, the beer expelling itself from his body. The vomit hit the ground with a loud thud that shattered the semi-silence. Connor's headphones and phone had fallen at the base of the tree, the faintest sound of Bowie singing about the girl with mousy hair echoing into the garden.

Chapter 24

Imogen was eating an apple at her desk when Gary sat down beside her. He had a massive grin on his face as he opened his laptop. Imogen stared at the screen, her own face looking back. There she was. The pictures were certainly better than anything she could have taken. Nevertheless she made a mental note to have Gary scrub all trace of them from the internet when this investigation was over. Gary had called her 'Cinnamon Shimmer' on the website and all the photos on her wall were in a sepia tone. She heard the faint sound of music playing from the laptop.

'What song is that?'

'"Fade Into You", Mazzy Star. Do you know it?'

Of course she knew it. 'What made you choose that one?'

'It was in the same playlist as the song Erica Lawson picked. I'm trying to give you that vulnerable and accessible vibe.'

'You're better at being a woman than me,' Imogen said. 'It's not what I would have picked.' She scrolled down the page; there were twinkle stars, GIFs, ornate borders, slideshows and a lot of activity. She could see that there were loads of people clambering to be friends with her – well, with Gary.

'Cool, isn't it? Do you like the name?' He laughed.

'I sound like a bloody shade of lipstick.'

'Well, you certainly are getting a lot of attention.'

'So I see.' Imogen looked at the transcripts of the conversations that Gary had been having, it was all so friendly and over the top.

'I've managed to connect with most of the people that are visible on Erica's wall. I've hidden them in among other players so that no one could get suspicious.'

'You think they could figure it out?'

'I've had to act like I have no idea what I am doing all day; it's been very frustrating. But I have been taken under a few of the big players' wings. It's strange how different people treat you online when you have a picture of an attractive woman as your avatar.'

Imogen ignored the compliment. 'Any leads so far? Did you put trackers in?'

'I've had a huge flurry of activity and so there are a few profiles coming up as local. Within fifty miles at least.'

'Fifty miles is not local.'

'Accuracy on trackers is not a hundred per cent, it's not like putting a pin in a map, it's more like dropping a sandwich on it. It all depends on where the hub is; sometimes it might not even be in the same country, and if you know what you're doing, then they're easy to fool. I'll dig deeper.'

Imogen nodded. 'OK. So, what's next?'

'Next is that we keep probing. I update and connect hourly, making sure I stay on the radar.'

Imogen's phone started to ring. She picked it up and held a hand up to Gary, not silencing him as such, but possibly still a bit rude. It was Adrian.

'Where are you?' Imogen asked. 'We were expecting you here.'

'I just got a call. We have another body.'

'What do you mean?'

'We've got another woman, like Erica.'

Imogen frowned. 'What do you mean like Erica?'

'I mean there are too many similarities to ignore. Woman at home alone, phone and other tech missing. It just feels like the same thing. I'm at the scene now.'

'When did the call come in?'

She hoped they weren't barking up the wrong tree with the social media game. It was the only real lead they had so far. It seemed to be such a huge part of Erica Lawson's life that it had to be connected.

'I didn't want to bother you with it, it was just a repeat noise disturbance call. One of the neighbours thought there was something really wrong. The woman in question, the victim, had a dog and it was barking like a lunatic for ages, then it was whining, then it stopped. The neigbour had collected several packages for her and she never went to get them. I just went to check it out, didn't think it would turn into anything.'

153

'OK, well text me the address and I'll be there as soon as I can.' She put her phone back in her pocket and nodded to Gary. 'I have to go. How are we with getting on with Erica's Facebook account?'

'I'll get onto them again today.'

Imogen rushed out and got in the car, leaving Gary tapping away at the screen. It was unlike Adrian to go off to a crime scene without her. At the very least she had thought she could keep an eye on him, but she wouldn't be able to if he started doing his own thing. As if she didn't have enough to worry about with Adrian, there was the distinct possibility they were dealing with a serial killer which meant more possible victims if they didn't act fast.

When she arrived at the scene, the uniformed officers were taping it off. Imogen showed her warrant card and went inside. Adrian was standing in the centre of the lounge, staring at a painting on the victim's wall. It was a beach scene and it looked familiar, like somewhere local, but she couldn't place it. Two large red columns of rock in the sea, the vague outline of caravans in the background. She didn't spend much time on trips to the seaside these days.

Adrian turned to her.

'First place I got drunk. Ladram Bay.'

'Looks a bit desolate,' Imogen said. She had seen the signposts for it a few times when driving around but this wasn't what she imagined.

'It was.' He didn't elaborate.

Imogen waited for him to continue, but he just looked

down. She didn't know what to say, what to do to make things better. It was a waiting game, grief, there was no way for her to speed things up. It took as long as it took to work through the pain that came with loss. She had lost people in the past, but never anyone that close, never anyone that was hers to grieve for, not in any real way. It was always someone else's mother, someone else's child, someone else's lover, someone else's friend. She felt their loss but never enough that it affected her everyday life. Not even the loss of her unborn child, too young to have been anything more than an idea, a future she never made it to. She knew how empty she felt without Dean but if she wanted to she could call him and change that. What Adrian was going through was so final, she could barely imagine how much it must hurt.

'Who is the victim? Where is she?' she said, trying to rouse Adrian out of the quiet moment.

'Her name is Alyssa Ward, similar age and look to Erica Lawson. Late twenties, living alone, not a huge amount of family around.'

'Was she strangled?'

'It looks that way, but same deal again, the body looks dressed.'

'Sexual activity?' Imogen asked.

'Won't know until the coroner's report, but there was a strong odour of bleach around the body. So it's probable.'

'You say there's no phone or anything?'

'No. However, Karen, the crime scene tech, just found a tablet. It was completely dead though. It has a cover that looks like a book sleeve which is why he probably didn't notice it. Gary should be able to get into it; we might find something out from that.'

'OK then, let's get it back to Gary.'

Chapter 25

Sleep had not been easy since Connor had seen what he'd seen. He had not been outside to the tree house either, his sacred space now tainted by the idea of what had happened in that house. What he had *let* happen. His first urge was to call the police, but then he thought about himself and how it had felt when he had been questioned by the police back home. When his neighbour had called them because of the noise, because of the screaming when Jacob had broken Connor's collarbone. It hadn't made him feel safe; for all Jacob's faults, he was good at people, when it mattered. He knew how to charm himself out of a situation. By the end of the day he had the police laughing at his jokes and writing the visit off as a misunderstanding. Connor, of course, had lied and backed up his father's tale of a loose floorboard and an unfortunate accident with the stairs. The whole scenario had made him feel even more alone, even more like there was no way out. So, no, he wasn't going to call the police. He had to think of some other way.

He paced the living room until he saw Selina come out of the house. Grabbing his rucksack, he rushed outside to catch up with her. As he walked alongside her, he felt her body tense. He matched her pace and walked in sync with her.

'What do you want?' she finally said after speeding up and slowing down to no avail.

'Hi.'

'Well? Is this some kind of joke?'

'What do you mean?'

'People don't walk with me . . . Connor,' Selina said, as if she were stating a fact.

'You know my name?' He smiled at her.

'Everyone knows your name, you're kind of a big deal in school already.' She seemed annoyed.

'I don't know why.'

'So, what is it you want?'

'I walk behind you almost every day to school, I figured we could walk in together.'

'Has someone put you up to this?' She looked around to check if anyone was watching them. 'Why would you do that?'

'Why wouldn't I do that? Is there something I should know about you? Are you crazy or something?' Connor smiled at her.

'I'm not clever or anything, I can't do your homework for you.' She tried to speed up.

'Is that the only reason I might talk to you?' Connor caught up with ease.

'People don't talk to me, Connor. You probably shouldn't either.'

'Why is that?'

'Because I'm weird?'

'So am I.'

She rolled her eyes. 'You don't look weird, I mean, apart from the tan and the perfect hair and perfect teeth and all that stuff. You look like I expect every boy in the school wishes they looked.'

'Is that not weird enough?' he muttered. The burden of being a commodity.

'We're almost at school, now would be the time to fall back. I won't be offended.'

'It's funny, you know, I just assumed you were shy and quiet,' Connor said remembering the sad girl he had seen. She was even more intriguing now that they had spoken. She didn't fit any of his preconceptions. 'You aren't though.'

'Sorry to disappoint you.'

'I'm not disappointed.' Connor smiled.

'How come you drive? You're not seventeen yet, are you?' Selina changed the subject, clearly uncomfortable with the compliment, if you could call it that.

'No. I passed my test back home in the US though. My dad doesn't care either way, it lets him off the hook if I run errands in the car.'

'Mum says she used to hang out with your dad.'

'She looks younger than him.'

'Because she injects mould into her forehead.' He could hear the contempt in Selina's voice, contempt for her mother. The end of her sentence was clipped, as

159

though she had more to say on the matter, but had decided it was better not to. He recognised the lingering urge to carry on the sentence with a list of every other fucked-up thing his father put him through. Something they had in common.

'Botox?'

'She's very insecure about her looks, especially now she's pushing forty.'

As they got close to the school, Connor saw Pippa and her gaggle staring at them both, confusion and a little anger behind their eyes. He knew what they were thinking: they were wondering why he was talking to Selina, or why he was letting her speak to him. Things weren't so different over here. No one was allowed outside of their little groups, and no one got to choose for themselves.

Selina smiled at him and started to walk off to the right as they approached his new group of friends.

'Hey, Con, are you still up for going out tonight?' Neil asked, thumping Connor on the arm.

'I'll see you later,' Connor called out after Selina, interrupting Pippa just as she was about to speak.

Chapter 26

That morning Adrian found himself driving out of the city again, only ten minutes out of his way. Ten minutes. He often went this way just to drive past the spot where they had found Lucy's abandoned car. He wondered if she had died there. The police had never been able to establish an actual crime scene for her murder. He felt connected to her somehow on this road more than anywhere else, even though they had never been there together. Ghosts were not something that Adrian particularly thought about, let alone believed in, but there was something on Langaton Lane underpass that made him catch his breath every time he drove through it. Knowing that she had been so close when she died almost made things harder. Like stretching out for something that was just beyond your fingertips, just out of reach.

Adrian pulled into the station and sat for a moment in the car. He needed to get his shit together, he couldn't keep doing this to himself. This was not him, not how he usually dealt with things. Having Andrea and Tom around was probably stopping him from dealing with things the way he usually did, which was to get drunk and sleep around, or go out looking for some anonymous violence. If this was what it felt like to grow up, he didn't like it.

He saw Imogen standing outside the station smoking a cigarette and reluctantly got out of the car.

'What are you doing here already? I called by your place, but you were gone?' Adrian said.

'Just wanted to crack on with this case. I hate the thought of that man out there, preying on vulnerable women.'

'You and me both. What's on the agenda for today then?'

'We see if Alyssa has any enemies. It's possible that Erica was just practice and Alyssa was the real target, or maybe neither of them are. There must be a connection somewhere. Gary will let us know if she's in the game, so for now we have to chase up some real-world leads.'

'I was looking through the database and Alyssa Ward's neighbours had made several noise complaints about her dog in the past. One said the dog bit them, but when asked to provide evidence they couldn't; they were trying to get the dog put down.'

'That seems a little extreme.'

'Well let's go and speak to them, see what they have to say about Alyssa.'

*　　*　　*

162

At Alyssa's house, there was police tape across the entrance and several bunches of flowers laid outside the front door that led straight out onto the street. People glanced at the tape as they walked past and carried on with their day. That was what struck Adrian the most about death, how it largely went unnoticed, how millions of people died every day and yet the world kept turning. Even grieving was frowned upon after a while, you just had to get back on that wheel.

'It's the neighbours at number sixteen that filed the complaint,' Imogen said. 'They called in over twenty times, most of the time outside unsociable hours, so there was nothing the officer on call could do, although it's been noted in the reports that the dog wasn't even that noisy and they were possibly a little irrational about the whole thing.'

Adrian knocked on the door. A man answered; Adrian noted his shoes before anything else. Slip-on moccasins with no socks, calf-length fitted trousers and a T-shirt with an extra-large V in the neck so the point was exposing part of his torso. The man had long red hair tied up in a bun and a very glossy red beard. Adrian held up his warrant card.

'Are you Grant Auster?'

'Yes, is this about that woman next door?'

'It is, yes. Can we come in?' Adrian said.

'I'd rather you didn't actually. My baby daughter is asleep upstairs, first proper night's sleep she's had in ages since they took that bloody dog away,' Grant Auster said.

'You made several complaints about the dog over the

last few months,' Imogen said. 'You even claimed that the dog bit you in order to get it put down, is that correct?'

'Look, I'm not proud of that, but we have a baby and that Alyssa woman next door wouldn't do anything about her stupid mutt; we were at the end of our tether. It was constantly waking the baby up, made it impossible to establish a routine.'

'Did you notice anyone going in or out of the house on the night of the murder?' Adrian said, feeling a little low on sympathy for the man who seemed to be wholly relieved that Alyssa Ward was dead.

'No, we never really saw her, I only knew when she was out taking the dog for a walk because we couldn't hear it. These walls are pretty thin.'

'But you didn't hear the murder take place?'

'I'm sorry, no. I put music on now when the dog starts. He started yapping uncontrollably and so I put the radio on, couldn't hear anything beyond that and the sodding dog.'

'Did you know her at all, Alyssa Ward?'

'Me and my girlfriend were friendly to her in the beginning, but then the dog came along. We tried to put up with it as long as we could, but as soon as we had our daughter, Esme, then we just had to say something. We asked nicely the first few times, but it didn't seem to make any difference, so we got the police involved. No offence, but your lot were about as much use as a chocolate teapot.'

'Did things ever get physically aggressive between you?' Imogen chipped in.

'No, of course not. Not that there weren't times I didn't want to go round and throttle that dog.'

'Did she have a boyfriend that you know of?'

'No idea, like I said, we didn't know her much except to say hello to in the beginning. I helped her bring in her shopping a few times when she broke her arm, to try and get onside, see if she would listen to me about the dog. Mostly though, she just kept herself to herself. I never saw anyone visit her.'

'Do you know how she broke her arm?'

'She told me it was a fall of some kind, I can't remember exactly.'

'And can you remember when she broke her arm?' Adrian asked.

'Seven months ago,' Grant said with no hesitation.

'How can you be so sure?' Imogen said.

'Because it was during the pregnancy; we came home after a routine examination and she had a sling on – I remember it was when my girlfriend was exactly thirty weeks,' he said, very pleased with himself. His smile revealed perfect white teeth, alarmingly white. Adrian often noticed how people suddenly perked up when they thought they had been helpful in some way.

A shrill cry of anguish pierced the atmosphere. The baby was awake. Grant Auster immediately tensed up, his laid-back hipster stance suddenly looking a bit more like a fraught first-time father and Adrian warmed towards him a little, remembering those first few months of fatherhood well.

'We won't keep you any longer,' Adrian said. They

stepped away and Grant Auster closed the door behind them.

'What do you think?' Imogen said as they walked back to the car. 'Do you think he could have killed Alyssa?'

'I think he would have killed the dog first.'

They both got into the car. Adrian started the engine and pulled away. He had to remind himself which way to drive back to the station; the urge to go past Langaton Lane was ever-present.

'The lack of technology is what bothers me,' Adrian said. 'Why remove it? That's what keeps leading me back to that game. If the killer's not that smart and can't delete a history, maybe removing the computers is the next best thing.' His statement was more of a commentary of his own understanding of computers than anything else, Imogen was probably more equipped to understand the situation than him.

'Or you know, most people leave all of their accounts logged in on their laptops; who can be arsed remembering logins and passwords and the like? I reckon he takes them so he can delete emails and photos and whatever – any apps they share. He could just go in from her side and delete the stuff that relates to him. He takes it away so he has time to go through more thoroughly maybe?' Imogen said.

'OK, that does make sense. Even with the information from the ISP we are unlikely to get a complete picture of exactly what she was doing on the internet,' Adrian said. He made a mental note to take another course on internet security, and maybe buy a laptop so that he had the foggiest what he was talking about.

'So, we need to find out what else Gary's got,' Imogen said.

This was one of the reasons Adrian admired Gary so much. Where Adrian had instinct for people, Gary had instincts when it came to computers. He always seemed to know what to do and where to look. Adrian wasn't jealous as such, but he did wish he knew more. He knew it was his own fault that he didn't, having thought of all of that as a waste of time. Ironic really, it's not like nobody thought the internet was going to 'take off' or anything. The best thing about Gary was that he wasn't condescending with it, he just knew his stuff and was happy to share. Adrian had worked with IT people before and it was quite a test of his character that he hadn't punched them in the face. Adrian was sure that Gary would have something, or have some idea of how to get it.

Chapter 27

Connor watched as Janet unwrapped his hand, the burn faded and the blister almost gone; it was still sore and he knew that some of the bandage was stuck to him. He braced himself for the feeling as she got closer. She was gentle though and it didn't hurt. He had other things on his mind. He couldn't stop thinking about Selina. Maybe Janet would be able to help her, or maybe that would make things worse still.

'Something on your mind, Connor?' Janet asked, as though she could read his thoughts.

He didn't answer, just fidgeted a little in his chair. Who was he to interfere? Was he allowed to bring her whole world crashing down even more than it was? He couldn't just out her. He needed to think some more. Knowing what he knew, he couldn't just leave it – he had to do something. Maybe this was his chance to atone.

'You know, whatever you tell me in here, stays in here.'

Well, he had heard that before, and he knew it wasn't true. A danger to himself or others meant the authorities were informed back in America; he expected it was the same over here. Connor suppressed a laugh. The lies people tell to get what they want.

'No, it's cool, everything's cool,' he said.

'Whatever it is, you can tell me?'

It was too near the surface, he hadn't absorbed it yet, hadn't learned how to lie about it, how to make it a festering knot inside him, like the rest of his secrets.

'OK, so maybe I know something,' he said slowly, reluctantly.

'Know something about what?'

'I can't tell you that.'

'Why can't you tell me, Connor?'

'Because it's not mine to tell.'

'Is it a friend of yours?'

'Not really.'

'Then why can't you tell?'

'I just saw something I shouldn't have.'

'When?' The pitch of her voice raised a little, he could tell she was trying to keep it under control.

'Last week,' he said. It had been a few days since he had been back in the tree house. He had walked to school with Selina that one time but hadn't seen her since either. Giving him plenty of time to think about nothing else.

'Saw something like what? Like a knife? Did someone bring a knife into school or something? If they did, then I have to alert the police.' She said, flustered for a moment.

169

So much for confidentiality Connor thought. 'No, nothing like that.'

'So maybe it was a crime you saw? Is that it?' Janet was staring at him intently. He felt uncomfortable.

'Sort of. Yes.'

'What kind of crime?'

'I saw someone get hurt.'

'I take it you didn't help them.' She said gently, as if to appease his guilt; but her words were like a slap in the face.

'It wasn't possible for me to help them,' he said. He felt like he was lying, he felt like there was something he could have done, even though he didn't know what that was.

'Are you feeling guilty because you didn't help?'

'I guess.' Connor looked at the clock, anxious to get out of there. He had said too much.

'If you're sure a crime was committed then you should go to the police, Connor.'

'I don't think so. I'm not sure what I saw. Not sure enough to go to the police,' he lied.

'Are they OK now?' Janet probed.

'I don't think so.'

'Why don't you ask them?' Janet said, the tone of her voice settling now; she knew he wasn't going to give her any details.

'I don't think they would want to know that I know, if you see what I mean. I think they might be embarrassed about it.'

'We can arrange for a police officer to come and speak to you here if you are nervous. It might be easier if I was with you. We have an officer coming at the end of the week to give a talk on drugs in assembly' She smiled; he could tell she was desperate for more information. 'If it's likely to happen again then maybe talking to the police will put a stop to it'

Connor nodded, looking down at his hands. Of course it was going to happen again.

'Can you stop it?'

Connor thought for a moment, then looked Janet straight in the eye.

'Maybe.'

The bell rang. Connor jumped up from his chair and grabbed his rucksack, leaving before he said anything else.

Chapter 28

Imogen was going through her game profile that Gary had set up for her; he had been running it for two weeks now. Adrian was sitting next to her, but his mind seemed to be elsewhere as usual these days; at least she knew where he was physically. What struck her most was how familiar these people online were almost immediately, they behaved as if they had been best friends forever. Even without trying, Gary had managed to elevate Imogen's status in the game to higher than Erica's position. She got the feeling he had played it before.

Her stomach turned at the content of some of the private messages. You could click on a symbol in the corner of a comment and the entire history of your interaction with the person in question could be seen. She clicked on a couple and saw that Gary had been working hard at forging friendships even though so many of the correspondents wanted to take things much further.

'At least they aren't sending you pictures of their junk,' Adrian said, looking over her shoulder at the screen.

'Gary said he hid all of those. Apparently I did get a few.'

'But nothing he thinks is very suspicious?'

'What does suspicious junk look like, Miley?' Imogen grinned. Adrian rolled his eyes. 'Let's ask Gary,' Imogen said, smiling as he approached, holding Alyssa Ward's tablet.

'Our new victim Alyssa Ward was a player on the game, too,' Gary said.

'She was?' Imogen felt instantly relieved that they had a foot in the game already, they might be on the right track after all.

'Yeah. She hasn't used this tablet in a while, but she has her login saved for the game, so I managed to get into her account.'

'That's brilliant. So, can you get into any of her other accounts?' Imogen said.

'Her game account yes, although she had changed her social media passwords since she last used the tablet so I didn't get much luck there. I cross-referenced her interactions with Erica Lawson's and they have a lot of overlap. We don't have a full picture of Alyssa's involvement yet and there were some bits of information missing, but she had taken several screenshots of when she hit value markers in the game on her tablet that were saved to file. I also ran a check on the speech patterns of the various users and there are at least thirty-five users that I can find who have multiple accounts which they use almost all the time.'

'You can do that?'

'Well, yes and no, different people write in different ways, just words that are repeated, quirks and anomalies; even you have your own way of writing. Stylometry is the analysis and identification of people through their language and writing style.'

'That's pretty cool,' Imogen said.

'Well, now it's just a case of figuring out who is who.'

'You're giving me a headache,' Adrian said. Imogen knew he had always been better with collectible games in boxes, covered in cling film for protection rather than games played online. Computers weren't really Adrian's thing.

'So, who do I need to get close to?' Imogen asked.

'There are seven guys who were active on both Erica and Alyssa's profiles, who I'm pretty sure are different people. We can start with them.'

'You think it could be one of those seven?'

'I don't know. I might need you to do some video calls or something. A couple of them have asked. I've emailed you your backstory and what I've told them already. I tried to stay as close to the truth as possible, so that it's easier to actually lie.'

'Video calls?' Imogen said. 'Where?'

'We can do it at mine if it's easier, I can dress a room.'

'Tonight?'

'Yeah. I suggest you have a couple of drinks first, loosen up.'

'I'd rather do it at mine I think.'

'Not a problem, everything I need is portable.'

'Am I invited?' Adrian said.

'Of course, it's work,' Imogen said, unsure whether he was trying to be funny.

'I'll tell them you finish work at different times, and set up some video chats. We should be able to at least eliminate a couple of them, if nothing else,' Gary said. 'Also, I got access to Erica Lawson's Facebook account. It was primarily a gaming account, she liked to play all the free games and a lot of them require you to have friends to click on things. As a result, she had over two thousand friends, but most of them did not interact with her.'

'Anyone stick out on there?' Adrian said.

'Yes, one person who hasn't said much. His picture is just something he's pulled off the internet, but it caught my attention because he's wearing a cowboy hat – you remember the song she had on her profile? "Where Have All the Cowboys Gone?" – maybe that's a reference to that. It's a picture of a model anyway, so it's no use to us. But in their personal messages it's obvious that they're communicating elsewhere as well, and a lot. They just seem . . . close.'

'What's his name?' Imogen said.

'A stupid fake name. Stetson Law – there's something vaguely dominant about it. It's possible that what happened, the strangulation, was just a horrible accident and he went too far,' Gary said optimistically.

'I might have agreed if it weren't for Alyssa,' Imogen said. 'It was no accident.'

'Do you think he'll do it again?' Adrian said.

'I do. Something has set him off though. There's no record at all of anything quite like this before.'

'We need to find this bastard quickly, before anyone else gets hurt,' Imogen said. She walked to the DCI's office and knocked on the door.

Mira Kapoor waved her in.

'Can I speak to you Ma'am?' Imogen said. DCI Kapoor looked up and raised her eyebrows, indicating she was listening. 'Has Gary filled you in on what we're doing?'

'He has. Is this the only lead you have at the moment?'

'There does definitely seem to be a connection between these victims and the game. Both women have accounts in this app, which we think is more than a coincidence. They had mutual friends on there; it's entirely possible one of these people is our guy. Gary thinks we should run through some video calls and try to eliminate some of the players.'

'Sounds like you have everything under control. Were there no witnesses to Alyssa Ward's murder?'

'There don't seem to be. She was quite reclusive by all accounts. It was only because of the dog's behaviour that anyone even noticed there was anything wrong. We spoke to the neighbour who had lodged noise complaints against her, but they had a newborn baby and were just fed up of the dog.'

'OK, well, thanks. Do what you have to do, just keep me updated.'

'Thank you, Ma'am,' Imogen said as she went to leave.

'Imogen,' the DCI called out. Imogen stopped and turned around. 'Have you decided whether you are going to apply for the DI position permanently?'

'I need a little more time to think about it,' Imogen said. There was definitely something blocking her from just going for it. Every time she thought about filling out the paperwork, a panic rose in her which didn't go away until she dismissed the idea. Was she scared of more responsibility? She didn't think that was it. She just didn't feel ready. At the same time, it felt so wrong to say no to this kind of opportunity.

'Fair enough. You've got two weeks, then I need to start looking to hire someone else.'

'Thank you.'

'Good luck with the op tonight. You may as well get home now and start getting ready.' DCI Kapoor smiled in a very final way, dismissing Imogen.

She knew what they had planned was for work and she knew she wasn't in a relationship, but it all felt very strange, pretending to be interested in guys on the internet, putting make-up on and getting dressed up for another man. A man who wasn't Dean. She pushed him to the back of her mind as quickly as he had appeared. She couldn't risk thinking about him right now, she had to force herself to get over him, no matter how hard it was. It wouldn't work, it couldn't work. One of them would have to change significantly more than either of them were capable of. *Sometimes*, she thought, *love just isn't enough*.

Chapter 29

In my naivety, I had forgotten how bad things had been. I had listened to JD's stories about their distressing childhoods and felt sorry for Rocket. I found myself being motherly towards him when he came over, and I thought that things had really moved on; I thought by being the bigger person and letting him back in to our lives that I was helping my marriage to grow, bringing me closer to JD. Things became less and less strained and eventually it was a manageable situation. Rocket seemed to be the only person that JD's father responded to in any way. I got the impression something had happened between them in the past. I found out later that there had been a physical fight between them and JD's father had lost.

My reality was uncomfortable at the best of times, living in a strange house with only one ally, the man I was in love with. JD's father was overbearing and controlling. He was like a dark shadow that cast out nothing but negativity. His mother moved through the house like a ghost, almost as if she wasn't really a part of anything. She never once intervened or spoke up. I could see JD disappearing into himself. The only time JD seemed like the man I fell for was when Rocket was around. I thought we had all got to a place where we could be together again. It almost felt like it did in those first few months when we were all hanging out, my allegiance being the only real difference.

We had almost saved enough money to put a deposit down on our own house; we would be gone from this place soon. I tried to convince JD that we could move anywhere, there was nothing keeping us there, but he couldn't see it. At dinner one night, surrounded by the men in my life: my father-in-law, my husband and my abuser – I mentioned that we were planning on leaving soon. As much as JD's father hadn't wanted us around, he didn't seem pleased by this. Rocket was even less impressed and made his excuses to leave early.

A few days after that, everything changed. One morning, with my head over the toilet basin as I threw up, I realised that I was pregnant. I was scared that if I told JD, he wouldn't want to leave, and might be afraid that we couldn't afford to raise a child on our own. But I knew I didn't want a child to be born into that house. It felt haunted at times.

I was unable to keep the pregnancy to myself because I couldn't stop being sick. I threw up from morning to night-time; I couldn't even smell food without running to the bathroom seconds later. JD was over the moon, and I felt a pang of jealousy towards the child in my

179

stomach because I knew that from now on I would not be the most important person in JD's life, and he was the only person in mine. I wasn't sure I was capable of being a good mother and I was worried that I didn't have enough love in me to give to a child. I had been right about JD's reaction. He said we couldn't possibly move now and I was angry. We argued and I accused him of not loving me, of never having any intention to leave. I said I didn't want the baby if it meant we had to stay, but he talked me round and promised that we would only stay for a little while, he would start looking for work elsewhere as soon as the baby was born.

It became obvious to us after a while that someone had been taking money from our savings as it hadn't gone up the way it should have. JD decided that we should hide the money somewhere else.

Our daughter was born in the winter and moving out seemed to get further and further away. We still had our small satchel of savings but we had to buy things for the baby and so no more money went in, until eventually we were having to take money out. JD got a promotion though and so it looked like we could get back on track again. I had been worried about my feelings for a baby without reason; I adored her from the moment I saw her face, so serene and innocent. But she didn't belong in this house any more than I did. All I wanted was to take my baby and leave.

Chapter 30

Connor's school day had been both predictable and uneventful. He spent most of the day wishing he could wear sunglasses as his head was throbbing. He felt like a worm was boring into his forehead as he stared out of the window onto the sports field and watched the other kids play sports. He was glad he didn't have to today; he really didn't feel up to it.

He was sat across the room from Selina; he kept looking for a clue on her face, but there was nothing. She was practised at being normal, like him. She was quiet and she kept her head down. He heard the muttered insults from the other classmates but she just ignored them. A few insults were nothing, he'd had them himself, back home. It didn't matter what anyone said because words didn't really hurt the way other things hurt. Like a father who hits you for wearing the wrong colour shirt, or a stepfather who puts his hands on you. He wondered how long it had been going on. He wondered if Selina's mother knew.

After the final bell, Connor rushed to walk home with Selina before Pippa had a chance to catch up to him. He wasn't interested in girls like her.

They didn't talk, just walked. Selina looked at him a couple of times as though she was trying to figure him out. It was nice to surprise someone for a change, not to just slot into the neat little groove other people make for you in the world. He wanted to make his own grooves.

'I'd invite you in but . . . you know,' he said as they reached his house.

'It's fine,' Selina said. 'Your girlfriend wouldn't like it anyway.'

'She's not my girlfriend.'

'Oh, but she will be. She has her eye on you and she always gets what she wants.'

'You're close then?' Connor said sarcastically.

Selina smiled shyly. 'You're smarter than you look.'

'She seems really friendly.' He raised his eyebrows.

'Friendly? She's just marking her territory. No offence, but she probably only wants you because you're the new boy. She doesn't want anyone else to get to you first. She may as well have just pissed all over your leg.'

'Well, thanks. You really know how to make a guy feel special.'

'Sorry, I'm sure you're a nice guy.'

Connor pulled his cigarettes out of his pocket and put one in his mouth. 'Not that nice.'

He offered Selina one but she shook her head.

'I don't smoke.'

'You drink?'

Selina shook her head again.

The sound of a car approaching made them both turn to see Selina's stepdad's car approach and pull up in front of the house. The smile disappeared from her face. Connor wanted to tell her to come to his place, but his dad wasn't the most hospitable of people.

Her eyes shifted to the ground.

'Better go . . . bye.'

Connor watched her go inside, exhaling to himself in frustration.

'Connor! How's it going?' Selina's stepfather called from the doorstep.

Reluctantly looking over, Connor nodded at him before clenching his jaw and walking inside his own house. He could smell the booze before he closed the door behind him. The mirror in the hallway had been smashed and the place was a mess. Something had gone down. He braced himself for what was about to happen. He toyed with leaving the house again until his father calmed down – but why delay the inevitable. Instead Connor dropped his backpack and headed into the lounge, which was in equally as disgusting a state.

Sitting on the sofa was his father, drunk again. He wondered if Jacob had even gone into work today. He looked at him with those cold eyes and Connor knew what was coming; he looked around trying to figure out why and then he saw the crumpled photograph on the floor – the picture of his mother. It must have fallen out of his bag this morning. He reached down to grab it and Jacob brought the full force of his foot down on his hand. Connor cried out in pain, his fingers bent under the wrong way.

'How many more of these have you got? I swear to god, Connor, I'll break your fucking spine. Where the fuck did you get this?'

'None, that's the only one. I found it when we were packing.'

'Where?'

'It's no big deal, Dad. I found it ages ago.'

'Christ, you are so ungrateful.'

'It doesn't mean anything, Dad!'

'Doesn't mean anything? Doesn't mean anything?! Maybe it doesn't mean anything to you, but it means a fucking lot to me. You may as well spit in my face.'

'Dad, please!'

Jacob cuffed Connor around the face hard. The pain exploded across his eyebrow, but he bit down, careful not to cry out. He didn't want to give Jacob the satisfaction.

'Please what? I thought I'd made myself clear on this subject. I told you I never wanted to see that bitch's face again!'

'But . . .'

'This is the respect I get from you? I practically raise you on my fucking own after your mother . . .' Jacob stopped, scrambling for the words to finish the sentence.

'Dad, I'm sorry, I didn't mean to . . .'

'She left you! She didn't want you anymore! I got fucking stuck with you.'

'Please, Dad, don't . . .'

Jacob lifted his foot off Connor's hand which had gone numb at least. Connor stretched his fingers out but before he could get up Jacob slammed his foot into Connor's shoulder and pushed him back. His head hit the sharp edge of the door, which still didn't distract from the pain in his eyebrow. Jacob got up.

'Here!' He tore up the photograph and threw it at Connor before storming out of the room. The front door slammed and moments later the car started, even though he'd been drinking and could barely stand up straight. With any luck he would crash the car. Connor didn't know where his father had gone and he didn't care.

Connor scrambled to pick up all the pieces of the photograph, his sore fingers finally regaining some feeling. He allowed the tears to flow now that his father was gone. With the pieces in his pocket, he rushed out into the garden, desperate for clean air. Outside, the moon seemed so far away tonight, but the sky looked darker than ever as he searched for the rungs of the makeshift ladder. He had an hour to get himself together before he was meeting Neil and the boys. Right now, he needed to stop the throbbing pain in his head. His eyes were puffing up and so he closed them. He hoped that was the last time he ever saw his father, in fact every time he saw his father he hoped it would be the last time.

Chapter 31

Adrian was reading through the crime scene reports from both Erica Lawson and Alyssa Ward. In both cases, the women were found a few days after they were last seen. In both cases, they had had sexual intercourse, and in both cases, they had been washed down with bleach and redressed after the murder, the bleach strong enough to slightly counterbalance the smell of decay. Was that why he did it?

What about the window? In both cases, one of the bedroom windows was open. Was that to confuse the time of death or was there some other significance? Was it to stop the putrefaction? Adrian wrote down each of these questions as they came to him. In a lot of cases, they would never find answers to all of the questions. How many more people would have to die before they figured it out? He thought about those women and it made him angry. He wanted to stop this perp before he got a chance to hurt anyone else.

DCI Kapoor walked towards Adrian and sat on the edge of his desk. He tried not to audibly groan. He was enjoying being alone.

'Ma'am?'

'How are you doing?'

'Getting fed up of being asked how I'm doing. Other than that, I am . . . OK,' Adrian said, instantly regretting how curt it sounded. 'I'm fine, really.'

'The offer of counselling is still there; you only went to a couple of sessions, you can have more if you need them.'

'I don't need counselling.' Adrian didn't want to have this conversation right now, he had a killer to catch and he wanted to focus on that. Anything but focus on the gaping hole inside of him.

'Don't suffer through this alone, Adrian. The death of someone close to you is about as tough as it gets.'

'I know, I just don't want it to bring me down. I want to keep going. If I stop and think about it for too long then it becomes hard to start moving again.'

'If you want to keep going then you need to start leaning on someone for help. There's no shame in it. You have friends and family who care about you. Promise me you'll stop bottling it up and start dealing with it?'

'Yes Ma'am,' Adrian said. He had absolutely no intention of dealing with it.

'What are you looking at?'

Relieved to be changing the subject, Adrian launched into a situation report. 'Crime scene documents for the Ward and Lawson murders. The reports show marks on the neck that indicate they were most likely left by the same hand. Looking for any other similarities, differences, seeing if I missed anything.'

'And did you?'

'Hard to know what's a similarity and what's a coincidence.'

'Just mark down all the things that are the same, and all the things that are different. You don't have to decide what's relevant and what isn't. God forbid we get another one, we can use that as a comparison against the first two,' DCI Kapoor said.

'OK. I'll just write everything down then.' Adrian tried not to sound like he was rolling his eyes. Nothing irritated him more than when someone comes and tells you to do what you're already doing as though it was their idea in the first place.

'What are your thoughts on this computer game?' DCI Kapoor said, seemingly oblivious to his sarcasm.

'You're asking the wrong person,' Adrian said. He didn't really have any thoughts on the computer game beyond the fact that he didn't understand it. Imogen seemed to appreciate what Gary was saying a lot more than he did.

'Do you think that's the connection between the women?'

'Seems that way. I trust Gary's work. He's about as close to a technical wizard as you'll find. He knows what he's doing. Just because I don't get it, doesn't mean it's not completely sound.'

'OK, his track record is impressive.' DCI Kapoor conceded.

'I think the way to investigate this is through the tech, that's how our perpetrator hunts and so that's what we have to work with. We aren't going to see him skulking around outside the victims' flats or at the crime scenes or anything like that. He's using the game to find people, which means that's where he spends his time hunting. So, we have to have eyes on it at all times.'

Just not his eyes, Adrian thought.

'Are you going over to Imogen's for the video chat tonight?'

'Yes, so I'd like to get on with this and get going if it's all the same, Ma'am,' Adrian said, hoping she would get the message and move away.

'Very good. I'll expect a report on how tonight goes,' she said, hovering. He could tell this wasn't about the case. He hadn't been himself, he knew that. He must try harder not to look too glum, he hated being asked if he was OK, in fact most people did when something was actually wrong.

'Gary is recording the whole thing, so you'll know what we know.'

'Great work, thanks Adrian, and make sure you don't rely too much on the technical stuff. He's not killing people through the computer, at some point there is a crossover into the real world.'

'Got it.'

'And promise me you'll at least talk to someone, a friend if not a counsellor. I understand it's hard, but you can't run away from grief, it sticks around.' She smiled and touched his hand before walking away.

Adrian returned to his list before he said something he regretted. This case was the only thing keeping him from falling apart at the moment and he didn't need people to keep reminding him of that. Maybe if he could stop this man then there was a point to it all. He looked at the information again and there was something about the open windows that bothered him. It wasn't really cold enough for the time of death to be massively affected; there had to be another reason the windows were left open in both cases.

Chapter 32

This was the first time Connor had been into a British pub. The Christmas decorations were up in The Swan already, foil garlands stretching across the ceiling and bulbous foil cascades at the corners where they intersected. It was shabby but cosy. It was nothing like the bars he had been to back home. His whole gang had fake driving licenses and the bar owners turned a blind eye to the rich kids spending their parents' money on drink, Connor hung with them and reaped the benefits of their monthly allowances. The pre-snowed Christmas tree in this pub had seen better days, with only a few strands of anaemic tinsel and a mismatch of cheap baubles with fake presents around the bottom. Neil and two other boys from the rugby team, Pete and Jon, had brought him here. It was a small, out-of-the-way community pub, different to the places he had seen in the city centre. No pretence. It probably hadn't been decorated since the nineties; everything was a little worn and rough around the edges. Connor wondered why they had chosen this pub of all places. It was clear pretty soon though, as they all sat with a pint of frosty local ale. No one cared that they were underage here, as long as they kept themselves to themselves.

To Connor's surprise, Selina's mother Diana was serving behind the bar, her eyes constantly darting over to the table where the boys were sitting, presumably trying to think of an excuse to come over. Something about her made Connor uncomfortable, the way she looked at him. Diana was attractive and her hair was done up like a woman from the fifties and tied with a red bandana to match her lipstick. She stood out so much in this place against the drab wallpaper and worn carpets. Nothing was left to the imagination in her leopard-print pencil dress. The men fawned over her and she lapped it up.

'It's your turn to get the beers in,' Pete said to Connor.

Connor could tell Pete was slightly in awe of Neil, who seemed to be the leader of the group. Connor knew he'd destabilised the group with his appearance. He knew they needed him to become their friend; they needed to keep an eye on him. He had had friends back home like this, until they realised he wasn't like them, wasn't driven by the same urge to be popular and so they made him prove himself. Friends that make friendship a test. This is how it had all started back home in America, with everything leading up to the incident. He had been trying to impress his friends, trying to fit in, prove he belonged with them and that he wasn't just the son of an alcoholic. So, he started off a chain of events that led to him being here, in this pub. For now, he would take this, he would happily play his part until he couldn't play it anymore – until they started trying to control him.

Connor stood up and walked to the bar. Diana glanced in his direction and then straightened up. Shoulders back, tits out.

'What can I get you, darling?'

'Just three more of the house ales and a Diet Coke, please.'

'You sure you're old enough?' She smiled; it wasn't a real question but she giggled at the look of concern on Connor's face. 'Oh, relax, love, you look old enough to me.' She winked at him and poured the beers. When she placed them on the bar, he handed her the money and her fingers lingered in his palm, brushing against his for as long as possible without it being weird, staring at him the whole time.

'Thank you.'

'So, how's that gorgeous father of yours?'

'Fine thanks,' he lied.

'I've seen you walking home with my Selina,' she said, leaning forward, 'but don't tell anyone in here I have a teenage daughter. I told them all I was twenty-five.'

He smiled nervously and picked up the beer before making his way back to the table. Neil grabbed the Diet Coke.

'You really don't drink?' Connor asked Neil.

'Nope. My body is a temple.'

'A life without beer? No, I don't get it. What do you do to unwind?' Connor said.

Neil shook his head with pride, a grin stretched across his face. 'Alcohol is not the only way to unwind.'

'No, but it's the cheapest,' Pete laughed and Jon smirked with him, some unspoken joke between them, presumably at Neil's expense.

'Shut up, you tool,' Neil said.

'What am I missing?' Connor said.

'Don't listen to him, he's an idiot. Inbreeding, it's big in Devon.'

'Fuck you,' Pete said.

'So, when's your next date with the Titanic then?' Jon smirked, looking at Connor.

'Titanic? Pippa isn't fat,' Connor said, confused.

'You are so jealous; it's pathetic,' Neil laughed at Jon.

'As if. If I wanted genital herpes I'd have sex with your mum,' Jon replied.

Neil punched Jon in the arm.

'Titanic?' Connor asked again.

'It's his shitty little pet name for Pip,' Neil said, rolling his eyes.

'Yeah, you only have to take her out once and she goes down on you after three hours,' Jon held his hand in the air and Pete slapped it in solidarity.

'She rejected him and he never got over it . . . sad really,' Neil sneered.

'He does have a point though,' Pete added.

'Yes, well last time I checked, "dick" was not one of the major food groups,' Jon said, holding his hand up yet again.

'You all need to relax,' Neil said, pulling a little bag out of his pocket and sliding it into the centre of the table. 'Anyone care to join me?'

'No, thanks. My dad checks my pupils when I get in ever since he watched some Panorama programme about teen tweakers,' Pete said.

Jon shook his head.

Neil offered a pill from the bag to Connor, who didn't hesitate. He put it on his tongue and washed it down with his drink. He didn't usually do anything harder than weed but his last altercation with his father had left him feeling as if a chemical escape might be the way forward.

A young woman walked into the bar. She had long brown hair that hung past her waist, and all the boys looked up at her – all of them except Connor, who could see her out of the corner of his eye. They were basically in the middle of nowhere, and she'd walked in alone. The pub was out of the way and most of the patrons seemed to be men. She was out of place. She leaned over the bar and spoke to Diana who pointed her in the direction of the public telephone.

'I wouldn't mind a go on that,' Jon said.

'You are nothing if not optimistic,' Neil laughed.

Connor kept his eye on the girl as she made her phone call; she was animated. Clearly angry at whatever she'd been told, she eventually slammed the phone down and stormed out.

'Are you with us?' Pete clicked his fingers in Connor's face.

'Have you never taken a Molly before?' Neil asked, referring to the pills.

'First time for everything,' Connor said.

Connor had the strangest feeling of déjà vu, as though he had already lived the moment before. The room started to contract and expand and the centre magnified as though he were staring through a fish eye. This wasn't the drug – this was something else – a familiar friend coming to say hello. His neck got warmer until it was as though someone was pressing a cigarette against his skin. He had felt this way many times before. Moving his hands was almost impossible, they weren't a part of him anymore. With great difficulty, he managed to get hold of his phone and get it onto the table. He could hear the boys laughing. His cheek twitched.

'Uncle Joel. Call my uncle Joel,' he said as his hands stiffened completely. *Ride it, and let it take you.*

'Jesus Christ,' he heard, unclear who from.

His thoughts got further away from him and his head hit the floor.

Chapter 33

Adrian was sitting in Imogen's lounge; Gary had arrived and set up the recording equipment and Imogen was dressed like a different person altogether. She had dark but natural-looking eye make-up on and her hair was blow-dried and full, not pulled back into a ponytail like she wore at work most of the time. He wasn't sure how he felt about this new Imogen; he was torn between missing the way she looked ordinarily and being uncomfortable with the uninvited feelings of attraction that were fighting their way to the surface.

They were setting up for the video calls from the other players in the game; players they thought might be connected to the murders of Erica Lawson and Alyssa Ward. There were two screens to watch the conversation as it took place. Gary had suggested Imogen be on her own in the bedroom when she took the call, in order to avoid making accidental eye contact with one of them.

'Stop looking at me, Miley,' she said to him.

'You look weird,' he told her.

'Yeah, well, so do you.' She smiled nervously.

'Don't worry. You'll do great.'

'Have you ever done the webcam thing?' Imogen said.

'I'm not sure what webcam thing you are referring to.' He raised his eyebrows; chatting online was not something Adrian really understood, if he wanted human interaction he was more likely to go to the pub and start a fight.

'I mean, do you video chat with anyone?' Imogen asked. 'Have you ever?'

'No, not really.'

'All right, hush up, I've added the first guy to the video chat. He will probably ring through in a second. Have you read through the transcript of your conversation with this guy, Imogen?' Gary asked, clearly excited.

'Yeah. Charming.'

'If you want to cut the chat at any point just tuck your hair behind your ear, OK?'

'Got it. Do I go into the bedroom now?'

'Yes. Also, if at all possible, can you get the guys to show you their faces . . . just in case they aren't guys at all.'

'Would a woman do that sort of thing?' Adrian asked.

'Oh yeah. Lots of them about. People like pretending to be other people, it's not a gender-specific thing. Especially not in a game where there are points at stake.'

'Go on, you better get in there,' Adrian said, his hand on her shoulder.

'We'll be in the other room watching the whole thing, but don't worry, there is no way they can get into this system, if that's what their game is,' Gary said.

'Oh God, OK,' Imogen said, looking nervous.

Adrian smiled at her. 'I'm just in the next room, you'll be fine.'

Imogen left the room and appeared on the screen in front of Adrian. The other screen was blank. The incoming phone call icon on the screen lit up and Imogen leaned forward to turn it on. Moments after she touched the symbol, the second screen filled up with the face of a man. Imogen put her game face on and got to work.

Gary and Adrian just sat back and watched with headphones on. It was strange for Adrian to see his partner being flirtatious. He scrutinised the face of the man talking to her; he could virtually see what he was thinking and it was unsettling. Adrian found himself getting angry as the man tried to pressure Imogen into cam sex. Is this really how it worked? They had barely spoken for two minutes before he suggested she show him her bra. Adrian had to remind himself that Imogen could take care of herself, as she would often remind him.

The man on the other screen didn't match the description of the man in the restaurant with Erica Lawson, he was much older, and so after a few minutes Imogen made her excuse and cut the call.

The next man to call was closer in age to the man that had been described to them, but he was not the best looking of men, even Adrian could see that, and so this call too was brought to a swift conclusion. The third man turned out not to be a man at all but someone much younger, barely eighteen at a glance, and so Imogen didn't even bother to play nice, she just hung up. The fourth man who called, known on the app as 'Magic Knight', couldn't get a decent connection but asked to see Imogen anyway. Adrian listened as Imogen told him she'd rather not do that, but when he promised to get it sorted for their next conversation, she let him see her for just a second at his request. He was obviously trying to verify that she was real. He tried to engage with her, but Imogen laughed him off and told him he couldn't watch her until he had a cam of his own. It seemed there was a whole world out there that Adrian had no idea about and he wasn't sure he wanted to. She continued with the rest of the possible suspects. By the end of the session Adrian had seen five faces that didn't match the description at all, and one penis which he could have done without.

Imogen re-emerged from the bedroom and slumped on the sofa.

'Do you want a coffee?' Adrian said.

'No, but I will have some wine. There's a bottle in the fridge.'

Adrian went into the next room to get her drink. When he returned with the wine and a glass, Imogen was pulling her hair back into a loose bun.

'You did great,' Gary said as he packed all his gear up. 'I'll just leave these things in the corner and we can try again tomorrow. I'll have done more analysis on Alyssa's account and we might have a couple more to go on.'

'What did you think of that guy without the camera?' Adrian asked.

'Definitely suspicious. I'll go through everything I can find on him, see if I can weed out some of his fake accounts, too. I'll chat to him tonight, try and suss him out,' Gary said.

'Be careful,' Imogen warned and held the bottle out to Adrian. 'Do you want some?'

'Nah, I should get home,' Adrian said, even though he wasn't relishing the idea of another night of happy families.

'Well, if you change your mind . . .' She poured herself a large glass and started to swig it.

Adrian stood up and got his things together. This whole evening had been unnerving, he didn't like watching guys hitting on Imogen; a primal urge to protect her had surfaced and he didn't know what to do with it. He couldn't put his finger on what was bothering him but he knew he needed to get out of there.

'Later,' he said hurriedly and walked out.

Chapter 34

Imogen flicked through the TV channels, trying to ignore the solitude. Her home wasn't a cosy little refuge anymore, it was empty. Without Dean. The decision had been made and once it was made it was easy. Switch those particular emotions off. She had never understood how people could do that, at least until now. It was like a part of her was just gone, dead on the inside, numbed to any feeling. She had kicked the habit, but now she was left with the hole that remained. She missed the feeling more than she missed him. He was like someone she had made up to find out if she had any feelings. Was it love? Was it lust? Surely if it was love it would hurt more than this, this . . . nothing.

She was on her second bottle of rosé, and it was late. She knew she should turn in, but she didn't want to go into the bedroom and think about how empty that room was, too. The emptiness followed her around; it was inside her. She drained the bottle into her glass and settled on a black and white movie. There was a knock on the door. An involuntary pulse of excitement rushed through her until she remembered it couldn't be Dean; he had promised to stay away and if there was one thing she knew about him it was that he kept his promises.

Imogen checked her face in the mirror before she opened the door; her hair was down and she had smudged mascara on her cheek, but the truth was she didn't care. She opened the door. It was Adrian.

'What are you doing here?' she asked, suddenly aware of how drunk she was as she laboured to push the words out.

'You're drunk.' He held up a bottle of whisky. 'Can I join you?'

She was glad to see him again so soon after he had rushed off earlier. 'What are we drinking to?'

'Being alone.'

'Why would we drink to that?' she said as she stumbled back to the front room, Adrian behind her.

'I'll drink to anything at this point,' he said.

He put the bottle on the table and went to fetch a glass. Imogen pulled her feet up under her and finished off her wine.

'Why are you here, Miley?'

'This may come as a surprise to you, but I'm not overflowing with friends and I just couldn't face being at home tonight in the end; it doesn't feel like my place anymore,' Adrian said.

'Family life disagreeing with you?'

'It's like I'm stuck in some ridiculous sitcom that I can't get out of. It's so surreal.'

'What about Andrea? Have you had sex with her yet? You've been holding a torch for her for years,' Imogen said bluntly, or maybe it was the wine talking.

'I know, and it's weird, because now that it's possible, now that I could, I'm not interested. She's not who she used to be.'

'You're not who she used to be either, I mean you used to be,' Imogen slurred.

'You are nothing if not wise.' He handed her a mug full of whisky, and they clinked their drinks together.

'How are you though? I'm serious. If you want to talk about Lucy then you can,' Imogen said gently. She watched as Adrian drained his cup and poured another one.

'I don't want to talk about her.'

'You really liked her then? I mean, did you think you had a shot at a normal life with her?'

'Is that what you thought about Dean?' he asked.

Imogen started laughing and couldn't stop. Normal? With Dean? No. That's not what she had thought at all. She didn't know what she'd thought. Maybe it was the fucked-up nature of it that made it more appealing. After all, she had grown up in an erratic environment where she never quite knew what was going to happen next. Maybe that's why she was drawn to Dean; the unpredictability of it all. Her stomach started to hurt, the muscles unused to the feeling of laughing. It had been a long time.

'I wish I was looking for normal. I don't like anything too easy,' Imogen said.

'Join the club.'

'I think I like being miserable.' She clinked mugs again, this time a little too hard. Hers fell out of her hand, whisky soaking the sofa cushion and her jeans, the smell hitting her nose. She shook her head, trying to shake free from the odour.

'How much have you had already?' Adrian asked.

'Not enough.'

'You don't look so good, Grey.'

'I'm fucking fine.' She felt the mix of whisky and wine churning in her stomach and clamped her hand over her mouth.

'Come on.' He put her arm over his shoulder. Her legs, that were working just fine a minute ago, had suddenly given up; the whisky had finished her off. She felt Adrian's hand on her waist, holding her close as he tried to walk her to the bathroom.

'I'm not going to be sick,' she said finally. She was almost sure she wasn't. 'I want to lie down though.'

He changed direction and took her into the bedroom. She could feel him trying to place her carefully on the bed, but she fell back anyway, her body had ceased to cooperate. As she lay there, the ceiling moved up and down, side to side, round and round. She could see the figure looming by the side of the bed; she knew it was Adrian but her eyes weren't working enough for her to see his face, the light was dim and he seemed to just be watching her.

'I'm not convinced to be honest. I'll get you a bucket,' he said.

She groaned and undid her jeans, they felt so tight

and she could smell the whisky on them. It was a huge effort, almost more effort than she could muster, but she did it, she kicked and kicked until they were off. Then she flipped over onto her front to stare at the carpet instead as she hung over the side of the bed. She saw her red melamine mixing bowl appear on the floor beneath her along with a glass of water. She reached up and grabbed Adrian's arm.

'Don't go. Sit with me for a bit. I'm fine.'

'I'm not going anywhere.'

She felt his hand on her back, rubbing her gently across her shoulders. She focused on the movement as much as she could; it was grounding her, bringing her back into the room and not leaving her floating in space.

'You're a good man, Miley.'

'Now I *know* you're hammered.'

'I mean it. I'm telling you because I don't think you know. I don't like people who aren't good on the inside. So, if I like you it means you're good.'

'You're too kind.'

'Don't do that. Don't brush it off – think about it. Think about what I just said.'

'You need to get some rest, Grey.'

'I know you think you have this shitty legacy from your father, that you're destined to be bad too. But you're nothing like him. Tom is lucky to have you. The fact that you even care shows how much . . .' She trailed off, trying to remember where she was going with this, but her mind was hazy.

'How much what?' Adrian said.

'How much better you are.' She tried to move. 'Help me up?'

Adrian moved her so that she was sitting on the edge of the bed; she wasn't quite sure how, because she couldn't figure it out for herself. Her head felt as though it were full of water, imbalanced, and every time she moved, it wanted to fall backwards or sideways.

'You should go to sleep.'

'I'm such a mess, Miley. What am I going to do?'

'About what?'

'About me!'

'There's nothing wrong with you,' Adrian said.

'My last two boyfriends have been nothing short of nuts.'

'We're all a little crazy, Grey.'

'Not you though. You're the most normal guy I know.'

'Ha!' Adrian exclaimed so loud she had to put her hand against her forehead to steady herself.

'I mean it.'

'I'm a little crazy too, Grey. I drink too much. I want things I can't have and I like getting a beating.'

'What?'

'I like being punched.'

'By women?' she said, surprised.

'No, not like that. I like getting into fights,' Adrian said.

Since Imogen had started working with Adrian he had occasionally turned up at work with a black eye or split knuckles; she had never asked him about it, she knew she wasn't supposed to. It was something that she had been curious about though. He had spoken to her before briefly about his father and the violent behaviour he had experienced growing up. Maybe now they knew each other better she could probe further.

'Why?'

'It's comfortable, I guess.'

'I understand. I find chaos comfortable.' She wasn't lying. She figured it was to do with childhood. It made sense that Adrian would have something similar, a comfort in a familiar behaviour, even if that behaviour made no sense.

She pulled herself further up the bed and lay in Dean's spot, wanting to feel closer to him in that moment, even if he wasn't there.

'I'll kip in your spare room.'

'No don't. Stay here. Lie next to me. At least until I fall asleep.'

Within moments Adrian was lying next to her on the bed; he smelled different to Dean, but she nestled into his armpit anyway. He put his arm around her and she curled up and closed her eyes, grateful for the warmth of human contact again.

Chapter 35

Connor was breathless when he woke up. His head hurt, not from the fall but from the overload of electrical charges to his brain. That moment before he woke up, the second before he remembered what had happened was his favourite part of the day. It was full of possibility but then he saw the faces of his friends, bloodied and dead, and he knew that this was just going to be another day to get through until he could sleep again. He couldn't remember getting into bed, he couldn't even remember getting home. He hadn't had a seizure for a while though. Maybe the ecstasy had exacerbated it. What a waste.

His first grand mal seizure had happened several years ago. The doctor suggested it might be from a head trauma and that was the last time Connor saw that doctor. Several seizures and even more doctors later Jacob just stopped taking him to get checked out. Jacob didn't like anyone pointing the finger at him, even though that was what he deserved, and then some.

There was a knock at his door.

'Hey boy,' his uncle Joel said.

Connor had only met him a couple of times over the years when Joel came over to America to visit. He looked like he imagined his father would look without the hate and bitterness. They couldn't be further apart in character. Joel was the sunshine where Jacob was the thunder. Joel seemed to give more of a shit about Connor than Jacob did, another crucial difference between the two men. There was something about Joel though, he was the only person Jacob listened to. He could whisper Jacob into a different frame of mind, something Connor had never seen anyone else do. He had seen Joel talk his father down from anger, knowing what words to say, what buttons to push. They obviously shared a history that Connor would never know about, neither one of them particularly forthcoming about life before he was born.

'Uncle Joel.'

'How's your head?'

'Did you bring me home?'

'Your friends called me, said you were having a seizure. Told me you took some E. That was dumb,' he said without judgement.

'I know. Does Dad know?'

'What do you think? Of course he doesn't know.' Joel smiled. There was something unfriendly behind the smile though, as though it weren't connected to anything, as though it were pretend. Like a crocodile's mouth with the curve at the corners that meant nothing. Maybe he wasn't so different to Jacob after all, maybe he was just better at pretending.

'Is he home?'

'No, he left already. I can't believe how big you've gotten. Stand up and let me look at you properly.'

Connor slowly moved, his head still throbbing; he felt like he could sleep for a week but he stood up instead.

'Do I need to do a twirl?'

'Just give me a hug.'

Connor wasn't used to getting hugs from adults. He wondered what it was that had made his father the way he was. Why was he so angry all the damn time? He couldn't remember the last time his father hugged him, or even touched him without some form of malicious intent behind it. Joel was calmer altogether, but there was something calculating about him, unlike his father. He had seen them argue before and Jacob had been the weaker one. Joel had a hold over him.

'Dad didn't see you bring me home?'

'He doesn't know anything, don't worry. Still giving you a hard time?' Joel tousled Connor's hair as though he were a small child.

'You know I messed up back home. I promised to do better here.'

'Well, let last night be a lesson to you. Don't do that shit again.'

'I won't.'

'I have to get back to work. I just wanted to check up on you. I'll come back tomorrow and we'll do something fun. Are you going to be all right on your own?' Joel frowned down at him. Connor nodded.

'I'm OK. Thanks. See you tomorrow.'

Joel left after his flying visit and the house was silent again. Outside, the weather was ominous, a grey cloud enveloping everything as far as the eye could see. It was going to rain and it was going to rain hard. Connor grabbed the sleeping bag from under his bed and slowly made his way downstairs, steadying himself against the wall. He still felt so weak. He took a bottle of water and some chicken and went into the garden before the rain started. He wanted to be inside his tree house, he wanted the fresh air and freedom. Even though the temperature had dropped to allow for the rain, Connor still felt claustrophobic inside the house, something driving him outside into the cold. He didn't want to be in when his father got home. His head still hurt and the last thing he needed was an argument.

Chapter 36

Adrian woke up to find Imogen draped over him. She looked peaceful, more peaceful than she had the night before. He desperately needed the toilet but he didn't want to disturb her; he knew she had been restless since Dean had gone.

As though him being awake had stirred her into waking, she groaned a little and started to snuggle into him, stroking his waist from his chest down to his hip, up and down. He had to admit, it felt good. He closed his eyes again for a moment and savoured the sensation. It had been a long time since he been touched like this, with affection, but it felt right. She hesitated for a second; he knew she had woken up and realised who she was lying with, but she didn't stop. She snuck her fingers under his T-shirt and continued to stroke his side. Adrian didn't know why, but he started to move his hand, too, across the breadth of her shoulder blades that he could feel under her top; he searched for the opening with his fingers and slid his hand down until he was running his bare fingers along her skin, gently tracing along the bones.

She was fully awake now, he could feel it, but she kept her eyes closed. Adrian knew he should keep his eyes closed too, unwilling to break the spell between them. This didn't feel sexual; it was something else. It was just . . . touching, being touched; not being alone. He could feel her warm hands exploring the side of his body, it felt so good, so natural, and yet something inside him didn't want to say anything, afraid that if he did then it would stop and he didn't want it to. Adrian's skin was alive with sensation, as though she were painting him with warmth. Then suddenly she sighed heavily and stopped. Reluctantly he pulled his hand out of her shirt.

They kept up the pretence of sleep for several minutes longer, even though they both knew the truth. Eventually, Imogen crept out of the bed and went to the bathroom. When Adrian finally heard the shower going, he got up and grabbed his shoes. He couldn't be here when she got out; they both knew that. Pulling on his jacket, he tried to focus on getting out of there. His mind was still reeling from what had just happened.

He put the mugs and her wine glass in the sink, the empty bottles on the draining board and kept hold of the remaining whisky, not wanting to leave a trace of himself. Was he being a bastard if he just left? He wasn't sure what the protocol was, so he put the kettle on and made a coffee, then popped some bread in the toaster. As soon as it was done, he heard the shower turn off.

Buttering the toast quickly, he spread some marmite over it and took both toast and coffee back into the bedroom, leaving them on the bedside table.

As he reached the front door, his phone beeped in his pocket. He pulled it out and looked at it; it was the DCI with an address. Duty called.

The bathroom door clicked open and he quickly made his exit. Outside, he got into his car and drove away as though the devil were chasing him, not sure what he was running away from, but knowing that if he hadn't left when he did, then he could have messed up the one good relationship in his life.

Chapter 37

As Connor and Joel arrived at their destination, the first thing that struck Connor was how different this landscape was to his home town in California. Everything was so much bigger there, wider and further apart. Even the horizon looked somehow shrunken here. He almost felt like he was in a miniature village. Everything felt smaller, prettier.

They had come for the Sunday afternoon to a coastal town called Beer, twenty-five miles east of Exeter. His uncle had brought him while his father was working on a contract that was overdue, to show him more of the country. It was unlikely that Jacob would have ever brought him here; brought him anywhere. Their relationship was devoid of moments like this. Connor had laughed at the name and wondered what kind of ridiculous place would have a name like that, but when they arrived, he saw nothing ridiculous about it. Even in the winter its charm was evident. It felt like a secret.

The hills that rolled and folded to deliver you to the sea. Stone houses dotted up the side of the south-facing cove – a picture. As they walked down, the bottom of the road opened out onto the coastline where the pebbled beach was strewn with rows of deckchairs facing the sea, row boats and fishing boats huddled together, like something straight off a postcard from the past.

'When the weather picks up we can hire a boat and go fishing one weekend,' Joel said.

'It doesn't look safe,' Connor commented; the sea looked angry today, the wind whipping it into spiked talons that grabbed at the sky.

'Some days you can come here and it's so still and perfect, you wouldn't ever want to leave.'

'It's certainly different to back home.'

Connor remembered the open spaces in California, the people too. Since being here in England he'd been struck by the lack of diversity. He blended in as long as he kept his mouth shut, but as soon as he spoke he felt the eyes on him. He couldn't imagine what it would be like to be a different race in a place like this. In the city, it was a little less obvious, but in small places like this he felt uncomfortable.

'How are you getting on at school?'

'Did Dad ask you to spy on me?' Connor said, smiling, but still not really joking. As nice as Joel was to him, he knew where his allegiances lay.

'It must have been tough, what happened at your school,' Joel said, trying to lead Connor into conversation.

It always came back to this for anyone who knew about

the shooting; they wanted the details, the details that Connor kept locked inside his head. Before they left America, Connor had been offered a sum of money to tell his side of the story to a documentary maker. For once Connor and his father both agreed that it should never be spoken of. But that didn't stop people from asking.

'I try not to think about it.'

'Sometimes things happen that just get inside us. There's no running away from them.' Joel stared out to sea wistfully.

'Unless you move to the other side of the world,' Connor said. It felt strange talking to Joel about it, or even around it. He didn't know how much Jacob had told Joel about what had happened.

'Your dad was trying to protect you. What happened scared him, he thought he was going to lose you.'

'No, he thought I took a gun into school and killed a bunch of people. He called the police and they questioned me for days about my involvement.' Connor struggled to supress his anger.

'Were you involved? You can tell me if you were. I promise not to tell,' Joel said. Connor tried to ignore the look in his eye; he seemed almost excited at the prospect. Connor must have been imagining it. A shiver ran up his spine.

'I couldn't hurt people like that. What he did, there was no good reason for it. There's no reason that could possibly be good enough to excuse it,' Connor said, staring his uncle straight in the eyes, eyes that seemed to dance. Perhaps it was just the breeze that was making them glisten.

218

'You don't think that boy had a reason?' Joel looked away again, the connection gone.

'In my father's eyes, I had a reason as well. Although he never quite explained to me what he thought that was. If I had done something like that, it would be down to him and the shit he's put me through.'

'You know your dad loves you, right?' Joel said.

'He's got a funny way of showing it,' Connor replied.

'Look, I know what he did was bad, calling the police on you,' Joel said, 'but I also heard what you did to that boy . . . what everyone thought you did. They never would have let you forget that. If you had stayed in America then who knows what would have happened. I'm just saying . . . he uprooted everything for you, so that you could have a chance at something better. His heart is in the right place.'

'It doesn't feel like it.'

'Growing up, your dad never had it easy. He's turned out a lot like your grandad. He always got the worst of it. Being treated like that messes with your mind . . . fatherhood kind of straightened him out.'

'Well, with all due respect, Uncle Joel, you don't know how bad it is.'

'I can have a word with him if you want.'

'You know I've heard this all a million times. Moving to a new house was supposed to change everything,' Connor said. 'Sometimes . . . the way he looks at me . . . I think he wishes I was dead.'

Joel put his arm around Connor's shoulder and rubbed it. He was more affectionate than Jacob, but there was still that feeling of being controlled whenever

219

he put his hands on him. Maybe Connor was just being paranoid.

'Have you made any friends yet at your new school?'

'Some. I'm trying to. I don't want to get stuck in the same rut, but it's like Groundhog Day. Doesn't matter what choices I try to make; I seem to have a place where I'm supposed to be. I'm supposed to be grateful that I'm popular, but I don't want to be. I just want to be left alone. I hate those people.'

'Good-looking boy like you, you've got no chance,' Joel said. 'But you know what they say: in order to get something you've never had, you have to do something you've never done.'

Connor frowned. 'Like what?'

'I don't know, that's for you to figure out. Just don't cut off your own nose to spite your face.'

'How's that?'

'Don't outcast yourself just to be different. Sometimes it's better to change things from the inside. Like at your last school, remember what it was like when everyone turned on you? How did that feel?'

'It was horrible. It made me realise I didn't have any friends. No one stood by me. As soon as I messed with their perfect image, they threw me under the bus. They couldn't wait to jam me up.'

Joel nodded. 'So be better.'

Connor looked down. 'It was an accident; I didn't mean for it to happen. How was I supposed to know what he was going to do? I've taken worse beatings than I gave Billy. I wouldn't in a million years have done it if I had known what he was going to do.

220

I know everyone blamed me when it came out, as if I made him kill people. I blame myself.'

'Just reach out to these kids until you figure out who is who. You blend in by being what people expect from you. Go against all of that and you'll stick out; people will be waiting for you to mess up. Just bide your time until you know who you want to be.'

Connor wasn't sure how much longer he could carry on in this destructive pattern. Maybe it was time to do something he had never done. He just had to figure out what that was.

Chapter 38

DCI Kapoor was standing in the centre of the road that ran through Farway Common when Adrian parked up in a layby at the roadside, each side of the road flanked by a ditch covered in brittle thickets with a stretch of fields to the left and some sparse woodland to the right. On the thicket side, police tape circled a large area and there was a gazebo-type tent over what he assumed was a body.

'Where's Grey?' she asked. 'I texted both of you.'

'I'm sure she'll be here in a minute. What's going on?' Adrian hadn't seen or spoken to Imogen this morning. He was dreading it.

'Someone called in a body – Mr Jeffries over there was out walking his dog when he spotted a deceased woman by the side of the road. She's been here a while. We don't know exactly how long yet.'

'Hit-and-run?'

'No, strangulation.'

'By the side of the road? You think it's something to do with Erica Lawson's murder?'

'Strangulation's not that common round here. I'd say maybe our guy made a mistake, maybe an opportunity arose and he couldn't stop himself.'

'Sexual assault?'

'No obvious signs of intercourse, but we'll have to wait for the body to be examined; we know how he likes to redress them.'

Adrian frowned. 'This whole set up seems so far removed from the others. It's outside, opportunistic and doesn't seem to be planned. I'm assuming from the way she was found, no care has been taken with the body – which we saw with both Alyssa and Erica. But she fits the physical description. Could it be a copycat?'

'Ugh – that's all we need.' DCI Kapoor shook her head. 'Ah, there she is.'

Imogen stepped out of her car and walked over to them. She nodded to Adrian, with not a trace of acknowledgment of what had happened between them the last time they were together.

'What's going on?' she asked.

'Woman matching the description of a missing persons report someone filed yesterday. We will have to verify, but if it's her then her name is Jackie Munroe. Her boyfriend reported her missing at around six in the evening; she wasn't around when he got home on Sunday after a stag weekend, and he hasn't seen her since Friday morning when he left. Check out his alibi, he says he was in Amsterdam with some mates, should be easy enough to verify,' DCI Kapoor said.

'Do we know anything else about her?' Imogen asked.

'Not yet – you should probably get on that. You can add these parameters to your little list and see where the crossovers are.' DCI Kapoor smiled at them and walked back over to her car.

Adrian found himself alone with Imogen and at a complete loss as to what to say. He weighed it up and decided that talking about the connection they had made would probably be a mistake. They couldn't let it impinge on their work. Yet he found it impossible to look at her, in case she looked back at him. The door had been opened. He cringed internally at the complication of it all. Without speaking, they both walked over to the gazebo. They had to step across the ditch; it had been raining the night before and so some wooden slabs had been laid out as a pathway to minimise cross-contamination of the grounds and preserve what evidence they could.

The girl was face down, with a mass of hair and unmistakeable purple bruising around her neck. Hopefully they would be able to match the hand size to the other two murders. The last thing they needed was another perpetrator altogether. Better to have more pieces to a puzzle than a new puzzle altogether. Karen Bell, the crime scene technician, was crouched by the side of the ditch taking photographs of the ground that she had mapped out with a grid network of string.

'Any news on your Magic Knight guy?' Adrian asked Imogen. He hoped she didn't notice the strain in his voice as he tried to sound exactly the same way as he had done before they had their hands on each other.

Unfortunately, he seemed to have forgotten how that was.

'Gary said he wants to try again. He also said he's found several other profiles that are all connected to this one account, and they all connect to Erica and Alyssa,' Imogen said. Adrian looked for a sign that Imogen might be feeling as awkward as he was right now.

Adrian frowned. 'Well, this seems completely different – chaotic, disorganised even. But physically, she matches the others. Athletic brunette, I'd guess in her late twenties. But we're twenty-five miles outside of the city, which is a break in pattern.'

'It's not unheard of for the method to change, but it is unusual. Maybe they knew each other? Maybe he knows we're onto him and he panicked,' Imogen said. 'If it was him, then we officially have a serial killer.'

'Deep joy. The press will love that. What do your instincts say?' Adrian said.

'I don't really trust my instincts anymore,' Imogen replied. Was she talking about the case, or him?

'Well I think we should check for CCTV, as usual, ask around. Did she have a phone?'

'Her phone was dead,' Karen informed them. 'It was in her handbag, it's been put into evidence with the rest of her belongings already.'

'Was she robbed? Did she have cash?' Adrian asked.

'She had a fiver on her, and she's also wearing a gold chain and some gold bangles. Given the amount gold is worth and how easy it is to shift thanks to all those cash for gold shops, I seriously doubt money was the motivation here,' Karen said.

'Why was she on the road? Was she killed here or was the body dumped?' Imogen asked.

'She wasn't moved here after death, she died here. Lividity is evident on the left side of the face, left hip, and on the areas of the left arm and leg that were closest to the ground. You see, the blood that was formerly flowing through the body is pulled to the lowest point in the body by the influence of gravity,' Karen said.

'Cheers, Karen,' Adrian deadpanned.

'Who was this boyfriend?' Imogen said.

Adrian smiled grimly. 'Let's find out.'

Chapter 39

I was sitting in the back garden with my beautiful baby in her Moses basket. Bluebells had started to appear at the edges of the lawn and the sun felt so good against my skin after what felt like the longest winter I had known. I lay my daughter on my shoulder and tried to read a book as she slept. I was relaxed because no one was home; these moments were few and far between and I relished them when they happened. Especially now that I was a mother, I longed for moments alone with my family, but with JD's work being so demanding I had to just settle for time alone with my little girl.

After a while, the doorbell rang and I placed her back in the Moses basket; she was sound asleep and shielded from the sun. I covered her in the mauve blanket we had bought for her and rushed to answer the door. It was Rocket, and this was the first time we had been alone together since the night that he attacked me.

I invited him in, trying to ignore the prickly feeling in my skin. He seemed agitated and he was looking for JD. I told him that he was at work and he wouldn't be back for some time. He asked to see the baby, although he'd seen her a few times already of course. I lied to him and told him she was upstairs asleep. I just didn't want him anywhere near her. He called out to JD's father and I told him that both of JD's parents were out. I asked him to be quiet so that he didn't wake the baby. I don't know how to explain what happened in the next few moments, it was like a snake shedding its skin, but the next time he turned to look at me, I felt those familiar old chills running through me. It was as though he had been given some kind of cosmic permission to do whatever it was he was about to do.

He pushed me against the wall and thrust his forearm into my throat, cutting off any air. My eyes started to roll in my head as I clawed at his denim jacket, the same denim jacket he had been wearing the day I had met him. I would have screamed, but I didn't want to wake the baby up and remind him she was there, besides I'm not sure it would have worked even if I'd tried with Rocket squeezing my throat so tightly. He leaned in and whispered into my ear. He told me that I belonged to him, that I always would and that there was nothing I could do about it. I remember feeling shocked, as though it were out of the blue, until I reminded myself that this was just who he was.

When I woke, I was on the floor in the lounge and my underpants were missing. I didn't know where they were. But I knew he had raped me again. I got my bearings and then I heard the crying from the back garden. I prayed to God that Rocket hadn't touched her as I got up and ran outside into the garden, my naked legs not working as fast as I needed to reassure myself that she was OK. I didn't even care if the neighbours saw me in this state of undress. I was half expecting to find my baby had tipped her Moses basket and was lying in the grass but she wasn't. She was fine. I picked her up and clung to her, holding her to me as though I needed her in order to stay alive. I rushed back inside and upstairs and took her into the shower with me. The water pounded against my back as I rocked from side to side, the rhythm soothed her and her warmth soothed me.

I didn't know what to do, I didn't know whether to tell JD or not; knowing how little support he had in his life I didn't want to add to his burdens. I'm not sure who I was protecting. He still didn't know about the first attack and I was worried that if he knew what had happened to me, he might think it was somehow my fault on both occasions, so I decided to just make sure he never found out.

It wasn't the last time though. Rocket came around in the day when he knew JD would be at work. He would bang on the door until I let him in. He would threaten to call social services if I didn't answer the door. Something had changed and I wasn't sure what it was. I couldn't fight him. I couldn't find enough of myself to fight him. When he was near, I closed so much of myself away that I had very little control over what was left of me.

JD was working all hours and so I was alone with the baby most of the time. Rocket would come for dinner still, he would be the perfect guest, the perfect friend. I felt the walls closing in on me and there was nothing I could do. My main concern was to keep my daughter safe and so I became unbearably overprotective. I knew I was pushing JD away but I couldn't bear to lie to him, so I just said nothing. The space between us became a chasm and before long we were essentially strangers. I wished the same could be said for me and Rocket.

Chapter 40

'It's definitely the same man.' DCI Kapoor slammed the post-mortem report onto Adrian's desk. 'Exactly the same hand positioning, size, amount of pressure applied. It's him. That's the somewhat good news. We are only looking for one attacker here which is the bad news, I'm afraid we officially have a serial killer on our hands.'

'We charged up her phone,' Gary picked up. 'She wasn't in the game, but she did have a social media profile that she used exclusively for gaming. She had several thousand friends on there. She posted a status at nine-thirty p.m. on Friday saying that her phone was dying and she was on her way home after a night out with her mates that ended badly. It was GPS tagged.'

'I'll say. Ended badly is an understatement,' Adrian said.

'Do we think the killer is one of her connections on there?' DCI Kapoor said.

'It's possible. I'll look through and see if anything

rings any bells. Needle in a haystack though. There are special pages you can go on where you advertise for more friends, like hundreds at a time. He might be on those. One thing is for sure, at the time of the murders Magic Knight was not playing the game. He is AFK for a few hours on each of the occasions,' Gary said.

'And AFK is?' Adrian asked.

'Away from Keyboard, someplace else,' Gary clarified.

'The boyfriend has a rock-solid alibi, he was on a plane back from a business trip in Ireland, there are time-stamped photos on social media. He got home and she wasn't there. He said he could tell she hadn't made it home so he called her friends and they told him she had stormed off,' DCI Kapoor said.

'Is she linked to Alyssa or Erica in any way?' Adrian said to Gary.

'No. I really don't think she's connected. Just unlucky.' Gary shrugged.

'Did anyone know where Jackie was? Where was she coming from? Where was she going?' DCI Kapoor asked.

'We spoke to her work colleagues, the women she was out with. They were at a bingo night in a pub on the outskirts of Exeter, The Crown. It was their Christmas work do,' Imogen said.

'The one on the way to Clyst St Mary?' the DCI asked.

'Yes, that's the one.'

'Why did she leave?'

'According to one of the women, there was some friction between her and another woman there. No one saw what happened, but they fell out in the bogs and Jackie left, made some excuse about her boyfriend coming home early, but the woman I spoke to said she could tell she had been crying. It wasn't until later they found out about the argument,' Imogen said.

'Why did they let her leave?' Adrian asked. Jackie was obviously incapable of taking care of herself; the level of alcohol in her toxicology report showed that she had had more than a few.

'She lied to them and told them her boyfriend was picking her up. Then she started walking back,' Imogen said.

'Why didn't she get a cab?' Adrian said.

'Apparently she was an outdoorsy type. She and her boyfriend were walkers, they would go on walking holidays all the time,' Imogen said.

'Say again? A what holiday?' Adrian stared at her.

'Walking holidays. It's where you go out to the country and walk a lot apparently.' She raised her eyebrows at him and he felt strangely comforted by the fact that things were definitely back to normal between them.

'That's a thing?' Adrian's idea of a holiday was being allowed to lie on the sofa for several days, binge-watching old sci-fi shows.

'Well, her boyfriend said walking back from there wouldn't seem like that big a distance for her. She walked for fun.'

'Now I've heard everything.'

'So why the change of style?' Imogen said, as though she were talking to herself.

'It could literally just be that he saw an opportunity and took it,' Adrian said.

'And then drove her to Farway Common before killing her? Why there?' Imogen said.

'Maybe he knows that area,' Adrian said.

'The time between this attack and Alyssa's is much shorter than the time between hers and Erica's,' the DCI said.

'Three weeks between the first two and less than two between Alyssa and Jackie,' Adrian confirmed.

'He's obviously highly agitated, something must have started this and, whatever it is, it isn't going away for him,' Imogen said.

'Are you still OK with playing this game? He's dangerous and now somewhat unpredictable,' DCI Kapoor said, a genuine look of concern on her face.

'I'm not afraid of him,' Imogen said. 'Besides, Gary is really the one playing the game.'

'So, what do we do now?' Adrian said.

'We go fishing,' Gary said.

Chapter 41

The restaurant was fairly empty, which was a relief for Connor; it also wasn't too fancy, which was nice because he already felt weird enough. His plate was empty, but Pippa had barely touched her food, eating only the side salad. Going out on dates wasn't really his thing, but it was what was expected, wasn't it? In an attempt to be more like everyone else he had texted Pippa and invited her after school; she had replied in an inhumanly quick time. They were in a small local bistro with muted, sophisticated decoration that made it look more expensive than it was. The waitress came over and cleared the plates away. Connor looked over at Pippa who had been looking at him almost without breaking eye contact since they'd arrived. The pretence of normality felt wrong, but his uncle was right, it was better to pretend, people wouldn't understand who he really was.

'Are you going to have dessert? Do you want to share one? The cheesecake here is amazing. Unless you don't like that. Do you know what cheesecake is? Do you get cheesecake in America?' Pippa said quickly without giving him a chance to answer. She could obviously sense that she was losing his attention, that he wanted the night to be over already.

'We get cheesecake.'

'Oh, OK I wasn't sure. Or like maybe you call it something else, because you know the whole jelly, jello, chips, crisps, fries, biscuits, cookies thing?'

'No, cheesecake is still cheesecake.' He smiled.

It wasn't Pippa's fault that she was the way she was, any more than it was Connor's fault that he was who he was. She was probably told she was beautiful every day of her life, if not by her parents then by her friends or boys who wanted a piece of what she had. From what she had said already, her father worked away a lot. She was starved of affection, but not attention, and to her those two things were interchangeable. Her uniform at school was never tatty, her hair was always washed and styled to perfection. She was the girl people loved to hate. She was an alpha.

Connor looked like an alpha too; he was all symmetry and sparkling teeth. Underneath it though, Connor was someone else entirely. But if there was one thing he knew for sure, it was that looks mattered. It wasn't until he had seen what Billy Wicowska had done to the people he hated the most for the way they looked that he realised how much it mattered to some people. It mattered enough for Billy to want them dead.

'Do you want to share a pudding?' Pippa said again after a long, awkward pause.

'No, I'm good.'

'Oh, I won't have any then.'

'Have some if you want some.'

He looked up at the clock and saw the time; his father would be waiting for him. He looked back at Pippa.

'Let's get out of here.'

Twenty minutes later, they were parked near Pippa's house in the back seat of the car. After the obligatory post-date sex, Connor scooched to the side and did his trousers up, his chest still heaving from the expulsion of energy; energy he didn't really have to spare. It was getting late and he just wanted to get home now. He wanted to be alone. He pulled out a cigarette and opened the window. He watched Pippa scrape her hair back into style, smoothing out the kinks. She took the cigarette out of his hand and had a puff before handing it back.

'Do you have any chuddie?' Pippa asked.

'Any what?'

'Chewing gum?'

'Oh right, yeah, in the door compartment,' Connor paused. 'Let's get going.'

'I just feel like you don't actually want to spend any real time with me,' she said, looking away from him.

Connor sighed. 'We just went out to eat!'

'Yeah, and you were clock-watching the whole time.'

'My uncle's over tonight and I haven't really seen him in years, that's all. I really wanted to hang out with him, but I spent the evening with you instead.'

'Oh.' She smiled, flashing a sideways glance at him. She grabbed her top and put it on. He was so torn

237

between what he wanted and what was happening. He was getting in too deep with Pippa and he knew it, but this was the only role he knew how to play and it came so naturally to him; even if it wasn't easy, it just felt like what he should be doing. He had to figure out a way to break the cycle. He had to give himself a chance to discover who he really was. Life just felt like constant noise, a cacophony of choices that he made without thinking, without deciding properly, just doing what was expected, what was easy. He desperately wanted that to change.

The light was on when Connor got home, and his uncle's car was still in the driveway. Connor peeked through the window and saw Jacob sitting on the sofa, his head in his hands. Joel was pacing, looking angry but measured; they had obviously been arguing for a while.

Carefully, Connor snuck the key into the lock and stepped into the house, making sure not to close it hard. He could see them through a sliver in the door, so he watched, wanting to see what his father talked about when he wasn't around.

'You need to tell him the truth, Jacob!' Joel was saying.

'No way! I screwed up his life enough already.'

'Yeah, you did, and you honestly think adding to all that shit with lies is helping anyone?'

'It's too late!'

'He's going to find out one day and that's the day you'll lose him forever.'

'He's the only good thing I ever did and all that crazy shit he did back home, I mean FUCK! He nearly killed that boy! That shooting was his fault and he knows it. You know . . . I was scared he was going to end up like her . . .'

Through the gap, Connor saw Joel sit down next to Jacob.

'That's not going to happen,' he said, his voice softer now. 'He's nothing like his mother.'

'I tried, you know? I really tried and I thought we were getting somewhere and then what happened, happened – it was like fucking déjà vu.'

'You have to stop blaming yourself for what she did, Jacob. She was crazy. And you have to stop blaming Connor, too.'

'She wanted another child so bad, and Shannon was such a good baby.'

Connor was confused, which baby were they talking about? He'd never had a sibling. Had he?

'It's not his fault, hell . . . it's not even hers, it's a fucking chemical imbalance. She was never right in the head, I tried to warn you.'

'Chemical imbalance? She killed our daughter!'

Daughter? What did he mean daughter? Connor clamped his hand over his mouth to stop himself from shouting out before the conversation was over.

'I read up on it, it happens to like one per cent of women after they have kids. She was already messed up, having kids just pushed her over the edge. You're just lucky he wasn't at home, too.'

There was a pause before Jacob spoke again. 'Sometimes

I wish we'd all died. How come she gets to escape all this shit and I'm still here to deal with what's left behind?'

'You need to stop feeling sorry for yourself and tell him what happened. He thinks she abandoned him, he thinks she's out there somewhere without a thought for him. He doesn't know what you did for him, that you saved him.'

The words swirled in Connor's head as he tried to make sense of what he was hearing. His mother killed his sister? His father saved him? None of this made any sense.

'I can't do that. He'll only hate me more.'

'I'll take you to the cemetery later in the week if you want.'

Connor recoiled; this was the first he had heard of any of this. What else was his father keeping from him? How did he not know he had a sister? How could his father lie to him like this? Make him think all this time that his mum had just upped and left, that she was out there somewhere, living a life without him. Why hadn't he told him the truth?

'What do I tell him? That she hated him? That having him made her crazy? Made her kill herself?'

Another silence. Then Joel spoke again. 'Maybe that's what he needs to hear.'

Chapter 42

Imogen pressed the buzzer to Jackie Munroe's flat. It was a large red-brick terraced house that had been split into two. The Christmas tree was in the bay window; they could see the outline from outside, although the lights weren't on. The rest of the street was aglow with Christmas lights. Jackie Munroe's house was conspicuous because it looked so sad and sombre. The icicle fairy lights ran along the guttering, but they were not turned on either. Christmas would never be the same for her boyfriend, always tainted with her death.

Adrian stood behind Imogen. She felt a little awkward because of what had happened between them, but she wasn't going to show it. What had she been thinking? As if she didn't have enough problems. And with Adrian? She shook it off before she had a chance to really think about what she had done. Thankfully he hadn't mentioned it either and so maybe it wasn't that big a deal. Maybe they could just forget about it and pretend it never happened. The door opened. Imogen held up her warrant card to the man standing in front of them. He had obviously been crying; his eyelids were puffy and glistening.

'Are you Keon Hunter?'

'Yes.' His voice cracked as he spoke.

'We're really sorry to bother you. We just have some questions about Jackie,' Imogen said.

'Come in.'

They followed him into the flat, his suitcase was open in the centre of his living room floor, clothes spilling out of it. It looked out of place because the rest of the flat was so pristine.

Keon slumped into the armchair and motioned towards the sofa. They both took a seat.

'We're sorry for your loss,' Adrian said. Imogen knew he meant it; he was sorry for the man. She worried about Adrian in this moment, there was no way he wasn't comparing himself to this man. Could he even be objective on this?

'Do you know what happened yet?' Keon Hunter asked.

'We are still investigating at the moment. We just need to ask you a few things about Jackie. Is that OK?' Imogen said.

'I wasn't here. I saw her Friday morning before I left for my mate's stag. Nothing was unusual, nothing was different. It was the same as every other day, except I was going away. I left her alone and now she's dead. I should have been here,' Keon said in a way that sounded almost rehearsed, but most likely because those were the words that had been running through his head over and over again. It was just easier to blame yourself.

'Do you know if Jackie was active on social media at all?' Imogen asked.

'She was obsessed with Instagram, used to keep a clean eating diary on there, took photos of food and stuff. I have no idea. She was a vegan and was trying to encourage other people to be vegan, too.'

'Did she ever meet people off the internet?' Imogen said, pulling her notebook out to take notes.

'Nah, most of her followers were in Australia or the States. She was trying to build up an international profile. She wanted to become a professional Instagrammer. Her online name was Jackfruit Sandwich.'

'Did she chat to people online at all?' Adrian said.

'No not really. Jackie was more of a transmitter than a listener. She made sure she posted three times a day like clockwork. Occasionally she would do a couple of extra posts. She didn't spend hours online if that's what you're asking. Why is this relevant?'

'Do you have any evidence that you were in Amsterdam over the weekend?' Imogen said.

Keon Hunter reached into his pocket and pulled out his phone. He unlocked it and handed it to Imogen. 'There's loads of photos and videos on there, there's also texts between me and my mates, a couple of texts from Jackie. I did a couple of Facebook live videos over the weekend of stupid things too. I'm in most of them. I know you have to check me out, but I couldn't have done this. I loved her.' Imogen could hear the pain in his voice.

'It's routine, sorry. It really is nothing personal,' Imogen said.

'I understand, I'll be as helpful as I can. I have nothing to hide,' Keon said, pausing for a moment as he looked up at Imogen 'Do you have a photo of her?'

'What do you mean?' she asked, bemused.

'I want to see how you found her, I want to see what he did to Jackie. My mind is racing with all the possibilities. He raped her, didn't he? That's why you kill pretty young women, isn't it? Because you're a sexual deviant.' He started clenching and unclenching his fist. They had watched him move from pain and guilt into anger, the third stage of grief. There was no telling how long he would be angry for, maybe until they caught the person who did this, maybe longer. Nothing they could tell him would quell his anger, only time.

'We can certainly show you a picture. I don't have an image with me right now though,' Imogen said.

'You didn't answer my question. Was she raped?'

'We'll know more after the autopsy,' Adrian said.

Imogen flicked through the photos on the phone. All date-stamped, silly fun. She imagined how Keon Hunter must have felt looking through these, knowing now that all the while this was going on, his girlfriend was lying dead in a roadside ditch at the mercy of the elements. She handed him back the phone.

'Satisfied I didn't kill her now?'

'We just have to check,' Imogen said. She was used to family members being defensive after a murder. She couldn't blame him for feeling the way he did about being questioned.

'Is there anything else you can tell us about Jackie? Did she have any enemies?' Adrian asked.

'No, she was nice, you know? Some people thought she was a bit vain and shallow because of her Instagram thing, but she wasn't. She did her online food diary because she enjoyed it. She used to have an eating disorder and the diary kept her on track with her eating. The doctors fully encouraged it. Who is anyone else to judge? People think they know what other people are going through but they don't.' He was really angry now and it was probably only going to get worse.

'I understand,' Imogen said.

Adrian stood up and held his hand out to Keon. 'Thank you for your help. We'll let you get on with it.'

Keon took his hand and shook it without getting up.

'We'll see ourselves out,' Adrian said, but Keon had stopped listening, he was just staring angrily ahead.

They left the flat and walked back to the car which was parked a little way up the street.

'Poor guy,' Imogen said. There was no easy way through that kind of pain, you just had to keep going. She had watched Adrian go through the stages of grief himself; he was still in the depression phase. It seemed strange to call it a phase or even to label it as anything other than just anguish. Maybe just the idea that there was a process to go through helped some people. Not being able to see a light at the end of the tunnel was never good.

'I got a text while we were in there.' Adrian pulled his phone out of his pocket.

'Me too.'

'Gary's set you up another video chat for tonight. He wants us to meet him at yours in half an hour.'

'Wonderful,' Imogen said. Not relishing the idea of being the bait but determined to get whoever was doing this. She could play the helpless vulnerable woman for now, it was a means to an end. Whatever got this bastard off the streets.

Chapter 43

Connor spilled out of the house, gulping for air. He clutched at his throat and rushed to the bushes in the front yard, throwing up just as he reached them. His eyes were burning and the tears couldn't come out fast enough. Wiping his mouth, he rushed back to the car and jumped in. He needed to get away from this, from the lie he was living. How could he not have known that his mother was dead? How could his father have kept this from him? His uncle knew. Who else knew? And Shannon – a sister? Was his mother crazy? Is that what was wrong with him? Is that why he couldn't keep his thoughts straight? Is that why his father hated him so much? He had so many questions and no way to get the answers. He couldn't trust his father. His father who had lied almost his entire life.

He got onto the road that led out towards Haldon Forest and drove as fast as he could, his eyes stinging so much that everything was a blur, especially in the darkness.

The light illuminated barely enough of the road ahead for him to take the corners, but he couldn't stop, wouldn't stop, until he was as far away from his father as possible.

This explained why there were no photos of his mother around. This explained why his father looked at him like he was shit; he had always said he looked like his mother. The woman who murdered his daughter and then presumably herself. Connor had felt crazy for longer than he could remember and suddenly it made some sense. What happened back home made sense. Everything did. Even Jacob's hatred of women, why he didn't like Connor having girlfriends. He had never seen his birth certificate; he had never been able to find it. It was as though his father were trying to remove all trace of her, as though without her there he could forget what she did, but Connor's face made him remember.

Connor desperately tried to clear the tears from his eyes, tears that wouldn't stop. He didn't even notice the warmth in his neck that crept up to his face. He didn't notice his cheek start to twitch. He was too upset to pay attention to the warning signs. It wasn't until the road changed shape in front of him and his hearing started to echo that he realised he was about to have another seizure. He had to stop the car now. He slammed his foot on the brakes so hard that he lost control and the vehicle slid across the lane, the wheel spinning through his fingers. For that split second between control and the total loss of it, he was relieved that this might be the end. That's when he felt his muscles start to tighten and the world went black.

Chapter 44

Imogen lay on her bed, wearing a red silk nightdress that had been billed as expenses. It was satin with a sweetheart neckline; not what she would normally wear. She wore a cardigan with it because she was cold and she didn't want to seem too eager, didn't want to tip him off. It was relatively high-necked but suggested a desire to take things to the next step. There was a tiny part of her that felt this was not fitting for someone who was looking for a promotion. Although she hadn't actually been looking, she had been asked. There was no logical reason why she wouldn't want the job. Maybe she felt she didn't deserve it because she hadn't definitively chosen her job over everything when it came down to it. Not right away at least.

Gary had been talking to Magic Knight a few times a week over the last three weeks since they'd started this course of action. Imogen had read through the transcripts and it was amazing how good Gary was.

She noticed parts of herself in his narrative of Cinnamon Shimmer, although she was nowhere near as friendly or light-hearted. It made her a little depressed to think of all these people out there having fun, just chatting to each other and getting on socially while she felt closed and unwelcoming. It was something she had tried to work on, but to no avail. Maybe that's what she loved about Dean so much, he forced her out of her shell. She shook her head, trying not to think about him.

She had two laptops in front of her; one had a chat screen open so that Gary could instruct her while she spoke to Magic Knight. She could see why the women fell for it, he was charming, attentive and funny. She watched Gary and Magic Knight's conversation unfold before her eyes, and she watched as Gary flirted until eventually the stranger was asked if he wanted to turn his cam on.

Gary opened the bedroom door and looked over at Imogen.

'Are you ready?'

She took a deep breath. 'Sure.'

'I'm just going to turn the light down a bit if that's OK? We want it to look relaxed and natural.'

'What if he wants me to . . . do anything?'

'Obviously, you don't have to do anything you don't want to do, and I wouldn't recommend getting naked as I will be recording everything and it will most likely be analysed in detail by everyone back at the station.'

'Oh God. Thank you for reminding me not to get naked, Gary. What would I do without you?'

'Very funny. Just remember I'm in the other room.'

'OK, let's do this,' she said.

Gary disappeared and Imogen took another deep breath, wishing Adrian was here too. Things had been awkward since they had slept in the same bed together. They still hadn't talked about it and it was almost too late to mention it now. Part of her wanted to know what he thought about the whole thing, another part thought that if they spoke about it, it may never happen again. She didn't want to have the conversation where they both admitted it was a terrible mistake under thinly veiled laughter. She would rather be stuck in this limbo. She wasn't sure why. She hoped he wasn't staying away because he felt awkward.

She saw Gary agree to go on camera with Magic Knight even though he made an excuse as to why he couldn't, and then the symbol appeared on the screen. They had decided that in order to keep him close she would do the video chat. He was the best lead they had at the moment. She clicked the button and her own face appeared. She looked different to how she imagined, it was strange seeing herself like this. She smiled and looked down, trying to seem soft, shy and vulnerable. Gary had passed the conversation over to her now, she had to respond in the chat box, try to remember everything that had passed between Gary and Magic Knight so that she didn't mess up as she was typing.

Magic Knight: Wow.
Cinnamon Shimmer: I still say this is unfair, I want to know what you look like.

Magic Knight: Soon, I promise. My cam is broken on my laptop.

Cinnamon Shimmer: I can't wait.

Magic Knight: You look amazing, I wish we could be together.

Cinnamon Shimmer: I don't even know what you look like.

Magic Knight: Does it matter?

Cinnamon Shimmer: I just want to know. I'm allowed to be curious, aren't I?

Magic Knight: I'll send you a photo if you want.

Imogen let her cardigan fall from her shoulder, hoping that might prompt him to take action.

Cinnamon Shimmer: I wish you would get your cam fixed, I really want to see you, talk to you.

Magic Knight: I'll get it sorted soon, I promise.

Cinnamon Shimmer: Tomorrow?

Magic Knight: I can't tomorrow, but the day after.

Cinnamon Shimmer: It's a date.

She blew a kiss at the camera and then clicked the button to turn it off. Moments later, Gary appeared.

'Why do you think he can't do tomorrow?' Gary said with a raised eyebrow.

'I dread to think.'

Chapter 45

When Connor's eyes opened again, he gasped; the white light was too bright and the noise hit him like a brick. As his eyes adjusted, he saw the doctors and nurses. He was in a hospital. His father and uncle were stood talking to the doctor standing at the end of his bed. They were so engaged in conversation they hadn't noticed he'd woken up. He closed his eyes again so he could listen without their knowledge.

'Fortunately, he had his seat belt on so the damage is pretty superficial. He was very lucky.'

'Thank you, Doctor.'

'There is something else that is concerning me however.' The doctor's voice became more sombre, as though he was preparing to say something serious, something Connor had heard so many times before. Connor recognised the tone and braced himself for his father's reaction. Depending on Jacob's mood, anything could happen next. Connor knew that Jacob knew what the doctor was going to say as well.

'What's that?' Jacob said calmly.

'Connor seems to have rather a lot of bruises and damage on his body; most of them look to be from before the accident. Do you know anything about that?'

He was waiting to hear what his father said to that, how he would try and deny it, how he would try and pass the blame onto Connor, how he would come out of this looking like the hero.

'He plays a lot of sports; I suppose it must be from that.' Jacob tried to play it cool. Connor wondered if the doctor would buy it – sometimes they did, sometimes they didn't.

'Not all of this damage is from sports,' the doctor said. There was no doubt as to what he was insinuating, he didn't recall any of the doctors back home being this direct with his father.

'What are you saying?' Jacob snapped.

The doctor's tone was stern. 'Why was he even driving a car?'

Jacob sighed and softened slightly, obviously aware that he needed to appeal to the doctor's concern for Connor's wellbeing. 'He took it. Look, don't call the police, he's been in trouble before and I just don't think they would let him off with a warning this time.'

'Well as he had no alcohol in his system, then I'm willing to give you the benefit of the doubt.'

Jacob had done it again, managed to avoid any kind of retribution for his behaviour.

'Thank you.'

'These seizures, how long has he been having them?'

'This is the first I've heard of it.'

Connor did remember more than one time when Jacob had taken him to the hospital about them. Jacob had a general distrust of doctors and he knew that Connor had battle scars the doctors would take a more than passing interest in. He was angry with Connor for them, that they jeopardised this mini cosmos Jacob had created that made it OK for him to hit Connor. As though Connor were somehow doing it on purpose to get him in trouble. So, to cover himself, he lied.

'He had one the other day, told me not to say anything,' Joel said.

'What?' Jacob snapped.

'Sorry, I didn't want to worry you.'

'You should have said something.' Connor could tell that Jacob was suppressing the anger that was brimming under the surface; he recognised the tones in his father's voice. It usually came a few hours before a beating. He rarely lost his temper with Joel though and so Connor was sure it would pass.

'Well, make sure he rests well over the next few days, he will have a sore neck. You should speak to his school about the sports he plays, anything that runs the risk of full physical contact is probably best avoided, at least for the time being.'

'Will do, doctor,' Jacob said politely, clearly relieved that the doctor seemed to have moved away from any suspicions about him.

Connor opened his eyes again as the doctor walked away. Both his father and uncle turned to look at him with entirely opposite expressions on their faces. Joel put his hand on Jacob's shoulder, either to show support or to hold Jacob back; Connor wasn't sure which. At some point, he was going to pay for this, he knew that much. This wasn't the first hospital visit that had resulted in a warning for Connor to take it easy. Jacob never took it well. He saw it as Connor trying to embarrass him on a personal level.

'I'll go pull the car around. Go easy on him,' Joel said before leaving.

Jacob walked over to Connor. 'You almost gave me a fucking heart attack.' There was that buried anger again.

'I wouldn't want to do that,' Connor lied.

Chapter 46

Faith Jackson was putting the finishing touches on her profile; she had changed it to show that she was taken, she was in love. The overall colour was a deep purple now and there was a Katy Perry song on in the background, 'Dark Horse'. She'd chosen it because it was very sexual; she wanted him to get hot and bothered whenever he visited her online, she wanted him to know that she was down with whatever he wanted to do. Tonight would be their first meeting.

She had just got back from getting a wax and a facial, and had had her hair and nails done too. He wouldn't be able to keep his hands off her, wouldn't be able to wait until after dinner. She had told him he could stay in her spare room, which wasn't a spare room at all. She hadn't told him she shared a flat with her work colleague. Not that it would matter; she had told Terri that she wasn't allowed to come home tonight under any circumstances and so Terri was staying over at her boyfriend's house.

Faith had never met anyone like this guy before, he seemed to know exactly what to say to tie her in knots. She had offered to pay for his ticket to come and visit her, unable to wait for the day when his hands were finally on her body. Since they had started talking it was all she could think about. He hadn't taken up her offer but had agreed to come down this weekend. She was so ready.

Hey, what time does your train get in? she messaged him.

I'll be there in fifteen minutes, he replied instantly.

I can't believe you're coming.

We'll see who's coming ☺

Don't, I can barely contain myself as it is!

I don't want you to contain yourself.

I don't even want you to speak when you turn up at my door, I don't want you to speak until after I make you cum.

Oh God, I'm on the train, you're making this so hard. Literally ☺

I've left a little something on your wall.

You shouldn't spend real money in the game, not on me.

I want everyone to know you belong to me.

I need to stop talking to you or I won't be able to stand up when we get to the station.

I'll be waiting.

His avatar went grey to signify that he had gone offline and she looked around the room to see what she could plump up or make more enticing. She lit the candles on the mantelpiece and rearranged the cushions on the sofa for the seventh time today. She rushed to the bathroom and sprayed herself with a dash of perfume that he had sent her in the post. She wanted him to know that she cherished it. Next, she checked the kitchen; there was a salad in the fridge and a cooked chicken in the oven in case he did want to eat, which she doubted. She grabbed her vodka from the side and took a swig, the acrid taste almost making her gag. She was nervous – excited and aroused, but nervous nonetheless.

Twenty minutes later and Faith was definitely feeling the effects of the vodka. All her edges were rounded, she felt smooth and silky, as though she were moving with grace. She had soft, slow music playing to add to that feeling. Vodka always made Faith feel sexy. He would be here at any moment. She took a couple of deep breaths and as if on cue the doorbell rang. Even though she had prepared herself for this, her stomach bubbled and fizzed with excitement as she put her hand on the door.

There he was. He stood on her stoop with a grin on his face but he had that twinkle in his eyes; she recognised the lust in him and was happy when it didn't falter as he ran his eyes over her body. She was wearing a black shift dress; she hadn't wanted to look too slutty, so she'd made the choice to have her legs on show rather than her cleavage. Her mother had always said you should choose one or the other. When she moved, if you were paying attention, you could see the tops of her hold-up stockings. She would make sure he saw them. She stepped closer and he raised his hand to reveal a bunch of white roses; she took them from him and placed them on the console table next to the front door.

They stood and stared at each other for a moment, then she grabbed hold of his shirt and pulled him inside, slamming the door and pushing him up against it, then planting her lips on his before he even had a chance to speak. This was the culmination of months of conversation and he was even hotter in real life than he had ever been on the screen. She couldn't wait to tell the girls at work. He returned the kiss and ran his hands down her body until they reached the tops of her stockings; he let out a tiny gasp of excitement into her mouth. Following his lead she pulled at his coat and shirt until he was topless in front of her. He went to speak but she put her finger on his lips while deftly unbuckling his belt. She grabbed hold of his waistband and pulled him towards the sofa which faced away from them. She hoped he wasn't put off by sexually aggressive women because she wasn't going to wait for him to make any of the moves.

They were up against the back of the sofa now and he pushed his knee in between her legs, arching her backwards. She laughed as she found herself suddenly laying on the sofa. He thrust his hand between her legs. She had debated whether to wear underpants or not, she figured that she would, because a little resistance can be exciting sometimes. Within moments the obstacle was gone and he was inside her. They had met less than five minutes ago and now this was happening. She smiled.

His hand came up and clasped her on the throat. She had told him she wanted him to, that it was something she liked. His fingers dug into her skin. He was doing it properly even though he said he had never done it before, even though he had told her he was reluctant in their messages together.

As they kissed and she felt his tongue exploring her mouth she also felt his hand tightening around her throat; she kissed him harder as he squeezed. His grip was too tight; he didn't seem to care that she was squirming – this didn't feel like a game, it didn't feel sexy. The room started to warp. She tried to think of the safe word they had discussed.

'Pyramid . . . Stop,' she said, but he didn't, he carried on.

'Shhh. It will all be over soon,' he said.

His voice became distant but he continued to whisper in her ear as he pressed his fingers harder into her neck. She couldn't make out the words but he sounded so angry, so full of hate.

Her legs kicked out and she thrashed against him; the struggle seemed to make him even harder. She bucked against him, thrusting her hips upwards and trying to push him away, but he just pushed harder against her, getting deeper. He had stopped kissing her now and instead he was grinning into her eyes. What she had mistaken for lust before had mutated into something else, excitement for something different. He was here to kill her. He was much stronger than his frame suggested; she couldn't fight back and she was losing consciousness.

'I know, I know!' a voice suddenly called as the front door slammed. 'We promised to stay away, but I left my phone on charge in my room, sorry!'

It was Faith's housemate Terri and her boyfriend. She felt a tear escape as she lost the battle and slipped into the darkness.

Chapter 47

On our baby's second birthday we had our first full argument and I was afraid of JD for the first time. To this day, I don't know if that was because of him, or because of the way I was. I was scared of everything, I was scared to stay home, scared to go outside. If it weren't for my daughter, I don't know that I would have even got up in the mornings.

I still found it impossible to tell JD what was going on with Rocket – it had been going on for months now and I could see no way out – and so when JD put his hand on me and I told him I couldn't sleep with him, for what must have been the hundredth time, he got angry. Not angry at me for saying no, but angry because he didn't understand what had changed between us and why I couldn't bear for him to touch me. He never ever forced me, but he would leave me alone in the house with his dysfunctional family which I decided was worse, and so eventually

I let him sleep with me again. But he knew things weren't right between us.

Yet again I found myself in an untenable situation. I wanted JD around me all the time, but I also felt so ashamed for lying to him, for not being able to tell him what was happening. I couldn't look him in the eye. The strain between us was palpable and I started to feel like he hated me. The visits from Rocket continued and I just accepted them, which made me feel complicit. He would come when he knew JD's parents were out at work. It was always over faster if I just let him do what he wanted. I would scrub my skin raw after he had left.

JD was getting fed up of my moods and so was I. I didn't want to feel anything anymore so I started to take my mother-in-law's antidepressants; she had hidden them in a cupboard after being forced to go on them by her husband. There were several boxes, all untouched. I wasn't sure if they would work, but I didn't care, I had to try something. They gave the world a different feeling, smooth around the edges. I was distant and distracted and JD thought I was suffering from post-natal depression; how could I tell him what was really going on? It got to the point where I started to resent him for not noticing, not caring enough to find out what was the matter with me. He doted on our daughter though; as soon as he came home he would scoop her up and then I would disappear to our room and go to sleep.

Sleep became my only refuge and so I slept as much as possible. The more I slept, the more I wanted to sleep; I was awake for a third of the day at most. As soon as our daughter turned two, we got three hours a day free childcare at a centre just at the end of the road. That was when Rocket would come over. I didn't always know which day but I was grateful for the fact that I knew when it was going to happen. At least with the window so small I was freer the rest of the time. Strangely, I started to feel a little better about the situation. It's only looking back on these things now that I realise how crazy that seems, that I could get used to those months of turmoil. Rocket didn't seem to like the fact that I was adjusting to the circumstances.

I realised then that it wasn't about him wanting me or wanting to be with me, it was about punishing me for rejecting him. I became a surrogate for all the people who had rejected him in the past; I was a thing to him, something for him to use and abuse. I wondered if he had ever loved me, or even liked me – if he was even capable of those things. I knew that my compliance and apathy were annoying him; I think I hoped I would lose my appeal to him if it wasn't upsetting me anymore.

I know the way I am describing this makes no sense, I should be more upset than this, but I'm not. A part of me snapped and I didn't have the energy to feel those things anymore. Or maybe it was just the antidepressants.

His visits became less frequent; he wasn't getting what he needed from me anymore. I started to come back into the real world, out of hiding. JD noticed a change in me, and we talked about the future again for the first time in a long time. He told me that he was *sorry he ever brought me to this house and that if I wanted to move away, we could. All he wanted was for me to be happy again. Finally, I could see a light at the end of the tunnel.*

Chapter 48

Adrian rushed into the station, past the access door and into the bullpen. Imogen stood up as he approached.

'Where are they?' he said.

'Interview rooms one and two. I was waiting for you,' Imogen said.

'And the girl?' Adrian said.

'Faith Jackson.'

'Right, Faith Jackson, where is she?' Adrian asked. He couldn't understand why he felt so invested in this case. Not that he was ever apathetic, but there was something about this one that made him angry. Targeting the lonely was low, people who thought they had found something special, only to realise they had been lied to and deceived. He couldn't help but imagine that moment when they realised what was going on, as the killer's hands closed around their throats. What kind of monster could do that to anyone? Adrian found some comfort in the fact that he was appalled at this behaviour, he had begun to feel numb to the job. Since Lucy had died he had felt a bit numb to everything. Now, finally he was starting to react to things, he was waking up again.

'Out of intensive care already, still not out of the woods though. The doctors had to put her in a medically induced coma. She's at Wonford with a uniformed officer stationed outside her door for now.'

'What about the suspect? Any leads on him?'

'Nothing yet,' Imogen said.

'What about evidence?'

'All of it.' Imogen smiled. 'We have her phone, her computer, everything. Gary's looking through it now.'

'Is it your friend? Is it Magic Knight?' Adrian asked, hoping they would finally have something concrete against him; if it wasn't him, then they had put Imogen in danger for nothing and they had no idea where the danger was coming from.

'I don't know. I haven't seen Gary yet. If there is anything there he'll find it,' Imogen said.

They walked into the interview room to see Theresa Johns, Faith Jackson's housemate, sitting staring at the wall. Adrian sat down and smiled. She looked nervous.

'You're not in any trouble, we just want to record this so that we have your testimony on tape,' Imogen said, and the woman nodded.

Adrian pressed the red button to start the recording.

'This interview is being recorded. I am Detective Sergeant Adrian Miles and I am based at Exeter Police Station in the Devon constabulary. Acting

Detective Inspector Imogen Grey is also present,' Adrian said for the tape.

'Can you state your name for the record?' Imogen asked.

'Terri Johns, Theresa Anne Johns.'

'Can you explain in your own words what it is you saw?'

'I was out with my boyfriend, Ray, but I had forgotten my phone, left it on charge in my room so we came back. I opened the door and at first I thought she was just . . .' Theresa took a deep breath and stared ahead, remembering what she had seen.

'Go on please, Miss Johns.'

'I thought they were . . . you know. But as soon as he saw me he got up and ran. He pushed me out of the way and punched Ray. His clothes were on the floor, well, he still had his trousers on. He grabbed his stuff and ran out. I ran to check if Faith was OK; she was unconscious and so Ray called an ambulance.'

'That must have been very upsetting,' Adrian said. He couldn't help thinking about Lucy again. How if he had been quicker then maybe he could have saved her. Even though Faith Jackson wasn't out of the woods yet, they had that glimmer of hope. He would do anything for that.

'Did you see his face? Could you give us a physical description?' Imogen said.

'Yes. He was a man in his late thirties, maybe early forties, with white skin and dark hair. Clean-shaven.'

'Wait. Dark hair?' Imogen said.

'Yes, it was kind of wavy and hung around his ears. He was . . .' She stopped and looked down.

'He was what?' Adrian probed.

'He was kind of good-looking,' Terri Johns said.

'Did he say anything?'

'Nothing. He just ran. We called 999 as soon as we could.' She sniffed but there were no tears. 'I just can't believe it. I don't want to go back there. He's been in our house.'

'It's highly unlikely that he will come back,' Imogen said, trying to smile reassuringly.

'Faith is impulsive. I encouraged her though, she was so excited about him.'

'Did he know about you?' Adrian asked.

'No, she told him she lived alone. She wanted him to think she was someone she wasn't. She lied about her age as well.'

'How old did she tell him she was?' Imogen said.

'Twenty-seven,' Terri said.

'And she was thirty-seven?' Adrian said.

'Yeah, she doesn't look it though. She looked good for her age. She never told anyone how old she really was.'

'Did she often meet up with men from the internet?' Adrian said, trying desperately not to make it sound like a judgement.

'She had done it a couple of times before. She said he was different though, she really had to play it cool or he would run scared. Some nights they would talk for hours on end, some nights he just wouldn't log on at all.'

'I don't suppose you remember the dates of when he wasn't online?' Imogen said.

'No, sorry.' Theresa frowned. 'Is she going to be OK?'

'She's in the best place and the doctors are doing everything they can. Thanks to you,' Imogen said.

'I didn't even do anything. It was just dumb luck,' Terri said, her voice drifting off into thought again.

'Dumb luck is better than bad luck,' Imogen replied.

'Sometimes dumb luck is all you need,' Adrian said. He stood up, needing to get out of there. He couldn't help but turn it around on himself, as though it were him that had failed by somehow not even being close to being able to save Lucy, not even really knowing she was in danger. Maybe he had come back to work too soon after she died. Everything that was being said he managed to somehow twist in his mind to slot into the narrative he had created. Was this what survivor's guilt felt like? Did he wish it had been him? No question about it. It should have been him.

He saw Imogen looking at him with concern; he must have looked as bad as he felt, thoughts hurtling through his mind at a rate that was entirely too fast to be in any way useful.

'Interview suspended at eleven fifteen,' Imogen said. She nodded sideways to Adrian, motioning towards the door. 'I'll be back in a minute, Terri.'

They stepped outside and Adrian began to feel calmer.

'Sorry,' he said.

'Are you OK?' She put her hand on his arm.

'I don't know what's the matter with me.'

'It's perfectly understandable, Adrian, cut yourself some slack.'

'I don't know why this is getting to me the way it is.

These women, he picks them because they are alone and vulnerable. He deliberately looks for the ones that would fall for his shit, ones that are so intent on finding that connection that they don't even notice what kind of man he is. Then they end up dead because of it.'

'This man isn't just sleeping around. He's killing them, too. You aren't like that, Adrian. Don't be so ridiculous. The man is fucked in the head.'

'I've done it before though, I've gone into a bar and looked for the lonely ones, the ones who are grateful for some attention. What kind of man does that make me?'

'You're probably flattering yourself a bit here. Maybe they just liked you. Maybe it wasn't just about your manipulation of them but about what they were looking for, too. Maybe everyone got what they wanted? Generally speaking: women don't just "go along" with sex because men want them to. We kind of like it, too. It's not always a coercion or a bloody mind game that you've won, some women deliberately act lonely and vulnerable to get guys like you. They know how to play to your ego. It cuts both ways.'

'We need to find this guy, before he hurts anyone else,' Adrian said. He wanted to put his arms around Imogen. She was surprisingly good at pep talks. The idea of this man, whoever he was, watching Imogen and making plans to pounce was nauseating. Adrian wanted to close his hands around the killer's neck and see how he liked it.

'Take a break. Get me a coffee. We'll go through what we know so far in a bit.'

He nodded and took off. Trying to stop himself from

272

thinking for a moment. He needed to get some power back, to feel like they had some of the cards in this case. So far it felt as though someone else entirely was in control. What if Magic Knight knew Imogen was a police officer? What kind of danger would she be in then? He couldn't let her down the same way he had let Lucy down; he couldn't lose her. Not Imogen.

Chapter 49

Connor lay on the sofa in his lounge; the room was clean and the cuts had almost disappeared from his face. His father had taken it easy on him, maybe because his uncle Joel was around to keep an eye on things. Joel had packed Jacob off to work and was there at the house, cleaning each room. Being the father that Connor wished for, together and in control. Even Jacob seemed to be calmer around Joel; Joel always seemed to know exactly the right thing to say to the point where Connor was suspicious of his sincerity. Joel could twist Jacob around his finger. Connor had never really observed them together before, but since they had come here from California, he watched and realised that his father had once been a very different man. Connor always had the opposite effect on Jacob, but he wasn't afraid anymore.

Connor couldn't understand it and he couldn't explain why, but it was like a switch had flipped inside him. Hearing the truth about his mother had lit a fire in his chest. A burning desire to get away. He had always felt trapped, stuck with his father, as though he couldn't abandon him because his mother had done the same thing. As though leaving would prove Jacob right. But since he had found out that she'd taken the easy way out, something he completely understood, something he had thought about more than once himself – well, suddenly walking out the door didn't seem so bad. When the time was right he would ask his uncle Joel if he could stay with him, and if that didn't work out then he would get a job or something. He would do his best in his exams and then he would go.

He had lain at home for the last few days and thought of nothing else but leaving. He couldn't believe his whole life was a lie. The nights he spent wondering why his mother had left him. The nights he spent wondering if she would ever come back, if she ever thought of him. The precariously Sellotaped picture of her wearing the David Bowie T-shirt and holding the baby, her face obscured, that was all he had of her, the edge of a face.

'Uncle Joel?' Connor called out.

Joel appeared at the door a few moments later, a tea towel over his shoulder 'Yes?'

'Do you have any photos of my mother?'

'What?' Joel seemed a little shaken at the mention of her. It wasn't something they openly spoke about.

'I have no idea what she looked like, not really,' Connor said, noticing the slight change in Joel's stance. He had tensed up.

'That's easy, she looked just like you.' Joel smiled, a wide smile, almost too happy.

'But I've never seen her face, not properly. I have half a photo held together with Scotch tape, but nothing else. I don't even know what her name was, before she was married.'

'I think it was Beckett, it's so long ago now. I'll have a look at home, I think I might have a wedding picture.'

'Thank you.' Connor relaxed and turned back to the TV.

'Don't tell your dad, for God's sake,' Joel said.

'No, of course not.'

There was a soft knock on the front door. Joel left Connor in the lounge and went to answer it. A few seconds later Selina was standing at the foot of the sofa. She was the last person Connor was expecting to see. He had put her out of his mind completely since their last conversation.

'Who is that?' Selina said, glancing around as Joel left the room.

'My uncle. What do you want?' Connor asked, wishing she would go away. If anyone could understand, it would be her, but he didn't want anyone else right now. He just wanted to be alone, to get away. There was something about Selina though, something that made him want to say things he didn't normally want to share with anyone else. Even in these few seconds, her presence felt like a magnet and he hated the powerlessness of it.

'I just wondered how you were doing,' Selina said, perching on the arm of the sofa, looking down at him.

'I'm OK, thanks,' he answered, knowing that he didn't have to be small around her, knowing that he could say the big things and she wouldn't look at him like he was crazy.

Connor switched the TV off and sat up, and Selina came and sat next to him on the sofa.

'Why did you do it? Why did you crash your dad's car?' she asked, whispering to keep the conversation between them.

'It was an accident, I didn't *do* anything,' Connor said, wondering why she had assumed that he had done it on purpose.

'I saw you, you were pretty upset.' Selina looked at him; he was drawn into her eyes. There was something there, a desire to be seen maybe. It was the same thing he felt in himself, he desperately wanted to be seen, for someone to look past all the bullshit to the things inside.

'What, are you spying on me or something?'

Selina looked down and took a deep breath before speaking. 'Was it because of your dad?'

'No! What do you mean?' The habit of lying, of trying to cling on to the life he knew, however fucked up it was, was ingrained in him. Connor was alone and the thought of anything beyond that terrified him; if he brought Selina into his confidence, then what? He didn't know how not to be alone.

'These walls are pretty thin. Sometimes I hear you arguing.' She looked up and their eyes locked. He wanted to tell her what he knew as well but figured now wasn't the time. He didn't know how to let go of

277

the lie. *Everything is fine. Everything is fine. Everything is fine.*

The realisation that she could hear their fights dawned on Connor. Embarrassed, he picked up his cigarettes and lit one.

'Thanks for stopping by,' he said.

'Why don't you talk to someone about it?'

He smiled knowingly at her. He could embarrass her back now if he wanted, expose her for who she really was. A victim just like him, someone who let other people take what they wanted and discard them when they were done. He could if he wanted to. He could make her feel smaller than shit, but that wasn't who he was, that was his father, the recognition of his father inside him. Making her feel bad was what Jacob would do. Find someone's weakness and make them hate themselves.

'It's not that easy . . . is it?' he said, vague enough to mean nothing.

Selina looked down at her feet. 'Are you afraid of your father?'

It was a valid question, something he had been thinking about these last few days, and the answer was simple.

'Not anymore.'

Chapter 50

Connor put his maths textbooks into his locker and pulled out the computing one. He felt a body press against him and cold hands cover his eyes.

'Guess who?' Pippa said.

Connor turned around and she pressed herself harder into him, kissing him on the lips and slipping her tongue in between. He eased her away.

'Hey,' he said breathlessly.

'It's good to see you.' She had a twinkle in her eye as she stared at his damaged face. 'I was so worried when I heard what happened to you.'

'Sorry I didn't call.'

'I assumed you couldn't. It's been boring as hell without you around. Do you want to hang out after school? I need my fix.' She dropped a shoulder slightly and pouted her lips the tiniest bit.

'I don't know if I can.' This game wasn't fun anymore. He was bored of pretending to be normal.

'Try, yeah? It's been a week, I'm beginning to think you're avoiding me.'

'My uncle's cooking something special for dinner, but I'll text you after that,' he lied.

'OK.' She seemed wounded by the idea that he wouldn't want to rush for a fumble with her. As though that would be what he would want most in the world right now.

The bell rang and Connor turned again and slammed his locker shut.

'I better get to computer science.'

'See you later then,' she called after him as he made his escape.

He got into the room and pulled out his textbook; they were continuing projects for their coursework and so there was no need for formalities or small talk today. He just wanted to get in and do his work. Connor logged into his personal student account and stared at the start-up screen. Instead of clicking on the app inventor, he clicked on the browser and typed in his mother's name.

It was a long time ago, so the hits were on the seventh page the search engine churned out. *Murder-suicide*, that was the technical term for what had happened. There was a picture of his father distraught, not the father he knew now, a man with pain on his face instead of anger. In his arms, Jacob cradled a small child. Connor knew it was him but had no recollection of the moment; he was too young to remember.

Sometimes, he thought if he closed his eyes for long and hard enough he would be able to remember his mother's face but he never could. At the bottom of the article was a picture of her; it was poor resolution and small, but there she was. It was the first time he had seen her face properly and he suddenly understood the looks his father gave him. She looked just like him, right down to the dimples and the lopsided smile. He emailed the picture to himself and quickly opened the app inventor just as his teacher wandered around towards his desk. After all this time, he finally knew where he came from.

At dinner that evening, the tension was palpable as they ate the meal that Joel had prepared for them. The first meal they had sat down together for since the car accident. The first time Connor had spent more than five minutes with his father. It was a lasagne; it tasted almost the same as the lasagne Jacob used to make back when he used to cook, back when he at least pretended to give a shit.

'This is pretty good,' Connor finally said.

'One of the many attempts to save my brief and failing marriage,' Joel said. 'I doubt you remember my ex-wife, your aunt Kathleen, but she made me go to a cookery class with her.'

'Why did you break up?' Connor said. He had never met Joel's wife; they'd stayed in the UK for the very short duration of their marriage. Neither man ever really talked about her, in fact they rarely talked about women at all.

'She left me for her yoga teacher.' Joel shrugged.

'Did he wear a leotard?' Connor laughed.

'Actually, it was a woman.'

He heard his father sigh a heavy sigh, presumably in exasperation. It wasn't like him not to be vocal about his grievances. He slammed down his knife and fork. 'Why did you do it?'

Connor looked at him. 'Do what?'

'The car. Why did you crash it?' he spat out.

'I had a seizure while I was driving. Apparently repeated blows to the head will do that to you,' Connor snipped.

'Don't you start blaming me for that shit. I took harder beatings than you ever got and I never had a seizure in my life,' Jacob said, his anger escalating. Joel put his hand on his arm and gave him a stern look. This seemed to stop Jacob from erupting completely. Connor wondered what information had passed in that look between the two men.

'Well, I guess that's just another way that you're better than me then.'

'Just tell me the truth, will you?' Jacob said, teetering on the edge of a full-blown meltdown.

'What truth are you looking for?' Connor said, no longer afraid to confront his father.

Jacob glared at him. 'What happened?'

'Are you asking me if I did it on purpose? Do you think I tried to kill myself?'

'I don't know what to think,' Jacob said, clearly a little confused by Connor's directness.

'Don't worry, Dad. I'm not the liar here.'

'What does that mean?'

'I'm going out.' Connor got up and threw his cutlery

down. The look of shock on Jacob's face was almost worth the insubordination.

Joel carried on eating without even looking up from his plate. He wasn't uncomfortable though, in fact Connor thought for a second that he was smiling.

'Sit back down.' Jacob slammed his hand down on the table.

'I'll be home later.' Connor left without looking back.

Chapter 51

Connor walked for hours, long enough for dinner to be over, long enough to calm down. He had to think about what his options really were. He didn't have many. It was cold and was only getting worse; the anger that was keeping him warm had now abated. He walked past Pippa's house, the only person who might be happy to see him right now. As he stood outside, he realised he didn't particularly want to see her, or anyone for that matter. He was alone.

Walking back to the house he realised he could do this until he worked out how to get away. As he rounded the corner onto his street, he saw his Uncle Joel putting his bag on the back seat of his car and rushed over.

Connor shook Uncle Joel's hand, holding on for a little longer than was probably acceptable, not wanting him to leave the house; not wanting to be left alone with his father. They held on to each other for a moment and yet again Connor wished Joel was his dad. He felt so much more connected to him.

'Do you have to go?'

'I'll be back soon, don't worry. I can't stay another night; I don't have any spare clothes.'

'I wish you could.'

'I've spoken to your dad and he's promised me he is going to try and get himself together. But you can always call me, I'm just a phone call away.' Joel put his hand on Connor's shoulder and squeezed.

'Maybe I could come with you? I hate him so much.'

'It'll be fine, Con, you know he's not the only shitty parent in the world. He's already paid a heavier price than most of us ever have to, why don't you cut him some slack? Give him one more chance. For me.'

'I just don't fit in here though.'

'Curse of the Lee boys, I'm afraid. Don't fit in anywhere.'

Jacob came out of the house and Joel pulled away from Connor, the warmth disappearing. It was as though Joel didn't want to be caught being nice to Connor. His demeanour changed so quickly and definitively that Connor was confused. The men shook hands and Jacob shot a look at Connor to leave them alone.

As Connor walked back inside the house he felt the dread return, like an old friend, familiar and ever-present. He shook it off and decided, not for the first time, that he wouldn't be pandering to Jacob's moods anymore. Something had changed between them, but was it enough? Was the barrier between them psychological? Could it be dissolved with a new mindset? Connor didn't know.

Jacob came back inside a few moments later and Connor could feel his mood. He was apologetic, looking for another chance. Another fresh start. There were only so many second chances though. Only so many times you can prove that your word means nothing, that you can't be trusted, that only a fool would believe you.

Connor took his coat off the bannister and walked back out the front door, the air filling his lungs as though he had never been outside before. Suffocating, that's what his father was. Whenever he was in a room, the world revolved around him – whether Connor was trying to make him happy, or attempting to avoid his anger, it was always about Jacob. Well, not any more.

Selina's mum Diana came out of her house dressed up for work. She kept looking impatiently at her watch, checking up and down the road. As soon as she saw Connor, she smiled and tried to inconspicuously make herself look pretty. She was tucking her hair behind her ears, tugging at the neckline on her dress to reveal more, standing in a way that made her legs look longer. All very subtle movements but Connor noticed things like that; maybe because he had never known his mother, he took a particular interest in how women moved, behaved, spoke. All pieces of a puzzle he could never complete. Who was she, the woman who had abandoned him? The woman who had chosen death over a life with her son.

'I hope the other guy looks worse,' Diana called over to him.

Connor looked at his house, saw his father watching

from the window and walked over to Diana with a smile on his face.

'You lost your cat again?'

'I'm just waiting for my stupid husband. God knows where he is! He's supposed to be giving me a lift to work tonight and he's already twenty fucking minutes late . . . pardon my French. I start at nine, so if he's not here in the next fifteen minutes . . .'

Connor looked back at his house. Jacob was necking a beer; through the lounge window, Connor could see that he looked annoyed and powerless. He knew he wouldn't come out and have a go at him while he was talking to Diana. First and foremost, Jacob was a coward; that was why he picked on kids, and it was probably what drove his mother to suicide. He didn't want to go back in there right now, in fact he didn't want to spend any more time in that house than he had to.

'I can take you if you like?' As he spoke to Diana, he looked up to see a large black cloud completely dominating the sky like a stain, obscuring all the stars. Very metaphorical.

A smile crept across Diana's face as she looked at her feet. He wondered what she thought this was.

'You sure you don't mind?'

'I don't mind at all.'

'Did you get held back at school or something? How come you drive?'

'I technically shouldn't, but I passed my test in the States so, what difference does my age make?'

'Damn right.'

287

Connor walked to his car; Diana tottering behind him in her stupidly high heels. She waited for him to open the door but he just walked around the car and got in. This wasn't a date.

As they drove along the lanes to the outskirts of town, Connor looked over to Diana, still wondering how she could be Selina's mother. They were nothing alike. She was preening herself in the visor mirror, plumping her lips out and dabbing the corner of her eye with the tip of her little finger. A light rain spat down onto the windscreen. She turned to face Connor.

'You look so much like your father. I know everyone says you look like her, but I see him in you.'

'You knew my mother?'

Diana nodded. 'Oh yeah, I knew her.'

'What was she like?'

'She was a bit older than me, as you can probably imagine. We all used to hang out together. Me and your father, Joel and your mother.'

'Were you dating my uncle?'

'Oh no, I was with your dad. Briefly, anyway. She was with Joel.'

'What?' Connor was surprised – neither Jacob or Joel had ever mentioned this before.

'Oh yeah. They were all over each other. It was such a surprise when she left him for your dad.'

How could he not know this?

'Why did they break up?' Connor asked.

'She just wanted Jacob. He was the real catch, you know. Joel's a lovely guy, life of the party, but there was something about your dad. I see it in you, too. A kind of intensity.'

Connor suppressed a sneer as Diana continued twiddling with her hair in what she obviously thought was a seductive manner.

'I bet you don't think Selina looks like me,' she said, looking sideways at him.

'No, she doesn't.'

'She took after her father, too. Her dad's inside . . . you know . . . prison. Good job too if you ask me. He was nothing but trouble . . . Can I have a cigarette?' She nodded at the packet that was sticking out of Connor's shirt pocket.

'Go for it.'

Diana reached over and ran her fingers across Connor's chest; he held his breath as she slid her hand into his pocket and pulled out his cigarettes. She lit up and inhaled deeply, her eyes fixed on Connor, willing him to look at her. The car started to fill with smoke and Connor opened the window. Diana leaned over and put the cigarette in Connor's mouth before taking out another one and lighting it. He felt the drop in the temperature as the clouds churned overhead.

'You know . . . I could possibly be a little later for work, the boss won't mind. We could stop off for a drink or something,' she said.

'I really should be getting back; Dad needs the car,' Connor lied, the moment marked by the lightning that broke the storm, illuminating the road ahead.

Diana put her hand on his thigh, and he shuddered involuntarily. Thunder cracked and the rain began to hammer against the windscreen.

'You cold, babe?'

Connor shifted in his seat. 'A little.'

'I can think of a way to warm you up.'

Diana leaned towards him, squeezing his thigh and slowly moving her hand upwards. He concentrated harder on the road as they pulled into the car park where she worked.

'We're here,' he said as he jerked the car to a stop. The movement seemed to snap her out of it and she tucked her hair behind her ears again. 'It's only going to get worse, you should get inside.'

'Well, thank you, gorgeous,' she said, a disappointed look on her face.

'You're welcome,' he called as she slammed the door behind her. What the hell was he doing?

Diana ran into the bar with her bag held high to shelter her from the rain. Connor looked across the street, and saw what looked like Neil's dad's car parked on the corner. The light was on inside, and Connor spied movement. Frowning, he pulled his car around and as he did so, he saw the familiar sight of Pippa in the back seat of the car. In the glow of his headlights, Connor saw that she was partially undressed. Presumably, Neil was the guy underneath her.

Connor lifted his foot off the clutch, still not used to driving a manual gear even though his father insisted he learn that way. The car stalled as it faced them, beams pouring through the window. The brightness of his lights caused Pippa to look up and she saw Connor, a wide-eyed stare across her face. She immediately scrambled to get out of the car and ran towards him.

'Connor! Wait.'

'Don't worry about it, Pip!' he called out as he desperately tried to restart the car before she could reach him. She was just wearing a bra and her jeans were unbuttoned.

'I'm sorry; I didn't know you'd be here.'

'It's not a big deal. Don't worry. I'm not mad or anything.'

'I never meant to hurt you.'

Connor smiled.

'I'm not hurt, Pip. Trust me.'

Pippa looked upset by this.

'Well I . . .'

'Listen, it was just a bit of fun, no big deal. Don't feel guilty on my part. I'm kind of relieved, to be honest. Besides, you and Neil are a much better match.' It had been obvious to Connor that Neil held a torch for Pippa. He could tell by the way Neil talked about her that they had history.

Pippa shrank away from him, crossing her arms over her bare midriff, her lips shivering.

'You should get back inside,' Connor said, 'you're soaking. You're going to get sick.'

He smiled at her and started the car. He pulled away before she had a chance to say anything else to him. He wasn't lying though, he was relieved. Now he didn't have to pretend to be interested, he could pretend to care that she cheated on him instead. Much easier.

In his rear view, he saw Neil come up behind her and wrap his coat around her. She was better off without Connor. Maybe everyone was.

Chapter 52

Imogen looked at herself. The mirror in the station toilets was quite unflattering, maybe because of the battleship grey walls. Her olive skin had taken on a sallow tinge. She smoothed her eyebrows and took a deep breath. The toilet flushed and DCI Kapoor emerged from one of the cubicles. Imogen jumped; she'd thought she was alone. The DCI washed her hands, leaving Imogen to break the silence.

'I've been meaning to talk to you about the job offer,' she said awkwardly. 'I know it's been longer than two weeks.'

'Which offer is that?' DCI Kapoor said, with a strange look on her face. A sideways look. Something had changed.

'For the DI gig, you asked me to tell you if I wanted it. Well, I spoke to Adrian and he's cool with it and so I would like to go for it.' Imogen couldn't think of one good reason not to do it, and so she decided to ignore her fears and crack on.

'Oh . . . That might be a problem,' DCI Kapoor said.

'What?'

'Well, I was hoping we wouldn't have to have the conversation just yet.'

'Which conversation is that?'

'Something has been brought to my attention; I was going to try and ignore it – and might have been able to do that if you didn't want to push forward with the DI job right now. If I had known about it before, then I probably wouldn't have offered you the position.'

'Brought to your attention by whom?' Imogen said.

'That doesn't matter, but it appears that you are involved with a material witness on a couple of cases, someone who was also formerly a suspect.'

'He was never a suspect.' Imogen felt her stomach sink, realising instantly that the DCI was talking about Dean. She had always known it would come out, but she wasn't ready for it. Not right now.

'Maybe he was never suspected by you, but in the files he was listed as a person of interest.'

'I'm not involved with him anymore,' she said, knowing that if she lost her job now then she wouldn't have to make a decision, she could just run to Dean and they could skip off into the sunset together. Maybe it wouldn't be so bad.

'But you were involved with him?'

'A bit, yes.' Imogen was embarrassed, embarrassed that instead of being terrified of losing her job, which is what she should be feeling, what she thought she *would* be feeling – she was feeling the tiniest glimmer of hope. It was as though fate, something she didn't believe in, were telling her it was the right thing to do.

'Well, we are going to have to have an informal chat about it. I wasn't sure how I was going to deal with it, but if, as you say, you are no longer together, then I think it's best if we just get it all out there. We don't want it to come back and bite us at a later date. When I got this job, I was given the authority to decide which disciplinary matters would be taken down the official route. I will listen to what you have to say and decide if there needs to be a formal investigation. This station has been through a lot in the last year and I've been asked to try and avoid any unnecessary scandals.'

'Will I lose my job?'

'Depends what happened.'

'I broke up with him because of the job, because it's too important to me. I haven't seen him in weeks.'

'Look, I understand your situation more than you realise, I'm not judging you.'

Imogen wondered what DCI Kapoor meant.

'So, what happens now?' Imogen said, confronted again with a feeling of relief that she wasn't expecting.

'I'll take a statement from you and we will have to corroborate your story with the other party, but as long as none of the cases were put in jeopardy we can talk about where to go from here. If he got information from you and acted on that information, then you're in more trouble than just losing your job, I'm afraid. There may well be an independent investigation, but I would like to avoid that if at all possible. But, if, as you say, it's over . . .'

'It is.'

'OK, well, now's not the time, but we must do it soon. As you know, it's not against the rules per se, but very much frowned upon. Providing everything checks out we can maybe talk about applying for the DI position at a later date.'

'Thank you.'

'Don't thank me yet. You should have told me about this, I shouldn't have found out from someone else. The biggest problem here as far as I am concerned is that you didn't declare it.'

'I won't make any excuses, it was poor judgement on my part.'

'The last thing you want is to become an officer who has a reputation for poor judgement. Just ask your friend DS Miles, it's taken him a while to recover from his own bad decisions and he's a good-looking white man. Unfortunately, as a woman, you may not restore your reputation so easily. We can't give the people who want to hold us back the stick to beat us with.'

DCI Kapoor offered Imogen a conciliatory smile before walking back to her office. Yet again the DCI had surprised her by the way she had handled the situation. She'd expected immediate suspension and not this soft approach. Imogen wasn't sure how she really felt about any of this right now. It would almost have been better if the DCI had thrown the book at her. Almost.

Imogen walked back to her desk to find Adrian going through all the crime scene photos from Erica, Alyssa, Jackie and Faith's cases again. Denise Ferguson was up a ladder hanging some tinsel around the clock, royal blue tinsel of course. A reminder that it was only a few weeks until the year was over, something she hadn't really thought about.

'What are you doing for Christmas?' Imogen asked Adrian.

'Working, you?' Adrian continued looking at the photos.

'If we haven't cleared this up, then yeah, I haven't had any better offers.'

'I think I'm expected for family dinner at home with Tom and Andrea.'

'That'll be nice, won't it?' Imogen said, knowing full well that that wasn't what Adrian wanted. It was going to be hard for him this year, without Lucy. Christmas made you thoughtful. The relationships you usually thrust to the back of your mind were brought kicking and screaming to the surface. Old mistakes were revisited and sometimes new mistakes were made.

'I don't know about that. I'm just worried that Tom is reading the situation wrong and he thinks we might be getting back together again. I mean, he's never known us to be together. I just hope that's not what he's expecting, because it's not going to happen.'

'Have you tried talking to him?' She smiled, knowing that he hadn't. Adrian didn't talk about things, it was why she hadn't mentioned what had happened between them. What *had* happened? It was something and nothing at the same time. It probably wouldn't happen again anyway. She tried to ignore the small part of her that wanted it to.

'He seems happy at the moment, we're getting on well, I don't want to ruin that. He's had a really tough time lately, tougher than most.'

'Tom's a sensible kid. You should talk to him.'

'Maybe.' Adrian paused for a moment. 'If you're at a loose end, you could come, too.'

Imogen smiled. 'Gee, thanks.' She wasn't sure if that was such a great idea, things were getting complicated between them and she didn't really know how to deal with it.

'I just mean . . .'

'I know what you mean.'

'You shouldn't be alone at Christmas,' Adrian said, head still down, but she could tell he wasn't looking at the photos anymore.

'I'm alone a lot of the time. What's so special about Christmas?' She hated the fuss around Christmas. Christmas time with her mother had been nothing less than an ordeal. She had come to expect nothing but some kind of heartbreak. She didn't get presents most years as a child, if she was lucky she got through it without her mother getting so wasted on pills and drink that she slept through most of it. Christmas reminded Imogen of how isolated Irene and she were, of how she hadn't had a father. The sooner it was over, the better.

'It's just a time for family and friends.'

'Right, then maybe you should spend it with yours,' Imogen said with a taut smile.

'I'm not cooking, if that's what you're worried about.' He teased.

'I'll see,' Imogen said. Adrian was as close as any family

Imogen had ever had, aside from her mother, and it would be nice not to be alone. She didn't want to give him the wrong idea though. It almost felt like any time spent together out of work was muddying the waters.

Adrian looked up and smiled, no awkwardness or discomfort on his face. Maybe she was reading too much into things. Maybe what had happened that morning wasn't that big a deal. Maybe this really was nothing in the grand scheme of Adrian's frequent intimate liaisons with women.

There was the conundrum of Dean though; speaking to the DCI had just made Imogen think of him even more. She knew he would be alone for Christmas and that didn't feel right. They couldn't be together though, so what was the answer? Putting him to the back of her mind wasn't working. Would it ever really be over? Just the mention of his name and she was beyond distracted again, full of hope for a completely unrealistic future where they got to be together. She fished her phone out of her bag and looked through the contacts, remembering she had deleted Dean's number – but it didn't matter, she knew it by heart. She put the phone away; maybe she would call him later and tell him that the DCI would want to speak to him about them. Maybe that was just an excuse to hear his voice again.

'Any news on Faith Jackson?' Adrian said, interrupting her thoughts.

'Still under, they said she's doing well though. They are thinking about bringing her round over the next couple of days; the swelling on her brain has gone down and her blood pressure has stabilised, too.'

'Are they going to call us?'

'I've told the officer watching over her to call me when it happens. She's still under guard, in case the perpetrator knows where she is,' Imogen said.

'Is that likely, do you think?'

'He's still too much of an unknown entity, we can't rule it out, I don't think,' she said. She was uncomfortable with the amount that Magic Knight may or may not know given that he was the strongest lead they had and they still didn't know very much about him. He could be anyone. He could be one step ahead of them the whole time.

'When are you speaking to your Magic Knight again?' Adrian said.

'I'll find out from Gary,' she smiled, 'but soon.'

'Is everything OK? You seem a bit . . . distracted.'

'I just spoke to the DCI, she's on the brink of launching an investigation into my relationship with Dean. Someone told her about us.'

'Well it wasn't me.'

'Of course not,' Imogen said – the thought hadn't even occurred to her.

'If you need me to back you up on anything, I will. Just tell me,' Adrian said without hesitation.

'Thank you. It doesn't look like I'm going to be your boss after all,' Imogen said. Still probably not as upset as she should have been.

'Just when I was getting used to the idea.' Adrian smiled. 'They will see that you acted professionally when it counted.'

'You mean when I accused my boyfriend of being a

child porn distributor on the record in a police interview?' She still cringed at the thought of it, but Adrian was right, that interview probably would be the thing that saved her job.

'Well, yes. That will definitely help your case.'

Imogen sat down next to Adrian and looked at the pictures.

'These poor women,' Adrian muttered.

'We'll get him, don't worry.'

She smiled and resisted the urge to put her head on his shoulder for comfort. She was exhausted at the prospect of being questioned over her relationship with Dean. She had always known that this was a possibility, more of a probability, but that didn't make it any less inconvenient. How was she supposed to get over Dean if she was forced to think about him? She couldn't worry about that anymore. She had to get her head in this case. Before the killer found another victim. Before she became a victim herself.

Chapter 53

Connor slammed the door as he entered the house. The TV clicked off as the door closed and Jacob appeared at the living room door just as Connor was about to go upstairs. He had managed to avoid time alone with his father since his uncle had left a few days ago; either he got home late enough that he knew his father would be too drunk to be awake, or he left a note saying he was in the tree house outside. Jacob never ventured far into the garden, stopping on the back patio. The uneven ground caused the pain in his leg to worsen.

'No hello for me then?' Jacob slurred. Out of the corner of his eye, Connor could see Jacob priming his fists by clenching and unclenching them at his side. Whatever Joel had said to Jacob to get him to ease up on Connor was wearing off.

'I've got nothing to say to you.' Connor went into the kitchen and reached for a beer, smacking the lid against the edge of the counter to open it.

Jacob blustered in, hands still tight by his side. Jacob could take anything but disrespect and Connor knew what he was doing. For the first time, he thought maybe he was deliberately trying to goad Jacob into hitting him.

'What the fuck is your problem?' Jacob said.

Connor pushed past his father to go upstairs. The anger was pulsating through him, he just couldn't stand to be around him anymore; he'd thought he could stomach it until he finished school but now he wasn't sure. He just wanted to leave. Jacob grabbed his arm, and Connor felt his fingers digging into his flesh.

'What have I told you about walking away from me when I'm talking to you?'

Connor turned and looked at his father, seeing him flinch as he registered the look on his son's face. He was glad that all his anger and hatred were being projected successfully. Jacob took a step back.

'Why don't you refresh my memory?' Connor said.

Jacob regained the composure he'd momentarily lost and lunged for Connor. He pinned him up against the wall by his throat, but for the first time Connor wasn't afraid, wasn't frozen in fear. Connor smiled at his father.

'Do you think I'm funny?' Jacob said.

'No, I think you're a joke!' Connor said, fighting to get the words out as his father squeezed. He welcomed the adrenaline as it coursed through his body, it felt different to usual, physically the same but not accompanied by fear. He was excited.

'Well your sides will be splitting in a minute!' he said, releasing his grip a little.

'Before you start there's something you should know,' Connor said.

'And what's that?'

'This time I'm fighting back!'

Connor took as deep a breath as he could before propelling his head forward. He heard a crack as it connected with Jacob's. Jacob reeled back, completely stunned. He let go of Connor and clasped his face as blood gushed through his fingers from his broken nose.

'Son of a bitch!'

Connor screamed and lunged toward his father, arms reached out with claw-like hands as he took his father down. On top of him, he bore down with his fists, hitting his face in a way that he remembered experiencing from the other side. Maybe he wasn't the coward his father had maintained he was for all those years, he thought as he watched his father shield his face and cry out with muffled screams. He remembered the way he'd felt when he was hitting Billy Wicowska. This was what he had wanted back then – to be attacking his father, not that boy.

Jacob finally managed to gain some traction and push Connor off him; he scrambled to his feet faster than Connor had ever seen him move before. He staggered a little before finding the wall and leaning against it, breathless.

'See, I think I like it better this way, how about you?' Connor heaved, suddenly hit with exhaustion from throwing punches.

'I've beaten bigger guys than you!' Jacob grunted.

'Really? I thought you just liked hitting kids?'

'I should have got rid of you when I had the chance!'

'I wish you fucking had!'

Connor swung for Jacob again, but he was too far away so he missed.

Jacob laughed, his face bloodied. 'Well, look who finally got some bollocks!'

Connor staggered forward a little and grabbed Jacob by the hair on his temples, smacking his head against the wall. Jacob reached up and put his hands around Connor's throat again, but without much pressure. It was suddenly as though he didn't care what Connor did to him, almost as if he wanted him to finish what he had started.

'I heard you and uncle Joel talking,' Connor rasped.

'I'm supposed to know what that means?'

'You lied to me . . . about Mum . . . about Shannon,' he pushed the words out, struggling for breath between each one.

Jacob loosened his grip and pushed Connor away, both of them leaning against opposite walls and trying to regain their breath, considering a second round. Physical fights were easier than talking.

'What did you hear?'

'You told me she left,' Connor said through gritted teeth.

'I had to lie to you, if you knew the truth . . . What difference does it make now?' His father shrunk as he spoke.

'The difference is you LIED!'

'You think I wanted to? I can't even bear to think about the truth!'

'You don't even know what that word means! I thought she left because of me! You told me she didn't want me. Why did you do that?' His heart was pounding, the anger growing inside him.

'How could I tell you the truth? I had to make you hate her. I couldn't have you looking her up and finding out what she had done.'

'I didn't even know I had a sister! How old was she? How old was Shannon when she died?'

'She was five years old.' Jacob hung his head and the words were barely audible.

'And the way you treated me all this time! Why did you do it? Is it because I look like my mother?'

'You need discipline! You hurt that kid! I thought you were losing your fucking mind like your mother did. I didn't stop her when I had the chance and she killed our daughter, would have killed you if I wasn't there!'

'Don't give me that crap! You get off on it! It makes you feel like a big man. Were you beating her too? Is that what happened? Did she finally get sick of your shit?'

'I never laid a finger on your mother!' Jacob shouted again, even though the fight had gone out of him somewhat.

'So why me then, Dad? Why do I get the special treatment?'

'Because I fucking hate you! After she had you she was never the same, she said you were the devil and I should have listened to her. She went crazy. I lost everything because of you and I wish to God you had never been born!' Jacob screamed. Connor was taken aback by the words and it looked like even Jacob was too.

He opened his mouth to speak again, tears in his eyes. 'Connor, I'm sorry, I didn't mean that . . .'

Connor balled his fists and moved towards Jacob. It was worth it for the look of fear on his face. He raised his hand and Jacob cowered. Disgusted with his father Connor stormed out through the kitchen and into the garden. He rushed up into the tree house and quickly wrapped himself in the sleeping bag. He looked out of the window back at the house; through the kitchen window he saw Jacob punch the wall. He really had to get out of there. It was only a matter of time now which one of them ended up dead.

Chapter 54

Adrian's lounge was full of boxes. The opportunity to sell off all his toys was too good for Andrea to miss. As soon as it had been suggested to her, she had started photographing and listing everything she could get her hands on. She loved the idea, it was a double win for her. She had always hated Adrian's toy collection and they needed a new place to live. Adrian knew it was a distraction for her: a way to avoid what was happening in her life. Both she and Tom had got caught up in it and were having a great time sorting through everything. It had been a while since Adrian had seen his bare shelves, but several times a day Andrea was making trips to the post office to send the items off. They had sold over half of everything he had collected over the years. It was a strange feeling for Adrian because it had been such a huge part of his life, and now it was over. What would he put on his shelves now? Maybe he could start reading books again.

'How much stuff have you sold so far?'

'A lot. I can't believe how much it's worth!' Andrea exclaimed with a smile spread across her face. Money always did make her smile.

'You seem to have a knack for it,' Adrian said.

'Amazing really when you consider that when you started buying all this stuff, eBay wasn't even really a thing.'

'It was a thing.'

'I know, but not like in the way it is now.'

'No, I suppose not.'

'This was really very smart of you, Adrian, I'm impressed. You're kind of my hero right now.'

'Thanks.'

She cleared her throat. 'Me and Tom went to view a place yesterday. I hope you don't mind.'

'I don't mind at all. Where?' He tried not to look so happy. He thought about the years he'd spent wishing that Andrea and Tom were living under the same roof as him. He lay awake thinking about it night after night when they first broke up, until eventually he rebelled against it and started sleeping around, getting back at Andrea, even though she didn't know or care. He never thought he would get over Andrea and yet here he was, desperate to get rid of her.

'Near here actually, about a ten-minute walk.'

'Near here?' Adrian didn't think Andrea would want to live in this part of town after her white regency period house in the hills overlooking the city. Maybe she had changed.

'It's a two-bedroom flat with a little courtyard garden, it's a good size anyway, a little smaller than this place.'

'Sounds nice. Does Tom like it?'

'He loves it, it's above a restaurant in town. Down the bottom end.'

'And you can afford it?' Adrian was surprised, the old Andrea would have turned her nose up at a flat above a shop.

'Thanks to you, yes. I've been saving up since we moved in as well, so I had some money, then with this toy money, we already have enough for a substantial deposit.' She started to cry. She was always so stoic that he couldn't handle it at all when she cried.

'Why are you upset?' he asked, concerned.

'I've just been such a bitch to you and now here you are, saving me.'

'I'm saving Tom, it's his money.'

'I know, but it's more than a lot of fathers would have done in your shoes. When we broke up I was horrible to you, I looked down on your job and kept you from seeing your son. I made you out to be something you weren't. It was all so twisted in my head. I can't believe I let Dominic manipulate me into marrying him, into treating you the way I did. I feel so stupid. I don't even recognise who I've become.'

'We all feel like that sometimes, Andrea, you can't beat yourself up over what happened. It's gone now. All you can do is deal with things from now on.'

'I know, and I will. I spoke to a mortgage advisor and if we can put down at least a thirty per cent deposit, which, thanks to you, we most definitely can, then we can easily afford this. I've been promoted at work, I'm now the category manager for my team so my wages have gone up. I'm also thinking about getting a second job; the restaurant under the flat is looking for someone, I spoke to them and they seemed keen to hire me even though I don't have any experience.'

'Of course they were. Look at you,' he said without thinking.

'What does that mean?'

'You're beautiful, Andrea, you know you are. They would be idiots not to hire you.'

'I don't see what that's got to do with anything.'

Adrian shrugged. 'It shouldn't matter, but it does. A good-looking person behind the counter is good for business.'

She shook off the compliment. 'Well, I thought it would be like I was home; I wouldn't be far away if Tom needed me and you are only a short walk away. Between us I think we can make it work. He's not a baby anymore.'

'I'm proud of you, Andi, you've really adjusted well, given the circumstances.'

'Not really. I'm still very much in denial.' She smiled.

'I sold several of your cards yesterday. I got almost three thousand pounds for twenty cards. There are loads more that I haven't even gone through, and I have a shop willing to pay pretty generously for any of them that I can't sell on their own.'

'Good for you.' Adrian looked at the clock. 'I better get some sleep. I'm on the early shift tomorrow.'

She grabbed hold of his hand for a moment and squeezed it. They had become friends, something he had never thought possible.

Chapter 55

Connor savoured the nicotine as it hit his lungs, the cold hard boards of the tree house comforting against his bruised back. He put his headphones in and turned on the music. Bowie sang in his ears and he remembered his mother again. She was not the same mother he had remembered all the other times he'd listened to this song. She wasn't the same hard woman who had abandoned him, she wasn't the same woman who was probably working in a bank somewhere, or driving around in her little red car. The stories he had made up about what she had done and who she had been since she left him all faded into nothing and he realised that he was happy. Happy she was dead, happy not to be abandoned. No matter what his father said, he knew that she didn't do it because of Connor. He knew the way his father made him feel and he knew the times he looked at a bottle of pills and thought about chugging the entire contents. No. Jacob was the cause and the reason. Not him.

There was a face now, too. Thanks to the article on the internet, he saw his mother's whole face. He had looked at his torn and crumpled photo a million times and tried to make out the colour of her eyes or the shape of her mouth; but it was never real. The face he had now looked nothing like the way he had imagined her before. She was different, but she was his. A serenity passed over him for the first time in his life. He finally had answers to questions he didn't even know existed. Safe in the knowledge that his father was a liar and he didn't have to listen to him or respect him anymore. A weight had lifted.

Out of the corner of his eye, he saw the faintest light come on from the house next door. He sat up. The light was coming from Selina's room. Multicoloured fairy lights were dancing on her headboard. He squinted his eyes to see what was happening in the darkness. He knew her mother was working late. He felt bad for looking but also like he should witness it, as though witnessing it was enough to make it real, to bring it to life, to stop the pretence that it wasn't happening at all. He had tried to ignore it and act like it wasn't happening but he couldn't pretend anymore.

Connor's pulse intensified as his eyes adjusted to the strange misty light in the garden, the rain abating for a brief moment although the air hung heavy. Above the garden, through the bedroom window, Connor could see Selina stood in her nightdress. It looked like a very long T-shirt and had a large cartoon animal on the front, maybe a penguin. Lenny, her stepfather, was standing behind her; he swept her hair to one side and started to kiss her neck. His hands travelled across the front of her body and down until he reached the hem of her dress. Connor started to have that feeling again, the warmth in his neck and the itching in his cheek. If he didn't stop watching, he would have another seizure. Then he would be no good to her at all.

He pulled away from the window, unable to look any more. When he glanced up again, the rain had started again, and the window was just a blur of colour and water as the huge droplets ran down. He could no longer see what was happening inside Selina's house. He didn't need to – he had a pretty good idea.

Connor composed himself and grabbed a piece of stray wood before he jumped out of the tree house and ran across the garden. The lights were off in his own house, his father must have gone out. His trousers were soaked through from the long grass and his shoes were muddy but he didn't care. He snuck down the side of the house and then over to Selina's front garden. Connor didn't want to alert anyone to what he was doing. He searched in all the obvious places and eventually found a spare key in the roof of the birdhouse that stood proudly in the centre of Selina's front yard. He unlocked the door. The silence in the house was claustrophobic. It wasn't real silence though, it was a mask for what Connor knew was happening upstairs. The silence somehow complicit in the violation. Connor imagined how many times this must have happened when Diana was at work. He shook his head to get the rain out of his eyes; his hair stuck to his face. He was cold but focused. He just needed to do this one thing and then everything would be OK.

He could see the Christmas tree in the lounge; he'd forgotten it was nearly Christmas. There was no evidence of it in his own home. Diana's Christmas tree was covered in pink baubles and warm white twinkling lights. The rhythm of the flashing lights brought that creeping warmth back into his neck. The stress of the evening had already made him more susceptible to a seizure and so he had to be careful not to get triggered. He pulled his gaze away and carefully mounted the stairs and made his way up. The layout of the house was identical to his own, so he knew where Selina's bedroom was. He stared at the door for a moment. He was really going to do this.

Connor could hear Lenny talking softly in the bedroom. The words were too quiet for him to hear but the tone wasn't. His hand ached as he clenched the wood so tightly he thought it might snap in his hand. He approached as slowly and quietly as he could, not wanting to give him any kind of alert. He needed to take him by surprise. Connor closed his eyes and pushed ever so gently on the door.

'We should make tonight special,' Lenny whispered. No response.

Connor burst in and made his presence known. 'It's going to be pretty fucking special alright, Lenny!'

Lenny jumped, unsure how to react to the sight of Connor, soaking wet and wielding a plank of wood. He scrambled backwards, away from Selina who was sitting on the edge of the bed clutching a blanket to her. Connor's eyes shifted briefly to the nightdress on the floor.

'How the fuck did you get in?' Lenny cried.

'That's what you're worried about?'

'It's not what it looks like, you've got this all wrong.'

'I don't think so.'

Connor raised the plank of wood and swung at Lenny, forcing him to crawl backwards into the corner of the room. Lenny raised his hands as soon as he was against the wall, shielding his face as Connor continued to swing at him. There was a loud crack as the wood connected with Lenny's arm.

He cried out in pain. 'What, are you fucking crazy?'

'That's a distinct possibility, Lenny,' Connor said, feeling pretty sane for the first time ever, released from his prison of fear. As the storm lit up the room, Connor saw the blood trailing down Lenny's forearm.

'Connor! Stop!' Selina cried. 'You'll get in trouble.'

He stopped swinging for a moment.

'Jesus Christ. When your father hears about this . . .' Lenny whimpered, peering out from behind his hands, still poised to defend himself. Just the idea that Lenny thought this was over was enough to make Connor spring forward one more time with the wood and crack it against Lenny's shins.

'I'm sorry, Lenny. That's not going to work.'

Selina turned on her bedside lamp and the atmosphere in the room changed completely. Lenny lay sobbing on the ground, clutching at his legs. His eyes, when they opened, fixed on Connor. Staring at him in the same way he imagined he stared at his own father. He felt powerful as he stood over this pathetic excuse for a man and again thought of his father. Was this the feeling that Jacob looked for when he swung for him? He could understand how one might get addicted to feeling like this; in a life when power was taken away from you, you had to take what little you could.

Connor reached over and held his hand out to Selina. She gathered the blanket around her and then took Connor's hand and stood up, slipping behind him. She was shaking.

'This is what's going to happen, Lenny,' Connor said calmly. 'You're going to pack up your shit and get the hell out of here. Got it? You're going to do that now, before Diana gets home.'

'No! I'm not doing that! This is my home!' Lenny said, sitting up.

Connor jerked the plank upwards and held it over Lenny's head. He flinched and cowered a little more.

'Whatever you say! Just don't hit me again. Please don't hit me!'

'Get out of here tonight and don't come back. You don't contact anyone in this house again. If you do then I call the police and you'll go inside. They don't like people who mess with kids in prison.'

'Oh god, I'll go, I promise!'

'If I see you within a thousand feet of this place, I'll cut your dick off.'

Connor let Lenny get to his feet again. He wasn't going to be a problem. People like Lenny only operated in the dark; they were like cockroaches. If you shined a light on them they scuttled into the shadows again.

Selina held on to Connor's arms and buried her face in his shoulder.

He turned and whispered to her. 'Come on. Let's go.'

Chapter 56

Connor and Selina dashed through the rain back to his house. Jacob's car wasn't in the driveway and the lights were off as Connor re-entered, but he didn't much care where his father was at this point. He took Selina up the stairs and she stood shivering in the dark. He switched the light on and rushed over to his chest of drawers, pulling out tracksuit bottoms and a rugby shirt. He looked at her and saw that she was cold and white, lips trembling and hair hanging in front of her as though she had just stepped out of a horror movie.

'Just a sec,' he said, grabbing a towel that was hanging over the banister and handing it to her. 'I'll wait outside for you to get dressed.'

'No,' she said quickly, before he had a chance to leave. 'Stay, just turn around. I don't want to be on my own.'

He turned and folded his arms, the adrenaline coursing through him at a slightly less alarming rate, the reality of the evening finally hitting him. Passive Connor, the one they walked all over, the one who just sat back and let people use him, had done something good; even though he was scared, he had still done it. There was a big part of him that just wanted to smile right now.

'Are you OK?' he asked.

'Ha!' She almost laughed. 'I can't believe you did that. How did you know?'

'I could see inside your room from the garden. I saw you once before. I felt bad for not doing anything.'

'I didn't do anything when I heard your dad beat the shit out of you.'

'So, we're even?'

'Not even close,' she said quietly. 'You can turn around now.'

She had the towel wrapped around her hair and the shirt on, but she was still holding the jogging bottoms in her hands. She had thrown her blanket in the corner. She stared at it with contempt, as though it were evil, contaminated.

'My dad's out, probably for a while,' Connor said. 'You can sleep in my bed if you want, I'll sleep on the couch.'

'Look at you.' She stepped closer, brushing his hair back and tucking it behind his ears. She leaned forward and kissed him on the cheek. 'Thank you.'

'I'll go and get cleaned up. Will you be all right in here?'

'Don't leave me alone,' she said as she sat on the edge of the bed and pulled the oversized rugby top over her knees.

Connor flicked the light off and sat down next to her, putting his arm protectively around her as she nestled into him. Rain continued to pound at the window, which was somehow soothing, and the occasional burst of lightning illuminated the room. They both leaned back against the wall and held on to each other until they fell asleep.

Chapter 57

Adrian, Imogen and Gary sat together with cups of coffee steaming in front of them. Gary had asked them in for an early morning meeting so that he could run something past them. Adrian watched Imogen fidgeting with the lid of her Americano; she was obviously worried about her meeting with the DCI later in the day.

'So, what did you want to talk to us about?' Adrian said.

'Well, there are a few things, the first being that I've been looking through all of the case files for Erica Lawson, Alyssa Ward, Jackie Munroe and Faith Jackson. I noticed something – not with Faith, but with the others,' Gary said.

'Like what?' Adrian said.

'I think he had intercourse with them both before *and* after he killed them.'

'What makes you think that? The forensics were

unclear. Have you spoken to the DCI about this?' Imogen said.

'I'm kind of seeing someone, she's a psychotherapist, and no I haven't run this past the DCI,' Gary said.

'You're seeing a psychotherapist? Are you OK?' Adrian said. It was obvious what Gary had meant but Adrian liked to make fun when the opportunity arose.

'I'm great, it's nothing like that,' Gary said, flustered by Adrian's remark. 'She's my girlfriend. She was telling me about lust murders.'

'What's a lust murder? Just like a sexually motivated crime?' Imogen asked.

'Not exactly, it's more about the murder being sexually arousing. I don't know exactly, you might need to speak to a specialist about this, but I looked into it a bit and it fits.'

'What does it mean?' Imogen said.

'It means that he could be a sexual sadist, usually a bit of a fantasist. He needs to kill in order to get off.'

'But we know he had intercourse with Faith before she was dead. Does that still fit? He didn't need her to be dead to perform then,' Adrian said, the thought of it making him sick. One of the many things he didn't understand. Sex was supposed to be a mutual thing, not just about ejaculating into something.

'That's part of the game for him, killing them while it's happening; torture is a part of what excites people like that. It's all part of the plan. From the moment he picks them and connects with them,' Gary said.

'And he has a type? Long brown hair, slim, pretty,' Adrian said.

'Dead,' Imogen said.

'It's almost certain that these women are all surrogates for someone else. Either mother or first victim or something like that,' Gary said.

'How does someone decide that that's what they are into? I mean, where does that come from?' Adrian asked.

'There's no definitive answer really, could be something to do with a trauma that was witnessed early on, or childhood abuse, a personality disorder – it might have even been an accident the first time,' Gary said.

'An accident?' How do you accidentally fuck a dead body?' Adrian said. There was no circumstance he could imagine where that might happen.

'I guess if someone dies mid . . . coitus?'

'Gross,' Imogen said.

'So, who are we looking for now? Has the description changed? I'm assuming this is a rare condition, are there any indicators we can look at from previous crimes? Is this an escalation of some sort?' Adrian said.

'Someone attractive but dysfunctional, although they will appear quite charming, higher than average IQ and very manipulative. Probably no obvious history of violent behaviour as they would be able to talk themselves out of any trouble. He takes his time with the bodies because he's overconfident, doesn't feel like he has to abide by the rules because they don't apply to him,' Gary said.

'What do you mean?' Imogen said.

'He sees himself as apart from the human race, above them, maybe even a little bit of a god complex. But as I said before, deeply dysfunctional,' Gary said.

'What about the bleaching? Both Alyssa and Erica were bleached, presumably the other two would have been too if he had had the opportunity. What's that all about?' Adrian asked.

'That might go back to the original trauma, assuming there was one. Or it could be something else. Maybe he was just trying to remove any DNA, which bleach doesn't get rid of anyway. So he might not be educated to a very high level,' Gary said.

'Why has he started now then?' Imogen said.

'Probably some kind of inciting incident. Something happened recently that's pushed him over the edge,' Gary said. 'Franka, my girlfriend, said it's likely he's recreating something in his past because it's been brought back to the surface.'

'Where did you meet Franka?' Adrian said. The idea of Gary in a relationship was not something Adrian had ever considered; he had always just been Gary to him. Some people just seemed happy single, like that's how they were meant to be.

'I've been going to classes up at the university.'

'What kind of classes?'

'I'm doing a degree in Forensic Psychology.'

'Since when?' Imogen asked.

'This is my second year, I had my points transferred over from Plymouth Uni.'

'I thought you knew everything already?' Adrian said, half-joking. Gary was always learning new things, full of surprises. 'You're making the rest of us look bad.'

'I like learning.' Gary shrugged.

'How certain are you and your girlfriend about this?' Adrian asked.

'It's a solid theory. Franka is convinced, and she knows her shit,' Gary said

'What's her full name?' Imogen said.

'Franka Novak. She's actually kind of a big deal; she's teaching the module I'm on at the moment. We kind of hit it off. She has a PhD in the relationship between coercion, manipulation and mind control and she's the head of Forensic Psychology at a university up North.'

'Mind control is a real thing?' Adrian said.

'Oh yeah,' Gary said.

'And you're dating someone with a PhD in mind control? That sounds kind of terrifying.'

'I think it's hot.' Gary beamed.

Imogen rolled her eyes 'So, what do we do now?'

'Look for previous cases. Necrophilia is pretty uncommon so there's every chance anything similar would be connected. Look at places where dead bodies are readily available and see if there have been any reports of anything untoward,' Gary said.

'Are dead bodies ever readily available?' Adrian asked.

'The university medical department, hospitals, funeral homes, crematoriums. Places like that. I had a quick look and couldn't see anything local. I'll try further afield,' Gary said.

'We'll brief the DCI and consider it. If the press gets hold of this they'll have a field day. They're excited enough about a murdering serial rapist,' Adrian said.

'I'll get onto the pathologist and see if they can be

any more conclusive on the necrophilia. Maybe the added psychological evaluation will make a difference,' Imogen said.

'Would Franka be able to come in and speak to the DCI and explain it, it might have more sway coming from someone official?' Adrian asked.

'I'll ask her, but she's not around for Christmas. Are you sure you aren't just being nosey? You want to know what kind of woman would go out with me.'

'You're a total catch, Gary,' Imogen said.

'Novak, that's a Slavic name, isn't it?' Adrian said, frowning.

'Croatian, actually. She's originally from Dubrovnik. I'm going to go now and have a look if there are any crimes or incidents that even remotely resemble necrophilia outside Devon.'

'Well, I can't wait to meet her,' Imogen called out as Gary left.

'When's your interview with Kapoor?' Adrian asked.

'Interrogation you mean? In about an hour.'

'Well, good luck,' Adrian said.

Chapter 58

It was the Easter holidays when Rocket decided to visit me next. I had had a whole six weeks without him and I was almost surprised to feel dread at the sight of him. My little girl was at home, and we were making a solar system model on the lounge floor. She shrieked in excitement when she saw him. He gave her a pound coin and told her that he needed to speak to Mummy. I made him wait while I put a film on, not knowing what else I could do to keep her attention.

He took me upstairs and I was angry; I slapped him across the face. How dare he come around when my daughter was at home? He explained that he would come around whenever he wanted and there was nothing I could do about it. I told him I was going to tell JD if he did that. This pushed him over the edge and he put his hands around my throat until I blacked out. When I woke up he was gone. I rushed downstairs to find my daughter had fallen asleep on the sofa and the credits for the movie were playing.

When JD got home from work that night, I told him we needed to leave as soon as we could. He said he would start looking for work somewhere else. Again. I told him not to tell a soul for now, that this had to be our secret completely.

After a few weeks of Rocket not coming around, his visits started again most days, often when my daughter was there. Rocket choked me the next time, too. That became part of it; I would black out and when I would wake up he was gone. Is it wrong that I preferred it that way? A tiny part of me hoped I would never wake up again and if it wasn't for my little girl, then I don't think I would have had the energy to stay alive.

We had started to save money again and JD had found some possible jobs he was more than qualified for. I tried to stay positive when he was around; I desperately wanted to turn back the clock, to the day I met them both. I wondered if all this would have happened if I had chosen him to begin with. My mind was flooded with what ifs and scenarios where I was free. To make matters worse, I ran out of my mother-in-law's disused anti-depressant medication and I was too scared to go and ask the doctor for any more. The world was coming back to me and I didn't want it. Not least because I couldn't ignore what was happening to me. I had a strange feeling in my stomach, a wringing feeling that I had only felt once before. I was pregnant again.

This pregnancy felt different, uncomfortable and

unnatural. I had not long come off the pills and my moods were erratic at best. I would snap at anyone who spoke to me and I started to cut myself across my thighs. I wasn't sure if the baby was JD's or not and the idea that I might have a part of that monster growing inside me made me feel ill. I started to drink, as much as I could without blacking out. I was trying to lose the baby, I didn't want it inside me. I didn't get away with that for very long because I started to show. JD was over the moon, but he was worried about me, he wanted me to go and see someone. I made him promise that we would still leave, that we would find a way to make it work somewhere else. I would get help if he would only promise me that one thing. He did.

My second child was born on a hot summer's day. I was so uncomfortable but so glad to finally get it out of me. I didn't even want to look at it when they held it up. I just closed my eyes and waited until it had been moved into another room. JD asked me what we should call the baby and I said I didn't care, that he could call it whatever he wanted. God help me, I hated that baby, that poor innocent baby that never hurt a soul. They bottle-fed it because I refused to even hold it; it was days before I really looked at it. I felt nothing.

We got home and I asked JD why we needed another child anyway. I suggested we put the child up for adoption and he was so angry with me I thought he was going to hurt me. He wanted me to hold the child but I just couldn't, I felt physically sick at the idea. This went on for a while. Even with the reprieve of Rocket's absence for the time being I was a mess. JD would *come home from work and the baby would be crying because I just couldn't pick it up. I would hold the bottle for it while it ate, but I couldn't do anything else. I wanted it out of my house, out of my life.*

This caused irreparable damage to my relationship with JD. He doted on that child, to the point where he hardly spent any time with our four-year-old daughter. She asked me why her father hated her and I was upset for her. I told him the baby was destroying our lives and that it had to go. I didn't look at what was happening, I had lost the ability to apply logic to a situation. I think it got to the point where everything was so broken that my mind struggled to come to terms with it and so I invented a scenario in my head where the baby was the Antichrist.

Chapter 59

The low winter sun poured in through the bedroom window, waking both Connor and Selina up. The silence in the house told Connor they were alone; his father wasn't home. He relaxed, too tired to face another confrontation right now. They had slept propped against the wall all night, his duvet pulled slightly over her legs. She pulled away, confused for a moment, but then she smiled.

'Good morning,' she said.

'Hey.'

She uncurled herself and sat on the edge of the bed, dragging her fingers through her hair to untangle it. She must have pulled the towel off in the night.

'I should get home.' She looked at the clock, it was past seven. Not long until school started.

'I'll walk you out. If you're sure.' Connor propped himself up on one elbow and looked up at her. This felt real, this felt natural. Connor felt more at ease in the world, maybe it was confronting his father, standing up for himself for once; or maybe it was getting rid of Lenny, standing up to someone else. Perhaps it was just having Selina here.

'I'd prefer to face the music sooner rather than later,' she said.

'I understand.' He picked up the jogging bottoms and handed them to her again.

She slipped them on and looked in the mirror. He jumped up from the bed.

'I'm such a mess.'

'No, you're not.' He turned her to face him and placed his hand under her chin, bringing her head up so that she was looking him in the eyes. He leaned in and kissed her, without thought, without anything else beyond that, just the kiss. He pulled back even though he didn't want to – he wanted to kiss her again. She looked at his lips before moving forwards and kissing him back.

'I don't understand . . .'

'What?' he said, his lips barely an inch away from hers as her head tilted back and he hovered there, on the cusp of kissing her again.

'You. You're perfect and I'm . . .'

'You're beautiful.' He kissed her.

'I really should go.' She whispered unconvincingly before planting her lips on his yet again.

Chapter 60

Imogen sat opposite DCI Kapoor in her office. Already she felt like she was being reprimanded. She supposed she deserved no less. The amount of times she had thought about what would happen if it ever came to this, she'd always actually thought there would be no discussion and she would just lose her job. This was better.

'I want to keep this as low-key as possible so I think it's better if we do it this way,' the DCI started.

'OK. Look, I'm sorry.'

'We'll get to that, but first off I think I need to know a few things. Just be honest and we'll see where we go from there.'

'I'll tell you anything you need to know,' Imogen said.

'When did you meet Dean Kinkaid?'

'On a case, a couple of years ago. I don't remember the exact date. It will be in my notes.'

'Did you know he was an ex-con?'

'Not straight away. I found out soon after though.'

'How long after you found out before you started a relationship with him?'

'That only happened recently.'

'After he got out of prison?'

'Yes.'

'And what was the nature of your relationship?' DCI Kapoor said.

'We were intimate, if that's what you're asking me.'

'Yes, that's what I'm asking you. And it only started after he got out of prison? Not before?'

'Correct,' Imogen said.

'Did you visit him in prison?'

'No, I didn't.'

'You know I can check that, right?'

'Go ahead, I didn't visit him in prison.' At least she knew she wouldn't get caught in a lie there. The fact that she hadn't visited Dean in prison had been the elephant in the room for most of their relationship. Even though they hadn't been together while he was inside, she knew she should have gone to see him. Especially after what they went through together.

'Is he the reason you transferred to Exeter from Plymouth?'

'No.'

'Did you live together?'

'No.'

'Did you share information from any of your cases with him?'

'No. But he did know some of the things I was working on,' Imogen said.

'He was brought in as a suspect three months ago. You questioned him. Were you sleeping with him then?'

'Not exactly, we hadn't done for a little while and our relationship ended soon after.'

'I'm not surprised, I listened to the interview.'

'Then you'll know I followed procedure. I didn't give him any special dispensation.'

'You certainly didn't.' DCI Kapoor raised her eyebrows. 'And you didn't warn him about the questions you were going to ask?'

Imogen took a deep breath before continuing. 'If anything, I think maybe I was unnecessarily hard on him.'

'It sounded like a very difficult situation,' DCI Kapoor said sympathetically.

'It was.'

'It's one of the reasons it's a bad idea to get involved with someone like that. Difficult situations happen. The rules are there to protect you, not just to ruin your fun.'

'That's not fair. It wasn't just about having fun.'

'So, you're not seeing him anymore?'

'No, funnily enough, the interview kind of put an end to that.'

'How often do you think you saw each other?'

'Why does that matter?'

DCI Kapoor scribbled something in her notepad and then sighed heavily before looking up again.

'You were involved in a serious incident together, which resulted in Mr Kinkaid going to prison, correct? He was originally charged with assaulting you, but you said he wasn't involved.'

'He wasn't. He was also assaulted during that incident; we were both victims. He was being set up to look like he had orchestrated it. But he absolutely didn't.'

'But he was involved with the beating of a material witness?'

'A man who was supplying drugs to underage girls that he was also sleeping with, yes, he was involved in that. But he served over half of his term and only had a couple of months' probation left when I got together with him.'

'I'll need to speak to him, I'll do it informally as well. I have left messages on the number he left with his probation officer, I trust those are his current details?'

'I'm not exactly speaking to him at the moment.'

'From what you've told me the biggest issue is your failure to disclose. As long as you weren't together while he was implicated in any crimes. Did DS Miles know about the relationship?'

'He knew about it afterwards, and he told me to report it.'

'That's your story and you're sticking to it?'

'It was my mistake, no one else's.'

'OK, Imogen. Better late than never. Make sure this doesn't happen again.'

Imogen cleared her throat. 'What do I do now?'

'You just wait. Once I confirm what you've said then I'll let you know. If you've been straight with me then this doesn't need to go any further. With all the turmoil this department has seen, I don't see the need to drag any more officers' names through the mud. If I can avoid taking official action, I will. You can go now.'

'Thank you.' Imogen stood up to leave.

'I hope he was worth it,' DCI Kapoor said, a little too flippantly. 'Just don't do anything like this again.'

'Don't worry, I won't.' She walked out of the room. She didn't know if he had been worth it, but the idea of it never having happened made her feel a bit sick. Even though it hadn't lasted that long, even though it was fraught with complications, it wasn't an experience she would want to trade in. She wondered how any other relationship could ever compare, and why she always seemed to be attracted to men that were bad for her. She wondered if being with someone who wasn't bad for her would even hold the same kind of appeal. Maybe she was destined to be alone. She shuddered at the thought, remembering her mother, all those years alone.

Chapter 61

Connor stood in his front garden waiting for Selina to come out of her house again. She had reluctantly gone home to change into her uniform before making her way to school. It was still dark out, late December and the sun was barely rising. He never did things like this. He was always coming or going somewhere, looking for the next place to hide. He pulled out his cigarettes and lit one, hoping his father would turn into the drive and look him in the eye again. He wondered if last night was a temporary feeling or if he really had broken free of Jacob's hold over him. The road was still though, there was no breeze, and everything felt strangely static in the morning light after getting used to the twinkle of Christmas fairy lights in the evenings. Houses covered in wires and bulbs and little statues; it all looked miserable in the greyish light of dawn when no one was around.

He started to pace, he needed more cigarettes and

had to walk off the agitation he could feel building up inside his arms. He heard the sound of shouting coming from Selina's house. The door opened and Diana threw a couple of black sacks onto the front yard, Selina's clothes spilling out onto the grass. Diana didn't notice Connor as he ducked out of the way. The next thing he saw was Diana pulling Selina out by her ear.

'I don't give a shit where you go. Go to your nan's house. See if she will have you. I don't want you here!' Diana cried, mascara streaking her cheeks.

'It wasn't my fault!' Selina cried, her eyes red and puffy.

'I've got to go into work now, you better not be here when I get back!'

'I'm sorry, Mum, please don't do this. He kept coming in to my room.' She tried to speak normally but her mouth kept catching on the words.

'Keep your filthy mouth shut. I am sick to death of your lies!' Diana clenched her eyes shut and screamed. She stormed up to Selina and slapped her hard across the face. The skin reddened immediately.

Connor clenched his fist into a ball. Stepping in now wouldn't help her, so he would just stay out of the way.

'Mum! Why won't you listen to me?' Selina pleaded.

Diana pointed a finger directly into her face. 'Whatever you leave behind, I'm burning!' She rushed back inside then and slammed the door as Selina scrambled to gather her clothes and put them back in the sacks. Connor rushed over and helped her.

'Are you OK?' he asked.

Selina stood up and took a deep breath, trying to

slow her erratic breathing. 'Well, she freaked out the second she realised he was gone.'

'Didn't she believe you? I can tell her what I saw.' Connor put his hand on her shoulder but she didn't seem to notice.

'You know, until today, I wasn't even sure, but now I think about it, maybe she knew what he was doing.'

'For real?'

'Just the things she was saying. I don't know. I have nowhere to go, I don't know what to do. I'll have to ring my nan.'

'Just come to mine for now. We don't have to go to school today. We'll figure something out.'

'Do you think anyone saw? God, I'm so embarrassed.'

'No one saw anything. Come on.'

He picked up two of the sacks and walked back to his house. He instinctively looked around for his father but he wasn't there. They went inside. Selina sat in the lounge and he went and got a drink for them both; remembering she said she didn't drink, he got her a large water.

When Connor returned to the lounge, he heard a car and went to the window to check outside. A cab was parked outside Selina's house and Diana rushed out and got in. She looked remarkably different to the screaming banshee on the front lawn just five minutes ago, her face now flawlessly made up and her hair immaculate. The cab pulled away and Connor relaxed.

'Your mum's gone now. So, what happened?'

'She was calling out for him, it got more and more frantic and so I told her he was gone.'

'Did you explain why?'

'The second she realised it was anything to do with me she just stopped listening. She accused me of all sorts of horrible things,' Selina said. She just stared at the wall as she spoke.

'You told her that I saw everything, and that that's why I came over? Right?'

Selina shook her head. 'I didn't tell her that you were there.'

'You can stay in my room for now. My dad won't come in there and if he does I will deal with him.' Connor sat down next to her and placed his hand on hers. 'You're going to be OK now. I won't let anything else happen to you.'

'Why did you do it? Why did you come and help me? He could have hurt you, you could have got in trouble with the police,' Selina said.

'I don't care, I'm glad I did. From the minute I first saw it, I knew I had to do something.'

'I feel like I owe you so much.'

She leaned over and kissed him. He pulled back.

'Sorry, I'm not thinking straight,' Connor said.

'Don't you like me? I thought . . .'

'It's not that, of course I like you . . .' He didn't know what to do. 'I just don't deserve someone like you.'

'Why would you say that?'

'I did something, back home, in California. A lot of people got hurt because of me.'

She stared at him. 'What happened?'

He took a deep breath before speaking, he wanted her to know the truth about him. 'I was mixed up with some people back home, they weren't very nice, but I couldn't see that at the time. I didn't want anyone to think of me as the poor kid, I was ashamed of where I came from. Still am really. They had it in for this kid in the school, Billy Wicowska. I'm not sure what he did, but he pissed the wrong person off. They kind of picked on him and, somehow, I got wrapped up in all of that. I guess I wanted to impress them. I wanted them to like me because I wasn't rich or cool. I thought they were my friends but I was wrong.'

'What did you do?'

'I started out pretending to be his friend for a while and then one day I got him alone. I hit him, more than once, made him piss himself. Humiliated him in front of everyone, for their approval. I made his life hell. One time I took a video of him in the showers at school; he was a scrawny kid and when everyone saw it he just got a really hard time. The more I did, the more they liked me. I destroyed him.'

'Wow, and then what?'

Connor held his breath, a lump forming in his throat; this was as far as he had ever got to talking about this in any detail.

'He got his dad's gun and came into the school, opened fire.'

'Oh my God,' Selina said, looking horrified.

'Then he shot himself. Eight people died.' Connor stood up and walked to the door. He was certain this was the moment she decided she was too good for him after all.

Selina stood up and reached out for his hand. 'I don't want you to go. Stay with me.'

Somehow, she was more confident than him. She wasn't what he expected; whenever they had spoken in the past she had said or done something unexpected and this time was no different. He found himself struggling to know how to behave. He couldn't hide behind the mask he wore around other people. He couldn't be himself, because for the first time he realised he didn't know who that was. He had been pretending for so long. He could tell she didn't blame him for what had happened, he could feel that her warmth towards him hadn't dissipated. That nothing had changed between them even though he had just shown her the darkest part of himself. The part he was running from, the boy that caused the massacre. The boy that everyone blamed after all the other possible culprits were dead. Billy had shot the instigators and the manipulators, he had killed the whole group who had orchestrated his humiliation, all apart from Connor. Connor had assumed that was because of the bond that had been forged between himself and Billy before it happened. But the more he thought about it, the more he realised it was because Billy hated Connor the most and he wanted him to live with the pain. He wanted him to suffer.

Connor came back and took Selina by the hand. He would keep her safe, he would make sure no one ever hurt her again. He would try to atone for what he had done, he would make better choices for himself, for Selina.

Chapter 62

Connor and Selina lay together in the bed, undressed and under the covers, skin to skin, her back pressed against him, his arms around her, holding her close. He saw her look at the bruises on his arms and he didn't care that she knew how he'd got them. If anyone could understand, it would be Selina; she would know what it was like to endure the worst out of necessity. He knew that people would ask why he'd never told anyone – they would probably ask her the same thing if they ever found out what she had been through. They might even ask why he didn't fight back, why he didn't tell a teacher. Whatever the question, the implication was always the same. *It's your fault this happened to you. You could have stopped it but you didn't.* How could you argue with that? How could you explain to someone who had never been under someone else's control? You couldn't. At least with each other, they never had to explain that one thing.

They could protect one another now, they could make sure nothing bad happened again.

'Come away with me,' Connor finally said, and Selina laughed.

'Come with you where?'

'Anywhere.'

'OK.' She kissed his arm and shuffled around, their legs intertwined inside his single bed.

'I can't take another minute here.'

'What happened with you and your dad?'

'It doesn't even matter anymore, *he* doesn't matter anymore.'

'What did you do to him?'

'Nothing. I wanted to though. I wanted him dead,' Connor said.

They interlocked fingers under the covers.

'You know last night, I knew you were coming. Maybe not you, but I knew when he started that he wasn't going to finish. I prayed someone would come. I wondered if you knew about me the way I knew about you.'

'Sorry I didn't come sooner. You can stay here as long as you want to, I'll deal with my father. I won't let anyone hurt you again. I promise.'

'I should go to my nan's really, she doesn't live that far away. I'll be fine,' Selina said, taking a breath as if to speak again, then hesitating for a moment. Finally, she spoke. 'Did you really want to kill him? Your dad, I mean?'

'More than anything. I couldn't have looked at his face any longer without sticking a knife in it.'

'I feel the same way about my mother.'

'She won't hurt you again. I promise,' Connor said before adding, 'Do you ever worry that you'll turn out like her? I mean . . . not that you're like her now, but I know I always worried I would turn into my father. I feel that rage burning in me sometimes. Like I'm just going to snap and really hurt someone.'

'You're nothing like him. You could never be anything like him and I would rather die than be like her.'

'You wouldn't miss her if she wasn't there?' Connor said, thinking about his own mother.

'How can you miss what you never really had?'

Chapter 63

Imogen had got the call to meet Adrian at the hospital. Faith Jackson had woken up while Imogen was being questioned by DCI Kapoor. She pulled into a parking space and got out. It was quite a walk from the car park to the entrance, and from her memory of the hospital it was a complete maze on the inside as well. She hated hospitals.

Adrian was waiting by the front reception desk when she got inside.

'When did she wake up?'

'About an hour ago. She's still not talking yet as they haven't extubated her, they are just sorting her out then we can go along. One of the porters is coming to take us down. She should be able to speak to us.'

They stood together for a moment, their shoulders touching and she couldn't help but think about his hands on her. Imogen tried not to reflect on what had happened between them, she had been trying to avoid it since that morning. Maybe it was her conversation about Dean with DCI Kapoor that had brought it to the surface. She was annoyed that it had ever happened, annoyed at herself for letting it happen, for making it happen. She had crossed an unspoken line with Adrian; some part of them would always be aware of that.

'Do we know anything else?' Adrian said.

'No.

At that moment Imogen turned to see the porter hovering behind them. He looked Imogen up and down, somehow making her feel a bit grubby.

'Follow me,' he told them.

They both walked through the hospital in silence; it always amazed Imogen how long the corridors were. People moved through with purpose, some visitors and some staff, and there was a low rumble of chatter but it wasn't noisy, almost like a generator in the back room. They seemed to be walking forever at the best of times in this hospital, but with the friction between her and Adrian, it really did feel like an eternity.

They arrived at the corridor outside Faith Jackson's room and the porter disappeared back into the hospital machine. Imogen pushed on the door and Faith glanced over, a haunted look on her face. She looked pale and there were marks on her neck, the drip diligently feeding into her arm. There were two seats by the side of the bed. Imogen and Adrian sat down.

'She may have slight aphasia which is normal after what she's been through,' the nurse told them. 'It's just a slight issue understanding certain aspects of speech and not remembering words like nouns or maybe adjectives. It happens after a loss of oxygen to the brain or a head trauma, but it should improve.'

'Can we talk to her?' Imogen said.

'Go ahead, just be patient,' the nurse said.

'Faith, do you know why you're here?' Imogen said.

'I was attacked?' she said, almost whispering, unaccustomed to speaking.

'That's right. Do you remember anything about that night ten days ago?' Imogen said.

Faith looked at the wall. Imogen guessed she was uncomfortable with Adrian's presence. She nudged him in case he hadn't read the situation.

'I'll wait outside,' he said, taking the hint.

Adrian stood up and left the room. Imogen saw him settle in the chairs in the corridor as the door closed slowly behind him and she turned back to Faith.

'How much do you remember about what happened?'

'He was in my house, we had some vodka.' She spoke in a monotone, as if she were reciting a shopping list. Completely detached.

'Do you mind if I write this down?' Imogen asked. Faith shook her head and so Imogen pulled out her notepad and started to make notes. 'Had you met him before?'

'No. First time,' Faith said. 'But we talked online quite a lot.'

'What was his name?' Imogen said.

'Ellis,' Faith said.

'And what was his handle? His online name?'

'LeChevalier.'

'Is that something to do with horses? Was he French?'

'It means Knight. No, he was English.'

Imogen felt her stomach sink. This couldn't be a coincidence – could the person Gary had been speaking to be the man they were looking for? The man who had seen her in her room? The man who she had been flirting with on camera? She suspected he'd told a lot of the same lies to Faith that he'd told her alter ego, Cinnamon. Maybe there was some truth buried among the lies.

'And how did you first make contact?' Imogen asked gently.

'We met online. He was so nice.'

Her voice got stronger with every word, the fragility starting to disappear.

'Did he tell you anything about himself?'

'He told me he was a doctor. I was so impressed and I couldn't believe it. Doctors don't fall for me. He sent me pictures of him in his lab coat and stuff – at first, I thought they were stolen. Something in the back of my mind didn't trust him, but I just put that down to me being paranoid. He knew all the right things to say and I forgot that I had ever been suspicious, just accepted everything he told me. I'm such an idiot.'

'Do you still have those pictures?' Imogen said.

'No, they were the ones that disappear after a few seconds. Snapchat.'

Imogen sighed. Of course they were.

'Why did you agree to meet him if you had suspicions?'

'I spoke to him on the phone and I saw him on video. I just ignored my instincts and eventually completely forgot.

He had an answer for everything. I just got carried away in how he looked, I think.'

'Over what period of time were you speaking to him?' Imogen said.

Faith thought for a second. 'About three months, I think. It started out just friendly, but then we chatted a lot and things got quite intense between us quite quickly.'

'Intense how?'

'I thought I was in love with him. I wanted to marry him. He just got me.'

'After three months?' Imogen tried to hide her incredulity.

'We talked for hours every day, and when you're online it's different, it's easier to type secrets out than it is to say them. I told him things I have never told anyone before,' Faith said. 'I'm so stupid.'

'No. We've all done it. These people know what they're doing. They know how to get that information out of you,' Imogen said.

'I knew though, part of me knew.'

Imogen shifted in the plastic hospital chair. 'Let's talk about the attack.'

'I don't remember much.'

'Anything at all could be helpful. We think that he has done this before,' Imogen said.

'What do you mean? There are other women? How many?' Faith said, surprised.

'Well, you are the only person we know about who has survived. There were three others who didn't make it, but you could stop this from happening to someone else.'

'Oh my God.' Faith started to cry. 'He came over, we started having sex and then it got rough. We'd talked about that before.'

'About it getting rough?'

'Yeah, I trusted him and so we talked about maybe trying some bondage or something, so when he put his hand around my throat I wasn't surprised.'

'Did you ask him to stop?'

'We had a safe word, but he didn't stop. That's when I knew it was all a lie,' Faith said. She was becoming more angry than upset now.

'You know these people are good at what they do, you didn't figure it out because he made sure you wouldn't.'

'I feel like I've been raped. Except I consented.'

'You stopped consenting though, didn't you?'

'I did.'

'Then you're right, you were raped. But don't get hung up on the labels here. The man assaulted you physically and sexually, he tried to kill you. You've been unconscious for almost two weeks . . .'

Imogen looked over and saw Adrian talking to a doctor in the corridor; it seemed like an intense conversation. Adrian took a sheet of paper from the doctor, then gently tapped on the glass.

'He can come in if he wants,' Faith said.

Imogen nodded for Adrian to open the door. He came in and sat back down, holding the paper in his hands. The doctor followed him inside.

'Hi Faith, I'm Dr Hadley,' the doctor said, her voice low and soothing.

'Faith, I need to ask you a couple of slightly personal questions if that's OK?' Adrian began.

She scoffed. 'This all feels very personal to be honest, so go ahead.'

'Aside from this man, have you had any other recent sexual partners?' Adrian asked.

'No, I haven't,' Faith said.

'And the time when he choked you, was that the first time you had been together sexually?' Adrian asked.

'Yes, I already said that. Why?' Faith said, trying to sit up in her bed.

'When they brought you in, the doctors did a rape kit, to get any evidence that may be left on your body,' Adrian said.

'That makes sense.'

'Well, there were no traces of semen. He didn't get to finish,' Adrian told her.

'He was wearing a condom,' Faith said.

'Doc?' Adrian said, looking up at the doctor with concern.

'Just tell me,' Faith said.

'Right,' Dr Hadley said. 'Well, Faith, the HCG levels in your blood are quite high.'

The doctor spoke softly, as though the tone of her voice could reduce the impact of the information in any way.

'I'm pregnant?'

'That seems probable, yes,' Dr Hadley said.

Adrian hesitated for a second. 'It's still very early to tell. It's been ten days since the incident. They ran all the tests again when you woke up, to make sure everything was OK.'

'They can tell this early?'

'We can tell from as early as six days after intercourse when we use a blood test,' Dr Hadley said.

'How is that possible?' Faith said, her eyebrows scrunched in confusion.

'The doctor will discuss the details with you, I just wanted to make sure we had the correct information,' Adrian said.

'When we were having sex, when he was choking me, he was whispering something in my ear, something about his baby. It's all a bit of a blur.'

'Can you remember exactly?'

'Saying I would never get away and that he knew about the baby. I think he was crying. I just thought he was confused about something.'

'It's just strange that, given the lack of evidence that was retrieved from your body immediately after the attack, you are actually pregnant now,' Adrian said.

'Can you get his DNA from the foetus?' Faith said.

'They don't do prenatal paternity tests at this hospital for ethical and moral reasons. It may influence whether a person wants to continue with the pregnancy. But also, it's a highly invasive procedure that puts the foetus at risk,' Dr Hadley said.

'What about if I had an abortion? Could they tell the DNA from the aborted foetus?'

'Then yes, with your permission they could test the DNA of the foetus, although at present it would be too early to do that,' Dr Hadley said.

Faith frowned. Imogen was impressed with how together she seemed; she wasn't fazed by the information, it was as though she wasn't personally or emotionally involved herself, as though she were talking about someone else. It was entirely possible that this would all hit her later on.

'Well, this is shit,' Faith said.

'You have up to twenty-four weeks to make the decision on an abortion, if the doctor confirms you are pregnant,' Dr Hadley said.

'More like twenty-two now,' Faith said.

'Are you ethically opposed to an abortion?' Imogen asked.

'No, but I have always felt the earlier the better. I'm not comfortable with the idea of letting the child grow inside me on purpose just to harvest some DNA later.'

'It's your decision, no one is going to force you to do that,' Adrian said.

'I know, but, it's important, isn't it? That the guy gets caught. Three women are dead, and I was almost killed, too. How do I go about my business knowing I could have stopped it if someone else gets hurt?'

'This is not a decision we can make for you. If the doctor confirms your pregnancy then it's up to you where you go from there. If you have an abortion and you give us permission to do a DNA test then we will. If you decide to keep the baby no one is going to judge you for that either. If we can get the DNA later on in the pregnancy that would also be helpful. I think people would understand whatever you decide,' Imogen said.

'I'm not worried about people's opinions to be perfectly frank. Life's all about the choices you make that you can live with at the end of the day.'

'Are you considering keeping the child?' Adrian said.

'I think I am. I'll talk to the doctor.' She glanced up at Dr Hadley.

'They will be sending in a counsellor when you're up to it. Maybe you could talk it through with them,' Adrian said.

'It feels very clear to me what I need to do. I need to keep this baby to help catch the man who did this. I'm looking forward to telling my child I put their daddy in prison.'

'Would you give the child up for adoption?' Imogen said.

'I don't think so. I don't know. I'll have to talk to my parents.'

'They have been contacted and are on their way. You have a lot to think about,' Imogen said.

'I suppose you've read through all of my conversations with LeChevalier?'

'We have,' Adrian said.

Faith let out a deep sigh.

Dr Hadley stepped forward.

'I'm afraid that's enough for now, Ms Jackson needs to get some rest.'

Imogen and Adrian stood up.

'I hope you get him,' Faith said.

'We may have some more questions for you at a later stage. If that's OK?' Imogen said.

'Of course.'

They walked out of the room and looked at the hospital signs, trying to figure out the best exit for them.

'This way I think? Follow the blue line on the floor

to get to the exit,' Imogen said, pointing at the guide lines on the linoleum. Blue for the main exit to the car park, green for Cardiology, yellow for X-ray and so on.

'I always wondered what those lines were.' Adrian rolled his eyes at her.

'What did you think of Faith?' Imogen said, changing the subject before Adrian accused her of patronising him, again.

'She seems remarkably together given what she's been through,' Adrian said. 'I'm barely that together when I wake up in the morning, let alone after ten days in a drug-induced coma only to wake up to find I'm pregnant with my rapist's baby.'

'The man who attacked her was called LeChevalier online; it's French for Knight,' Imogen said.

'Son of a bitch. We've got him,' Adrian said.

'Technically Gary has. I wonder how the killer would feel if he knew he was talking to a bearded ginger man.'

Adrian smiled. 'I'm looking forward to telling him.'

Chapter 64

Connor had taken his father's car again. He didn't even bother asking any more. They had successfully managed to avoid each other in the couple of days since their confrontation. The bumper had taken most of the impact when he crashed it but it was still roadworthy. Besides which, his father was usually too drunk to drive. He stared at the outside of The Swan pub that was situated at the end of the road for a few minutes before getting out. There was a large inflatable snowman lit up on the roof along with various other Christmas decorations.

Inside, the place was quiet. Diana was cleaning up and there were a few stragglers in Santa hats finishing up their pints, reluctant to leave.

'Bar's closed!' Diana called out as the door closed behind Connor. She was wiping down the dark wooden surfaces, but looked up at the sound. When she saw him, a wide smile spread across her face. Bingo. 'I'll make an exception for you, would you like a drink?'

'I was passing by and I thought you might be finishing soon,' Connor said. 'I could give you a ride home if you want.'

Diana looked genuinely moved that someone had even considered how she was going to get home. Connor could tell that she was reading a lot into his presence in the pub. Which was exactly what he wanted.

'I finish in about thirty minutes,' she said. 'Come and sit round here on the stool, I'll get rid of these people and we can go earlier.'

'Sounds good.'

'Why are you here? Just to give me a lift?'

'Something like that. I've been thinking about you a lot,' Connor said.

She smiled 'Well it's good to see you here. It's a nice surprise. Got any other surprises for me?'

'Maybe one or two,' Connor said flirtatiously. It was unnecessary to flirt with Diana, she took everything with a pinch of innuendo, regardless of what you were saying. She was a sexual person, he could tell. There was something about her that seemed very available, always switched on and ready to receive.

He moved around the bar and sat down out of the way as he watched her gather the glasses from the last hangers-on and hurry them out of the door. They left and she locked up behind them.

'Do you have a cigarette?' she asked as she slinked towards him, slowly, running her palm along the bar in an overtly playful way.

'Can you smoke in here?'

359

'Now it's shut I can. You're not going to tell on me, are you?'

'No.' He pulled out a cigarette and lit it in his mouth before putting it in hers; she caught her breath at this, as though she couldn't believe her luck.

'What made you change your mind about me?' she asked him.

'Who says I've changed my mind?'

'Something's changed. If it's not your mind, then what is it?'

'Like I said, I've been thinking about you all day, about this.'

She moved in closer to him as he perched on the stool. She wore polka dot capri pants and she pressed her crotch against his knee, making sure he knew what she was offering, the bend in his knee nestled comfortably between her thighs. She usually got what she wanted, he could tell. He stared at her mouth, the universal signal that you wanted to kiss someone.

'You're not making fun of me, are you?' she asked, a hint of worry crossing her face.

'I'm deadly serious.'

She leaned over, her pubic bone impressing on his leg as she planted her lips on his, barely waiting a second before sliding her tongue inside his mouth. He parted his lips further, allowing her to explore, her lips thick with a pink gloss he could feel transferring onto his own mouth. His eyes stayed open during the exchange; he looked for traces of Selina on her face, but there wasn't even a hint of resemblance.

She pulled back and he smiled, resisting the urge to

wipe the greasy residue from around his mouth. She stood on her tiptoes and reached past him, pulling a full bottle of Scotch off the shelf behind him, thrusting her breasts in his face. She smelled of sweat and cigarettes, masking the faintest odour of worn-off cheap perfume. Diana unscrewed the lid of the bottle and took a swig, making sure he noticed her wet lips around the neck of the glass. This probably worked on most people, but Connor wasn't here for that.

She handed him the bottle and he took a drink; he needed it. Everything about this was making his skin crawl. She pulled away from him and walked over to the jukebox. She keyed in a code and chose a song. He remembered thinking how predictable it was that she would choose Amy Winehouse; she had that faux fifties glamour thing going on. He cringed inside for her when she started to dance in his direction, moving closer, cigarette in hand. She blew out the smoke and rested what was left of her cigarette on the edge of the bar. She started to unbutton her off-the-shoulder retro gypsy top. Connor stood up and put the bottle in her hand. She took a swig, all the while swaying her hips to the music on the jukebox. He could tell that she thought it was a done deal already, that she was irresistible. He knew she would want nothing more right now than to feel as though she wasn't alone; she would get in the car with him, he would drive her home – it would be almost too easy. He had her right where he wanted her. He took the bottle again and moved forward so that she was pinned against the bar, pinned under him. He could feel her breasts heaving against him, and knew that she was turned on.

He gulped down the drink, its warmth spreading through him and giving him the courage he needed. He reached behind her to put the drink on the bar as he kissed her, almost gagging at the force with which she thrust her tongue inside his mouth again. He dropped the bottle and it smashed against the tiled floor behind the bar. She went to speak but he put his finger on her lips before pushing right against her. Her back arched, eyes looking down. She was attractive, sexy even, but just so ugly on the inside. She pressed her oily wet lips against his again, propelling him back slightly, giving herself room to bend her knee and slide it between his legs. She reached down and cupped him, he instinctively pulled back but quickly disguised his revulsion by kissing her neck.

'You're shaking, there's no need to be nervous,' she whispered before taking his earlobe in her mouth.

'I've never done this before,' Connor said.

She moved up against him even further, pressing until he was almost up against the back counter of the bar. The bottles behind him clanked together as she slammed him against them. She moved her knee even further upwards, rubbing against him.

'Don't worry. I'll show you what to do.'

She kissed him hard, forcing his lips apart with her tongue. He had to sell it, he had to make her believe he wanted her. He had pretended to want girls before so it wasn't so difficult. He moved his mouth to her neck and she moaned. He grabbed at her breasts, she closed her eyes and whimpered.

The jukebox music stopped as he continued to kiss her.

'You have a very pretty neck.'

'I think you told me a porky,' she said breathlessly, her hands rubbing up Connor's thighs, fumbling to find his flies. 'This is not your first time with a woman.'

She got on her knees and pulled on his buttons.

'I think you misunderstood what I was saying when I said I had never done this before . . .' He moved his hand behind him and closed it around a bottle of rum. He brought it down on her with full force. 'I meant I had never killed anyone before.'

The glass shattered as the heavy base of the bottle connected with her skull.

She crumpled to the floor and groaned as the blood seeped from the wound. She grabbed hold of his ankle and tried to pull herself up. He swept all the bottles behind him onto the ground and they smashed around her. She pulled herself towards his ankle and tried to bite him, but it didn't matter, she was running out of energy and before long she went limp, her arms lacerated from all the shards of glass on the floor. She still had a faint pulse, he checked.

The adrenaline coursing through him, he lit a cigarette and placed it on the ground next to her unconscious body, watching as it caught against the alcohol. He wiped down the bar quickly before the fire took hold of the wooden shelves behind the counter. The flames spread faster than he could have imagined. He had to get out. He left through the back door and scaled the wall; watching from the top of it for a few moments. At first the pub continued to look silent and empty, but the orange glow grew and in no time the flames were licking at the windows. Before Connor had time to react, his muscles tensed and the rigidity took over as he fell to the ground, teeth clenched and jaw locked, the long overgrown dead grass cushioning his fall.

Chapter 65

'Here you go,' Adrian said as he pulled up outside Imogen's place. A few of the houses on her street had Christmas trees up with less than a week left until Christmas Day. The twinkling lights were bouncing on the wet pavement. It had been a long day of waiting for Magic Knight to contact Imogen's dummy game account; Gary said he had been silent for a while. Now that they were convinced he was the right man they couldn't lose him. The worry was that he was already working on someone else. That they would be too late again. They had spent the best part of the evening watching Gary play the game. Magic Knight's account had been inactive for four days now. What was he up to? It seemed less likely that Magic Knight would turn up as time went on and they left the station. Gary had said he would continue at home and call if anything happened. Adrian had offered Imogen a lift and so here they were outside her home. The rain started to pick up and thrash against the windscreen. Adrian shivered involuntarily.

'Come in for a beer if you want?' Imogen said without looking at him.

He wanted to go inside but he shook his head. 'I should get back.'

'Fair enough, I'm pretty tired anyway.' She got out of the car.

He turned off the engine and got out too.

'Actually, Andrea has her book club over tonight, so I can hang here for a while, if you want,' he shouted over the rain as she rooted around in her bag for her keys.

'Suit yourself.'

He pushed any awkwardness he was feeling to the back of his mind as he went inside, hung his coat on the peg and followed her into the lounge. She immediately picked up the remote and flicked the TV on, something to break the silence between them. She disappeared into the kitchen.

'What food have you got in? I could cook something?' he called to her as he shook the wet from his hair.

'I've got some Weetabix and a mango. Not sure what you can do with that,' she shouted from the other room.

'Well, you should eat. I'll order takeaway.'

'I'm not that hungry to be honest. A liquid dinner will do me.' She came into the lounge with a box of beer.

The air was heavy, electric. So much that wasn't being said. Adrian took the beer and they both drank as they watched the TV, feigning interest in a documentary on some mega bridge in South America.

Adrian finished his drink and put the bottle on the

table. Were they going to talk or did he come here for more? He hated to admit to himself that that's why he was here, this was what he wanted. To be close to someone. He knew though, he knew he wasn't allowed to talk about it.

She opened two more bottles and handed one to him. Dutch courage? Who for? If he had one more beer he wouldn't be able to drive. He would have to stay here. She would offer him the couch or the spare room and he would say yes. Or maybe she would say she was tired and needed to sleep. How much longer did he have to pretend to be here for a drink? Here goes.

'Is it all right if I sleep in your spare bedroom? The rain's crazy out there and I probably shouldn't drive in it.' He thought it was better to get that sentence over with.

'Go ahead. I was just about to head off to bed now actually, I'm beat.' She still wasn't looking at him properly. She put her unfinished beer on the table and stood up.

'Goodnight,' he said as she disappeared into her room.

What should he do now? Go in there? The door was closed. Maybe he had been wrong. He looked at the clock; it was ten p.m. It looked like it was going to be an early night for him after all. He got up and went into the spare room. He took his trousers and socks off, then got into the bed; it was cold, the whole room was cold and the sheets against his skin made his skin prickle with goosebumps. After a while, Adrian had just about warmed up enough to hope to fall asleep, even though his mind was whirling with thoughts. Was she waiting for him? Did anything even happen between them last time? Had he imagined it? Was it a dream? Why was he dreaming about her?

Just as the noise in his head started to abate, he heard the click of a door followed by the padding of Imogen's feet on the hall floor. He held his breath and waited, then heard the faintest sound of a hinge creaking as Imogen opened his door. Seconds later, she was in his bed. Her body was warm, her bare legs hot against his. She flinched slightly as their skin touched, obviously noticing how cold he was. He kept his back to her for a moment. He wanted to see why she was here. He felt her hand on his waist again, straight under his shirt this time, the heat of her fingers warming him. He let her do this for a few moments before noticing her breathing was slightly jagged. She was crying. He slowly turned but kept his eyes closed, those were the rules.

She lifted her head and allowed him to slip his arm under so she could rest it there, her face sticky, moisture seeping through his T-shirt immediately. He stroked her hair out of her face and wiped her tears away, her breathing calmed and she exhaled heavily. She moved her hand outside of his shirt and started to touch his face, running her fingers along his lips. She wanted him to put his finger on her lips, that's what that meant. He placed his finger on her mouth, still wet from the tears on her face. She opened her mouth and took his finger inside, sucking it clean. He opened his mouth because he couldn't keep it closed, the air inside him desperate to escape. As his lips parted, she slid her finger inside and he suppressed a groan, he could taste soap and the salt of her skin. Her tongue was soft and wrapped around his index finger as well.

Oh God. He had to stop this, or at least slow it down. He removed his hand and slid it back under the covers; it brushed ever so slightly against the front of her pyjamas. *Don't think about that.* He pulled her in close, moving his head at the same time, making sure she took her finger out of his mouth. Adrian embraced her and she read his signs, because she stopped touching him and relaxed into hold. *That was too close.*

He tried to drift into sleep, aware that this would start again in the morning. It was inevitable. There were too many things that were inevitable now. He felt powerless to stop it because he didn't want to. His curiosity had always been there, but now it felt like something beyond that. They were on that train now. There was no getting off.

Chapter 66

Amidst the chaos, I had resolved to make the best of my situation. I had yet again adapted to a new normal, a normal where I hated my son and that was OK. At least Rocket hadn't visited in a while, he had started dating a girl he worked with and that put a stop to his visits with me for the time being. I didn't know how long his absence would last but I knew that his return would push me over the edge in my fragile mental state. I became increasingly paranoid that the child was trying to cause us harm. I would go to the church near the house and pray for my little family; I found myself in there often, searching for answers. JD stopped leaving the baby with me and I felt calmer when he wasn't there. It was only with this space that I started to realise that there was something profoundly wrong with me. More than ever, I could feel myself losing my mind. On the occasions when I had to look after the baby if he cried, I would do nothing. I hated myself for it, I couldn't even tell you what the baby looked like, to me it was an intruder, a parasite in my home. It wasn't until my mother-in-law commented that the baby looked exactly as JD looked as a child that I even considered I might have been wrong about who the father was. She pulled out an old baby photo of her son and, sure enough, when I checked my own child's face they looked so similar. I was overcome with relief, but also shame.

When JD got home from work that day I was cradling our son in my arms. Once I had accepted him into my heart he had completely taken a hold of me. I had been crying for hours, staring into that little boy's face and thinking of the weeks I had missed, the weeks he had gone without a mother. JD carefully took the baby from me; I was reluctant to let him go, but I knew he would be safe with his father. He asked me what had happened and I wanted to tell him everything, but the words stuck in my throat like lead weights. I promised that I would get help and that I would tell him everything someday, he just needed to be patient with me and we needed to leave. I told him that leaving would fix me.

He told me that he had applied for a job in America, asked me if that was far enough away and I threw my arms around him. Finally, my nightmare would be over. It was a year-long position with a British construction company who were renovating some offices out in Silicon Valley, California. The job came with accommodation, childcare and a car. It would be a better life than we had in the UK, certainly a better life than I had. We even had enough money for the flights saved.

For the first time in what seemed like forever, I could see an end to the madness. I went to the doctor to get some antidepressants; I didn't want to, but I knew that if I wanted my life to change then I couldn't be a slave to my emotions anymore. I hadn't cared enough about myself before to get the prescription, but now I had a reason to change. I had to be composed enough to make sure JD knew I was serious about getting better.

We had less than a month left and I could feel the excitement rising in me. It felt like we had passed the point of no return and that finally things were going to go my way. I was going to get my family to myself and then maybe start building a life where it was just the four of us. It had never been just the four of us. I was filled with hope for a future I could almost taste.

JD left his job and we announced to the family our plans to move away. We had three weeks before it was time to leave. I had already packed and given away most of the children's things to charity shops. Clean slate. I was refreshed and revived and life was full of possibility. Our bedroom was sparse; it had been our home for five years now and there was a part of me that was sad to say goodbye to it. Not sad enough to stop me from going though. Nothing would stop me from going. This was our last chance to make it as a family.

The children were out with their father when I heard the door slam. I knew who it was and I knew that he'd found out I was leaving; JD must have told him. I felt defiant and strong; let him do whatever he came to do, I thought, and then he could leave, I would *be shot of him soon enough. Sure enough, his hand was around my throat within moments and he had me up against the wall. He hissed and spat his displeasure at me, but I smiled and let him rant to his heart's content. He told me he was going to tell JD that I had been sleeping with him and that his son wasn't his son at all, he couldn't be. I laughed then and that seemed to anger him even more. Without JD, Rocket had no one who cared about him and I knew he wouldn't throw that away, not just to get back at me. He told me he would see me dead before he let me take JD away from him. He reminded me of the promise he had made all those years ago. That I was his. That he would never let me go.*

That was last night. I believe him. I realise maybe that he is in love with JD, that his feelings are more than platonic, that he knows there is no way it could ever be reciprocated. I sit here waiting for the end of this chapter to come now, counting down the clock and waiting for this all to be over, either I will get away or I won't; somehow, I suspect it's the latter. I'm writing everything down because I'm worried I'll disappear and he will get away with it. He has a way of getting away with things. So now, little book, my confessor, I am going to hide you somewhere in this house. I'll come back for you one day, but if I don't, then someone will eventually know what happened to me, I won't just be forgotten. If this is to be my last entry then so be it, come what may, I have told you everything now.

Chapter 67

The sky was glowing orange; it took Connor a moment to remember what he had done. He only hoped there was enough damage by now to have destroyed the evidence of him being there. Cold, he got to his feet and managed to make it down the road to his car, still shivering and sore, exhausted from the seizure. He drove home.

The light from the TV was illuminating the hall in bursts, although the volume was down. He steadied himself against the wall and breathed deeply, trying to get enough energy for the inevitable confrontation, when really all he wanted to do was climb up the stairs and into bed. He just wanted to go to sleep. He didn't feel guilty, he felt nothing.

'I can hear you,' Jacob called from the lounge.

'I have nothing to say to you. I'm going to bed.'

'Please, come here,' Jacob said. He sounded different, softer.

'Fine.' Connor stood up straight and walked in to see his father, perched on the edge of the sofa, in a strangely thoughtful pose.

'Listen, what I said before . . . about hating you. That wasn't true. You and your sister were the best thing that ever happened to me. It's been so hard; I know I haven't been a good father. I'm sorry. Please understand.' Jacob looked up at Connor; he had been crying.

'Fine, OK,' Connor said. He would say what needed to be said to get this conversation over with. He needed to sleep.

'Let's talk about your mother,' Jacob said. 'I mean properly talk about her. I should have told you what happened but I just couldn't.'

'Why now?' Connor said, unsure about this version of Jacob, it was not something he was used to dealing with. He grabbed the beers from the coffee table and put them on the dining table, then sat down. Connor cracked open a beer, he knew drinking was a bad idea after a seizure, but he really couldn't face this sober.

'Because I can't lose you too. I just can't.'

'So why did you lie? You must have known one day I would find out the truth.'

'Because I'm stupid, and because, despite what you must think, I love you. How would you have felt knowing that? Knowing that your mother killed your sister, that she killed herself?'

'You think telling me she left because of me was the answer?'

'No. I know that was wrong. But you just push my buttons.'

375

'That's not good enough,' Connor said.

'Before both of you were born, your mother and I were happy. Then something changed, I don't know what it was. We had your sister and then we learned that you were coming. Your sister was so excited when you arrived. A couple of weeks passed and I knew, I knew something was wrong, but you know how it is, suck it up and everything will be fine . . . Your mother stopped feeding you, left you to cry and cry, tried to keep everyone away from you.'

'You're lying.' Connor didn't want to listen to any more of this.

'Swear to God. Then she started saying some really crazy shit . . . I don't even know who she was. She said we needed to get rid of you, that you were evil, that she got raped by the devil and . . . Fuck!'

'Shut up!'

'I thought it was just a phase, that she would get over it, but it got worse. I took her to the docs, but they did nothing. I may have downplayed it a bit, probably should have told them some of the things she was saying but I was embarrassed. She started going to church twice a day, even left you there a couple times.'

Connor necked his drink, and Jacob handed him another one.

'So, what happened? How did they die?' Connor couldn't take all of this in. This couldn't be true. Could it?

'I got home one day and they were both lying in bed, holding each other. She had closed all of the windows and turned the gas on. The police said she suffocated.

She told me she wanted to end it, too, but I just never took her seriously.'

'Where was I?'

'I had you. I didn't like leaving you with her. I never really thought Shannon was in any danger. They were so close. She did seem to change towards you just before she died. Before she killed herself.'

'Maybe it was an accident?'

Jacob shook his head, tears rolling down

'Is that why you hate me?' Connor asked. 'Because I made her crazy?'

Jacob put his head in his hands. 'Don't you get it, Connor? She was going mad and I did nothing! You started messing up, taking drugs, getting drunk, fucking your life up . . . then you did what you did . . . I had to do something . . . I was scared you were going to hurt someone! I was scared you were going to hurt yourself.'

'So, you thought you'd hurt me instead?' Connor looked at his dad, his face softening slightly. 'You really fucked things up between us.'

'I know I did . . . I didn't know what else to do . . . please, just give me one more chance. I promise this time it will be different. I'll stop drinking . . .'

'It's too late for all that. Far too late. Why didn't you just tell me the truth?' Connor couldn't believe a word his father said anymore. There had been too many lies told to give him the benefit of the doubt.

'I didn't want you to know your mother was crazy. That woman, who she became those last few months, that wasn't my wife, and maybe to protect my memory of her, I just couldn't admit it to myself. She changed so much.'

'You didn't know why?'

'She was insane, always hiding, constantly taking photos or scribbling in her notepads. She didn't talk to me about anything. She cried all the time. I didn't know what to do.'

'So, what was it? What was wrong with her?'

'Some kind of psychosis, happens to some women after they give birth, when she had you . . .'

'So, it was my fault?'

'No, it wasn't your fault, it wasn't anybody's. After she died I took you away from here and we went to America. I had a job lined up and I didn't want you growing up around my family.'

'You lived here together?'

'We had to. We couldn't afford our own place and your grandparents had room for us. I never would have moved back here, but the timing was perfect. That I should inherit it now felt like fate.'

A thought struck Connor. Knowing what he knew, he had one question left to ask.

'Where did she die?'

'Here, upstairs.' Jacob looked away, unable to meet Connor's gaze.

'Where? Which room?'

'It doesn't matter.'

Connor knew, his father didn't even have to say it. They suffocated in his bedroom. They might have even died in his bed.

Chapter 68

The Swan pub was a burnt-out shell; it had been burning all night. Thick black smoke bellowed into the sky. The firefighters were packing away the hoses. Selina stepped off the bus from her grandmother's house and walked towards the pub; she would get the next bus to school at eight-fifteen. A police officer stepped in her path.

'Whoa there, missy, where do you think you are going?'

'My mum works there.'

'Well I'm afraid you can't go in there until the firefighters have finished their investigation, and even then, there's nothing left.'

'Was anyone in there?' Selina stared at the building, tears falling down her cheeks.

'We have recovered one body in the fire, a female. I'm sorry.'

'Oh my god . . .' Her hand went up to her mouth,

she couldn't believe it. It must have been her mother. She remembered Connor's promise. Had he done this?

'Are you going to be OK? I can get a counsellor to speak to you, we can contact the school for you. Is your father home? Did he contact the police about her not coming home last night?'

It wouldn't be the first time her mother hadn't come home. Before she met Lenny, she was always out. Selina had spent countless nights alone when she was eight years old. She remembered the loneliness, and how she'd thought it was the worst feeling in the world. Then her mother had brought Lenny home and she longed for those long lonely nights where her fear was imagined and never materialised.

'It's just me and my mother. I have a test today; I was studying all night. How did it happen?' She didn't want them to know she had been kicked out. She just wanted to get away from here.

'We're not sure yet. Someone will be in touch with your family soon, we'll know more after the post-mortem.'

'Post-mortem?'

'That's all I can really say at this point. Do you have somewhere to stay?'

'My nan's, I can go there after school.'

'Could you tell me your mother's name?'

'Diana Dilley.'

The police officer nodded in acknowledgment and reached into his pocket, pulling out a business card before handing it to Selina.

'Here's the number of our counsellor, she can help you get your head round all this. Do you need a lift to school or home or anywhere? Can I call some family to come and get you?'

'Thank you, no. I need to get to school.' Selina took the card out of his hand.

She walked away from the scene. She wasn't as upset as she should be, her initial tears had gone already, she should have broken down and cried, she should have felt something other than relief.

She waited patiently for the eight-fifteen bus to take her to school. The last day of school before Christmas. She had a few hours to work on being sad, for when she had to speak to other people about her mother. They would expect her to be sad. No one would expect anyone to hate their own parent; no one would expect a child to want her mother dead and not feel a stitch of sympathy to learn that she had died in such a horrible way. Sympathy was more than Diana deserved.

Chapter 69

Connor walked behind Selina in the school hall; he wanted to reach out to her and take her hand, check that she was OK. She was walking with the same focus and determination that she always had, trying to keep her head down and avoid any kind of eye contact with anyone. The news must be around the school already because Connor had noticed the way people were looking at her. Focus was sparse enough on the last day of term; add in a scandal and everyone was pretty much useless.

When Connor entered the maths classroom, she was sitting at her desk already. She turned her head slightly away from him as he approached, but he deliberately dropped his book and knelt beside her desk.

'Are you OK?' he whispered, looking up at her. She refused to meet his gaze and he could see tears in the corners of her eyes. He couldn't help but feel hurt and confused. Had he done the wrong thing? Had he completely misunderstood the situation?

As he stood up, no longer able to maintain the pretence of picking something off the ground, Pippa walked up and stood in front of him.

'We're all going to hang after school. Do you want to come?'

He looked at Selina as if he were waiting for permission but she didn't even move her head. He didn't want to get her in trouble if it came out that he was involved in her mother's death, he didn't want to take her down with him. If people knew about them they might suspect that the death wasn't an accident. For now, in public, things would have to stay the same.

'I'm not sure, maybe.'

'I still want to be friends, Connor. I hope we can be.'

'Sure, yeah, of course.' He looked at Selina again, her face was still expressionless and staring straight ahead, poised for their upcoming maths test.

'I know that thing with Neil was bad.'

'I told you, it's fine. I don't hold it against you, against either of you.' He really didn't mind.

'It would mean a lot to me if you came,' Pippa said.

Connor felt trapped. 'Sure then, of course.'

He'd lied to get her off his back. He couldn't face socialising right now, couldn't face pretending to be interested in anything those people had to say.

Satisfied, Pippa went back to her desk. Selina didn't look at Connor once, so he took his seat, a weight on his shoulders. For the rest of the day he couldn't get Selina's attention. She seemed to be ignoring him. When the school day ended, he saw her get in a taxi outside the gates. At that moment, Eric, Pete and Pippa appeared behind him.

'You OK, mate?' Neil said awkwardly.

'I'm good, I'm good.' Connor smiled, feeling a little awkward himself; he genuinely liked Neil, he seemed to be a nice guy, not constantly trying to prove himself like the others, like Pippa.

'Did you hear about the Swan? It's gone! Totally levelled.'

'What happened?' Connor said, trying to look surprised.

'Fire gutted the place. What a pain in the arse, it was the only place that didn't check for ID.'

'Bummer.'

'Are you coming to the park? I've stashed some cider there.'

'I'll be there, just going to go and dump my stuff off first.' He smiled. 'See you in a bit.'

The day had been so confusing that Connor wasn't sure about anything anymore. They thought he was one of them, but he wasn't sure he was one of anything anymore, he didn't fit anywhere. He had actually killed someone, not just been inadvertently responsible like with Billy Wicowska. What was worse was that he didn't regret it. He just hoped that Selina didn't hate him for it.

He walked home to an empty house, something he was relieved about after last night's conversation. He wasn't sure he could take any more revelations. He went outside and looked up at the tree house; he didn't feel like going in there today, knowing that Selina wasn't home. Instead, he walked further into the garden, past the tree to his grandfather's old shed. Inside was as he had left it a few weeks ago. Knowing now that his mother had lived in this house, he remembered the old photographs he had seen and looked for the box. Uncovering it, he rummaged inside until his fingers felt the familiar glossy texture and he pulled the photos out. Some were stuck together; most were dusty and none of them seemed to be of anything in particular. Flowers and the occasional cat. He recognised the surroundings as the garden, but unlike now, it was tidy and well kept. The shed looked almost new, freshly painted and still in use. Even the brickwork on the house seemed less tired, less worn and dishevelled.

Eventually he found some photos of people. His father and grandfather. His grandmother that no one ever seemed to mention; the men were very much at the forefront of his family. A baby being cradled by a slightly older child. It must have been Connor and his sister. He put the photo in his jacket pocket. He found a few more pictures of his father, young and smiling, happy with his arms around his mother, Victoria. Some of his father with Joel. He took a few of the photos and picked up the red exercise book he'd found on that first day he arrived in England. He sat down on the small stack of crates and started to read. Before long, he realised that it was no story.

Chapter 70

Adrian came into the station a little after midday. It was Christmas Eve and everyone was handing out their Secret Santas. On his desk, there was a small box wrapped in purple with a large green bow. It almost looked like a prank gift from the Joker. He opened the box to find a silver necklace, a pendant with St Jude on it, the patron saint of lost causes. It wasn't a tacky necklace and so he assumed whoever had given it to him wasn't being facetious. He looked around to see if anyone was watching him, but no one was. Whoever had given it to him must have known him pretty well, and they had spent well over the ten-pound budget.

'We've got a problem,' Gary said as he hurried towards Adrian's desk holding his laptop open.

Adrian had hardly ever seen Gary in a panic before, he was usually very laid-back and calm. If he was worried, then something must be wrong.

'What is it?'

'Its Magic Knight. Where's Imogen?'

Adrian had snuck out of Imogen's house before dawn two days before and he hadn't seen her since then. With no new evidence on the case both of them had somehow managed to avoid coming in to review the case files at the same time. He hadn't slept a wink that night. He'd spent the two hours before he actually left her wrestling with his thoughts. After leaving Imogen's place, Adrian had gone home and fallen asleep on the sofa for a few hours. If he had stayed at Imogen's, he was sure it would have gone further and he realised he didn't want that, not while they were both so vulnerable. He was still grieving for Lucy and he didn't want Imogen to be the collateral damage. But there was a part of him that just wanted more. Was it her he wanted or just sex? He had to figure it out before he did anything. It was like the fuse had been lit though, as if there was no way back from this.

'Hello? Earth to Adrian,' Gary said, jolting Adrian from his thoughts. 'Imogen – where is she?'

'I haven't seen her. I only just got here,' Adrian said, hoping that she had left already. He could deal with this after Christmas.

'There she is,' Gary said suddenly, putting his laptop on the desk as Imogen approached, completely blanking Adrian.

'Afternoon, Gary, Adrian.' She said his name without looking at him.

Adrian's chest tightened. Was she angry that he'd left? Angry that he'd even stayed at her house the night before last? He didn't know what to do, but he couldn't speak to her about it, not now.

'So, what's this big problem then?' Adrian said, trying to distract himself.

'Magic Knight's gone,' Gary said.

'What do you mean gone?' Adrian said.

'The game was shut down for twenty-four hours to update, everyone's been in a mad panic on the message boards. Anyway, when it rebooted this morning he was gone, not just him but all of his messages, gifts, everything. He must have deleted every single thing. Also, two of the other accounts that I suspected were his have gone as well.'

'What does that mean?' Imogen said

'Maybe he's just sick of the game,' Adrian said.

'I don't think so.' Imogen turned to Gary. 'Do you think he knows who I am?'

'I have no idea. How would he know? We have been careful,' Adrian said.

'To remove any trace of himself within such a short space of time takes some skill, I mean we are talking everything. And you can't just remove a block of messages, you have to remove them individually.'

'How could he be onto us?' Adrian said.

'Maybe he saw you. Maybe he's been in the station. Maybe he did facial recognition on Imogen and found some old police articles online. Maybe it's nothing to do with us, someone else could be onto him,' Gary said.

'That's a lot of maybes,' Imogen commented.

'I'm just saying, we will look into it, but all we know right now is that he is gone.'

'So, what's changed since the last time you spoke to him Gary? When was it?' Imogen said.

'About four days ago. But sometimes he was off for a few days at a time. There didn't seem to be any pattern to it. Not one that we could figure out anyway. It might have had to do with a work rota, assuming he had a job. It could have been family commitments, although according to Franka he's not likely to be married or have any children,' Gary said.

'Why does she say that?' Adrian asked.

'He's looking for a connection. He can't connect though. Maybe he genuinely wants these relationships to work,' Gary explained.

'So, what's happened between four days ago and now?' Imogen said. She still hadn't looked at Adrian.

'Faith woke up. It was on the local news,' Gary answered.

'She's the first talking witness we have had. Do you think he's going after her?' Adrian said.

'She's surrounded by uniformed officers at the moment. It's unlikely he would try. He attacks vulnerable women, he's not brave enough,' Gary said. 'It's more likely that he's gone to ground. Planning his next move.'

'So, we're flying blind now?' Imogen said.

'We always were, to a point. In terms of actual physical evidence, we have very little,' Adrian remarked.

'OK. I'm going to go speak to the DCI and update her, then we can go through everything we have again, step by step.'

'I thought you were off until the twenty-seventh? Gary said.

'It's no big deal. I don't have any plans, I'm just using up my holiday before the year is out because I can't carry it over.'

'Just go. We'll call you if we find anything.' Adrian said.

'I'll send you regular updates, I promise,' Gary said.

'If you're sure.'

'We're sure,' Gary and Adrian said in unison.

'OK. Fine. I'll call and make sure there's still officers at the hospital after I update the DCI, then I'm off until after Christmas,' Imogen said. 'Have a good one, boys.'

'Don't forget, Imogen, you're welcome at mine tomorrow. If I'm not still at work, I'll text you the time,' Adrian said, not willing to let the tension between them change anything.

'Merry Christmas.' Imogen smiled and walked over to the DCI's office.

'Is she alright?' Gary said, making Adrian feel like even more of a shit.

'Can we cross-reference these four cases and see what overlap we have? I feel like there is something we're missing. I'm going to keep looking through the details, but if you could have a look through any conversation transcripts you have with him. Make sure you didn't spook him.'

'I didn't,' Gary said, affronted.

'Well just check and see if you think there is anything hinky going on.'

Adrian had to keep looking. Now that they had no clue what the killer was up to, he was even more concerned that he could strike again at any time. He looked at the facts once more; he would keep reading them over and over until something made sense to him. Sometimes it was that simple. There must be something he was missing. What did all these cases have in common?

390

Chapter 71

Adrian was revisiting all the case files, the photos, the lists he had made, any data pertaining to the case. He looked at the clock; it was two a.m. on Christmas morning; he should have gone home hours ago. He'd explained to Tom and Andrea that he would be working on Christmas morning, but the truth was that he'd actually volunteered. He didn't know why, but he didn't want to be with his family right now. He couldn't help thinking about the Christmas he might have had if Lucy had survived. Would they still be together? he wondered. Maybe, maybe not. But there was something about the ritual of Christmas that made him miss her even more. It seemed stupid, but he felt as though he deserved to be alone; if she couldn't celebrate Christmas, then he shouldn't either.

Denise Ferguson, the Desk Sergeant, walked into the office.

'I'm just clocking out now, are you sure you're going to be all right?'

'Anything happening?' he asked.

'The usual, some pub disturbances, nothing particularly taxing.'

'Well, merry Christmas, Denise. Have a good one.'

'Actually, if you're bored, there's a kid out there. Looks a little lost.'

'What's he here for?'

'Not sure, Bri is talking to him now, but maybe you might be better, you know what Brian's like.'

Brian Myers was the other regular duty manager on the desk, they brought him in on the nights when they had the belligerent drunks because he didn't mince his words and it took a lot to crack his tough exterior.

'OK, thanks Denise, I'll check it out.' He paused. 'Denise? Were you my Secret Santa?'

'Nope, that would be Imogen.' She smiled and walked out.

Adrian opened his draw and picked out the pendant from the box. Knowing it was from Imogen, he wanted to put it on. What the hell was happening? He closed the drawer before his mind started wandering again. He walked out to the main entrance and saw the young man sitting in the waiting area. Brian was busy dealing with a couple who had got into a fight. By the sounds of it, the man had kissed a waitress under the mistletoe and his wife had taken objection to it and assaulted the waitress with hot food. Another normal Christmas day at the station.

The teenage boy was biting the quicks of his nails and clutching a red book.

'Can I help you?' Adrian asked.

'I need to talk to someone about something,' the teenage boy said, with an American accent.

Adrian nodded. 'What is it?'

'A murder.'

Adrian stared at him for a moment. He seemed shaken and slightly wide-eyed, as though he were struggling to process something. Adrian knew that feeling well. 'You'd better come with me. I'm DS Adrian Miles.'

Adrian led the boy through to the liaison room, wondering where on earth he'd come from. He got a can of Coke from the vending machine on the way into the room. They sat opposite each other on the sofas. The boy unrolled a notebook that he had crumpled up in his hands. Without speaking, he handed it to Adrian. He hadn't seen one of these books for years, but he remembered they used to sell them at his local post office, next to the airmail envelopes that always looked so important. Adrian always wished his family were well off enough to know someone who lived abroad. Those envelopes seemed like such luxury.

The boy grabbed the book back and opened it to a page somewhere in the middle. Adrian started to read an account of physical and sexual assault. He looked up at the boy.

'Who wrote this?' Adrian asked.

'My mother, I think. When she was alive.'

'I'm sorry. Your mother passed away?'

'I was told she killed herself, but after reading that, I don't think she did.'

'What makes you think this isn't just a story?'

'It's not a story, just read it.'

'How long ago did she die?'

'When I was a baby. I'm sixteen now, so about fifteen years ago I expect. My sister too, she was a few years older than me. Sorry, I don't know many details, this is all news to me as well.'

Adrian continued to look through the hand-scribbled book. The writing was erratic and somehow became more so as the story went on; she seemed to have written it all at once, like some kind of suicide note. He could only read snippets here and there. The second half of the book was water-damaged and stuck together, but there was no denying that it was chilling, and had a ring of truth to it.

'Who do you think would have killed her?' Adrian asked.

'I don't know . . . Maybe my dad . . . he knocks me around, a lot.'

Adrian's jaw clenched at the thought of it. 'You think your father killed her?'

'I wouldn't be surprised.'

Adrian skipped back to the beginning and read through a little more.

'What's your name?' Adrian pulled out his notebook and pen.

'Connor Lee.'

'Where and when did you find this book?'

'I found it yesterday afternoon. I read it, then came straight here. You need to find out what really happened. He needs to be locked up.'

'And what happens to you when he's gone?' Adrian looked up. He remembered his own violent father and knew what the answer would be. But what was the alternative? Leaving this boy with his abuser? With the man he thinks killed his mother?

'I'll be better off, trust me. You need to arrest him.'

'I'm afraid there's no evidence that this is a true account of something that has actually happened.' Adrian said. It wouldn't be the first time a kid from an abusive background had tried to get their abuser put away. He could have made this up.

'Then look into it. I don't care what you have to do. He can't get away with it.'

'Did you read all of it?'

'I couldn't, there's a lot of damage. Maybe you can though. I don't need to read every word to know what my father is capable of.'

'Have you been drinking?' Adrian could smell the beer and cigarettes on the boy.

'I don't see what difference that makes.' Connor was getting anxious. Adrian could tell this boy had been through a lot, he had all the classic signs of a victim of prolonged physical abuse. Hypervigilance, agitation and shaking hands from alcohol withdrawal.

'I'll get someone to look into it and then we can decide how to proceed.'

'He strangled her and raped her!' Connor shouted.

'Excuse me?'

'That's what he did, it was his game, strangling her and raping her when she was unconscious. You can't tell me that's OK.'

Adrian stared at the boy. It couldn't be that easy, could it? They had been searching for this man for weeks and now a boy walks in with the key? What were the chances that this boy's father was Magic Knight? Was his mother the first victim? Adrian tried not to get ahead of himself. They needed to verify this was genuine evidence first.

'What's your father's name?'

'Jacob Lee.'

Adrian wrote the name down. 'What was your mother's name?'

'Victoria Beckett. She would have been listed as a suicide. My sister was called Shannon.'

'Do you have a picture of your mother?'

The boy pulled a few photos out of his pocket; he looked through them quickly and pulled one out to give to him.

Adrian's heart thumped as he looked at the photograph. The woman in the picture had long dark hair – she looked like the victims so far . . . she looked like Imogen. Adrian's mind was racing.

'OK, do you have somewhere safe to go tonight?'

'I'll be fine at home. I'm over sixteen.'

'Are you sure?'

'Promise you'll look into it?'

'I will, I promise. Write down your contact details for me and I'll contact you as soon as I know anything.'

'Thank you,' Connor said, scribbling his address and phone number on a scrap of paper and handing it to Adrian.

The boy left and Adrian picked up the phone immediately. He remembered begging the police to arrest his father when he was younger and half the time he was probably right. Maybe the boy's instincts weren't completely skewed by his hatred for his dad though.

'Gary, are you busy?' Adrian said quickly as the line connected.

'What do you need?' Gary's voice was a dry rasp, he had obviously been asleep.

'I have a book here with pages stuck together, how do I unstick them without damaging what's on them? There's no one in the lab for the next two days and you seem to know everything else.'

'It's a bit time-consuming.' Gary paused for a moment. 'Where are you?'

'I'm still at work. A teenage boy just came in with a book he thinks his mum wrote fifteen years ago.'

Gary sighed. 'Don't you have enough to do?'

'In the book, on the pages that are legible, she talks about being strangled and raped. I wondered if it might be connected to our case.'

There was a pause. 'I'll be there in half an hour.'

'You don't need to do that, just tell me what to do.'

The line clicked dead before Adrian had a chance to protest any more.

He started to read the book from the beginning. A wave of futility swept over him as he read about the girl whose life got progressively worse with every day. He thought about calling Imogen but he didn't want to wake her up until he could get the full story; there was no point both of them being up and waiting. He was tired, hungry and struggling to ignore the emotions that were trying to work their way to the surface. He didn't want to think about all the things he should be doing right now, he just wanted to get through Christmas and into the next year; put a full stop on this one and move on.

Chapter 72

Imogen ran along the road towards St Thomas's church, the dawn light making it look even more imposing than usual. The city was strange at seven in the morning, quiet and empty, almost like a photograph. She thought about Adrian's offer to go over for Christmas dinner as she passed the end of the adjacent road. He would be at home with his family, probably preparing vegetables or stuffing or something like that. She didn't want to intrude. She had left a message for Dean, even though she had promised not to reconnect with him; they still hadn't managed to get hold of him at the station, so she'd called him, and before she knew it she was inviting him over for Christmas dinner. Not a traditional dinner, a fish fingers and mash kind of dinner, but it wasn't about the food. Adrian had told her it was about family and he was right, there was no getting away from the fact that Dean was a part of her life, and even if they couldn't be together then she had to be there for him as a friend. It was Christmas Day and she knew he didn't have anyone else.

But for now, all she wanted to do was run. This was her idea of Christmas; she had started running as a way to get outside, to feel free. Family was not something she had grown up with, unless you counted her mother. There were no grandparents and quite often no presents. It wasn't something that massively bothered her; although if she was honest, it was nice when she did get something but she wasn't expecting anything this year. Christmas running was Imogen's gift to herself.

It was a mild day with a bite in the air when she left the house, but the occasional breeze that nipped at Imogen's thighs had got stronger. The temperature had dropped and it smelled like rain was imminent. She had been running for almost an hour now and was starting to get tired; this was usually the point where she would push herself harder until she found her second wind, but she decided to make her way home instead, to see if Dean had called her back.

She rushed into the house and kicked her shoes off, realising as soon as she got in the warm just how cold her skin was. She needed to get in the shower before she started shivering. She looked at her phone to see a missed call and a text from Adrian, but nothing from Dean. She looked at the text from Adrian; he might have a lead but he was still waiting on more information, nothing to deal with right now. She wondered if he knew she had bought his Secret Santa present. He didn't mention it. In fact the message was very professional, almost cold. Things were getting complicated between them and it was frustrating. Why was it so hard for them to deal with the situation like adults? She put Soundgarden on the MP3 player through the Bose speaker, turning it up to full; she didn't want to hear her own thoughts right now.

In the kitchen Imogen took the potatoes out of the vegetable basket – if she put them on now they would be ready by the time she got out of the shower. The water on the stove was at a low simmer, she had plenty of time before she would be hungry, but it felt strange not to prepare anything on Christmas Day, even if it just had to be heated up in a microwave later on. She made extra, just in case Dean turned up out of the blue; it was entirely possible.

She got into the shower and peeled off her sweaty clothes. Instantly the warm water soothed her as it trickled over her skin, white with red blotches from the cold; it wasn't as mild outside as she had thought. The soap was soothing as she rubbed the lather into her aching muscles and behind her ears. Imogen took her time in the shower, it was Christmas after all. She loved the feeling of the shampoo soaping up between her fingers as she scooped all her hair on top of her head and massaged her scalp, allowing her nails to scrape the surface a little. Once she was fully rinsed, she twisted her hair tightly until all the water was out. Her skin rejuvenated and warm, she wrapped the towel around her and got out of the shower. Ready to get dressed up for Christmas dinner for one. At least she would definitely win the cracker pull.

Chapter 73

Adrian looked at the clock; it was ten in the morning. He picked up his phone and dialled Tom's phone.

'Dad. Merry Christmas,' Tom said. He sounded happy.

'Merry Christmas, how was your morning?'

'Mum made pancakes.'

'Did you like your present?' Adrian had bought Tom a Nintendo games console for his room in their new home, when they eventually moved in. Most of their belongings from before were being held in evidence.

'You didn't need to. I love it though, obviously.'

'It took all my strength not to buy a boxed Star Wars toy.'

'I would have liked that too,' Tom said.

'Sorry I can't be there right now, but I'll be back later on. I'd better get back to work. Is your mum OK?'

'She's making some kind of vegetable sculpture. I'll see you later. I love you.'

'Love you, too.'

As Adrian hung up, Gary approached. He had spent the last few hours in his lab working on the book, painstakingly trying to restore it to a readable condition.

'The book is looking pretty good. I re-soaked it in order to peel it apart and then I've put fabric intermittently throughout the pages, it should be ready soon. I've stuck it in the dehumidifying tank downstairs.'

'Thanks, Gary, I feel terrible about this, what with it being Christmas Day,' Adrian said.

'It's fine. Stop going on about it. I wasn't doing anything else anyway. Franka has gone back to Croatia to be with her family so it was this or a day playing Skyrim. I have been looking at the rest of the case though. There's something I found that was pretty interesting. Looking through all the girls' records, they all spent some time at the Royal Devon and Exeter Hospital, Wonford, in the last few months. Which is not totally abnormal, but when you think about how often most people go to the hospital, then it's kind of strange.'

'What's that got to do with the game?'

'Well – Faith did say that he was a doctor. You usually find them in hospitals.'

'So, what are you suggesting?'

'The precise cleaning of the body, cut fingernails. OK, the use of bleach is a little extreme, and that's probably to get rid of evidence, but what if it's not? Bleach doesn't actually remove DNA and a doctor would know that. What if it's someone who cleans bodies? Redressing a body is not easy, he might have practice. Posing and redressing bodies is an indicator of a lust murderer.

There are jobs out there where you can get paid to do that shit.'

'You think it's someone who works in a morgue?' Adrian said.

'Or anywhere in a hospital. You would see things, and if you really wanted to, you could copy them.'

'I guess that makes sense,' Adrian said.

'Well, you know they assumed the window being open was done deliberately to confuse the time of death? I also found out that when someone dies on a ward it's standard to open a window to set the spirit free.'

'What?'

'It's just a superstition they practise in a lot of hospitals.'

'Would that usually be done by a doctor?'

'It could be anyone, probably more likely to be a nurse or a porter.'

'So how does this relate to the game?' Adrian asked. 'How did he know who to target?'

'I was thinking about that and I decided that maybe he took a picture of the person when they were at the hospital.'

'That seems a bit far-fetched.'

'Facial recognition software is very available. There are plenty of really basic facial rec apps out there. Even in Facebook it can take facial markers and throw up some possibles. For someone with some patience it wouldn't take long at all. The information is all out there. People just aren't that careful.'

'So, you think he finds these women at the hospital then looks for them online? That's pretty lucky, isn't it? That they were all in that game?'

404

'There are literally millions of people subscribing to these games and thousands of people pass through the hospital, maybe these are just the women he manages to locate online. Sometimes you can locate profiles through email addresses; if these women filled out forms at the hospital he could have access to those documents and then search for them that way. The game may not be his only social media hunting ground, either. Jackie Munroe wasn't on it as far as I can tell.'

'Thank god I'm a luddite,' Adrian said.

'He gets to be whoever he wants to be online as well. If he works at the hospital, he probably knows enough to pass himself off as a doctor. Enough to impress a woman,' Gary said.

Adrian shook his head in disgust. 'He gets off on that?'

'Exactly. Remember he would be a total fantasist. If he was quite low down on the ladder in a hospital then he might really want to play up and be something better than he is. He would totally revel in the idea of deceiving someone.'

Something was bothering Adrian about the way Magic Knight's profile had completely been removed, something about the timing of it. It happened just after they had interviewed Faith.

'We were at the hospital when we interviewed Faith – what if our perpetrator saw Imogen and realised who she was?'

Gary nodded, frowning. 'That may explain his disappearance from the game. Maybe he saw her and got spooked.'

'Do you not think this all sounds like a bit too much of a coincidence?'

'It's only a coincidence to us because we don't think like that. The man is a psychopath and will find ways to engineer his way into people's lives just to destroy them. He can't do it when he's being himself. Even though he's good-looking and feels like he's above everyone else, it all stems from a massive inferiority complex about his position in life, about the way he thinks women perceive him. Like he's not good enough. He wants to teach them a lesson.'

'So, have you spoken to Imogen about this?'

'No, I thought I should speak to you first. I don't want to overreact.'

'I think we need to speak to the DCI, I'll call her now.'

'At Christmas? Good luck.'

Chapter 74

Imogen looked through her wardrobe, but it was mostly full of the clothes she wore to work. She went into the spare room and looked at the free-standing clothes rail she had in there. Finding a navy blue dress, she pulled it over her head; it felt alien to dress up, but she wanted to make the effort for Christmas Day, even if she was going to spend it alone.

The potatoes were boiling when Imogen got back into the kitchen. She looked at the clock; it was only eleven. After pouring the cream, she put the pan on the counter and started to mash, the music still loud enough to filter out her thoughts. Even this, even being alone, was better than the Christmases she had had as a child. Her mother would either invite any strays over, who would end up stealing half of their stuff, or she would forget entirely, maybe sleep through it. Imogen learned a long time ago not to get excited about Christmas.

She turned the oven on ready for the food. It wasn't

really even lunchtime yet; she would give it another half an hour. She went back into the bedroom to finish getting ready.

After lunch she might drive round to see Adrian; she knew Christmas would be hard for him this year. She needed to put any awkward feelings aside and be a good friend right now. It was a time to think about the connections she had and the ones she had lost – a reminder of who was important in her life, like a stock-take. Adrian was important.

Maybe she could wear some make-up, not that it really made much difference but it was nice to feel like she had at least tried to look party-ready. In the mirror, she untangled her hair with her fingers; the kink in it was more pronounced than usual. Normally when she washed it, she tied it straight up, got it out of the way, but not today.

The make-up she had was cheap and at least four years old, quite dusty and most of the lines had since been discontinued. She didn't need foundation or concealer or anything like that, but she swept some mauve powder across her eyelids and found a lipstick that complemented it, one of the three lipsticks she owned and the only one that hadn't been mashed into the lid.

She looked in the full-length mirror; that would have to do. She smoothed her dress down and preened a little more. It wasn't that she was looking for perfection, more just some approximation of effort. She tossed her hair forward to shake the layers loose even more and give it some volume, then pushed it back away from her face. Doing so, she noticed that there was a red smudge across her cheek. Confused, she looked at her hands; there was blood along the side of her palm and up the side of her wrist. Where had it come from? She ran her hand up the side of the dress and felt the warm wetness that she somehow hadn't noticed before, it hadn't saturated the fabric. She pulled the sleeves up and checked her arms but she wasn't cut, and she wasn't in any pain. Her heart began to beat faster. There was someone else here and they were bleeding.

Chapter 75

Adrian was reading through the red book Connor Lee had brought in, a knot forming in his stomach. Gary had photocopied the legible pages and Adrian had underlined the passages on the copies that he felt pertained to the crime they were working on. They did this to keep the integrity of the original document intact, in case it was needed in a trial. The station was operating with a skeleton crew and eerily silent. Most of the officers were on call but not required to be in unless it was absolutely necessary. The station Christmas tree was beginning to look a little threadbare; it was an artificial one that had been used ever since Adrian had joined CID and even then, it had seen better days.

Gary was walking over from the lift. 'I found an old newspaper article from fifteen years ago. Mother and daughter, murder suicide. The mother suffocated the daughter with a pillow before turning the gas on and taking her own life. I looked through the police files and found the officer who investigated the case,' Gary said, putting some of the papers in his hand on the desk.

'Who was it? Maybe we can ask them about the father?'

Gary hesitated before speaking. 'It was DI Harold Morris.'

'Oh,' Adrian said. Hearing the name sent an involuntary shiver through Adrian. His old DCI, no longer alive. 'I guess we can't ask about the father then.'

'I checked out the father, Jacob Lee, he works in construction. As far as I can tell, he doesn't have anything to do with the hospital,' Gary said.

'Has he done any construction work on the hospital?' Adrian said.

'No. Also, they didn't arrive in England until a couple of days after the first murder. They moved here from California. Did you speak to the DCI about it?' Gary said, leaning over and pulling a flight manifest from the pile of papers on the desk and handing it to Adrian.

'I left her a message but she hasn't got back to me. Jacob Lee's middle name is David, so I am assuming he is the JD in this story, but there's another man too. I don't suppose Connor would have been able to read those parts as they were the most damaged. I think he's the man we are looking for.'

'How do we find him?'

'I'll go and see the boy.'

Adrian pulled up to the house at the address where Connor Lee had said he lived. He knocked on the door and waited patiently until Connor answered.

411

'You're here?' he said, looking surprised. 'I didn't think you'd come.'

Adrian nodded at him. 'Is your father here, Connor?'

'No, just me,' Connor said; he seemed relieved.

'Can I see those photos you had of your mother again?' Adrian said.

'Did you read the book?'

Adrian nodded. 'We got most of it apart and managed to read a lot of it. She talks about two men in there, any idea who the other one is?'

'My uncle Joel probably.'

'No this will be a friend, not family.'

'They aren't real brothers; they've just been friends forever.' Connor pulled the photos out again and showed them to Adrian. There was a photo of Victoria Beckett with both of the men.

Adrian studied the photo in Connor's hand; there was no indication that there was anything wrong. No indication that Victoria was unhappy, no indication that she was being hurt. Maybe this picture was taken before that happened.

'So, this man is your father?' Adrian pointed to one of the men in the picture; he was wearing a stone-washed denim jacket and a playful smile. There was something about the man that Adrian recognised.

'No,' Connor said, 'that's my uncle Joel. Joel Martin.'

'Where does your uncle work?'

'He's a porter at Wonford hospital. Why?'

Adrian took a deep breath and studied the man's face again, trying to imagine him older, trying to remember if he had seen him.

'I just need to ask him a couple of questions.' Adrian couldn't help looking at the patch on the man's denim jacket, the little red rocket. 'Is he working today, do you know?'

'I think so, he phoned to cancel coming over today.'

'Thanks. Listen, don't tell anyone you've spoken to me, not your uncle or your dad or anyone, OK?'

'I won't.'

'And don't tell anyone about the book or its contents. I'll be back in touch. Will you be OK?'

'Yes, thank you.'

'I'll need to speak to you about your father. See if we can get you into a better situation. He's not allowed to hurt you.'

'I don't want to be put into care or anything. I'm not a kid.'

'We might not have to do that. We can explore your options,' Adrian said. Connor wasn't a kid; when you came from that kind of home, you did a lot of growing up fast.

'I can take care of myself,' Connor said.

'I know, but you shouldn't have to. Take care, Connor.'

Adrian got back in the car and made his way to the hospital. He picked up his phone and called Imogen again; it wasn't like her not to call him back, even if he had told her not to bother.

Chapter 76

Connor had run out of cigarettes again; he went outside to breathe in some fresh air. He felt like he was suffocating, drowning, just waiting for his father to turn up, waiting for another confrontation. He wondered if the police had found him, if he was being questioned right now? Or maybe he was in a pub somewhere, drowning his sorrows. His father not being here was the best Christmas present Connor could hope for. It didn't matter much to him now anyway; he'd told the police what his father had done. Maybe now something would happen. Maybe something would change. The police officer had asked about his uncle Joel, maybe he was going to interview him about Jacob. Maybe he was going to ask him if Connor could live with him. Things were definitely looking up.

As if he had been called outside by something bigger than pure claustrophobia, he saw Selina being pulled towards him by her grandmother's Red Setter. Was she going into her own house? The house had been empty since Diana had died; Selina had been staying with her grandmother and he hadn't had a chance to talk to her. Would she ever want to speak to him again after what he had done? Maybe there was something in his blood that made him think killing Selina's mother was the only way he could save her. He had seen in the news that the fire was being treated as an accident; the alarms at the pub were found faulty and so blamed for no one being alerted to the blaze before it was too late. He felt sick at the thought that he had hurt Selina, just like he had felt sick when he realised how much he had hurt Billy Wicowska. She walked past the entrance and straight towards him. He braced himself for a slap; not that it would hurt, but it would definitely sting.

Selina looked around, checking that no one was watching from their houses.

'Can we go inside?' She walked straight into Connor's open house and he followed behind her. When they reached the lounge, she dropped her bag and wrapped her arms around him. The dog settled on the hallway rug as though it had always lived there. Her face was buried in his shoulder and when she pulled away gasping for air he could see she had been crying. A lot.

'I'm sorry. I'm so sorry,' he said.

'Don't be sorry. I didn't know, until I was out of that house, I didn't know how bad it was. It was like it was normal, just the way my life was supposed to be. Did you do it? Was it you? The fire . . .' Selina whispered.

'I thought that was what you wanted.'

'I didn't say that.'

'I'm sorry.' Had he got it completely wrong? Had he made things worse?

'Connor, no one has ever done anything like that for me. I had no idea what it could be like without them.' She smiled through the tears.

'Are you angry with me? When you blanked me at school I wasn't sure if you hated me.'

'I don't think I could hate you if I tried. I love you.'

Relief swept over Connor as she said the words; he had done the right thing after all. There was no trace of guilt left for what he had done, the only speck of guilt was attached to the possibility of hurting Selina and she had just taken that away. She loved him.

'What happens now?' he asked.

'I don't know. I'm living with my nan, she only lives over on Chestnut Road.'

'I have no idea where that is.'

'About four streets over. The police have spoken to her. So far, they think the fire was an accident. I heard my nan talking about it, she reckons it was an insurance job because the landlord was in the shit and his fire alarms were faulty. I don't think anyone suspects what the real reason was.' She smiled. A wave of relief passed over Connor.

'It's good to see you,' Connor said, his voice thick with emotion. He wanted to kiss her. He had always thought he wasn't really interested in having a girlfriend because he wasn't interested in the girls he had before. He wanted be with Selina though, he wanted to tell her to stay, she made him feel at ease with himself.

'I should get back, I said I would take the dog for a walk and I can't be too long,' she said.

Connor could see that the dog was getting restless. 'What's she called?'

'He. It's Barney.'

He smiled at her. 'I'll see you tomorrow?'

'I'll come by again.' She kissed him on the cheek, letting her lips linger for a few seconds. 'Merry Christmas.'

Connor desperately wanted to tell her what he had learned about his father, about his mother, about the book, but he thought it might scare her. She was his only way out now. Maybe saving her was enough to save himself.

Chapter 77

Heart thumping, Imogen stood with her back against the wall in her bathroom. The second she'd realised someone else was in the house with her she had found it hard to breathe. She was reminded of the time not so long ago where she had walked into an ambush, been cut and left for dead. Now that she knew, she could feel the blood on her hands. Whose blood was it? She was nowhere near her phone. Her mind was reeling with all the possibilities of who could be there and why. Why had they not announced themselves? The music continued to play at almost full blast, and what had been a blessing before was now making her feel more afraid. He could be just around the corner, he could be watching her, he could be anywhere.

She closed her eyes and tried to concentrate on her breathing. There was a technique they had learned in yoga, but she was struggling to remember it; all she could think about was the fear. Facing death, contrary to what she had heard, had not made her stronger. It had made her vulnerable, it had made her weak. She didn't know what to do, couldn't think properly. All she knew is that if she stood here for much longer she wouldn't have a chance.

Once she had composed herself, she pushed herself away from the wall, and started to walk towards the door from the bathroom into the hallway. She couldn't even lock herself in the bathroom because the lock didn't work and there was nothing to prop against it. Because she lived alone, she just hadn't seen the need to fix it.

After a minute or two, her police training began to kick in and she felt her body taking over where her mind was letting her down. She needed a weapon, something she could use to protect her. She gave the kitchen a cursory glance to check there was no one in there and then scuttled across the hall to get inside before she was spotted by whoever had invaded her space.

She scraped the skin of her upper arm on the kitchen door frame and winced, clenching her teeth together so she didn't cry out. The song had come to an end and she could hear the phone ringing. She had no way of getting out of the house without exposing herself. A new song began and drowned out the sound of the telephone, the telephone she could not get to. In the kitchen, she rushed to the sink and pulled out the knife she had been using to cut the potatoes. She then rushed back to the door and looked around. Where had the blood come from? It was still wet so it couldn't have been there long. She tried to ignore the panic; it had been a while since she'd had a panic attack but the familiar feeling was as unwelcome as ever.

She approached the lounge, terrified of what was waiting for her, but knowing she had no choice. As in all sticky situations that she'd found herself in recently, she wished Adrian was by her side. The lounge was as she had left it earlier on with no sign of any disturbance. This should have been comforting. Maybe he was gone. Why was the blood on her dress? There were only two rooms left in the house that she hadn't yet checked. The spare room or her bedroom, where her phone was. She had been in the spare room earlier and not noticed anything out of the ordinary. But the undeniable fact was her dress had blood on it, fresh blood. She turned the music off and an eerie silence perforated the atmosphere. She was torn between running for the door, and staying to fight. She picked up her phone, the screen was smashed. Whoever was there had obviously wanted to make sure she stayed alone. It was still on, so she could probably take incoming calls. But there was no way that she could use it to dial out. She just had to hope that Adrian would call her again before long.

Now that she could hear every movement, she listened out for any anomalies; there was nothing but silence. With her phone stuffed neatly into her bra she walked towards the spare room. The hallway was a good vantage point but she wanted to find him before he found her. She was suddenly grateful for the lack of stairs in her modest flat. Less places to hide. She put her fingers on the handle and took a deep breath, pushing forward.

Inside, the room was dark, the curtains had been drawn and she couldn't see into the corners. She carefully slid her palm across the wall and felt for the light switch, then quickly turned it on. The bed was made, and there were petals strewn across it. She had been in this room not fifteen minutes earlier and it hadn't looked like this. Someone was definitely in the flat. Whether they were in her bedroom, she didn't know, although the hiding places were sparse in there.

There was no avoiding it now, there was only one place the intruder could be. At that moment, she felt shivers down her spine. Before she had a chance to turn around and leave the room she could feel someone breathing behind her.

She turned quickly and swiped with the knife; the man ducked out of the way and pushed her; there was something familiar about his face but she couldn't place it. She slammed hard against the wall and felt the wind being knocked out of her. She kicked out and managed to knock him off balance. Rushing into her bedroom, she closed the door. She noticed the photograph of her mother was knocked over on the chest of drawers beneath the window. He had obviously climbed up onto the flat roof of the building next door and opened it. It was a sash window that she never locked, just pulled down. She leaned against the door, still clutching the knife, ready for him to break it down, ready for him to come at her. She thought about the bed in the other room and wondered what he had planned for her. Was this Magic Knight? Was this the man who had stared at her lying on the bed with the red negligee on?

The handle jiggled on the door and she felt him pushing against it, trying to get inside. He started to push harder, ramming his shoulder against the door to throw her off balance. She was running out of options now, he was going to make it inside, he was going to hurt her. She couldn't hold the door any longer and so she scrambled across the bed to hide on the other side. She had to believe that Adrian was on his way, she had to believe that he knew she was in danger. It was unusual for her not to call him back. The faintest smell of burnt fish fingers hung in the air; lunch was the least of her problems. Suddenly, the door burst open and the man was inside. Imogen's fingers were going numb, but her grip on the knife was paramount.

He lunged for her and managed to grab a handful of her hair. She screamed as he bashed her head against the bedside table and she fell to the ground, disoriented. The blurred image of him hovering over here was all she could see. He leaned down and put his hand around her throat, squeezing gently, as if he were testing it for size. She couldn't get her arms to fight him, she was still dazed. She was no threat to him, he knew he had her now; she could tell because his urgency had gone away. He was confident that he would win this fight and so he left her on the ground. The room was spinning. Her attacker flicked on the light switch and Imogen's eyes began to adjust. Her head throbbed and she wasn't sure she had enough strength to get to her feet. The knife was not in her hand any more, it must have gone under the bed. She moved her hand slowly across the carpet until she felt the handle. It was sticky and wet; as she pulled it towards her she realised it was covered in blood. She couldn't quite see under the bed and she wasn't sure she wanted to know what was there.

She squinted to try and see what was happening, her eyes still hurting from the knock against the bedside table, her focus still off. That was when she saw him, lying underneath her bed, blood saturated the carpet under his face, under his arms, under everything. He was grey and there didn't seem to be any sign of movement, any sign of life.

It was Dean.

She felt sick but, more than that, she felt angry. She wasn't sure what her attacker was doing or where he had gone but she stood up. He wasn't in the room any more, he must have assumed that she had passed out. Imogen could hear the bath water running, she could smell the bleach. She didn't have time to wait any more. She couldn't allow this to happen and she needed to get Dean to a doctor. He must have come over while she was out running, which meant he had been lying there for at least two hours. She absolutely had to save his life. If she didn't, then she would never forgive herself. Her mind flashed to Adrian and the pain he was feeling over Lucy. If she didn't save Dean, she would never be able to move on.

Suddenly Imogen felt like she was in control, as if she was the hunter. Shaking off the dizziness, she moved with confidence towards the bathroom. Her attacker was in there. Through the gap in the door she could see he was looking at himself in the mirror; he was saying something, but she could not hear him – quite frankly she didn't care. He was oblivious to her, lost inside his own ritual. Now was her chance. She held the knife up, swung the door open fully and ran towards him. Imogen plunged the knife into his back, pulled it out and stabbed him again and again. He was clutching his head, trying to get into the foetal position, but she just kept attacking him with the knife. The blood poured out of him with each knife strike. She was surprised at how little resistance the bone gave, she was surprised at the force she was using. She felt a hand on her hand, gentle and compassionate. She turned to see Dean, weak and soaked in blood.

'Hey. Hey, it's OK, I'm OK.'

Imogen gasped. 'I thought you were dead.'

'You should know by now it takes a lot to kill someone like me.'

Imogen looked down at the body of the attacker; he lay motionless, the blood flowing steadily from the lacerations to his body. She burst out crying and threw her arms around Dean, who winced at her touch. He carefully removed the knife from her hand and placed it on the sink. She kissed him on the lips, his lips were cold.

'I thought you were dead,' she sobbed.

'I'm a survivor.'

'I stabbed him, Dean, I stabbed him in the back. I'm going to lose my job. I gave you up and am going to lose my job anyway!' She couldn't stop crying.

'No, you won't.'

'There's no way of getting away with this, this isn't just self-defence. It's overkill.'

'If this isn't self-defence I don't know what is.'

'I have to call this in and call an ambulance, you look terrible.'

'I won't argue with you there.' Dean slumped against the wall and slid to the floor. He had lost a lot of blood.

Imogen had to secure the perpetrator before tending to Dean. She had to make sure he was down. She grabbed the wrist of the man on the floor, his pulse was weak and fading, he wasn't going to be hurting anyone else today. Grabbing a towel from the side of the bath, Imogen pulled Dean's shirt up and pushed the towel against his wounds to slow the blood flow. She looked at her phone again, it was futile, there was no way to dial out. Holding onto Dean, she wrapped another towel around his waist and tied it off, hoping that would help. She didn't want to leave him alone at the scene and so she rushed to the next room and opened a window.

'Help!' she screamed. 'Someone call the police! Somebody help!'

Chapter 78

Adrian had just received the call to say there was an altercation going on at Imogen's house. A neighbour had dialled 999 and an emergency response had been dispatched to the scene. Imogen was flagged as a police officer and Adrian was contacted immediately. He had just been to the hospital and spoken with Joel Martin's boss, who had confirmed that Joel had not been working on the nights of any of the murders. He had his home address and he was just about to go and visit when the phone call came.

He should have known when Imogen didn't answer her phone for the third time that there was something wrong; he was cursing himself for not paying attention. He should have been there for Imogen, he should have gone to see her. The uniformed officer who had called him couldn't give him any details and so he didn't even know whether she was OK. He would never forgive himself if she wasn't. It being Christmas Day, the roads were empty and it was a smooth run all the way to Imogen's place. When he got there, there were two ambulances waiting. He lifted the police tape that had already been distributed and rushed towards the entrance. There was an officer standing by the door; Adrian didn't recognise him. He was young, new, eager to impress.

'Where do you think you're going?' The uniformed police officer put his hand up to stop Adrian.

'I need to get inside, that's my partner in there. I'm DS Adrian Miles. My partner DS Imogen Grey lives in that building. I was called to the scene.' Adrian patted down his pockets for his identification.

'This is an active crime scene. I'm afraid you can't go in until it's been processed. Also, there are paramedics inside who need space to work. You understand,' the officer said.

'Can you at least tell me what's happened? Is anyone hurt? Please,' Adrian implored. He finally found his ID and showed it to the officer who adjusted his demeanour accordingly.

'We've got one fatality, one critical injury and one other.'

'Do you know which one is which?'

'What did you say your partner's name was again?'

'Her name is Imogen, DS Imogen Grey.'

'Right, the female – she wasn't seriously injured.'

A wave of relief washed over Adrian. Imogen had been injured once already under his watch. He had promised himself that he would never let that happen again. He had to find out who the two men were. He guessed that one of them would be Joel Martin AKA Magic Knight.

At that moment, Imogen walked out of the building. There was blood on her face and hands. She had a ghostly, wide-eyed look. The kind you only get from a brush with death but he'd never been happier to see her. She saw Adrian and a half-smile escaped from her mouth, not a comfortable smile but a small expression of relief to see him. He rushed over to her but was stopped by the same officer before he could put his arms around her.

'I'm afraid your partner needs to be processed first, she is covered in evidence,' the officer said. Adrian was embarrassed that he even needed to be told.

'What happened in there?' Adrian asked Imogen.

'He was there waiting for me. I didn't even notice until it was too late. He's dead.' She spoke quickly, almost manically. 'Dean is hurt really badly; the paramedics are working on him now. I wanted to stay and make sure he was OK, but they won't let me. Please stay with him, Adrian, I'm not sure he's going to make it and I don't want him to be alone.'

'Of course I will, you just worry about yourself.' Adrian wondered what Dean was doing there, he had thought they were finished. Given the circumstances he felt like a shit for even thinking about that but it just popped into his head. Was he jealous?

'I'll be fine,' Imogen said, but Adrian wasn't sure he believed her.

'I'm sorry I wasn't here.'

'Don't be ridiculous, Adrian, I don't think any of us

thought this might happen. How were you to know? Do we even know who he is?'

'I think I do and I'll tell you all about it later. We still need to tie all the evidence together.' He paused for a moment, then looked at the bloody state of her clothes. 'I should have been here. If you had been hurt, I would never have forgiven myself.'

'I'm fine, seriously, I don't even have a scratch on me!'

He could see she was lying, there was a gash on the side of her head that had been taped together and a large plaster on her arm. She looked pale and was clearly in a state of confusion.

'I stabbed him, Adrian, I stabbed him so many times.'

'Do you have a lawyer?' Adrian said. The officer was out of earshot now, talking to someone over his walkie-talkie, but Adrian knew all too well that it was times like this when you said things that could be taken out of context and used against you. He didn't want her to say anything that could be incriminating, not even to him.

'My father left a number for me to call if I was ever in trouble. I guess I'm in trouble.'

'I'm afraid we need to get going now, Detective Grey.' The police officer had come back.

At that moment, the paramedics wheeled Dean out of the house on a gurney. Adrian had never seen skin so white. They lifted him into the back of the ambulance.

'Wait. I need to come with you!' Adrian called out.

'Who are you, are you family?' the paramedic asked.

'He doesn't have any family, but I'm a friend.'

Adrian pulled out his warrant card and showed the paramedic.

'Fine. Get in.'

Adrian got in the back of the ambulance, his eyes fixed on Imogen as they closed the ambulance doors. The siren started and they left the scene. He looked down at Dean's colourless skin with the flashes of burgundy streaked across it. The paramedic in the back of the ambulance just sat and stared at the monitor, making sure the bleeps were keeping the rhythm, ready to spring into action if they changed in any way. Adrian took Dean's hand in his and squeezed, making sure he knew he wasn't alone. His mind drifted to Lucy's last moments and how he had wished he could have held her hand; the least he could do was be there for Dean, for Imogen's sake if nothing else.

Chapter 79

Adrian sat in the chairs in the hospital waiting room. Dean had been taken in for surgery, and it had already been four hours. Occasionally a flurry of nurses would rush in or out of the room but he hadn't heard much of anything yet. The automatic doors opened and Adrian saw Imogen standing there. She was wearing a grey tracksuit; her clothes obviously having been taken in to be processed as evidence. She looked defeated as she slumped in the chair next to him.

'Hey, you, that was quick,' Adrian said.

'And very thorough.' Imogen ran her hand through her hair. 'My whole sodding place is a crime scene now. Just when you thought your Christmases couldn't get any more fucked up. Is Dean OK?'

'He's in theatre, they reckon it'll be a few hours.'

'Thanks for staying with him. How was he, did they say?'

'He lost a lot of blood but they stabilised him. They said they were optimistic.'

'Who was the perpetrator?'

'One of the porters at the hospital. Joel Martin. He was DOA at the hospital. We think he recognised you the other day when we came to see Faith. He must have figured it out, which is why he deleted everything online. He was the porter who showed us to Faith's room.'

'I remember him, I remember thinking at the time that there was something funny about the way he was looking at us. Then again, I am quite paranoid at the best of times.'

'Just because you're paranoid, Grey, doesn't mean they're not after you.'

'Why did he do it? Do we know?'

'A young lad came in with his mother's diary. It took us a while to decipher it as it was badly damaged. Gary worked his magic and managed to restore much of the text. The short version is that he was a violent man who terrorised her and most likely killed her. The DCI has signed an order to exhume her body; she died around fifteen years ago but it was ruled as a suicide. The boy and his father moved back into the area and it's possible their return triggered something in Joel Martin, brought back memories.'

'Joel Martin was Magic Knight?'

'Yep, and the boy's mother had long dark hair, looked just like the women he was targeting. We don't know if he killed her accidentally, or what happened originally, but hopefully an autopsy will tell us more.'

'God, I'm so tired.' She stretched her legs out in front of her.

'Did you eat yet?'

'No, he turned up in the middle of when I was cooking my sodding fish fingers. Completely ruined my day,' she sulked.

Adrian smiled. Only Imogen would have fish fingers for Christmas dinner. 'Well you can come to mine for dinner.'

'I can't, I have to stay here.'

'Look, I'll take you back to mine, you can eat some dinner and then you can have a shower, get changed and I'll bring you straight back here. Andrea will have something you can borrow. He's not going to be out for hours. He won't even know.'

'But I'll know.'

'Come on, Grey, stop punishing yourself, this is not your fault.' As he said the words he realised his own hypocrisy over Lucy's death. If this wasn't Imogen's fault, then he wasn't to blame for what happened to Lucy. He made a mental note to forgive himself later on.

She half-smiled at him. 'Is Andrea a good cook?'

'She's improved. She's better than you.'

Adrian stood up and held his hand out, and Imogen looked at it for a moment before taking it and pulling herself up, using him as leverage. They walked along the corridor, the hospital deserted apart from a few nurses crowded around a tin of Quality Street at the front desk.

In the car, Adrian turned the radio on, and the usual cheerful Christmas tunes accompanied them on the way back to his house. They had barely been partnered together for a year, but already she was family. Last Christmas Adrian had been completely alone and despite all the crazy things that happened he looked around him and for the first time in a long time was grateful for what he had. What doesn't kill you makes you stronger. Adrian felt like after the year he had had, he could take on anything. Bring it on.

THE END

Acknowledgements

First of all, a huge thank you to everyone who has read and enjoyed the books so far; I am totally humbled by the reception they have been getting. Thank you as well to everyone who leaves a review online – I read every single one of them.

I'd like to thank everyone at Avon books, particularly Phoebe Morgan, my editor who has to read through my raw unedited thoughts (yikes). A big thanks to my agents at Diane Banks Associates – thank you Diane and Kate for all your great advice – and thanks Chloe for reminding me of stuff I have forgotten to do.

Thanks to Tracy Fenton and Wendy Clarke for running two of the best book groups on Facebook. And a huge thank you to the book blogging community who are always singing my praises. I can't name you all but you know who you are!

Thanks as well to my family. I swear I don't just sit around in my pyjamas on the internet all day. A big massive thank you to my cousin Jason who sends me cards telling me how wonderful I am, I like that.

I would also like to mention the many crime writers I have met since I started these books and how wonderfully supportive (and distracting) you all are. Also a sad farewell to the amazing Helen Cadbury who passed away recently – you are missed.

Please do drop me a line through my Facebook author page if you have any questions, I try to answer them all.

Go back to where it all began . . .

The Teacher

A lesson you'll never forget

KATERINA DIAMOND

The first smash-hit crime novel from Katerina Diamond.
NOT for the faint-hearted . . .

Those closest to us can hurt us the most . . .

'All hail the new Queen of Crime' *Heat*

The
Secret

Everything
you *think* you
know is a lie...

KATERINA DIAMOND
SUNDAY TIMES BESTSELLER

The Queen of Crime returns in her second
Miles and Grey novel.

The truth won't stay locked up forever . . .

'All hail the new Queen of Crime' *Heat*

The
Angel

Some things can't be forgiven...

THE *SUNDAY TIMES* BESTSELLER
KATERINA DIAMOND

The Queen of Crime is back in the third bestselling
Miles and Grey novel.